THE LAST DAYS CONTINUE

Chris Ayala

To My Grandmother,
Your Light Will Never Fade.

CHAPTER ONE

Light. So much light. It stung Adam's eyes. When he tried to look away, he couldn't because his body wasn't his own. It was happening again. A precognition.

The circle of light scurried away, pointing in different directions. It was a searchlight from a helicopter. Flying high up in the sky, the chopper flew along the eerie clouds. The moon hid in the darkness. Six other helicopters came into his vision. Their whirs were instantly drowned out by a shock of thunder, radiating through the air and his body. Hairs on his arms rose. The future looked more tormenting with every visit. Buildings had been so blanketed in soot, that it looked like a paint. Blood stained the sidewalk red and sticky. Black drops of rain came down and wobbled on Adam's eyelashes.

His head looked away. With no control of his future's motions, it felt like living in a virtual reality video game. As an observer, he felt intrigued and yet nervous. What was happening? People were everywhere. Practically shoulder-to-shoulder. They walked in total silence. The flood of heads bobbed up and down. There must've been thousands. Maybe even tens of thousands. Mucky faces stared straight ahead as they marched in unison. Their teeth hadn't been brushed in weeks and showers had eluded them even longer. One stranger next to him wiped dirt off a metal bat, smiling with wide eyes. Everyone's eyes were the same; that same savage thirst for blood.

A man behind him, with dreadlocked hair so crazy Adam was afraid he'd turn to stone for staring too long, whispered, "Shouldn't we have brought signs?"

Next to Adam, a girl spoke. He recognized her, even with that short haircut that made her look like a boy. It was Royal Declan. She said, "We're done protesting."

The thunder again. Lightning lit up the night. Adam could see the crowd for that brief second. Everyone was armed and ready to fight. Besides bats, there were shotguns, blades, and one woman even gripped a frying pan. Whatever it took. More surprisingly, Adam and his companion Royal were at the head of this massive wave. He didn't recognize the area. Street lights were dim, no roadway signs, not even a single car on the street. Homes had been made inside the buildings' ruins, with no roofs and blankets instead of doors. Posters lined up every street corner, with that familiar emblem of a dolphin. *The Union Offers Hope.* Adam had seen those propaganda signs in a prior precognition. Somehow the idea of a global government still didn't make him feel hope. Hope certainly wasn't in the eyes of this crowd. And whatever hope the Union offered didn't fan out to this area. They walked past homes. Citizens either shut their doors or joined the crowd. A man with a shotgun exited his home, his crying wife's hand tugging his shirt. This was the final fight, the war to end all wars. Tonight's enemy was government.

Adam turned to Royal again. She was so tiny, no more than five and a half feet; the bat secured to her back was almost as tall as her. Adam hadn't known her...yet. This was his second vision with her in it. "Marcel Celest must be shitting his pants," Royal mumbled.

Three police vehicles pulled up to block the front of the storm of people that was more dangerous than the storm above. The mob kept walking, climbing over their cars as though they weren't there. The cops stepped out, shrugging their shoulders at each other. Their uniforms were frayed and layered with dirt. One cop looked back at Adam. He bit his lip then holstered his gun. Expecting the policeman to fire, Adam was shocked at what happened next. In one swoop, the cop disgracefully tore his badge off and tossed it to the ground. It clanked against the concrete. Then he joined the mob, standing next to Adam. The other two nodded in agreement and joined as well. Apparently, even law enforcement had had enough. Anyone could join this rebellion. The only enemy was the Union.

There was a flash of lightning. He caught a glimpse of a castle in the distance, on top a steep hill. It must have been a good three mile walk. The castle was immense with four towers surrounding it.

Next to him, the cop's radio crackled. "SWAT en route. Just spray them with water. They'll stop." The dispatcher's voice was so nonchalant and bored; it made Adam grasp his fist. They still had no idea what was in store for them.

The walk continued. Some men went inside and recruited more for this battle. It was working; the crowd grew to an untold amount.

Two SWAT vehicles pulled up in front of them, a mere two blocks away but no one stopped marching. Officers dressed in riot gear stepped out. The SWAT team's shoulders were low and solemn, as though this was as routine as driving a car. They connected a large hose to a fire hydrant. One officer, with a cigar dangling from his mouth, turned it on. It sprayed hundreds of gallons of water onto the crowd to stop the horde. Some fell over from the high pressure. Others screamed obscenities in defiance. Then there were some who just laughed at this feeble attempt at ceasing a war.

Adam watched one officer yawn and then he raised his arm to the mob, using some type of hand signal. Someone stepped forward; everyone moved out his way. The man was dressed in a mechanical suit with a massive gas tank on his back. The hydraulic system pulled up two hoses and connected them to each of his hands. He giggled manically. A fierce burn scar covered half his face, a glass eyeball wobbled in different directions. "Burn, burn. Fire, fire," he kept mumbling.

The SWAT team's smirks fell. The man in the mechanical suit

ignited the hoses with a press of a button. Two flame throwers spewed a fire that put the SWAT's water hose to shame. They tried to dash out of the way, but it was too late. The SWAT officers were on fire. One of them burned to the ground so quickly, he couldn't run. The stream of flames reached out a hundred feet and ignited the two vans. An explosion blinded Adam. He could feel the heat. The fire attacker enjoyed every moment – his giggles just got louder. "Burrnnnnn!"

In seconds, more vans lined up the streets. Dozens of men in SWAT gear stepped out with riot shields. Adam ran forward, everyone following in a furious dash. The officers were overcome; some ran away. It was too late for those that faced this crowd. He slammed into enemy. A SWAT officer dropped his riot shield. Adam flipped over and grasped it. He spun around, with almost rehearsed precision, and banged the riot shield into the face of another officer. He could hear the crack of every facial bone. Then Adam spun again and smashed the shield into another officer. He swiftly grabbed the officer's baton. Adam threw the shield into another officer's stomach. Then he used the baton to break another officer's skull.

The mob was being just as ruthless, using shotguns and bats to slaughter the opposing officers. Even the rebellious cops showed no remorse in ending the opposition's lives. Adam looked to his right – a man's fist continued to punch the officer's riot helmet. Bloody knuckles made it through the glass and continued to pummel the unconscious enemy. To his left, a wild lady swung her frying pan up and down. He had never heard what a cracked skull sounded like until now. It was like using a sledge hammer to open a walnut. Overkill, yet satisfying.

Madness gripped this crowd. The only fear was in the eyes of the opposing team. Adam had never seen such violence, but according to this vision...he will experience it firsthand soon. His body leapt up and fought more officers. It was so easy. A kick here. A punch there. Adam didn't know how to fight like this. His marital arts training belonged in a drunken kung-fu comedy. This was unique.

A kick to the back sent Adam to the ground. He turned to see a SWAT officer with raging eyes raise a baton to strike Adam. Then another SWAT officer came from behind him and snapped his neck. Even the bad guys were turning against each other. The now-ally SWAT officer extended his hand to help Adam stand. There was no bias in who joined this uprising. He grabbed the officer's helpful hand and got up. They both looked forward to see eight more vans coming in front of them. "Union Keepers!"

Black SUVs swung into the scene, creating a perfect barrier. Men in unrecognizable uniforms stepped out with semi-automatic guns. Adam wanted to holler out a terrified whimper, but only his soul inhabited the future, not his body.

"Adam! Nelson's here!" Royal screamed, pointing to the sky.

Adam's eyes looked up. There was a fighter jet flying overhead. With all black and grey neon lights around the trim, it almost seemed from another planet. He felt his future self give an enormous grin. Then the fighter jet fired missiles onto the Union Keepers. Their SUVs exploded in different directions. One of the vehicles flipped over and landed on top of one of the Union Keepers. Another vehicle flew into the side of a building.

The war ensued. The Union Keepers punched and shot who they could in desperation. There were just too many people. In moments, they were stomped on. Spat on. Kicked in the stomach. Blood spewed up and smacked Adam's face.

"Fucking shit!!" Adam's curse echoed throughout the empty forest. Birds flew away. He heard hooves as a herd of deer scurried away with the baby running ahead of the others. With his back to Adam, Declan's shoulders fell. The bow and arrow in his hand dropped to the ground. "That was going to be our goddamn dinner until you scared them off!"

He wished he could scamper away like the deer just did; Declan's fury was worse than the deer's fear of Adam's outburst. He suddenly felt dizzy and turned to vomit. Declan sucked his teeth. "And you just wasted your goddamn lunch."

It was crispy squirrel and chewy raw snails. Adam wasn't going to miss it. He could still taste the dirty nails in it. Declan walked over and grasped his collar. He tossed Adam back up against the tree hump. In all the years he'd known this man, never had he felt so bullied. Declan was his mentor, trainer, and the only father figure he had. But so much had changed. Six weeks after a nuclear attack destroyed three-quarters of the United States and left the rest without electricity, simple things became complex. Like shaving. Declan's raggedy beard couldn't hide his disappointed face. "Did you have another vision?"

Adam tried to catch his breath. He could only nod.

Nelson dashed up to them with a bundle of twigs to build a fire. He seemed concerned. "What happened?" To see concern from the former President of the United States made Adam feel honored and yet embarrassed. Before he could utter a word, Declan spoke. "He's fine. He screams like that after a vision. I don't know what the hell is wrong with this boy."

Nelson's gray, scruffy beard couldn't hide his concern. "You saw the future? What was it?"

Adam's chest heaved up and down. "Light. Helicopters. People. Blood. Fire. Jet. Frying pan. Castle."

Both sets of eyes squinted at him. This must've been how the scientists looked at him the first time his precognitions began. Adam was a science experiment. An embryo from the future that travelled with past memories. He had been studied all his life. Yet, it was still awkward to be eyed like this.

"Catch your breath, son," Nelson said, laying the twigs down. Dusk was falling. Normally a night fire would be a bad idea in a vast forest filled with predators like bears and wolves. But the nukes wiped out most of the wildlife. Sure, there were no dangers, but Adam's grumbling stomach also reminded him there was no food either. Declan had already lost enough waist line that his pants drooped.

"Okay," Adam said. "It was a mob of people. Like a rebellion or something. Everyone was attacking officers. Royal was there."

Declan's eyes shot out. "What was my daughter doing there?"

"I don't know – it hasn't happened yet, remember? Or...actually it has happened to the future me that uploaded these memories...argh, my brain hurts." Thinking of the confusing time loop made Adam rub his temples. Only a month ago he had learned he had memories from his future self and still couldn't accept this strange phenomenon.

"Anyone else you recognize?" Nelson began to rapidly twist twigs together to create a small smoke.

"Well," he thought, "*you* were there."

Nelson stopped twisting the twig. "Me?"

"I didn't actually see you. But you were in a jet. Really cool looking jet, actually. Black with gray lights around it."

Declan turned to Nelson. "Is that the..."

"Just in blueprint phase, the last I heard." The President stared at a twig, grinning. This had been the only time he had smiled on their adventure through the Maryland forests. "I haven't flown in over fifteen years. And I get to fly a theoretical jet?"

Thunder rumbled in the distance. Adam jumped a little too much. It looked like another rainy night by Mother Nature attempting again to clear the impurities left by the devastation. The branches above could only blanket so much of the brown rain. It was going to be another sleepless night. The clouds had been black every day.

Declan coughed up a mouthful of mucus and spat it on the ground. This man used to be Secretary of Defense. Now, with his uncombed hair and a layer of tartar on his teeth, he resembled a vagabond. "Who else did you see? Was I there?"

Adam shook his head. He hadn't expected Declan's mouth to morph into a frown. In fact, he had never seen him in any of these future visions. Whether it meant Declan would be dead or separated from him soon, no one knew. "There was some crazy guy there with a nasty burn scar. He was lighting up people with flame cannons. Had this weird glass eyeball."

"Are you kidding me?" Declan stood up, his knee popped. "Barley was there?"

"*That* was Victor Barley?" Adam questioned. Before Nelson

asked, he answered. "He's on Servo Clementia's kill list. In fact, he would be good to have tonight. Victor would've had that fire going by now."

A little puff of smoke appeared from Nelson's twig and fizzled away. He blew on it more. Lucky for them, the ex-President knew a little about surviving in the wild. His prior military experience got him Adam's vote. But the madness caused by governments a month ago left Nelson the most hated President in history. His vow to join Declan's terrorist organization Servo Clementia was his only option. Adam was born in the organization; unfortunately he never had the choice.

"Wait a minute," Nelson said. He carefully used leaves to build the fire's potential. "Maybe you're right. Maybe he is useful."

"I told you," Declan barked, "everyone must die on that list."

"How did you get this list?"

"I already told you that too, Nelson! Does no one listen to me around here?" Declan plopped his sleeping bag from his backpack. Though the two had been best friends even prior to working on the administration together, Adam could see by Nelson's expression that he hadn't experienced such disrespect. Up until now, Adam always heard Nelson be referred to as "Mr. President."

Before another argument began, Adam intervened. "Okay, here's how it works. Servo Clementia made a vow that if time travel was possible, we'd send an embryo back with information. An embryo can hold a terrabyte of data. So 25 years ago, little ole me showed up in a lab test tube. My data included memories. They grew me up into this handsome guy you see in front of you. And you know...Servo Clementia created a kill list from my visions and started...well... offing the people on the list them to avoid the last days."

The fire crackled. It grew so flawlessly, it was like the air needed the warmth too. Adam's bones began to shake less. Since the nukes, the air had a constant bitter chill. He couldn't even remember the last time the sun peeked out past the dark clouds.

Nelson said, "Why was it assumed to be a kill list? Adam isn't the violent type. Maybe it's a list of people to recruit. That could aide in the final war. You said it yourself – the pyromaniac was helpful in the final fight."

Declan snatched up something small moving in the bush. A caterpillar. He sucked it down like the last bite of spaghetti. "Because," he spoke as if Nelson was five years old and not in his late fifties, "that was part of Servo Clementia's agenda. *If* time travel were possible, we'd send a kill list and not a goddamn friend list from Facebook." He rolled out his sleeping bag. "Now that we're done chit-chatting about Adam's useless vision, let's get some rest while we can. We're almost at the bridge." Laying down with his back turned to the group, Declan began to snore almost instantly.

Nelson pulled out a water canteen and handed it to Adam. "You vomited a lot and have to keep yourself hydrated. Drink what's left of mine."

They barely knew each other, but he felt an immediate bond. Adam smiled and guzzled down the water. With the warm fire and cold liquid, he finally felt at ease. "Thank you, Mr. President."

After a slow sigh and roll of his eyes, Nelson said, "I told you. I'm not this nation's *savior* anymore."

"Really? Because in my precognition...you seemed like a savior to me."

A dimple poked inward from the right side of Nelson's cheek. The fire reflected in his glazed eyes. Circles sagged below the eyelids.

"You gonna sleep tonight?" Adam asked this every night this week, though he expected the same blunt answer.

"Don't worry about me."

After a subtle nod, Adam must've fallen asleep because he opened his eyes to see Nelson moved somewhere else. Standing and looking up at the sky, searching for the missing moon. Then Adam's eyes closed and reopened. Nelson was in a different spot, picking his teeth with a twig. After a quick slip into unconsciousness, he awoke to Nelson making a pile of leaves and forming it into the shape of a human. He lied down to cuddle with it. Adam waited and listened. Then a gentle snore escaped Nelson's mouth.

Thunder knocked on the clouds like an unwelcome visitor. Just like the thunder in his vision. The question that kept knocking even louder on his mind was...why was *he* leading the rebellion?

Building technology on a weak power grid is like building a house of cards on a wobbly table.

-*Victoria Celest*

CHAPTER TWO

Being the President had its advantages. Every morning, Nelson was greeted with a ring from the telephone next to the bed. It mimicked the sound of bubbles coming up to the surface. His wife one time mumbled, "It's like they don't want us to wake up." Then he responded, "Maybe we shouldn't." He'd grasp her and hold her tighter. Wishing he could bury himself in a grave like this. First thing in the morning, his wife smelled liked fresh sunflowers. How she accomplished this he never knew...and never would know. Then the ringing would continue until it got on one of their nerves. Usually him. He'd pick up and listen to the polite greeting from kitchen staff, "Good morning, Mr. President." Then they'd read off the same menu. Three years and they still didn't seem to remember his request. Coffee then breakfast later. Tea with cream for the First Lady. She would check the tablet for the children's security cameras. And then smile that they were sleeping soundly and safe. Nelson once said, "Secret Service will keep the family safe." Her reply came quickly, "No. It's our job to keep the family safe." The kitchen staff would bring in two cups on a titanium platter. They'd pour his coffee gently into his favorite Atlanta Falcons mug.

The sound of liquid dripping into a mug turned into something else as Nelson awoke from his dream. It was now Declan urinating on the remaining fire from last night. He sucked in all the mucus to the back of his throat and coughed out the black chunk. This was always the worst part of waking up, the black soot resting in their throats.

His pile of leaves, that had the curves of his wife Victoria, had flattened into a mess of brown shades. Nelson sat up and yawned. He may have only slept a couple hours, but it was enough. The military taught him in times of need, sleep could be done in hour-and-a-half intervals. His staff sergeant would mumble the same motto about how Albert Einstein slept in short bursts and look what he accomplished.

There was no feeling of accomplishment in a while. Wandering endless fields of woods got dull. Trusting in Declan's plan got even duller. The risk taken, the day the missiles hit 98 spots around the United States, to fake their deaths and leave the government behind didn't seem to pay off. When Declan revealed himself to be part of a terrorist organization, Nelson should've called for Secret Service to arrest him. But instead he had been convinced the Servo Clementia had a purpose. If it was to stop the apocalypse from getting worse, then it had failed miserably so far.

"Okay," Adam said, appearing with a handful of colorful berries.

Seemingly fresh out of college, the kid seemed the most naive of the group. He barely knew him but was fascinated to meet someone who had the ability to see the future. He got butterflies in his stomach. In the vision, Nelson flew a top secret jet. He hadn't flown a plane since the ISIL war, when he was in his young prime age. But now, Nelson was reaching 56 years old. Did he still have it in him to fly at 328 mph, slicing the atmosphere in a 180 radius, spinning until the oxygen became too much?

"What about this one?" Adam asked, holding up the first berry between his forefinger and middle finger.

Squinting his eyes and searching his mind, he focused on the berry. Nelson said, "Elderberry. Causes vomiting."

After piercing his lips, Adam tossed it aside and held up a different berry. "This one?"

"Climbing Nightshade. Attacks the nervous system."

"Okay, this one can't be bad. It looks delicious."

"American pokeweed. Causes respiratory failure."

Adam dropped his arms and all the berries tumbled out of his hands. Defeated. Another morning without food. He wiped the remnants on his crusted jeans. At this point, Nelson was more concerned with a shower than eating. They'd worn the same clothes for three weeks. Any clean water they found had to be saved for canteens, not a bath.

"When are you guys going to start taking this serious?" Declan grumbled. "We are in the middle of the goddamn apocalypse and you're talking about berries?" Throwing his backpack on and turning away, he mumbled, "Let's go."

Charles Declan had been his friend for almost two decades. He thought he knew him. Now, Nelson wasn't so sure. Starvation brings out the true nature of most men. For a man that ate five meals a day, Secretary of Defense Declan must've been losing more than weight…he was losing his sanity.

It took them several minutes to catch up to Declan. Even though he was a heavyset man, his legs could move faster than a thirsty camel. Nelson and Adam were only able to catch up once Declan stopped to gather clean water from a gardening hose. He lifted it up and the water slowly poured into his canteen.

Only when they all were gathered did Nelson even noticed the kid had been talking to him the whole time. Stress made Declan irate but made Adam talkative.

"Yeah, so, what do you think?"

This happened to him in press conferences all the time, but Nelson knew a trick for renewing the conversation without seeming like he hadn't been listening. "Explain further."

"Well, I was thinking where would a castle be around here? Maybe my vision gave us a clue where Marcel's home base will be. Where he'll run the Union."

It's our job to keep the family safe. His wife's words still poked at him. Was it a dream or a message?

"I doubt any castles survived the nukes."

"So," Adam stuttered, "so...like...is your son...I mean, Marcel...did he have an eye on a certain castle as a kid?"

Anytime the name Marcel was mentioned around him, it tended to be a stutter. Nelson had a difficult time accepting his son would eventually become a menacing world leader with the power to control elements. He remembered Marcel's teenage years. His obsessions were school and Nintendo. That innocent boy would never hurt a fly. "No, not really."

After Declan finished sucking the water from the garden hose, he walked away. Nelson tried to suck any leftover water from the hose, but came up empty.

They travelled down a hill with the chatter of Adam continuing. "Can you guys believe I was able to fight like that? I mean, I was doing some amazing martial arts. Brent taught me a lot of cool stuff, but nothing like that."

"You and my son were close friends?" Nelson asked. Either join the conversation or wallow in his dark thoughts... Nelson chose the former.

"*Best* friends! Sorry, we kept it secret from everyone."

Apparently, his son Brent kept a very secret life from him. Even the fact he was an assassin for a terrorist organization. At least Marcel and his daughter Janice always remained honest to him. Or did they?

It's our job to keep the family safe.

"Hey, Mr. Declan," Adam yelled out to the small spot at the bottom of the hill that was their leader. "Can you teach me how to break a man's neck with one hand?"

"Sure! I'll be happy to try it on you."

Adam forced a giggle out. Nelson didn't buy it. "Oh, Mr. Declan. You're just kidding. Right?"

The air seemed to get thicker as they approached the bottom of the hill. That familiar taste of ash clogged the back of Nelson's throat.

"When you were in the war, how did you find the courage to

fight?"

"Courage isn't something in a cage you can unlock with just any key at your convenience. It takes the right one to free it."

Something crunched underneath Nelson's sole-less shoe. He moved his foot to reveal a severed hand. There was a wedding ring on it. Fresh painted red nails. Nelson immediately covered it with a pile of dirt. Just like with every dead body, he gave a short whispered apology. "I'm sorry I let this happen."

Adam caught up to him. "What was that?"

"Nothing."

They walked together down the hill and caught up to Declan. He munched on a box of donuts from a flipped over trash compactor. Apparently, it didn't occur to him to share. Nelson found himself growing frustrated.

Adam searched through the trash. "A toothbrush!" He began brushing his teeth immediately, with a satisfied grin.

Nelson surveyed the area. A canal surrounded the city. There was no water in it, just the manmade structure. It was Baltimore. The bridge in the distance was the Francis Scott Key Bridge.

"Don't even think about it," Declan mumbled through protruding cheeks of glazed donuts.

Adam stopped brushing his teeth and stood next to the Nelson. They stared at the bridge. "Is that...is that the way to your daughter's home?"

Over the Francis Scott, follow the Peninsula Expressway and a right on Merrit Boulevard. Janice repeated these directions to Nelson when she first moved to that home. She must've invited him eight times and he never made it there. Her home looked nice from the pictures he saw. Becoming a President made him forget how to be a father. How could he have not made it to her Christmas parties? What had honestly been more important?

"Nelson," Declan grumbled, "are you listening?"

"Yeah," he lied.

"We've already been through this. The Servo Clementia has only one focus. Family isn't part of that. Come on, let's keep moving north."

But she was right there. Maybe there was a chance his daughter's alive.

It's our job to keep the family safe.

"No," Nelson said. "I'm leaving."

Their eyes met. Nearly eight years in the White House together, Declan knew when Nelson locked on the eyes that there was no arguing allowed. The decision had been made.

"Fucking coward." Declan turned to Adam. "And you? You going to turn your back on the organization that raised you? Go ahead. I don't care. I don't need either of you. I'll find and eliminate the targets myself. I'm going to change the future. Both of you can go fuck yourselves."

Adam looked back and forth. Nelson then Declan. Nelson then Declan.

Without hesitating any longer, Nelson walked toward the bridge. Without even saying a simple goodbye to his old friend Declan. And leaving Adam indecisive.

His family came first. If they were dead, he wanted to cover them in a pile of dirt.

CHAPTER THREE

I've suffered because of you.

That voice. Marcel cringed. It was the element of water. He looked down to see he had stepped in a puddle of murky liquid. He backed out and watched the water settle. Its voice couldn't enter his mind unless it was in motion.

From his pocket, he pulled out a cigarette from a crusty used pack that had been in a trash can. Holding up the lighter to his mouth, the flame ignited without him touching the flint wheel. Fire adored him. Did anything he wished. On cold nights, Marcel wouldn't even have to ask; fire would surround him in warmth.

The trek to this point hadn't been easy. Only ten miles from their destination, the limousine ran out of gas. Marcel insisted on finding some, but his loyal Secret Service agent refused the offer. It had been four hours and Marcel felt concerned the agent wasn't returning.

Wind blew into his ear drum, streaming along the freeway. It said nothing. Like always. It was timid, shy, and possibly untrustworthy. Perhaps, as water, it blamed him for their infestation worldwide.

A month had past since he bonded with the voices of the elements. And the only thing he discovered was how to quiet them by settling them. But control was his goal. Besides fire, they were unruly children. Never listening to his commands.

"Mr. Celest, sorry for the wait." The Secret Service agent ran up carrying a gas can. His suit and tie were wet with sweat; stuck to him like he just swam in a pool. It must've been 40 degrees Fahrenheit outside. Apparently, his loyal protection ran the entire way. "I had to syphon some out of an abandoned car."

"Once the Union gets funded, oil will be centralized and controlled. No more reserves."

The gas filled the empty tank and sounded like water pouring into a jug. Marcel finished his cigarette, hoping Wind would whisper to him. Just once. Of all the elements, it would be the most useful.

"So," he tried to end the awkward silence, "have you gotten any radio chatter?"

"Very little," the agent said, plugging the ear piece further into his ear. His breaths created clouds in the chilly air.

"What's the last thing you heard about my brother?" Marcel flicked the cigarette, watching the gust push it away magically. Wind didn't like smoke apparently. That made him grin.

The agent patted the gas can, making every drop land in the tank. "Nothing new. Brent Celest is still being held in a phantasm cell until the judge sentences him. Without electricity, prisons are limited. Don't worry, the bastard won't get near you ever again."

Marcel climbed into the backseat and shut the door. His agent went into the driver's seat, rubbing his hands together for warmth. Seeing Marcel's distress, the agent asked, "Sorry, Mr. Celest. Did I say something wrong?"

"I realize my brother tried to kill me...and I shouldn't forgive him. But I just wanted the family together for this moment. The Union is finally becoming a reality. One simple worldwide government. My father would've been proud."

The agent nodded. "We will find the President and your sister, Mr. Celest. It's only a matter of when."

After a big sigh, Marcel leaned back in the seat. The vehicle moved forward as they drove off. Ten more miles to go. It had taken over a week to travel from the caves in Maryland to the East River in Manhattan. "Do you think they'll be happy to see me?"

"The UN is going to be ecstatic. Everyone is convinced you're dead."

Dead. It had a whole new meaning to him. Marcel had been swallowed into a coma then visited the realms of darkness. He shook hands with Lucifer to gain the ability of persuasion. Somehow hearing the word *dead* triggered no fear in him. The only fear now was failure.

Marcel visited Manhattan as a child. Even then he felt it was overcrowded. Too many cars. Too many lights. Just too many people. It created this frustration amongst everyone, ruining the vacation. Even Dad said he never wanted to make a trip here again. For 25 years, Marcel had avoided this place.

The agent took back alleyways. His concern was for carjackings. Rightfully so since Marcel had already lost two agents after Doomsday thanks to violent attacks from refugees. In the driver's seat, he could hear the agent click the holster to release his gun. Without any further movement, he held onto it. What triggered this behavior slowly came into Marcel's view out the limo window. A man, bundled in three blankets, walked barefoot on the icy sidewalk. He glanced up but showed no sign of retaliation. Only sadness. When they passed him, the agent relaxed and let go of his gun's holster.

"Stop," Marcel whispered.

"Mr. Celest, that would be a terrible idea. There are citizens -"

"Stop." Marcel only repeated himself once. That was the rule with his staff.

The agent stopped and pulled aside. Marcel stepped outside. He could see the blanket man walking so slow, it looked like he wasn't moving. It didn't take long for him to catch up to him. Startled, the man fell over on a garbage can.

"I'm not here to hurt you," Marcel insisted.

Hurried puffs of cold air escaped the man's mouth. His wide eyes beckoned Marcel to leave. But he couldn't. He bent over and untied his shoelaces.

"I know they might be a little too big, but you'll get used to them," he said, placing his black Dockers on the man's callused feet. They wouldn't stop shaking, from fear or the cold. Perhaps both.

After tying the knots, the man seemed more relaxed. "Thank you," he stuttered. "You're Celest. Marcel Celest. I read you were in a coma."

"I'm back."

"Why are you here? What do you want?"

Marcel recalled a moment in his travels to Hell. A moment he asked Lucifer the same exact question. And like the Devil, he recited the most peculiar answer. Marcel repeated it. "I want to save the world."

With one finger, Marcel combed his mustache. It was itchy. He read somewhere that world leaders garnered more favor with a full mustache. Acceptance would always be his goal.

Outside was nothing but piles of rubble. FEMA vans and trucks had been abandoned with open gas tanks. Time Square's billboards lied flat on the ground. "How long until we get there?"

"We are here, Mr. Celest." The agent said slowing the vehicle down.

His eyes squinted. Where was the UN building? And how had a Time Square billboard been flung this far? How strong had the nuclear explosions been? Reality kept slapping his face everytime he left the safety of his hotel. He stepped outside, reminding himself to keep his mouth closed; the foul air also had a foul taste. Every step he made, shards of glass cracked on the ground. Only from a sideways angle did Marcel finally recognize the building. The flags of the nations were gone, but the poles still managed to stand erect. What he first assumed was the wall actually was the roof. The entire building toppled over like a set of Legos.

"It's all underground now, Mr. Celest. I think I know the way."

Marcel followed his Secret Service agent who clumsily wheeled along a black luggage bag. After a small slope into the parking garage, he found himself bewildered by the set of cars on their sides. They were all bundled into one corner. Down a set of stairs, Marcel found himself in another parking level. There, several men and women sat on folding chairs, each one screaming and pointing fingers to one another. The languages were mixed. He didn't need a translator to hear the animosity. Without tailored clothes, it didn't feel like a UN meeting. More like a set of gang leaders vying for districts. They hadn't noticed them. His agent set down the luggage bag and whispered, "I count about 60 of them."

"That's all?"

With 193 members in the United Nations, this was undoubtedly the smallest number to show up. Most had no means of transportation probably; airplanes had strict routes to avoid the heaviest of the dark clouds. Most members were probably dead. Finally, one person noticed him. It was the Vice President of the United States, Peter Emerson. Or now, the official President of the United States, since Dad had still been unaccounted for. "Marcel?"

Everyone quieted and turned in unison. Smiles appeared across most of their faces. These were not only colleagues, but friends. Each leader stood their ground, instead of running for a hug. Professionalism was virtue.

"I am glad to see most of you are well." When Marcel planned that entrance in his head he expected further grins, instead there were frowns. Perhaps no one was *well*. "I escaped out of my coma just before the US was attacked. I had gone into hiding to avoid another assassination attempt from the terrorist group Servo Clementia. Unfortunately, my absence caused a set of rumors worldwide. Some said Syria plotted my death. Others said Russia. Then the proposal for the Union agreement sank. Several attacks happened around the globe. And now, nearly three billion people worldwide are dead because of the reckless behavior of elected officials." This time, Marcel did expect frowns and bowed heads. He wasn't let down. The world leaders showed nothing but shame.

His agent opened up the luggage bag to reveal 150 copies of the Union Proposal, bound and wrapped in a leather folder. Originally, he thought 150 copies wouldn't be enough but the turnout had been dismal. Marcel continued, "Complexity is what obliterated a third of the human population. I'm offering the opposite of complexity: The Union. Surely some of you have studied this document word for word; others left their copies in a pile to read later. I've worked on this for nearly 10 years, making decisions based on feedback. It's simple. One government. One law. One economy. One education. One world."

A clap. Then another clap. The applause spread and soon the parking garage was filled with content. All except one. Marcel's eyes met with Vice President Emerson, whose hands stayed in his pocket.

"That was convenient," he muttered.

The applause died and heads turned to the only opposer. Emerson folded his arms. "I've known you since I joined your father in the White House nearly eight years ago. And things with you always seem so...*convenient*." He said the word again with a slower sarcasm. "I mean, just in time to save humanity...the Union is here to help."

Before this buffoon in a suit jacket (two sizes too big) spoke any further, Marcel had to act. He locked onto Emerson's eyes. Right where the soul met the connection. Darkness grew, making a tunnel into the Vice President's mind. Marcel could see all the light and all the dark. He could feel the worst of times and the best of times. But right between these entities was the gray mist. Where Lucifer taught him to strengthen certain thoughts. Time sat still, awaiting his command. There it was, hiding in the light. A thought that perhaps the Union was a spectacular idea. Marcel made it grow and become one with the gray.

Emerson stumbled on his words. "What am...that's was weird...I guess I'm just tired...I don't know what's wrong with me...How could I possibly oppose such a fantastic plan? The

Union will combine our economies. We should start immediately on a headquarters. Don't you think? I'm so thrilled. I want to be the first to sign the proposal. Yes! You have the support of the United States."

Lucifer had been right. Persuasion was the greatest power in the universe. Marcel smiled.

CHAPTER FOUR

A mechanical snake slithered through the rubble, stopping every so often. Its outer body clung magnetically to the ruins. At first, Lloyd wasn't sure what the snake-like creature was. A figment of his imagination?

Only when it stopped in front of him did he get a clearer image. Covered in an aluminum body, the snake stood up like the King Cobra about to strike. On the center of where its skull should be was the emblem for the New Jersey Fire Department. Two red beams of light shot out of its eyes and scanned a 180-degree angle.

Then it looked at Lloyd. Its eyes turned bright green. An maybe-too-loud alarm sounded from the robot. A polite female voice spoke. "Citizen, please remain calm. Your location has been uploaded to the nearest rescue crew."

Like waking from a long slumber, he felt lost. He wanted to look around, but couldn't. Trapped below piles of steel grating, the chaos began to take shape.

"Citizen, please remain calm. Elevated heart rate causes more use of oxygen."

Where was he? The last thing he remembered...

Driving? Lost. Somewhere. I-95? No, another road. 195 North? Garden State Parkway? Yes, that was it. Stopping for directions. Ended up somewhere. In Tom's River? Lakewood? Brick? No, Atlantic City. He suggested a stop at the casino. Him and the wife needed to relax for one night. Then an explosion. A missile from the sky hit the ground. Light. Suddenly, light everywhere.

Wait a minute. Nina!

The rubble didn't budge. He couldn't get up and look for his wife. "Nina!" he screamed.

"Citizen, please remain calm. New Jersey's Fire Department is on its way. No need to panic."

"Nina!"

Finally, her voice echoed inside the pile of the destroyed building. "Lloyd! Help!"

Her father used to lock her in a basement. Nina hated closed spaces. She must've been panicking. Lloyd couldn't stand the thought. He could barely move his hands. It was like a vast foot had stomped on him and wouldn't walk away.

"Lloyd! I'm scared! How do we get out? Lloyd!"

The robot device continued. "Citizen, help will be here in..." It paused to receive wireless information. "...six hours, 39 minutes."

They wouldn't last that long.

"Lloyd? Honey? Please! Do something! Help!"

He searched around. His hands were free, but that was it. There was no hole to crawl through. Only steel beams, slot machines, and dead bodies. He felt behind him. Something on his back seemed familiar. Like rubber. A car was inches above him. Maybe there was a way out. With all the strength of a man in his fifties, Lloyd turned his body around. He could see below the car. Unfortunately, no entrance into the vehicle could be seen. With so much rubble, there was no telling which way was up or down. Lloyd learned a survival trick on a show. He spat out and gravity made his saliva dribble down his cheek. Good, he was facing up.

"I'm coming, baby!" he lied to Nina. It was never right to lie, but he had to reassure her.

Then he saw them. All over the bottom of the car. White ants. "What the..." Lloyd whispered. There was no such thing as white ants. But they covered almost every inch of the car's frame.

Perhaps termites? He stared longer. Maybe he needed glasses.

"My God..." he whispered. It was neither.

They were specks of light. Dots that floated around like the seeds of dandelions. He rubbed his eyes, but they didn't go away. There was no consistent movement to them. He waved his hand in front of them. The specks followed his hand.

"Lloyd? Lloyd!"

He crunched his hand into a fist and the specks of light tightened. When he pushed forward, the ball of luminance lifted the car slightly. "Woah!" he exclaimed. Then the car settled back down. From around him, more white dots appeared, coming from every open crevasse where any light had been. They gathered up at Lloyd's command.

Impossible. What was happening? These balls of light seemed to speak to him. He pushed the car with his palms and they helped. The car began to rise slightly. More balls of light appeared and shoved agains the vehicle.

Suddenly it shot upwards, slamming against the rubble, and flipped several times before stopping. Lloyd stood up slowly. He was convinced this was all a lucid dream, because that seemed like the only place he could lift an SUV. The car spun on its roof a few hundred feet away. Around him was a landfill of rubble. Was this the Golden Nugget Casino?

"Lloyd!"

He heard her voice and rushed to where she was. Panicked screams echoed below a slew of metal pipes. Lloyd tried to lift one pipe but it wouldn't budge. He could see her eyeballs, scrambling for a way out and panicked. "Honey, listen to me. I know this may sound crazy, but search for any light source around you. Concentrate on it. Do you see balls of...light?" His speech sounded more crazy than he intended.

An objection should've followed, but it didn't. Nina stayed quiet. After a minute, Lloyd began to wonder if she had stopped breathing. Then the rubble below his feet began to rise. He backed away. The metal pipes rolled away, opening a hole for Nina. Specks of light exploded out and fluttered away into the air.

He ran up to hold her tightly. His wife's gorgeous face had been covered in dirt and tears. After a few deeps breaths, Lloyd tried to take in the situation around them. "What happened?" His wife asked the question on his mind before he could, like always. Their eyes met and she flinched. "Oh my God. You've got a beard."

He touched his face. Weeks of facial hair streamed between his fingers. "How long were we under there?"

Nina stood up and looked at the sight of what used to be Atlantic City. Her hands cupped her mouth. Wind blew her long gray and auburn hair. They blinked several times, hoping this optical illusion would leave. But it didn't. The cities had been in ruins. She whispered, "The Light."

Then Lloyd's memories surfaced. Warmth. Blinding luminance. White everywhere. Kind souls. Choices given. A gift given. A gift of persuasion. An agreement made. He smiled, "The Light."

"The people need our help," Nina said.

CHAPTER FIVE

Since the end of the 1800s, society had grown accustomed to making a simple phone call. Now that luxury was gone. Janice Celest had to decide how to contact the clinic's doctor. Even the days of phone books were gone.

She trampled into a city street. Her calves were getting quite a workout climbing over piles of debris. At least FEMA had been kind enough to bulldoze streets for a clear pathway.

Janice's foot got stuck in a bicycle wheel. It took a good yank to finally release it. Out of breath, she stopped to look at her map. The backpack gave a thunk as it hit the ground. Next adventure she needed to bring fewer supplies.

This map cost her 120 dollars and it was drawn with a blue crayon on yellow paper. That guy made a big business out of knowing the area, thanks to years of truck driving. Too bad his handwriting looked like Egyptian hieroglyphics. He had scribbled the word "white" with a square next to it. That was her destination. White house? White box? Maybe white mailbox? Janice scanned the neighborhood. Sure enough, a white mailbox was at the end of the street. Tossing the backpack over her shoulder made her lose balance and fall aside. Her hand landed on a gooey mess of hair. A dead cat. She sat up quickly and wiped her hands like they had just been dipped in folic acid.

"We can share if you want?" a male voice behind her pled.

Janice grabbed her can of mace and turned in one swoop. It

was a tiny frail gray-haired man in a bathrobe. "The meat isn't so bad. Almost like chicken." His hands were cupped together.

"Doctor Michael," Janice said after a few breathes to calm her racing heart. "Do you remember me? Janice Celest."

His eyes stared at the dead cat then finally up to her. "My goodness! Yes, I do remember you. It's been months. We denied your application to be impregnated. What on Earth are you doing out here?"

"I've been looking for you."

"Why?"

Even after several weeks of knowing, it still didn't feel right to say it. The Population Control department decided who could bear a child nowadays; their female implants were 99.99% effective. Maybe this would be a little shocking for this doctor to hear. She struggled then cleared her throat. "I'm pregnant."

✧ ✧

The placenta excreted the hormone human chorionic gonadotropin. It then bonded with the antibody indicator. Dr. Michael stared at the "miracle" or "incovenience" as Janice would call it. Judging by his face, it was a marvel to an era where population was under the control of government scientists. "I don't believe it. This is impossible. You are pregnant. Even with the vaginal clip."

Not as impressed, Janice wiggled on her cardboard box chair. The actual chairs blew away with most of the Department of Proper Procreation. They were lucky to have a roof over the lab.

What was that smell? It snuck again into her nostrils and made her stomach bubble. Maybe the excrements of the dead cat on her jeans.

"Our internet is down for...God knows how long...I can't check the database. Are you sure you were clipped as a child?" he asked.

Selective Service was easier to get away with than a woman not being clipped. Though they promised it was painless, sleeping the wrong way would give quite a sting in her uterus.

"I'm positive. So tell me, how far along?"

"Somewhere between 10-16 weeks. This is just incredible." He pronounced every syllable slowly in the word *incredible*. The doctor looked again into the telescope. Being used to seeing children bred in enormous aluminum tubes and not in a uterus, this situation must've been a wonder for him. The doctor was in his late 50s. That meant he hadn't seen an unexpected pregnancy in almost 25 years since the world governments decided who became fit parents.

"Your husband, what was his name? Gerard? He must be thrilled. I remembered his determination to apply for a child."

10-16 weeks was a long estimate. How many men had she fooled around with in that timeframe? Five? Six? If only she had remained that civil housewife society taught her to be, then Janice wouldn't be impregnated by an unknown father. She certainly wasn't going to admit to this doctor the mystery of who-was-the-daddy hadn't been solved. Maybe it had been her student Adam, who turned out to be a Christian terrorist. Maybe even her half-brother Marcel. Neither seemed a good choice. "Yes." It had been all she could think of saying.

"This is remarkable. We will have to run some more tests." Doctor Michael pulled out a notepad and began writing notes. "Then we will have to perform a C-section to remove the clip from the uterus. We'll also need to somehow generate enough power to run an ultrasound machine. Oh Lord, where are we going to find an ultrasound machine? Hopefully I can find one on eBay. Gosh darnit, what am I thinking? There's no eBay anymore."

That smell again. She placed her backpack on her lap, covering the cat's guts on her jeans. But the smell didn't dissipate. What was it?

Her husband Gerard went on this almost exact same excited rant when he found out she was pregnant. Neither man had seen the big picture. Janice said, "Doctor, I'm not here to have a baby. I'm here to *not* have one."

He dropped his pencil and it rolled off the lopsided desk.

"But...I mean...Are you sure?"

In all her years as a college professor of Evolutionary Studies, Janice had been asked many stupid questions. *I thought evolutions class was about physics? Isn't evolution against the Bible or something? So did some dude have sex with a chimp and that's where we came from?* But this doctor's question took the top prize. "Let me make sure I'm understanding correctly. You are asking me if I want to have a child when two-thirds of the United States is still smoldering from a nuclear attack six weeks ago?"

"Well..."

"When just an hour ago you asked if we could cook a dead cat? Or how about this, I can take care of a child in the motel room that has no warm water because my home evaporated into a million pieces and all that's left is a basement?"

After a moment to let her breathing calm down, the doctor finally spoke. It was so low, she struggled to hear him. "But, Miss Celest, your child is a miracle. Population Control is over for now. That means your womb carries the only new child in the entire country. Possibly the world."

It had never occurred like that to her until now. Janice felt a little woozy. She stood up. That smell became predominant. Like rotten cheese, vomit, and eggplant had been mixed together then left out in the sun for a week.

She knew so little about being pregnant. Did the child already have arms and legs? Was its brain formulating as they spoke?

"Well, I haven't performed an abortion in over 30 years. The department did have some cases of unwanted children, but they were given to other parents. Gosh, I would have to do some studying. But it's so early in your pregnancy. Why not take time to decide, sweetheart?"

"What do you think I should do?" Hearing an honest answer would clear the rippling waters in her mind.

"That's for *you* to decide, Miss Celest."

Janice sniffed the air. That smell was coming from down the hallway. Without a ceiling, it shouldn't be so strong. Curiosity finally got to her. "What's that smell, Doctor?"

Dr. Michael fiddled his fingers and searched his desk for more paperwork. "I'm going to work on a schedule for you to meet with me."

He obviously heard the question, but didn't answer. "Doctor? What's that smell?"

After clearing his throat, he still didn't say anything. Janice recalled her visit to this facility before the nuke hit. The hallway to the left led to the waiting room. The hallway to the right led to the exit. That meant the hallway in front of her led to... "Oh, my God." Chunks of stomach acid grumbled in her stomach.

The doctor mumbled, "We haven't been able to clean them all out since the power outage."

Test tubes. That pungent odor was from the babies in test tubes. Dead infants. The foul smell entered her mind and would be identified forever. Janice rushed out of the office, knocking over the broken door before exiting. She made it out into the cold air and vomited into a battered bush.

CHAPTER SIX

Such a strange phenomenon. The sky flawless, not a cloud cast a shadow on the world. Warm air caused a bead of sweat to travel down Brent's neck. Sunset left a trail of gorgeous shades of orange. A group of birds flew by with calming calls. He took in a breath of the air. It smelled like the grass had been cut minutes ago. Also, there was a faint taste of salt in the air. The ocean wasn't far.

Five men continued a game of basketball leisurely in front of him. Brent had watched for over 15 minutes. Not one man missed the hoop. They even seemed perplexed by their accomplishments. It was all perfect. Too perfect. Looking up to the sky, he noticed something very odd. Brent's pleasant smile turned to a curious frown. Glancing around, he saw they were alone. A park, no matter where, tended to be packed in an overpopulated world. This was a charade. Almost immediately, the farce had been revealed to him and he slumped down onto a bench. A fake bench. The only reason it felt real was because the computer told him it was real.

"You guys are a bunch of retarded jack asses. There's no one else here except us. That's because *it* can't create new faces. Copyright laws."

The men stopped their game. Their laughs died down. They looked over at Brent, like they just noticed him there. Bigger than him, stronger than him. Shaved heads. Curled lips faced him.

Their brute didn't matter in this place.

One of them, a boy probably not old enough to drink yet, turned to face him. He had a shaved head and a tattoo running down his cheek. "What you say, hombre?"

"You guys are fucking idiots. Don't you notice anything?" The routine had been the same. Brent lifted his finger to the sky. "Birds." At that moment, a flock of birds flew above them. He then pointed to the trees on the grassy plain to their left. "Wind." A wind blew the trees, creating a calming sound that resonated throughout the field. "Cool breeze." Just then, a breeze came through and dried the sweat on their brows.

Aggravation grew in Brent when blank faces stared back. People are so naive. He stood up slowly and grabbed the basketball from the ground. "You can't miss." He turned with his back to the basketball net and threw it. The basketball landed perfectly in the net.

"Like it wasn't obvious that the whole country just experienced a nuclear Armageddon and there's isn't even a cloud in the sky." Brent grabbed the basketball and began dribbling as he continued. "In 2018, a media company created the most realistic video game possible. They could hookup wires to the part of your brain that controls your visual sense of the world. They created a utopia. The government asked: What's better? Two men to a cell or 15 men in a cell wired to a computer? Even rehabilitate them with happiness."

Brent stood in the center of the five men. He grasped the ball in his hand tightly. He looked up to the sky, speaking to the god of this imitation world. "I'm going to ask again...I want a real cell. Not this fake shit. This is your last chance."

Only serenity answered with the calls of seagulls.

After closing his eyes and sighing, Brent began his rampage. He smacked the basketball into one of the guy's faces. It bounced and hit another in the nose. Blood splattered on the court. The ball landed on the ground and Brent kicked it. It smashed into someone's genitals. He flipped backwards as the ball ricocheted. It flew into someone behind him, hitting him in the neck.

All five men were down. Brent ran and jumped onto one of them. He began punching the man's face repeatedly. Teeth flew out. He could see the inside of their nose. Blood spewed in different directions.

Zip.

He felt like he was pulled backwards, but his body didn't move. Then Brent was somewhere else. He was naked, lying between two metal gratings, in a compact room. The ceiling rose higher and higher. Nothing but a spiral of naked men locked in the same fashion as him. Wires were plugged into their heads. It smelled like piss and shit. The humidity felt like an underground sewer.

Horn-rimmed glasses looked down at him. He didn't know his name. And didn't need to.

Brent whispered, "Inmates really fall for that?" His tongue felt like sandpaper. A metal mask covered his nose, giving off fake smells for the computer program.

The lab coat geek running this digital prison just smiled. "Yes, unfortunately they do. Think about it. We can create any world. Isn't that what everyone wants? A perfect world?"

"I want a cell. Without a window, so I don't have to see what I let happen to this world. Without a toilet. Without a door. I want what I deserve."

After a crack of his knuckles, the creepy nerd rolled his chair back to the central computer. With a few presses of buttons, he rotated one prisoner over and sent him back up towards the ceiling. Inmates were now in an assembly line.

"I rarely get to have any challenges. I work with some of the most homicidal maniacs in the world and nothing exciting ever happens. We don't even use guns. I'm the warden, the correctional officer, and..." Drops of defecation hit the aluminum floors behind him. "...the janitor."

Brent tried to motion his hands to release the cuffs. The warden giggled. "Oh, trust me, you won't get out of those chains. I really like you, Brent Celest. I admire you. But did you honestly think killing Marcel Celest would've changed anything? He's a blessing to this world. Imagine if he didn't survive."

The words *Marcel* and *blessing* didn't belong in the same paragraph. Yet, everyone felt that way. Brent didn't need convincing; he knew what the future held. Marcel had to be stopped. Unfortunately, it wouldn't be him to do it. "I want my cell," he grumbled.

"I can even create one with chalkboard so you can color on the walls for the next nine years."

"A real one!" Brent's voice echoed up the endless ceiling.

The warden laughed again, wiping snot from his nose onto his sleeve. "Who thought Brent Celest was so mental? I mean, even worse than me. Of all the prisoners in this room, your rage is the hardest to tame. I can't wait to see what'll happen next. By the way, how on Earth did you figure out that one was fake right away? I mean, it's the perfect code. But you saw something in the sky, at first. What was it?"

Brent grinned. " It was dusk and Orion's Belt could be seen. The stars weren't aligned correctly."

"Very, very smart. I forgot the President's son wanted to be an astronaut, didn't you? I could put you on a different planet? How about Jupiter?"

"I want a filthy cell with a stench I can't find and yellow water dripping from the faucet. At least it's real."

"Sorry, cells are a little packed right now. Remember? *Armageddon* is happening." He laughed as though the world wasn't ending outside the prison walls.

"Then transfer me."

The warden snorted. "I never said I was a secretary too."

"I'll keep hurting inmates."

Typing rapidly into the computer, the warden spoke firmly. "Now *that* we cannot have. Last thing I want is inhumane charges against me. So, you're going to be all alone until I can find a nice digital prison you'll like."

Brent shrugged. "Give me your best shot."

CHAPTER SEVEN

Wind came alive. It didn't have much to say. But Marcel could feel its content. He'd never heard it whistle through his ears so harmoniously.

Atop the cliff, he let the air push against him. It reminded him of the moment after his mother died in a horrific car accident. For only the second time in almost sixteen years as the President's son, Marcel had escaped the Secret Service. He traveled for almost an hour. The darkest hour of his entire life. The image of his mother's mangled, bloody body never went away. Then there was the Arlington Memorial Bridge. He climbed to the very top and wondered what it would feel like to hit the water. Would it be a quick death or a slow one?

Marcel looked over the edge of the cliff. Water smashed against the shore and sharp rocks. Much more lethal than the calm waters below the Arlington Memorial Bridge.

Jump. The water element begged.

"You'd like that, wouldn't you?" Marcel grumbled.

A voice behind him said, "You talking to me?"

It was the President of China. *Former* President of China. Joining the Union meant forgoing titles. "Nothing, Mr. Wen." Marcel turned away from the cliff and back onto the bluish green grass.

"Aren't you cold?"

The cold bothered Marcel about as much as a hot desert day

bothered cacti. Not a single goosebump popped out of his skin, while Wen wore a wool coat. He made a mental note to use a jacket. Short-sleeved shirts looked awkward to several people. If they had visited the depths of Hell, like Marcel, this chilly weather would mean nil to them also.

Without answering his question first, Marcel asked, "What do you think?"

Mr. Wen looked around. They were on an elevated island. Not much occupied it. The flawless green grass reminded Marcel that not every part of the country fell victim to the nukes. On one end were the ruins of an old castle, destroyed by time, not by the attack.

His sister wouldn't leave his mind. Janice would've loved this view. But it wasn't too late.

Wen gave a long sigh like exhaling a trail of cigarette smoke. "Well, I'm not sure a headquarters should be so remote. There's only one bridge onto this property. Seems like a way to corner yourself."

"Corner myself from what?"

"Maybe opposition?"

Marcel laughed then patted his comrade's shoulder. "Don't be silly. Who would want to assault the Union? We're here to help, remember?" His dad used to say the same thing about the United States. *Who'd want to attack America?*

Since Lucifer showed Marcel the future home of the Union inhabited a castle, he'd been obsessing over the locations. Instead of staring into Mr. Wen's soul to convince him, Marcel decided to try convincing him the old-fashioned way. He continued, "Of course, we would need a crew to reassemble the building. It hasn't stood in over a hundred years. But the foundation is still solid." He patted the solid ground below them. "Castles were built to last millennia."

The walls had been stacked with layers of solid cement blocks that must've weighed 100 pounds apiece. Vines and dead leaves gripped the building, as though to suck it into the ground.

Mr. Wen looked at the bottom of his shiny black shoes. Animal feces stuck to the bottom. "But Far Rockaway? What is that? Thirty miles from Manhattan? So close to all the refugees? And a castle? It just seems odd."

What seemed odd was why Wen did what he did. Marcel had seen the dark energy in Wen's soul. The bastard tricked Iran into launching 98 nuclear missiles on the United States. Three entities battled in Marcel's head. One wanted to throw Wen into the hungry sharp rocks at the bottom of this cliff. Another wanted to make peace with China's leader. The other, a gray mixture of both, wanted the help of China to build the Union and leave revenge for a better time.

"Absolutely. *This* is the home of the Union. A castle."

"It would take a lot of my country's money." A tone like money still meant something in an apocalypse. Marcel fought a roll of his eyes while Wen tried to pretend he was in control. "A king belongs in a castle. The Union proposal is derived of three members, but not a king."

"I wrote it, I'm aware." Marcel didn't mean it to sound so sarcastic, so he quickly reiterated. "The Union won't be a dictatorship. Republicans and Democrats are a good example of how two sides couldn't decide what's best for the people. But three members can. Nice and simple."

"Except for the third person, if it's a tie between two decisions. I assume that's why you'll be taking the position of Third Mark?" The side of his lip curled up along his fat cheek.

Marcel smiled. Wen wasn't a typical world leader. He couldn't be fooled. "You've already won the Union members' vote for Second Mark. We will hold another vote for First Mark next month." They made their way back down the hill where two limousines and armed guards waited. "So for now we can agree on the location of headquarters? Don't get me wrong. We appreciate your generosity. The Hyatt Regency is immaculate. But it *is* temporary."

Mr. Wen looked back at the castle ruins. His eyelids lumped. "Yes. Okay. I'll forward the funds to the Union's account tonight."

They shook hands. He felt the lotion on the President's skin. "You have made a wise decision."

"I make many wise decisions. I'd make an excellent Third Mark, wouldn't you say?" Wen's eyes narrowed even more.

Marcel grinned. In politics, it was all about climbing the ladder. World leaders enjoyed power. But no one would have more power than Marcel. "Let's just start the Union before we alter it."

"We have to discuss our pay."

Wen's attitude was like Brent's. Marcel's conversations with his brother followed the same pattern. Like tip-toeing on the edge of a building, wearing a blindfold. One wrong step meant tragedy. Verbal abuse had led into physical abuse. Marcel woke up sometimes to memories of Brent in his all black uniform. Dressed like an assassin with the intent of murdering him. He still had doubts that Brent would go that far, but he did.

This situation he could control. Wen wasn't an out-of-control psychotic, but an in-control psychotic. Which was worse? Besides this wouldn't be the first outburst regarding salaries. Marcel's rebuttal was the same. "We are all paid the same, per the Union agreement. For now anyway."

"How do you figure we all deserve the same pay? I work much longer hours than..."

"At this moment, it is balance. That's what the Union is about. Money isn't the drive anymore. Peace is. Everyone gets treated the same. The Union will be built on a barter system. More work equals more luxuries. Bartering built this great country and money flattened it to ruins."

"Peace?" Wen sounded like he spat out a slew of raspberries. "I'm not convinced you are the man to garner peace."

Shock came over Marcel rather than disdain. "Excuse me?"

"How are you supposed to create peace when you can't even do it with your own family?"

The politician was right. Marcel had never been so insulted by wise words. The Celest family hadn't been at peace for years, after his mother's death. He'd have to prove to not just everyone but himself that he was capable of it. "I'll bring my family together. And we'll be happy. The Celests will become the most honored family in the world."

Prepared to use his dark power of persuasion if another objection came from Wen's lips, Marcel held his breath. But none followed. "Prove yourself worthy as I have throughout the decades, Mr. Celest. Prove you are a leader." Wen bowed in Chinese tradition, and then Marcel did the same.

After another moment of breathing the grassy air, he turned to the cliff. A boy stood at the top of it. Someone he hadn't expected this day. Marcel turned to his guards and held up a hand, signaling to give him a moment.

The boy smiled when Marcel walked up to him. His red tie seemed to glow more. The black suit almost meshed to the approaching dusk. Marcel stopped only a few feet from him. "What are you doing here, Lucifer?"

Not until this moment did Marcel realize the darkness around Lucifer had become more prominent. Water calmed and receded. Wind subsided. The elements were in the presence of a deity. Thunder filled the sky.

A few raindrops fell. Wen left with his security crew. Marcel turned back to the representative of Darkness. "I didn't call you."

"But your subconscious did. It's been a full cycle of the moon since I've seen the presence of my avatar. You've done well. But I must bestow three advices upon you. The same as I have for your predecessors in their time with my energy."

Three pieces of advice or three rules? Marcel didn't like rules. Especially from someone he'd agree would not be in control of his decisions. "I'm listening."

"You shall not allow anyone to have knowledge about our covenant."

After rolling his eyes, Marcel spat out. "Of course. I wouldn't want anyone to think I'm nuts. Making a deal with Satan wouldn't bode well with the masses."

"You shall not cause harm on anyone with your abilities."

Not being a violent person, Marcel shrugged that off. He hadn't hurt anyone physically since his martial arts training, where a little slip broke the trainer's nose.

"And lastly," Lucifer looked out over the cliff, "you shall not allow anyone to discover your elemental powers."

Crossing his arms, Marcel scoffed. "Then what's the point of having them?"

Lucifer snickered. "Rasputin uttered those exact words over a century ago. He ignored my advisement. Hundreds died. And more were killed to keep the legend of what he could accomplish as...a legend. Our power of persuasion is meant for humans, not the elements. Understood?"

"You have no control over me. Do I have to remind you of our deal? You can't touch me. You can't make my choices."

In a puff of black smoke, Lucifer appeared from the edge of the cliff to behind Marcel. "I am aware of the particulars to our agreements. I only offer recommendations. Guidance. We used to be comrades. The destruction, no doubt, caused spite toward me. I wish to rekindle our conviction. Question anything, I will attempt an answer."

The only question he couldn't find an answer to came to his mind. "My family," he whispered. "I want to know where my family is."

Like asking a car salesman to buy a boat, Lucifer stared back at Marcel. "You are inquiring if I can find a diamond at the bottom of the vast seas? A connection must be made and I have none with your family. I cannot answer."

Even ruling dark matter had its limits apparently. "Okay. Then tell me if they are alive." Marcel's attitude was becoming demanding. He reminded himself to get more sleep. Not to turn into an irate person like his brother Brent.

"Yes, they have not entered purgatory. I can verify that. Your..." Lucifer turned pale, "...*love* is thriving. Janice." He practically vomited out the word *love*.

Closing his eyes, Marcel gave a sigh of relief. Chance was all he needed. A chance his adopted sister could be his again. Maybe he could persuade her to share the bed. Waking up to her supple lips smile at him, blonde hair covering the pillow like a silk blanket on the floor. Then he imagined seeing his father greet him at breakfast with a strong pat on the back. Even Brent would be welcome to stay in this castle; all would be forgiven at the sight of his brother bowing to him for absolution. It was all possible now. "I must find them."

"And expect what? A bond? That has drifted into the domain of memory. You are disparate now."

Lucifer had been nothing but a teacher and philosopher. But this felt like bullying. Marcel never took bullying lightly. "Different? So what? Difference doesn't mean separation."

"That's precisely its denotation. Marcel, it is been the identical for the Darkness and the Light. Light brings forth healing and life, while darkness brings forth death and destruction. Divergent of each other and separate. Ultimately leading to balance. Leave your family be. Their fates cannot match yours."

The raindrops became heavier. Marcel let his clothes get soaked while he absorbed Lucifer's words. Perhaps he was different. But to suggest leaving his family to their own fates? "No. I will find them. And together the Celest family will create freedom."

"Freedom?" Lucifer shook his head and took a deep breath. "Perhaps I chose the wrong human with my powers. Freedom is not your objective, Marcel."

Marcel's blood boiled. "It's not?"

"You have much to learn if you plan to rule what is left of humanity. Do you ponder it a sterling tactic to be leaving the people to do whatever they want?"

This was becoming an argument between a trainee and a manager. Lucifer had the knowledge. Marcel just needed to listen. He straightened his back. "Of course not." Then the thought hit him. His crunched eyebrows loosened. "So the opposite of freedom would be...control? That should be my goal?"

Finally, a proud grin from Lucifer. "There's the human I chose. You need to assemble *control*."

The only way to keep balance on a see-saw is by giving as much as you receive.

-Victoria Celest

CHAPTER EIGHT

Sirius Dawson scoffed when he tried to turn the handle and the door didn't open. It didn't budge even after shoving her shoulder against the door several times.

A large rock flew by her and shattered the glass window next to her. "Oh my God, Royal! You almost hit me!"

Her companion, a rough country girl that dressed like a model for K-Mart, wiped her dirty hands on her even dirtier jeans. "There ain't doors anymore, sweetheart. No power, remember?"

How could she forget? When Sirius' life was about chasing the next scoop, she wrote a story about the havoc created by the loss of electricity. Editors said they wanted a realistic article to print. The irony.

With maybe a little too much skill, Royal wrapped her hand in a towel and knocked out the remaining glass shards. In one quick swoop, she was inside the store.

Willie applauded with a sequence of hard, slow claps. "Now that's a damn good throwing arm, you know what I'm saying? She's a natural. Should've played for the Mets!"

When they first discovered Willie Cooper in the Wells Fargo Center in downtown Philadelphia, Royal suggested leaving him there. But Sirius couldn't. Willie was on the verge of death. He held onto the body of a dead little boy. If he hadn't snored, they would've thought he was dead too. *He better not rape us,* Royal had said and shook her head when Sirius gave him the last of her food and water. A week later, no one mentioned who the boy was. Some things were better left unsaid.

It took Sirius a little longer to climb through the broken window. CNN never taught her how to break into places.

"Can you give me a hand?"

Willie didn't hesitate to offer a hand. "So yeah, what's the deal with this place again? I mean, Office Depot don't have no food, am I right?" He took off his New York Jets cap for only a second to wipe sweat, and then placed it back on.

Sirius climbed inside. Willie needed no help. His arms were thicker than her legs. He said it was from construction work; Royal had her doubts. Like she did with everybody. Sirius knew guys from Manhattan. They were all tough on the outside and soft on the inside.

Once inside, Sirius took a look around. It was perfect. She smiled for the first time in four weeks. "This is it. Perfect. We are going to create the first step to a revolution."

Aisles of office supplies had remained untouched. The only store so far that hadn't been looted. Royal was already in the printing area, checking the equipment. "Willie, how long before you can get the power on?"

"Gotta go up to the attic. I'll get started, boss." He walked away, zipping up his Philadelphia Eagles jacket.

Royal didn't reply with a simple *thank you.* "So I'm thinking it wasn't Iran," she said, her flashlight bouncing around the store. Sirius remembered her poor cat. He would've loved chasing that light.

Sirius dropped the 40 pound backpack and immediately felt her sore shoulder. "God, I hope they have some Tylenol."

"Did you hear me?"

"Yeah, Royal, I heard you." Sirius caught a whiff of annoyance in her voice. As a reporter, the trick was to turn the conversation back around before anyone noticed. "So you, like, think Iran was a patsy? Not exactly a great country, you know."

"It's just too easy, ain't it? I mean, why would they attack us?"

"You mean why *wouldn't* they attack us."

Royal screamed. Before Sirius could run to her aide, she said, "A Snickers bar! Wanna split it?"

Rubbing her shoulder, Sirius sighed. "No, I still got a can of peanut butter for dessert." She used a lighter to see better and began her search.

Shelf after shelf. Pens. Markers. Paper supplies. Folders. Boxes. There must've been a pharmacy aisle. Of course not – why would an office store have something like that? But maybe the employee breakroom.

Sirius found the door marked EMPLOYEES ONLY. Polite manners taught her to knock first, but this wasn't that type of world anymore. She pushed the door open and entered. Along the wall was a vast corkboard. Next to it, opened lockers with items scattered everywhere. At least some people escaped before the first blast hit.

She bent down and saw a bottle of aspirin. Not as strong, but would have to do. Sirius chewed them and scarfed them down. It should've been a bad taste. But after having a cooked raccoon for lunch last week, nothing tasted disgusting to her anymore.

The couch felt like a king-sized Tempur-Pedic. Her shoulders praised her as she sank down into it. Sirius couldn't help but look up at the corkboard.

Employee of the Month! Three times in a row!

The girl looked young. Her big smile showed bright in the picture. Maybe just out of high school. Sirius wondered if she was still alive. There were some Post-its scattered around it. *Great job! You're the best! You got a bright future ahead of you!*

There were other pictures pinned to the wall. Halloween, and the silly costumes, were the best. For Christmas, everyone dressed up like elves. On President's Day, two men dressed like Abraham Lincoln and George Washington. Sirius chuckled. All of them so young and full of life.

Royal's voice could be heard through the open door. "So do that mean Iran take the blame for everything? The chemical bomb in Russia? The killer locusts? The virus? Who is gonna pay for all those government sons of bitches and their actions?"

Sirius whispered to herself, staring at the corkboard. "Looks like we are." She stood up and looked inside a locker. There was a makeup bag. She stopped herself from screaming like Royal did when she found the candy bar.

With makeup bag in hand, Sirius went to the mirror above the kitchen sink. *Employees wash your hands often!* These people were fans of Post-its. After several minutes of applying concealers and blush, the mirror wasn't boosting her spirit. Makeup did minimal coverage to the scars on her face. This was turning into a worse disaster than the time she tried to put together that IKEA dining table. The scars looked like fault lines along the Rocky Mountains, her face having been smashed into a glass window while a nuclear weapon tilted her entire building over. The blemishes would never go away. And neither would the memories.

With a dish towel, she wiped away the makeup. Her once bright red hair had turned a dark shade of brown. Cleaning it with stagnant water never seemed to bring any vibrancy to it.

The refrigerator had the funky rotting smell. She didn't bother to see if anything was good to eat. Back in the hallway, she made her way to Royal. Better to have company when the mood got like this.

Royal was sitting on top of the cashier counter with a notepad. Her hair in the usual dull ponytail. If Sirius even suspected that her tomboy friend enjoyed makeup, she'd offer it.

"Them world leaders led their countries into shit. That should be our motto. 'World leaders are shit'." Royal hardly cursed. She crumbled the paper and threw it aside.

"You're wrong. The *press* leads the country. Not politicians," Sirius said, taking a bottled water from the drink display by the cashier drawer.

"Press?"

"Yeah, like, we ran *everything*. We had the power to over-exaggerate issues and the ability to dig up dirty secrets. Even sometimes make them up. Politicians were scared of us. The media had power." Sirius found herself in control of that power again. This store was just the beginning of their propaganda.

"Well," Royal said staring at the notepad, "what should we print on the posters then?"

There was no answer. The thought never crossed Sirius' mind. Just on cue, to give her time to get out of the conversation, the lights turned on and the heater ignited. The printing machines blinked on and off.

Willie was a genius.

"So, Miss Sirius Dawson," Royal grinned, "you ready to start some propaganda?"

CHAPTER NINE

"This has got to be it," Lloyd sighed. Scratching his beard, instead of his head like most people did when in thought. His wife buried her head on his chest. They held each other. Lloyd was six feet tall, Nina a mere five feet and four inches. Her head always laid perfect on his pec. Right next to his heart.

She may have cried; Lloyd couldn't tell. He kept his eyes closed. Maybe the sight of Caesar's hotel would go away. Instead, he imagined it when he was a child. Chasing his father along the boardwalk until Dad got tired, and then he'd chase his mother, who never got tired. It was the first moment Lloyd felt content his parents weren't alive. They'd shudder at the home of Atlantic City now.

"At least the Servo Clementia won't chase after us now," Nina said, always trying to find the positive. Even in the world's destruction.

The terrorist organization had been after them for over two decades; the chase may have ended anyways. Lloyd and Nina's combined ability aided their escape many times. Their ability to feel the emotions of those around them. Undiscovered until they met each other, the phenomenon frightened them both. The accuracy of sensing danger before it happened seemed out of a fantasy television show. But that power was insipid compared to speaking to elements and controlling light.

"How are we going to do this?"

Nina's question had a few interpretations. How were they going to garner followers to the Light? How were they going to eat tonight? How were they going to sleep? Didn't matter which interpretation, Lloyd had no answer. Twenty-two years as a psychotherapist and he finally reached a question with no answer.

She hid her hair up in that bandana she found. With no hair dye around, Nina stood her ground. A woman never showed her gray. Lloyd remembered the first time she saw the first strand come in. From then on, she stated her age as "50-ish" because it implied early 50s. To him, she was timeless.

You seem sad.

Not until he felt Nina stiffen did he realize she heard it too. Lloyd looked around. They seemed alone. Was that a voice? It sure didn't sound like a human voice. But he understood it.

"Hello?" he asked to the nothingness.

I'm right here.

In the corner of the building, a water pipe had burst open. It pushed out gallons of sewer materials. The smell was awful. Lloyd tried not to gag.

Nina was braver than him. She walked toward the burst pipe.

Hello.

Lloyd recalled his visit to the Light's realm. A brief explanation that the elements would adhere to them. It was the water talking to them.

Nina knelt down. Suddenly, streams of a clear liquid escaped the sewer water. They floated in the air before collecting together into one entity. The entity was no bigger than a python. It had no face, but Lloyd could somehow see its emotions. Nina covered her face with both hands, then immediately let them down to reveal a big smile. She laughed in wonder. "My God, you are beautiful."

Marcel never compliments me. I like you already.

Lloyd watched as Nina turned to him with a confused look. "Who's Marcel?"

Every time he'd ever go to the store for a newspaper, his wife would politely ask for a copy of a knitting magazine. Lloyd didn't even know they made knitting magazines. While he studied every political article, she would practice something more important to her. Nina could use those skills to make them clothing, but Lloyd could now use his skills to answer her question. "Marcel Celest. He's the President's son. Father of the Union Proposal. I heard he was in a coma before the missiles hit. Must be who the darkness chose to lead their side of the war."

You look thirsty. Come.

The water entity slithered along the ground and encircled the puddle of sewer liquid. The color began to change from a dark brown. Impurities rose out of the liquid, twinkling. Like when Nina would dust inside their house and the sunlight would reflect off the microscopic beings.

Clear water filled the puddle now, better than any beach the Atlantic side could create. The water entity disappeared. While Lloyd questioned if they should even drink it, Nina cupped it and sipped. "Oh my God," she whispered. "It's pure."

Show-off.

Another voice. "Did you hear that?" they both said at the same time.

The wind blew harder.

Wait until you see what I can do.

"Air!" Nina exclaimed, covering her smile up again. "They're speaking to us."

Then an interruption. Two boys, barely old enough to reach the bar counter, ran out of a club. "Hurry up," one of them said, "they are about to start the beating." The boys ran toward the town square area.

"Beating?" Nina said.

Lloyd felt it too. Fear. Terrifying fear from a man in the distance. Someone was about to murdered? Or beaten? Their ability never clearly explained the reason for the emotion.

Before Nina had the opportunity to show bravery again, Lloyd grasped her and they walked toward the town square.

✧   ✧

On one hand, Nina was thrilled to see so many people alive. Being taught to see life through only a positive filter, she found herself in trouble at times. The forced negative filter in her mind noted that these citizens could be a danger. Hundreds flocked the town square. So dense, she couldn't tell what the commotion was in the center. Her husband held her hand tighter. Being his way of protecting her, even though she didn't need it, Nina followed behind him carefully. They could have knives, guns, whatever to attack and steal. But this ado's focus wasn't each other, rather something peculiar in the courtyard.

It wasn't every day that a man would be tied to a fence post to be mocked. The visual made Nina's heart race even more. The crowd didn't have kind words either.

"Fucker!"

"Thief!"

"Who do you think you are?"

The poor soul had been handcuffed to the post. His face covered in tears and mucus flowed down from his nose. This shamed man emitted the emotion of panic. Nina felt it. Judging by the bruises, the people had already punished him but they wanted more.

"Back off!" a police officer shouted.

The cop's shirt was untucked and unbuttoned. His white t-shirt underneath had been blood stained. He held his gun's holster as a warning. No telling if there were bullets in it or not. People listened, rather than take a chance.

From the police car, the officer pulled out a bullwhip from the back seat. The crowd quieted, like the ball had just been served during a tennis match. Nina felt the shamed man's trepidation. But could also sense the cop's hesitation.

His hands shook as he grasped the bullwhip. The cop circled and spoke to the crowd. "*I'm* the only law left in this town. You listen to my rules." He eyed the imprisoned man. "Clean water costs money. Money you gotta cough up. You know that. Why'd you steal that crate? Now these people got nothing."

The cop ripped the shamed man's shirt off, exposing his boney back.

Lloyd whispered to Nina. "We have to stop this."

Do you want to see what I can do?

The wind. It was talking again to them. Just the slightest breeze in her ear, but it sounded like out of a loudspeaker.

"Ten lashes," the cop said.

Objections spewed from the people.

"That's it?"

"I got no water for my family tonight!"

"You got to send a message!"

Lloyd stepped forward, past the invisible circle the officer adamantly built in a minute ago. The cop reached for his gun. "I said to you all...stay back!"

Hands up gently, her husband spoke softly. "If you don't want to do this, then don't."

Daring and confident, Nina had never seen this in Lloyd before. The Light gave them confidence.

"This is my job. I have to do something. I got no one left to help me." The cop's voice cracked.

Sensing the police officer's anguish, Nina had so many things she wanted to say. But her husband was the expert speaker. He once talked a man from jumping off a bridge. In an even softer voice, Lloyd said, "This life is like a rain forest, every corner has a danger. You cannot place control over such disorder. But you can learn to live with it and survive with it. It's not necessary to burn the forest down."

The cop's hand shook more. "The prisoner will just do it again." He unraveled the bullwhip. "Twenty lashes instead!"

Applause shot out from the crowd. Lloyd backed away. The cop wiggled the bullwhip, preparing the first strike. Tightening himself to the post, the prisoner tried to cover his face.

You sure you don't want my help?

Lloyd looked into Nina's eyes. His pupils expanded. She gasped and covered her mouth. Why did his pupils open like that? How? Slowly, he turned back toward the bullwhip. Lloyd whispered to the chilly wind, "Stop this, please."

The cop raised the bullwhip and lashed it forward.

In the middle of the strike, the bullwhip froze. Hovering in the air, it vibrated and emitted tiny sound waves. The cop let go and fell backwards. Dirt flew up as he tried to kick himself away from the frightening phenomenon, but he couldn't get away fast enough. Gasps and screams came from the citizens.

Lloyd had his hand extended, guiding the wind to stop the bullwhip. He slowly placed his hand down and the bullwhip fell to the floor. A spark had been created from the lash of the whip. It stayed, suspended in the air. Lloyd walked up to it. He grasped it like a fragile butterfly. The spark pulsed and danced in his grip.

Nothing could be said. The people just stared in disbelief. Someone rubbed his eyes to make sure this wasn't an illusion.

Proud of her husband, Nina smiled. The Light had blessed them with undeniable power. And now they had a duty to show it was nothing to be scared of.

Lloyd eyed the crowd with those enormous pupils. His long face straightened up; his lengthy curly hair subtly blew with the breeze. "We are witnesses of the Light. Witnesses to what it can do. Witnesses to what it can offer. There is a final game between two transparent entities. Liberty or imprisonment." The horde glanced at the quivering handcuffed man. "And *we* are the chess pieces of this game. You will have to choose your side."

Her husband released the spark in his hand. It moved toward the police officer. "Get that thing away from me!" He pulled out the gun and pointed. The cop fired, but with no bullets the gun continued to click. Showing no surge to attack, the spark floated in front of him. It began to strobe.

Finally giving up on firing the empty chamber, the cop dropped the gun and stared at the light ball. Slowly becoming more mesmerized than terrorized, the officer reached out a single finger.

As though he was putting his hand in a campfire, the cop poked it then backed away. This time he extended his hand and grabbed it into his fist. The officer closed his eyes tightly. Then a smile. "It's so warm."

Nina spoke up. "You no longer have to be afraid. We can show you something that will combat this darkness. And it welcomes you."

CHAPTER TEN

The Death of Education.

If Janice was a painter, that's what she would call this scene. Fire had smoldered Baltimore University into a pile of black ruins. Black walls. Black fence. Black trees. Perhaps it wouldn't make a colorful painting at all.

She shifted through the wreckage of where her classroom used to be. Though cracked, Janice found her diploma. She remembered grasping that PhD like everything depended on it. Because it did. Shortly afterwards, the postdoctoral fellowship and teaching assistant work became tedious. But this diploma remained in its frame. Until the day she was called *Professor* Celest, Janice never forgot the ladder she climbed to cloud nine.

Her baby moved. Or maybe kicked? Was it possible the thing had feet already? Was it politically incorrect to call it a *thing*? Certainly it wasn't *he* or *she* yet.

Janice shook her head. Time to remain focused. Maybe she'd be lucky and find her tablet. The generator could charge the battery for a little bit. All her books were in that tablet.

The university had an actual library with books. How could she forget? One of the last schools in the nation to have one, actually. Janice scoured the site. The library was small but easy to find. East of the science wing. North of the three pillars that used to be the medical wing.

Shifting through the rubble, she was able to find a portion of a book that hadn't been burnt by the school's fire. It was *Jurassic Park*. Her peak of interest in evolution blossomed after reading this book. She used to read it over and over. While the other orphan kids experimented with sex and drugs, Janice would read until the sun set. Now the sun seemed to set all the time, leaving the world in a permanent dusk. The progress of human evolution had led to this.

Tucking away what was left of the books into her backpack, she continued on her journey home. Home? A motel that got shut down for selling drugs, prostitution, and child porn. That was her home. Didn't seem right to call it that. The house she and her husband Gerard built together landed somewhere in the fields of Maryland. The basement may have been intact after Doomsday, but it didn't stay that way. After the foundation caved in, they had to find a new temporary home. So this was what being homeless felt like.

She almost forgot. They needed gas for the generator. Without her phone's reminder list, things constantly slipped her mind.

The university's parking lot had eight cars. Two upside-down, three on their side, and three in the trees. From her backpack, Janice prepared a siphon. It took several days of practice with Gerard to get the hang of using a siphon. She may have mastered calculus, but that didn't mean she'd mastered how to suck gasoline out of a tank.

She checked the first two vehicles. Stupid anti-theft locks on the gas caps with full fingerprint scan. When gas prices soared years ago, her father had no reason to not sign a bill to place latches on vehicles to protect the gasoline. No reason until now anyways. Two more vehicle checks revealed they were electric. That was useless. Finally, one vehicle had a broken gas cap. Janice inserted the tube and sucked on the other end. She spat out a mouthful of gas; it tasted sweeter than she would've thought. Then again, when starvation entered the mind...everything tasted somewhat delicious.

✧ ✧

Should she tell anyone? If she did, would the decision of an abortion make her a strong woman or a vile one? Eventually Janice wouldn't be able to hide it. A woman's body changes when the *thing* grows in it. Still didn't feel right to call it a thing. Baby. That was a more proper word.

Do abortions hurt? Of course, they must. Especially without technology. How would it be done? Wasn't there a book she read where a woman used a coat hanger?

What about having the *baby*? Raise it on breast milk until it was ready to eat and then...then what? Feed it raccoon meat? Or possum entrails? Or any of the other awful things she'd tasted over the last couple months?

Questions streamed through Janice's head like a stock market ticker. Now she felt agitated. Her options were slim – either bring the child into this wretched world or not. One of the questions, without an answer, was why this was such a hard decision. Janice would be a terrible woman to bring a child into this world. On the other hand, she would be a terrible woman *not* to bring a child into this world.

Just like pulling petals off a sunflower and reciting "he loves me, he loves me not," Janice recited "have it, have it not" to the sounds of raindrops.

The motel came into view. Her feet throbbed and calves pulsed with heat.

Before she could make it to the door, her husband rushed out to take her backpack and gasoline can. Such a good man to be staring out the window until she returned.

Gerard grumbled, like he had any say in her decisions. "I can't believe you left without me. I told you it's unsafe. Just yesterday one of our neighbors got attacked by a bear. A freaking bear, Janice. In the middle of Baltimore!"

Inside, she slumped onto the mattress. The springs bounced for several seconds before she lied completely still. What little sun there was began to disappear and darkness creeped into the room. Already Janice could feel the goosebumps starting.

A plate with a candle was set next to her. It gave a little

warmth. Then Janice's eyes focused. Not a candle at all actually. "Is that...a crayon?"

"Purple is your favorite, right? It's actually called *lilac*, if you can believe that. Doesn't really smell like it though."

Her favorite flower. It was moments like this she should feel blessed to have such an attentive husband. And the crayon actually burned fairly brightly.

Gerard sighed, "I haven't figured out what to do for food tonight."

"I'm not hungry."

"Yeah, me neither," he lied. He spoke in rapid sentences when he lied. Lifting the gas can, Gerard shook his head in approval. "We should have enough to maybe last a few days. I just gotta figure out where Marcel is. He'll take care of us. Radio says he was last spotted in New York, scouting for a Union headquarters. I'll know more tomorrow."

Janice lay on her back. It was a night to either wallow in sorrow or find a positive note. The rain poured hard outside. She had to speak louder. "I think I felt it kick today."

Gerard brightened, smiling through his mangy beard that only ever grew in patches. He sat on the bed and put his ear to her stomach. "I think I can hear him."

"Him? Not her?"

"Of course it's a boy. And he's going to grow up to be a bad ass, like his dad."

If only Gerard knew that he wasn't the father. Until Janice could get a clear answer who actually was, being quiet had to be the only option. He cuddled in the bed with her, holding her womb.

"Cody. That should be his name."

She scoffed and smiled, "Cody? Sounds too much like *cuddy*. He'll be made fun of." It was the first time she spoke of the baby like it had a chance in this world.

Then a knock on the door.

Gerard shot up so fast, the bed bounced up and down. He reached for a drawer. Before Janice stood up completely, he had a shotgun in hand and pointed at the door. "Don't shoot," she commanded. It could be a harmless person, looking for shelter.

Rain smashed down so hard, she wondered if it was their imagination. Thunder rumbled.

Then the knock again. More agitated.

Gerard stepped toward the door. He put the barrel on the door and slipped his finger over the trigger.

"Janice?" a familiar voice beckoned from outside.

Frozen in place, she could only open her mouth in shock. Gerard knew that voice. He swung the door open.

Completely soaked and shivering, Nelson stared into Janice's wide eyes. "Hey, pumpkin."

The water was filthy, even after he had emptied it and refilled it twice. His fingernails had grown so long, he had been chewing them to keep them at an acceptable length. As he munched on the edges, he watched the water go down the drain. It spiraled around and around. A black goo, weeks of anguish in the woods were swallowed up. How much he had accomplished in that time gave him a sense of pride, considering his final days in the Oval Office were lazy and unproductive.

A knock on the motel bathroom door. "Daddy, there's a robe on the door. It matches your hair."

Nelson smiled. *It matches your hair.* His wife used to say that. Janice always had a way of bringing the spirit of her mother back. He stood up and put the robe on. When he opened the door, his daughter hugged him again. Her third hug this evening. Nelson would never get sick of it.

"Sorry, the water heater is still busted. Cold baths aren't ideal."

He hadn't felt cleansed in over a month. "It's fine, pumpkin. Not nearly as cold as it is outside."

"How did you find us anyways?" Gerard asked, making a bed of blankets on the ground for Nelson.

Nelson sat down at a lopsided table in the room. "Well, you weren't at home. So I figured you'd stay at the nearest motel."

Gerard nodded. He placed his arms on his hips, looking the bed up and down. "Needs more blankets. I'll be back."

The moment her husband left, Janice took a deep breath. "Daddy, I'm pregnant."

DPP, the Department of Proper Procreation, had decided pregnancies for almost three decades. So to hear those words, Nelson's immediate reaction was skepticism. "That's not possible. You didn't make it past the interview process."

Janice stared into his eyes. No words needed to be said. She was sure.

As President, he was trained to react properly to shocking statements. During his presidential debate, he was questioned if he found his job as Vice President boring and useless; Nelson quickly answered no, when actually working at an ice cream stand was more exciting. Years later, he was told his son Brent's a Christian terrorist. To which Nelson quickly replied to find and question him. But at this moment of hearing his daughter was pregnant, his mind couldn't find the right thing to say. So he said nothing.

She looked at the door and then lowered her voice. "Should I...you know...*have* it?"

"Pumpkin, that's not a decision I can make. You have to make that."

It wasn't the answer she wanted, because she crossed arms and leaned against the wall. Janice mumbled, "That's what everyone is supposed to say."

Again, he was at a loss for words. Thankfully, Gerard came back in to break the silence.

"So," Nelson said, standing up, "I guess he didn't follow me."

"Who?"

"This college youngster I met on my travels here. He said he knew you."

Janice squinted her eyes. "Are you talking about...Adam Durham?"

Nelson nodded. He immediately noticed her cheeks brightened. She went to the window and peeked outside. "He must've left with Charles instead. The three of us were in the woods together."

Her face was so close to the window, he could see the condensation pulses from her nose. Gerard interrupted, "So, Nelson. What's the plan? You going to take back the President's seat? I heard your predecessor is a jackass."

"No, the focus is on finding the family."

Quickly nodding, Gerard said, "You see, Janice. Even your dad thinks we should get to Marcel. We have the car and enough gas to make it there."

"I didn't mean Marcel. Not yet anyways."

Gerard's shoulders sagged. Janice never turned away from the window.

Nelson continued, "He'll be the easiest to get to. It's Brent I'm worried about. He's still a fugitive. We're not even sure he's alive."

"He's alive," Gerard mumbled, unpacking more blankets for Nelson's bed.

Janice glanced away from the window as though she had just found out her husband had been hiding a refrigerator of food from them. "Brent's alive? And you didn't tell me? Why? How do you know he's alive?"

This was turning into that awkward moment when Gerard would say something stupid and Janice would raise her voice. Nelson went back to chewing on his nails.

"He's in prison. He got captured trying to attack Marcel again," Gerard said. His lips tightened and his eyes narrowed. Even Nelson knew that face. It meant he wasn't going to explain any further. His son-in-law had a knack for keeping secrets. Probably would've made a better politician than a detective.

Janice recognized that look too and turned back to the window. Why was she so intent on seeing if Adam would appear? She said, "You found Brent before the nukes hit, didn't you? Decided to let him go?"

And Janice would've made a better detective than a teacher. Gerard said, "Wrong. I found him after the nukes hit. Since Marcel is alive, that means Brent didn't succeed. Therefore...he got caught. He failed. Do you realize what I'm going to have to do to fix this?"

"What does that mean?" Janice huffed.

Making light of the situation, Nelson stated, "Well, this is good news, actually. I know where we need to go, first thing in the morning."

"Where? We don't have much gas." Gerard's eyebrows were crunched up, just like young Brent would do when Marcel won his father's respect.

"Not far. The White House. The Vice President hasn't been sworn in. That means I'm still in charge. We'll find and have Brent pardoned."

That sense of pride rushed over him again. Nelson could finally feel hope after weeks from its absence. He laid down on Gerard's creation of a bed. Much more comfortable than the forest floor. He looked up to see Janice still peeking out the window. "You okay, pumpkin?"

With the smallest whisper, she said, "I just would've liked to see Adam."

After a long sigh, Nelson had to admit he missed the chatters from the goofy kid. "Me too."

CHAPTER ELEVEN

Adam's knuckles were red. Blood piled on top of the scabs.

"Again," Declan said without looking up from folding his sleeping bag.

Pop-tarts, Toaster Strudels, or maybe a bowl of Frosted Flakes. Followed up by a warm coffee by the computer. But punching a tree with his bare fist? That was not a usual morning routine for Adam. Maybe he shouldn't have asked for more martial arts training from Declan. Maybe he should work on a different path besides his precognition. Maybe he should've followed Nelson instead.

Pieces of tree bark split with every punch. He imagined his vision. The flawless fighting skills from his future self. It took something more than punching a tree for twenty minutes every day.

"Alright, enough." Declan didn't even offer a towel to wipe the blood off Adam's hands.

He tore a piece of his sleeve off, feeling the cold breeze cool the sweat on his brow. Today was going to be another uncontrollable chill. Adam wrapped his torn sleeve around the knuckles. The shirt went from white to red instantly.

Declan was already halfway down the hill. Adam dashed to catch up. He placed a toothbrush in his mouth, scraping away the remnants of his apple that morning. It was the best breakfast he had in a week. Trying to spit became increasingly difficult.

Adam's body didn't want to let go of any moisture, so his mouth was dry as sandpaper.

A public park could be seen in the distance. No swing sets, but plenty of knocked over lunch tables. Sandboxes were empty. The nuclear winds had been so rough, the sand probably landed in Los Angeles by now. There was a set of public restrooms. Declan went inside.

Adam stood at the door. "Water? Do you think there's any —"

Declan screamed, "Goddamn waterless urinals. These were supposed to save the world. Bullshit!"

Then crashes and glass shattering. Afraid to look, Adam peeked slightly through the door. Declan's tantrum looked worse than Godzilla's. The bathroom was in ruins. Luckily, he busted a pipe and water dribbled out from the sink. Declan stopped to fill up his canteen. Adam got his out. The water was a light brown. Probably not drinkable. But he felt himself licking his lips.

Moments later, they were sitting on top of an upside-down picnic table. Adam tried to think of a topic as they guzzled down the cool water that tasted like a dirty penny. "So who trained you in martial arts?"

It was none of his business and Declan's face said the same thing. After a grumble and pick of his nose, Declan answered, "Back in the day, Servo Clementia had training camps high in the mountains. We'd spend years there."

"Years? Wow. Must have been cool."

Adam felt himself struggling through this conversation worse than Declan. This man had been in his life for over twenty years, yet talking was so difficult. His chats were also short. He'd check-in with Adam's foster parents about my behavior. Then maybe swing by on Christmas to gorge on egg nog and fruitcake. Maybe he should've stayed away from the stuffing on Thanksgiving – his double chin grew every year. Now, it had a beard on the top one and none on the bottom. Fat already began sagging off his belt arms.

"Let's go," Declan stood up.

"Alright, Dad," Adam whispered.

After he said *dad*, he paused. Why did he just say that? Declan turned slowly toward him.

"Did you just call me...*Dad*? Are you fucking insane, Adam? I'm not your father. And I told you that once before, you little punk. I hate repeating myself and this will be the last time."

Adam bowed his head like a puppy caught peeing on the floor.

Declan's voice got louder. "The only child I have is possibly dead or wandering the city streets by herself! I think about Royal all the damn time. I could've made this world safe for her. Because I'm *her* father. Not yours! Your parents don't exist because you were born in a fucking petri dish. You have no family. Accept that and stop being such a pussy!"

Without looking up, Adam answered, "Yes, Mr. Declan. I'm sorry."

He was right. Adam felt like a pussy. His precognition showed a tough man, ready to beat anyone down. And all he could think about was how much he wanted a family. It was silly. Adam cleared his throat and threw his backpack on.

Their walk ended at the top of a hill. Mostly in silence besides the usual loud grumble from Declan, like he had pulled every back muscle. Adam peeked over. It was a downward slope filled with rocks, dirt, and cacti. Would be a tough climb down.

"About earlier," Declan coughed out black mucus again. "I haven't eaten in three days."

The best apology Adam was going to get.

A train pulled up below and stopped on the track. Though just a small speck in the distance, it was pleasant to see other people. Adam couldn't see what they were doing. They were collecting things from the side of the tracks. Straining his eyes didn't help to see what was being collected.

Declan pointed to the train. "This train goes directly into Philadelphia. And *you* are going to board it alone."

The word made the hairs on Adam's arms stand up. Alone. "But..."

"I'm going for the Forger, by myself. It's the way it is. We've already lost Nelson's help. Servo Clementia still has a mission to accomplish. And we are slowing each other down."

Being abandoned should've been easier. His first three foster parents left him. Janice left him. Hell, even Brent left him. But Adam had never been this terrified. He looked down towards the train. It was moving at a slow pace; black smoke from the coal colored the horizon.

"You know your target's name, right?"

"Yes," Adam stuttered but not from the cold air. "Yes, Mr. Declan."

"He's going to be hard. He's a conduit. Can manipulate electricity." Declan stuffed a photograph of the target in his upper pocket. "You are going to see things that are going to surprise you. Are you prepared?"

"Yes, Mr. Declan."

The train rolled away, followed by an endless line of containers. "Go, before the train leaves."

Adam's feet couldn't move.

"Go, goddamnit." Declan shoved Adam down the hill. All he could see were streaks of the cacti and rocks. Dust around him blinded him even more. The spinning seemed like it would never stop, until he slammed into a rock. Adam was sure that cracking sound when he stood might've been his pinky finger. His lip bled; he touched it then looked at the blood. Atop the hill, Declan looked down. Adam must've tumbled over a hundred feet. He'd been bullied, but never thrown down a slope. If Brent were here, he'd climb back up that hill and break three of Declan's teeth. But Adam wasn't Brent. He just stared as Charles Declan walked away forever.

The best goodbye Adam was going to get.

The train's horn blew. He walked toward it. It couldn't have been moving faster than three miles per hour. Probably conserving all the fuel they had. Adam grasped a handle and climbed into one of the tram cars. He threw his backpack down, staring at the ground as though it had an answer for why Declan just left.

Twenty-four years old and he didn't realize until that moment he'd never rode a train. It was bumpy, even at this speed. And dark. Very dark. He felt the wall of the container. Did these things even have light switches? He could feel the grooves of the aluminum walls, but no switch. The smell was rancid.

"Got another one!" a man screamed from outside.

It was better to hide. Adam went to the corner. The train stopped and the door opened. Light poured in. Adam's hand covered his mouth, masking the scream. Cargo was thrown in and the train continued. The cargo was a dead body.

Don't be such a pussy!

Declan's words scowled at Adam in his head. The entire tram car was filled with dead bodies. That's what they were collecting. He slipped on blood and landed on another pile of corpses. A bone cracked, but it wasn't his.

Their skin had already lost elasticity, sagging with every bump of the train. Teeth protruded from every gaping mouth like in a permanent shock. Eyeballs were mostly closed, but some stared at Adam. Stared into him and asked why he let this Doomsday happen. He foresaw the future but did nothing to prevent it.

They're corpses, dumb ass! They don't talk!

Flies circled around for a bite to eat. Adam tried not to breath. He found a ladder and climbed up quickly. The lid opened. It was the only time the ash-filled air brought him comfort. He sat on top of the container, looking straight up. Hoping to see one star tonight. Just something normal for one day.

Declan left him with the worst member of the kill list. An electrician that Servo Clementia could never take down. Because out of all the supernatural abilities on the list, this target had the most deadly. Maybe the organization was right. If all those on the list were dead, Doomsday may not have happened. Adam could do this. He had to do this.

His target's name was William Cooper. Also went by the nickname "Willie".

CHAPTER TWELVE

The queue was finally done. Lloyd should've been exhausted. But quite the opposite. He wanted more.

He sat outside his tent, on the cold ground. Six hours ago, they counted eighteen people in line for their healing. Now, none. It was better anyways. Night creeped in and the light became weaker at that time. The encampment hustled with excitement. People put together their tents and shared with the less unfortunate. Just like the drum circles during the fall equinox. Lloyd had realized it then and enjoyed it now...the feeling of peace. Light had done many miracles today. Even he had been surprised to see the polio victim walk out of his wheelchair.

"I have a boo-boo," a tiny voice whispered next to him.

The girl may have been no older than 7. Her hands behind her back, head ducked to the floor, and a pink ribbon tied her hair in a ponytail. Lloyd couldn't help but smile.

"May I see?"

She nodded and held out her index finger. The cut was small enough for a Band-Aid to heal. Lloyd playfully gasped. "My goodness, you are a strong woman to endure such pain!"

Gently, he placed his hand over the cut and then opened his pupils. The emphasis of light grew around him. Like turning up the brightness on a digital photograph. The girl was so bright. Children always were. Lloyd willed the light to heal the cut. In less than a second, it was gone.

"You feel better?" he whispered, returning his pupils to normal.

"Mm-hm," the girl nodded quickly. "Mommy says you are angels. Are you angels?"

"Oh, I wish! They are much more powerful. I'm only using the light that's in you. They can use it from *anywhere*."

She twisted back and forth, like dancing to an unheard song. "So um, can you mean I can fix my own boo-boo?"

This little mind understood more than the adults. He had spent the full day explaining this with responses of confused faces. "Yes. You can fix your own boo-boo. With the light inside you. You just have to trust in it."

Though Lloyd wasn't sure she'd understood, she nodded. Followed quickly by a tight hug. It had been the third one today. He could never get sick of this attention. The girl ran off to her tent.

"She has her eyes," Nina said. He hadn't noticed her standing by the tent, picking apart a flower nervously. Any memory of their daughter did this to Nina. Made her sink into a quicksand of regret.

It was time to change the subject and keep Nina focused. "Did you do a full body count?"

"68."

He stood up and placed his hands on Nina's arms. "It's working."

"Not fast enough. We need thousands."

Nina was right, of course. Word spread of their presence rapidly. But they needed more. A worldwide approach. "If only we had the internet or even telephones. We could reach out to more."

Pull on the strings, silly.

The wind's familiar sarcastic attitude blew in his ear. Nina heard it too. "Strings?" She looked around, as though the answer would be that easy. Wind never gave an easy answer. It enjoyed toying.

They're everywhere. How can you not see them?

Hand-in-hand, they walked deeper into the wooded area. Nina reiterated, "What strings?"

Lloyd held up a finger. "I vaguely remember a story about when Columbus first landed in what he thought was the East Indies. The locals repeatedly said they didn't see the boats until they had already landed. Such huge structures were somehow hidden to them. It's because our minds don't recognize unfamiliar things. Even if they are staring into our faces."

He opened his pupils. Nina did the same. They concentrated on everything around them.

She gasped. "Air was right. There's one of them."

Lloyd looked to where she pointed. No thicker than a nail, a long string hung in mid-air. There were no ends. Like a long spider's silk. When Lloyd held out his hand, using a light from his palm like a flashlight, it even glimmered like spider's silk. The different arrays of colors were almost hypnotic. He reached out a finger and touched it. It was solid. But moving.

"Are they wormholes?" Nina asked.

"The possibility seemed likely. Einstein probably didn't imagine them to be so tiny."

Another gasp from Nina. Lloyd looked around. Now they could be seen everywhere. An artful display of vibrant colors. Each string reaching in different directions. Up and down. Left and right. With no ends.

He closed his eyes and touched the string again. Something strange happened to him. He couldn't help but grit his teeth.

"What is it, Lloyd? Does it hurt?"

"No. It's just," he searched for the word, "overwhelming. I can vision it, but it's going so fast. A map, sort of. Terrains and land and water." Lloyd let go, feeling woozy. His head wobbled.

Grab it. Your predecessors weren't afraid.

Being bullied by the element of air didn't seem likely to Lloyd just a few months ago. But he had to admit, the feeling was intriguing. A wormhole to anywhere. This was how they could reach the masses.

Nina seemed to agree with just a simple nod. They both

reached their hands out, ready to grasp the string. "On three," she said. "One...two...three."

The vertigo became so overwhelming, Lloyd grasped Nina to keep from falling over. Judging by her swaying, she was no better. He crunched his eyes closed. The ringing in his ear made it impossible to concentrate.

After only a few seconds, his equilibrium calmed. Then water crashed against the shore. So loud, it silenced the ringing sound. Lloyd opened his eyes. And he wished he could never shut them again. Even to blink. Because the view was breath-taking.

They stood on top of a pure white glacier. The brightest white he'd ever seen. Water splashed the cliff below them, like a child begging to climb up. A slice of the glacier broke off, making Nina grasp her chest before the heart shot out. It slid down, vibrating the ground below them and diving into the endless ocean. It was dusk, the sun hid along the straight line of the horizon.

"Antartica?" Nina stuttered.

It must've been. The glacier went on for miles in each direction. As the sun receded, the stars sparkled. Lloyd sighed in relief. Seeing a dark cloudy sky everyday became monotonous. The stars were up there. And more striking than ever. "Teleportation. I think we found the way to reach more followers."

"I don't feel cold at all. The light must be keeping us warm." Nina grasped Lloyd's arm.

He scratched his long beard. "As much as I want to live the rest of my days with this view, I think it's time we leave."

Their pupils opened to emphasize the network of wormholes. Nina let go of his arm. "Honey, I think we should separate. Cover more ground that way?"

The idea had crossed his mind. This wouldn't be their first situation to go different directions. Servo Clementia's hunt for them was often obscured by their separation. He trusted her decision, without any objection. "We meet every night at midnight. Atlantic City. That's our home."

She nodded. After a slow kiss, Nina grasped one of the wormhole strings and zipped away. Lloyd wanted one last look. The full moon seemed to smile at him. This world was worth dying for. He held onto a string and left Antarctica.

The vertigo was less. The ringing less. Lloyd squinted his eyes, not from the motion sickness but the sand. He was in a desert. The pebbles blasted in every direction. He put his hand up to block it. The airflow stopped immediately. Pebbles fell to the ground as the sandstorm ceased.

You're welcome.

He took a big breath and sighed. Just like his mother at family dinners. Never even got the chance to say thanks before the sarcastic reply. Lloyd said aloud to the emptiness, "Thank you."

It was sort of convincing.

In one direction, the desert didn't seem to have an end. Neither in the other direction. But when Lloyd turned, he was shocked at the sight. There was an outdoor tiki bar nestled next to the dirt road. The road snaked around the mountain behind it. Certainly many people didn't visit this tourist spot; there were more tumbleweeds around it then stools. Patio furniture had tumbled on the side and was covered by the sand. The wood floor creaked as he stepped on it. "Hello?" Not even a bartender to serve the alcohol behind the bar? Nothing felt right about this.

Just then, he saw them. There were a few people here. All lying on the ground with their faces down and covered in the leftover sandstorm. This wasn't a proper burial for these poor corpses. Lloyd walked over and knelt next to a dead body. He remembered a prayer, taught to him in the Catholic Church. It was a general prayer for those that have passed.

"By thy resurrection from the dead, o' Christ, death no longer hath dominion over those who die in holiness. So, we beseech –"

"I'm not dead, you idiot."

Lloyd leapt back, grasping the side of the bar before he fell over. The body began to move. "My God, I thought you were dead."

"Might as well be," the man grumbled, wiping away the sand off his clothes. It was a strange accent. Australian? English? Lloyd couldn't tell.

"What about these other poor souls?"

"Dead? Naw. Not yet. Get your asses up. Breakfast is about ready," the man said, stumbling to the bar. He reached over and pulled out a large jar of pickled eggs.

Just then, Lloyd caught a whiff of the whiskey breath. Then the grumbles of less than a dozen people getting off the ground. "I'm sorry, but...are you all drunk?"

"*Were* drunk," the man at the bar whimpered. He rubbed the temples of his head, then swallowed down a pickled egg, presumably without chewing it. Through the stains of sand, Lloyd could make out a nametag. This man was a bartender. Max.

"Water," a lady begged as she tumbled into a patio seat. The bartender handed her a beer.

"That's not water," Lloyd said, sounding like the designated driver at a keg party.

"It's 97% water." The lady swung the beer up and guzzled the liquid. Afterwards, she flung the empty bottle at the desert. As though it was at fault for this situation. "Another bloody sandstorm, eh! Is that all you got?"

To convince these people about the Light was going to be harder than convincing them to jump out of an airplane without parachutes. Lloyd sat at the bar.

"And how in the hell did you get out here, mate?" the bartender slurred, as though he just noticed Lloyd there. Pickled eggs and whiskey made a unique odor. He leaned his head back to avoid the smell. "The roads finally open, so we can get the hell out of here?"

"I don't think so."

"And what are you? That's a stupid accent. You must be... Ah, you can't be... American? Are you kidding me? In South Africa?

He's a freaking American. I betcha gonna say 'I always thought Africans were all black'. Stupid Americans." The bartender tried to read a whiskey bottle through one eye, bringing the bottle closer then further. After a shrug, he drank the alcohol. "Even at the end of the world, they still want all the attention. Nukes? Shit. That ain't nothing."

The bartender's burp was loud. Somebody mumbled, then fell back asleep on the floor.

Then the most peculiar sound echoed. It sounded like a freight train blew its horn. In the desert?

The bartender dropped his bottle of whiskey. "Ah shit."

"What is that?"

"Ah shit," the bartender began to shake the patrons. "Get your asses up. We got another swarm!" He kicked one man several times. "Swarm, you fuckers! Wake up!"

"Swarm?" Someone sat up, eyes wide like pearls.

Everyone stumbled up, grasping onto chairs. Lloyd looked out into the desert. The sound got louder. Closer. More consistent. It made him cover his ears. Then, at the horizon, a large shadow appeared. Like a large brown boomerang. Whatever it was, it kept a v-formation like birds in the sky. "What is going on?" Lloyd looked around; the patrons covered their mouths with any cloth they could find. From bar towels to t-shirts.

The bartender spat out, "Have you been under a fucking rock, American? It's the locusts. Cover up!"

"Yes, I've been under a rock," Lloyd lied. Easier than having to explain he teleported here through a wormhole. "Explain what's going on."

"The nation's president lost his mind and released these crazy locusts to kill all the crops. But our blood tasted better. And my blood..." The bartender drained the rest of the whiskey bottle. "...is going to fuck them up if they get a taste of it."

The brown mass closed in. They were right. Locusts. He heard their wings drowning out every sound around them.

A woman unhooked the bra under her shirt, screaming to be heard. "They can only see your breaths. How long can you hold your breath when you swim, American?"

"I can't swim." Lloyd didn't feel the need to lie about that.

"Oh, you're fucked, mate." She placed the bra across her mouth.

The swarm closed in. Lloyd took in a deep breath. The locusts entered the tiki bar. There must have been thousands. Each stopped to scour the area. They searched around the bottles, tables, and stools. Lloyd could already feel himself running out of air. He was never good at holding his breath. A locust floated in front of his face. Its large bubble eyes circled him, looking past the long stinger on its nose. They had long threads from their wings, like golden hair. Almost majestic, if not deadly. Lloyd could feel their hairs landing on his clothes and searching. One crawled underneath his shirt sleeve. He couldn't hold his breath much longer. The woman next to him began turning blue.

Humans are so weak; no wonder you die so easily.

Wind. Lloyd closed his eyes, the locusts buzzed next to his ears. He thought to himself, *Destroy them.*

The air element snickered. *Why should I?*

His eyes opened, pupils wide. He held out his palms, grasping an invisible ball of air. He thought to himself, *Because I'm not asking!*

Okay, jeez.

Every locust became frozen in their spot, unable to fly any further. Lloyd watched in amazement as a tiny bubble, covered in mucus, came out of a locust throat. It floated in mid-air. The locust's breath had been yanked out of it; then it stopped flapping its wings. The same happened to every locust. One by one, until there were thousands of bubbles floating. Lloyd took in a deep breath. He grasped his palms in. The bubbles floated in a whirlwind around him.

"Holy Jesus," someone whispered.

Thousands of dead locust carcasses spun around Lloyd. He flung his hands out and the locusts fell to the floor. The tiny bubbles around him burst; mucus fell to the floor.

The tiki bar became whisper quiet. All eyes on him were wide.

"I take back what I said about Americans," the bartender whimpered.

Lloyd's pupils stayed open. Everyone stared into them. "There's still light in all of you. And I've come here to teach you how to use that light. I am a witness of its true power. And we will use it to start a war with the Union."

So much fog. Nina looked around, but couldn't make sense of her surroundings. She could be anywhere. Before touching the wormhole, she had a glimpse of white homes along a mountainside. All clumped into one spot, like it was the only area with running water. The same brown roofs on each one and they were made of bricks that looked on the verge of tumbling, yet settled. Definitely a foreign land, because the trees were still green.

England had a lot of fog. Maybe that's where she was. But wasn't that just a cliché?

Spain.

Nina jumped. It was the water element again, speaking through the fog surrounding her.

Didn't mean to scare you.

"That's alright," she said, imagining how crazy she looked talking to nothing. No crazier than her conversations with plants. It did help them grow, a proven fact. "Where in Spain?"

Just north of Barcelona.

The more she concentrated on the voice, the more she was convinced it sounded almost child-like. "Can I see you? See what you look like?"

I can take millions of forms.

It seemed like a silly question now. Nina decided to rephrase it. "How would you like to look? If you were one of us?"

Droplets of water fused together in the fog and created the outline of a little girl. She could see through the formation, but it felt so real. Nina covered her mouth to giggle. The water element spun in circles and laughed too. "You are so exquisite."

So are you.

Water danced around then leapt into the fog.

Your predecessors only want to boss me around. No one wants to be my friend.

"I don't have any friends. We can be friends."

Really? Great!

It danced around even faster, clearing away some of the fog. Nina's eyes became more focused. The ground was made of cobblestones. She walked forward and came upon a sold waist-high wall. A bridge.

Coughing interrupted her train of thought. Someone was here. She spun. "Hello?" The coughing became more raspy. The fog was still too thick to hear the source of it. Then footsteps rapidly approaching her.

"Where is he?" a woman's voice shouted from the distance. More voices came from the same vicinity.

"I don't see him!"

"He's going to infect us!"

"Hurry!"

"We have to kill him!"

The footsteps sounded louder. Nina backed away, feeling her heart about to beat out of her chest. "Hello?"

Then a man lunged at her from the fog. She banged her head on the cobblestone floor. The stranger grasped both her hands. "You one of them? Trying to kill me?" He was speaking in Spanish, but somehow Nina understood him.

"No," she answered, trying to free herself from his grip.

He leaned in. His face reminded her of a zombie movie she watched as a teenager, peeking through the slit between her fingers every so often. Boils covered most of his chin and throat. Dried lips had cracked so bad, they left scabs on the edges. Fresh mucus spewed from his nostrils. His eyes had a gooey crust in the lids.

"Let me go!" Nina demanded.

"You are one of them! If I'm going down, you are going down with me! You can suffer from this too!" he screamed.

Leave her alone!

It happened so quickly, Nina had to shake her head to understand it. All the fog had swallowed in and turned into ice, securing the attacker in place.

With the air clear, Nina could see her surroundings. Spanish men and women were on both ends of the bridge. Some carried guns, others carried kitchen knives. But all their mouths had the same look of shock.

The frozen man tried to free himself from the ice prison, but there was no use. Nina stood and faced him. His face hung out of the ice block and cried for help. "Please! Free me! I did nothing wrong! I didn't want this flu!"

It's not the flu.

It just occurred to Nina the power water had. Community College had three courses in human anatomy. Blood was made up of over 70% water.

"Then what is it?" Nina asked.

Something I've never seen. Man-made virus, I think. Can you see it?

Her pupils opened, letting more light in. She scanned the man's body, concentrating on seeing deeper. His heart beat rapidly. She followed the flow from the heart, past the basilic and renal veins. There it was, lying still in the iliac vein. A cluster of black dots. "Nanos," she guessed.

The attacker yelled, "A witch! Witch! Look at her eyes. She created ice! Kill her! Not me!"

No one moved when Nina looked around. They only blinked very fast, like she was one of those optical illusion paintings that needed to be figured out. She failed her Spanish classes, but for some unknown reason...she understood them so far. Perhaps the Light had taught them every language. She cleared her throat and then spoke in Spanish. "I can heal him. The Light can heal him. Please give me a chance."

Their silence didn't answer her plea. There must've been hundreds of them, now that Nina could see their lights. This would be her only shot. She held her hand out, where the cluster of nanos crowded in the Iliac vein. "This is going to hurt," Nina warned him.

Each nano sparkled with just a hint of electricity. She pointed her finger and moved it up. The nanos followed. The attacker hollered and then gritted his teeth.

Up the renal artery and through the gastric vein. Every cry of pain made Nina's eyes water. This was why she didn't make a good nurse. Even if it's for the best, she's never comfortable with causing agony. There was only one way this cluster of nanos could get out. From the gastric artery, the bundle entered the stomach. Nina backed away as the man vomited onto the ground. More foul than the smell was the sight. Black specks mixed in with the red stomach acid. Nina could see the dwindling lights of the nanos.

The man took a few short breaths from his mouth before settling on deeper breaths. Then he inhaled through his nose, like it had been his first time in weeks. "My God," he whispered.

"It's safe now," Nina told the water element.

Ice melted around the attacker. He was able to stand. "I feel better," he whispered to himself. Then spoke louder, "I feel better." He turned to the crowd, "I feel better!" On one knee now, he grasped Nina's hand and kissed it.

With her pupils still wide, she faced the crowd. "I have witnessed the realm of the Light. And it has blessed me with the power to save us all."

CHAPTER THIRTEEN

"I'm a huge fan," the hotel's porter said. The third time he said it. The third time Marcel blushed. Almost two decades of the political life and he could never get sick of the attention.

His hand autographed the Hyatt Regency Hotel's letterhead paper. Even adding: *The Union thanks you!*

"Please don't tell anyone I asked for this," the porter whispered, checking the hallway behind him.

"Lips are sealed." Marcel patted him on the shoulder and handed him the autograph. The porter took the pad of paper like it would disintegrate. "So, I'm just curious about something. Have all the world leaders arrived?"

His voice broke when he spoke. "Yes, Sir."

Marcel gave another pat on his shoulder and slowly closed the door. He sipped the coffee. Sixth day in a row and still not enough sugar in the coffee. But this wasn't the time to be ungrateful.

Chanting sounds came from outside. He passed the white leather couch and marble dining table. Pressing his head against the window, Marcel looked down. It reminded him of visiting the Statue of Liberty as a kid. *The people are so tiny down there*, he had told his mother then. Her answer stuck with him forever. *So are the stars in the sky.*

Hundreds crowded the entrance of the hotel, 13 floors down. Police didn't seem enthusiastic, chatting with each other instead of keeping the peace. Marcel smiled and searched his office desk for a pen. The fans were going to break down the door soon. He had to decide what suit to wear. The blue suit accented his piercing ocean eyes. The black suit matched his hair. The brown suit was neutral and welcoming.

"Share the wealth! Share the wealth! Share the wealth!" the crowd demanded.

His smile faded. He listened again to make sure that he understood the chant.

"Share the wealth!"

But that was the plan. The Union would change everything. Everyone would be equal. What was happening? Marcel touched the soft plush robe he wore. It must've cost over a thousand dollars to make this thing. And he lounged around in it, while these people didn't have a home. And he sipped coffee, while these people didn't have water to drink. And he took a warm shower, while these people cleansed themselves in the rain.

This was just a phase, right? Something that took time for people to trust. Like Obamacare.

An alarm sounded on his watch. It was time. His cup of coffee clanked on the table as he threw it down. He went to the walk-in closet and searched drawers of folded socks...when the protestors were barefoot. Hangers with starched shirts...the protestors wore torn shirts or no shirts. He went to the kitchen and picked up the landline phone. Thank goodness for landlines.

"Yes, Mr. Celest," the front desk clerk answered after the first ring.

"Is my first interview here?"

A pause. "Yes, he's been here for an hour."

Punctual was good. Too punctual was odd. "Send him up please. I need a distraction."

Hundreds of interviews in the last decade of a political life. And for once Marcel was the nervous one. He offered water, coffee, tea, and soda. His candidate turned down all three with a simple shake of his head. Besides the mumbled "hello", this man had said nothing else in the last five minutes of Marcel's explanation of the position. This man acted like he was at an interview for a receptionist, not a job like the Union General. At least it was a distraction. The noise from outside protestors had been drowned out.

"You don't say much, do you?"

General Vanderbilt leaned forward, resting his elbows on his knees. Marcel contemplated leaning back. This office in his penthouse seemed stuffier now than it had ever been. The general spoke in one monotone flat tone, as though he was at the low end of a trumpet. "I've admired you since the day your daddy took office. You have potential. He didn't."

A compliment and insult at the same time. Marcel decided to neither smile nor frown. His father was a blessing to this nation. Wasn't he?

He looked down at the file for the third time. Vanderbilt had an impressive resume. Five star general for nearly 18 years. He fought in every major war and didn't have a single scar. His head was shaved to the skin and looked like a shiny bowling ball. At 61, the man looked ten years younger. Muscles bulged from his plain white t-shirt. This would be the first time Marcel didn't interview someone in a suit. If it wasn't for this file, he might've asked the candidate to leave. "Well, I guess I wouldn't need you to say much. Or even do much. Union General should be a simple position."

"Why's that?" Vanderbilt gave a confused expression. The only expression he had given this entire time.

"Because in my vision of the future, there are no wars. It's peace. Your position was just something the world leaders required before signing."

The interviewee's face tilted like a dog hearing an unfamiliar sound. Marcel searched the file for something else to ask. It was all just a formality, he told himself. "So let's talk about salary —"

"How's that possible?"

"How's what possible? A salary?"

"No. No wars?"

In all his optimism, Marcel never prepared an answer for this question. "The goal of the Union is to create peace. I will NOT have blood on my hands to do so."

"That is how to create peace. With war." Vanderbilt sat up. "Do you hear that?"

The protestors outside got louder with each moment of quiet. Chanting. Shouting. Louder. Stronger. Angry. Bitter. Marcel could insert thoughts into people's heads. Make the elements cower with the darkness. Slow the perception of time when his adrenaline rose, thanks to nano technology. Heal himself at an expedited rate. Yet that sound made him sweat and his lip quiver.

Without any emotion, Vanderbilt said, "That's how it starts. With chants."

Everyone offered advice when Marcel didn't ask for it. He leaned back in his ergonomic chair. "It's just a misunderstanding. They need time. That's all." His voice squeaked. Since meeting his adopted sister Janice, his voice hadn't done that.

"Do you like Halloween, Sir?"

An odd question from someone who sounded like the butler from the Addam's family television show. He was practically a Halloween character himself. "Yes."

"What kind of candy did you like to give the trick-or-treaters?"

"Twizzlers."

"You know what I gave them? Dental floss, Sir. Every year."

Marcel pictured himself, dressed up as Abe Lincoln, expecting a slew of tasty candies. Red hots. Milky Ways. Snickers. And then receiving dental floss. The thought made his eyes squint. "Why?"

"Millions of children suffer from gum disease and tooth decay because of candy. Dental floss is essential to healthy teeth. Many people may not like me, but I am a necessity. It's my job. It's what I was born to do, Sir."

He was strange. But strange wasn't a bad thing. And no one else had this resume in the world. Marcel muttered, "You're hired. Welcome to the Union."

There was no "thank you" or mumble of gratitude. Vanderbilt stood, shook hands, and left the penthouse.

Marcel didn't accept that as rudeness, but as confidence. That man overqualified himself for a position like this. He knew he had it. Just the way Marcel felt in his position. But for the first time, he was noticing how uncomfortable his neck and back felt. He had stiffened during the interview. It wasn't fear of Vanderbilt, but something else. Something said. Something he couldn't whisk away with the power of persuasion or the elements.

"Yes?"

Marcel jumped at the sound of a child's voice. Lucifer sat in the darkest corner of the office, meshing like a chameleon. "You scared me."

"Scare? Do you comprehend the gravity of such a thing? Without being scared, humanity becomes that man. Sauntering this planet as though it belongs to him. Thinking that he can dominate his fate. Oftentimes, that'll deviate you from your path. So be scared."

"I'm not," Marcel shrugged.

Only the whites of Lucifer's eyes could be seen as the darkness grew in the room. "We shall have to work on that."

Marcel rubbed his fingers in his palm; they were wet. Lucifer appeared on his desk without moving. His back facing Marcel, he said, "So you summoned me here? Maybe you aren't handling things *perfectly*."

That tone sounded like Brent. Three years younger than him, but much smarter at Science class. During High school exams, he asked for Brent's help then figured it out for himself. His brother even used that same sarcastic word: perfectly. *You did it perfectly on your own.*

"There's something bugging me about what he said. War."

"There most certainly will be a skirmish. That would be like swimming the oceans without encountering a shark."

He rubbed his fingers again. More sweat. "A resistance? Why? The Union helps people."

"The same could be said for religion, but humans fight for that."

No one liked admitting defeat more than Marcel. But he had to calm the storm before it blasted his door. And the ruler of black matter must have a plan. "What do I do?"

Lucifer climbed off the desk and turned to him. "My realm has been weak for centuries, sitting at the bottom of a scale. Like a goldfish in a sea of sharks. Finally, darkness has prevailed and the scale has risen. For once, the Light is perturbed. Because I am superior. War isn't about winning. It's about making the shark feel less superior."

The phone rang. Marcel jumped again. He closed his eyes and sighed heavily. When he opened them, Lucifer was gone. The answer was a good one. Marcel essentially had nothing to worry about, as long as he stood taller than this forthcoming opposition. He answered the landline phone, "Hello?"

The front desk clerk answered. "Sir, I have some good news for you. We received an anonymous call. It's about your father and sister."

"I'm listening," Marcel stood.

"They are on their way to the White House."

CHAPTER FOURTEEN

Gerard liked plans. The trick was to start from the outcome and work backwards. Like, for example, High School prom. He wanted the most gorgeous girl as his date. Her name was Janice Celest, the adopted child of the newly elected (at the time) Vice President Nelson Celest. With all that Secret Service around, she was timid and practically embarrassed. He had a plan then. All it took was some money. Gerard paid off three jocks to ask her out, knowing damn well Janice Celest was too damn smart for their tastes. Then he took home economics class with her. Coming off as being a friend, he suggested a few more dweebs to date. It took more money than usual to pay those kids off, but they promised to act like jerks. So then, when the time for prom came around, he didn't even have to ask her. *She* asked him.

Now, sixteen years later...she was driving him nuts. Her attitude had been getting worse since the apocalypse. Who could blame her? But this pushed his limits. He stuck to plans. The plan, reiterated four times to her and Nelson, was simple: drive straight to the White House, no use of heater in the car or it might burn out the battery, keep the vehicle at a low RPM to conserve fuel, and by all means...don't stop ever. So far in the first hour of driving, Janice demanded they go above 30 MPH (*It's a freeway*, she says), complained about the cold until Gerard turned the heater on (*The battery will be fine!*), and now...telling him to take the next exit.

"What? That's not the way towards the White House," he grumbled.

"I lived there for almost a decade; I know where it is. That's not where we are going."

His father-in-law, who usually pretended to sleep during their bickering, decided to sit up from the back seat. Nelson asked, "Wait a minute, are we going to..."

"Yes," Janice quickly replied. "Gerard, turn the next exit."

She didn't even ask.

The sign read Maryland National Cemetery. He rolled his eyes, "If you wanna see dead bodies, they're at every exit." It wasn't until he saw Nelson in the rearview mirror, staring out the window and biting his nails, that Gerard realized he stuck his foot in his mouth.

Nelson whispered to Janice, "God, I hope she's okay."

Victoria Celest was buried there. His guilty conscious forced him to take the exit, not his nagging wife. Driving these roads was a complete hazard. Fallen trees, upside-down cars, and boulders from the mountainside. Gerard took it slow, driving around each obstacle with his high beams on. They reached the gate. It was made out of castor iron, but had been completely bent back. Damn, those nukes did some crazy damage. With no security guard or way to open that gate, it was time to walk.

Janice and Nelson were already out the door before Gerard could grab the flashlights. It was like they wanted to be ambushed by lunatic townspeople. He grabbed the flashlights from the glove compartment and his gun. Full clip and semi-automatic pistol that turned green with his fingerprint. He loved this weapon.

Gerard climbed over the bent gate and hopped onto solid ground. He'd never been here, even when Victoria died. It had been awkward, since he barely knew the woman. But she meant a lot to Janice. And Janice wanted to be left alone during the funeral. One of the many times in their marriage that she *needed room.*

Something cracked under his boot. His flashlight scurried to see what it was. A skull. A human skull. He scoured around. The sight made him a little queasy. The wind blast nuke had turned up all the dirt from the cemetery, tossing gravestones and caskets. All that money spent to bury these poor souls and they were scattered like tree branches after a hurricane.

After calling out her name and it being ignored, Gerard found Janice. She and her father were just staring at a tree. He knew nothing about trees, except people whined about saving them all the time. But he had to admit...this one was fascinating. It must've reached thirty feet high and still had several perfectly green leaves at the top. How the hell was that possible? Were they held on with super glue? The branches sprouted out like two arms offering a hug. Weird.

Nelson fell to his knees and pressed his face against the tree. Janice rubbed her father's head. She whispered, "Thank God, she's okay."

A metal emblem had been secured to the side of the tree. It read: For every life that ends, a new one begins – Victoria Celest.

Gerard heard about this once. Some type of technology where a person's ashes could be fed into a tree. Basically becoming one with the tree...or some other mumbo-jumbo. But it was definitely a miracle to see her still standing. And a relief to be part of a miracle, for once.

"We should go," he whispered.

Janice nodded, "Come on, Dad." They both began to head back towards the gate.

Another miracle. His wife actually did what he said.

CHAPTER FIFTEEN

An Open/Closed sign spun back and forth in the breeze. It was the sixth diner since Declan parted ways with the coward Nelson and the even more cowardly Adam. His stomach grumbled. During his trek, he had been careful to stay away from people. The last thing he needed was someone screaming: *Hey, it's that bastard Secretary of Defense! This attack is his fault!*

Declan put his nose up against the glass doors. Pancakes. It was a Denny's, the first he'd seen in all these weeks of travel. There was no need for a menu; he knew what he'd want to order. Grand Slam with two eggs over-medium, two sausage links, and two crispy pieces of bacon. As usual, he would leave the side of pancakes as a dessert, making sure to have a spoonful of butter melting along the slip-n-slide of strawberry syrup. His stomach grumbled again. If Declan could barely recognize his own reflection in the glass of this window, maybe no one else would recognize him either. The chance was worth it.

He entered the restaurant and flung his large duffel bag on an empty table. It was surprisingly not busy considering the sparse food in a 20-mile radius. Three men sat at the table across from him. One of them drank from a bottle of ketchup like it was a beer. The other two just stared at the table, maybe wondering if the wooden chairs could be edible. One female sat alone at the corner of the diner, munching on a bowl of croutons. Instead of quick crunch and swallow, it was a slow chew and savor.

Then he saw the menu and it became clear why so few patrons. Several meals were blacked out with a felt-tip marker. Every item needing any type of refrigeration had been omitted; even simple pancakes needed refrigerated batter. Might as well just eat out of a garbage can for dinner tonight.

Not until the shadow over his menu moved did he notice someone standing there. The waitress seemed less than thrilled, arms crossed and chewing gum. She said nothing.

"I guess I have a choice of bread, coffee, or..." Declan flipped the page. "...a banana. I'll take all three."

"Bananas went bad," she said so dull and quickly that it sounded like one word.

It crossed his mind to ask how bad. He'd eaten several rotten fruits from trash cans and had become accustomed to the taste. "You must have at least some jam and peanut butter? To add to the bread?"

"Cleaned out. No gas. No delivery trucks." She blew a bubble. Maybe he could ask for a piece of gum for desert.

Declan reached for his wallet. The three men poked their heads up and tried to take a peek. There was nothing to see. A running joke of cobwebs in his wallet became a reality. Convenience of credit cards took away the need for cash. He pulled out his American Express.

"Cash only."

"How the fuck am I supposed to get cash with no ATMs?"

"How we supposed to run a card with no internet?" she said in a rehearsed speech.

The smell of toast filled his nostrils. It smelled divine, like that smell cookie shops emit. They had a generator. That meant warm toast and coffee. The deal became even more spectacular. Declan pulled off his watch. He placed it on the table, softly. It was a gift from Nelson, when they won re-election. She picked it up and examined it. "White or wheat?"

Overcome with joy that he had a choice, Declan whispered, "White."

The waitress whispered, "And I'll just see if I can find some peanut butter and jam, but don't tell no one."

Behind the counter, she pulled out a radio with a windup lever. After a few twists, music began to play. "Tears in Heaven", whispered by the graceful voice of Eric Clapton. Declan closed his eyes. What would it be like? Heaven? Would it be whatever the heart desired? He pictured an all-white room with an endless table to choose what wine to drink and several full cakes. Red velvet was his favorite. He'd have his muscular body back before his appetite got the best of him. The women would be fighting for attention, asking him if any gal had stolen his heart yet. Declan would grab as many women as he could fit in both arms. He liked to hear them giggle. Yes. Heaven would be amazing.

The table clanked as the plate was set. The waitress was kind enough to include the peanut butter and jam with Declan's white bread and coffee.

"Thank you," she said walking away with the gold Rolex on her wrist.

The song ended and a radio announcer came on. Declan hadn't heard the news in a while, so if this rock hard bread wouldn't suppress his appetite...at least his appetite for current events would be fulfilled.

"The Union is calling for a quick election to the Third Mark. The seat will be filled by a vote of the Union members. Rumors have our very own Vice President to be in the lead for the third seat. All representatives of the Union will be meeting on June 30th at the former Capitol Building in Washington."

Declan was already licking his fingers. He had eaten the sandwich so fast there was no memory of its taste. The announcement made him pause for a moment. With one finger still in his mouth, he began to question what he just heard. Was this true? *All* Union members were going to be in the same building? At the same time?

This could be his moment. To finally put this apocalyptic future to an end. To complete Servo Clementia's plan. And it wouldn't take a kill list. Declan had an idea how to destroy the

Union.

CHAPTER SIXTEEN

A handsome man stared at Brent. Blue eyes and hair so black that tabloids asked if it was dyed. Permanent circles under his eyes, no matter the cosmetic surgery. Muscles practically tearing through his orange prison jumpsuit. Brent was peering into his own reflection. But it was eerie. Like it didn't belong to him.

Focusing his eyes up, the sky had no atmosphere. Just an endless darkness with the brightest stars imaginable. He squinted to make sense of it. These weren't the usual constellations. And not a single cloud blocked the view. Or even the faintest of smog in the highest layer of air. Where was he? The ground was solid ice, reflecting the polka-dotted skyline. A blue liquid rippled below the ice, moving throughout the land. No, not land. Just ice. Everywhere. No civilization. Was this a dream?

Brent jumped. He hovered for several seconds before hitting the ground. Laughing, he ran and leaped. He gained even more air, landing with the softest thud. Such a thrilling feeling. He did it again. And again. Higher each time. He landed and then slid skillfully across the ice. Beneath, the blue waters glistened with the stars' light.

Just as he expected...this wasn't Earth.

Like a child circling in a candy store, Brent looked around then stopped in awe. It only took a moment to find it. Jupiter rose above the horizon. A mixture of orange and red hues, so enormous he reached out as though he could touch it. Sparks emitted every so often on its surface; he could only imagine the sizable storm to cause them.

He was on Europa. One of Jupiter's 63 moons. With a scene like this, Earth faded from his mind. The nukes wiping out two-thirds of the United States...faded. His mother's death...faded. Dad's constant disappointment look...faded. All the assassinations for the Servo Clementia organization...faded. His failure at killing the one man who will cause Armageddon, his brother Marcel...faded. They all melted into the swirls of Jupiter's surface.

A plume blew out water. Instead of it falling back to the ground, the water kept going. High up into space. What a sight. Brent took a breath of fresh air.

I'm breathing, he thought to himself. That didn't make any sense. Europa shouldn't have nearly enough oxygen for him to be alive. This, so far, was the only thing that didn't make sense.

It wasn't real.

But this couldn't be a dream. Since he was old enough to dream, Brent imagined living on other planets and moons. But never in this much detail.

His lip curled up. The system almost tricked him that time. He looked to the sky. "You devoted an entire computer server for just me, Warden? I'm honored. Really."

No answer.

Brent looked to the ocean below the surface of the ice. "You're not allowed to let prisoners harm each other – I get that. But you're also not allowed to let prisoners harm themselves." He knelt down and felt the icy floor. Europa's surface was fragile, if the computer followed the specifications right. That meant it could crack with just enough force. Brent raised his fist and began to pummel the ground. Over and over again. Blood dripped off his fist and colored the ice red. He continued, seeing his reflection. Punching himself for all the mistakes he made. Joining a terrorist group, killing dozens of targets, lying to his family...

The ice crackled then split. He took a step back. The split

widened and he fell into the water. Currents swept him underneath. He had to focus. This wasn't real. But he found himself clawing at the ice, trying to get back out for air. Certainly the warden would have to release him from this digital prison. Right?

Brent's air was running out quick. He could feel the craving to just take a deep breath, fill his lungs with the chilled water. As his vision faded, he got to see one last glimpse of the stars sparkling through the ice.

His eyes opened. He was somewhere else. Back in the prison, a high tunnel of prisoners connected to a mess of wires. All of them smiling in their farce worlds. Brent would rather face the real one. He remained strapped to a gurney-like device, tighter than usual. There was a Playboy bunny icon drawn with a red marker on his stomach. The warden got bored with no one to talk to. He sipped on a cup of coffee next to his vast computer and monitors. Brent's body was brought down closer, using the prison's hydraulic system. He was stood up with a loud mechanical whir.

After another long sip of coffee, the warden peered at Brent with crunched eyebrows. He poured the rest of his coffee on a computer server next to him. The server sparkled as its internal boards fried and smoke poured out. Their eyes never parted. The warden, through his thick horn-rimmed glasses, whispered, "You know how long I worked on that Europa project? It was flawless. There was no way you could harm yourself."

"Apparently not. You forgot about the thin ice."

"What do you want, Playboy? Your own cell again, I presume. I just handed you a perfect life."

"It's not real," Brent stressed, as though he was chatting with one of those stubborn Republican congressman at Dad's presidential inauguration. "Give me my cell with one toilet and no sink. I deserve it."

After an angry sigh, the warden muttered, "Fine."

CHAPTER SEVENTEEN

Silent treatment had been Gerard's way of driving for the last hour. Janice knew her husband to only be quiet in two situations – watching football or when he's upset. She probably deserved it. Maybe it was the baby or the "end of the world", but she felt sick of the constant worry.

Her dad would try to break the silence with some fond memories. *Remember when I tried to take you to that expensive restaurant for your birthday party and the news asked what about the starving children on the streets? Remember when you got so nervous on the campaign, you puked in that tree? Remember when Brent went to that strip bar the next day after I won re-election and Twitter crashed?* All these memories would have to remain in their minds, because rubble replaced the locations.

Pilots had ended their lives to fly jets into the final nuke over Washington DC. Their sacrifices were in vain. Sadly, the remnants of the explosion didn't cause all this destruction...mankind did. Shop windows had been busted in; Best Buy had been looted to the point of even taking the outside advertising monitors. Sprawled in spray paint across the MLK Jr Library read: 'What did we die for?' Another spray paint read: 'The rest of us are dead.'

An ambulance could be heard. Gerard, with that curious crunch eyebrow thing he did, decided to take a corner toward the sound. Maybe he had hoped to see some civilization. Janice hadn't seen a person since that little girl sifting through the trash can at Columbus Circle. Gerard, of course, refused to stop.

Now they were at the corner of 13th and Pennsylvania. The ambulance sat in the center of a bombardment of cars. Still no people around. It seemed the traffic jammed so bad, the paramedics gave up. Gerard pulled aside and stepped outside. Janice and Nelson did the same, making sure to keep a few steps behind her husband. He was, after all, a Capitol police detective and could handle a violent civilian.

After circling the ambulance three times, Gerard shrugged. He switched off the whir and the ambulance quieted. "None of this makes sense. So people just rioted and suddenly...left? Where?"

"To go see the light," an answer came from behind them.

Janice turned to see a gun pointed at her face. She had never seen a gun before. Especially not up this close. The sight almost excited her. Hands up in the air, Janice backed away. Nelson and Gerard did the same.

"Wait a minute. Natasha McKinney?" Gerard said, behind squinted eyes.

The black woman coughed into her hand, loosening her grip on the gun. Janice thought she should grab it, but if Gerard wasn't making a move...then the opportunity was not there. Her husband trained in six martial arts and even implanted nanos into his system to speed up his reaction times. Honesty may not be his virtue, but safety was.

The woman's grip tightened, holding the weapon with practice. "Gimme the keys. I see you driving up here. Gimme the goddamn keys."

Gerard's lip curled. He reached into his pocket and tossed out the set of keys. Natasha caught them without even blinking. "You all just got me my ticket to see the light. They is going to heal me. Get rid of this goddamn cough."

Nelson took a step forward. "Natasha, we can get you help —"

"Step back, motherfucker. I ain't afraid to shoot any of you all. *Especially* you, Mr. President. I ain't fucking playing. Step back!"

Her father listened, thankfully. The crazed lady continued,

behind wide eyes. "They can do magic in Atlantic City."

"Everyone does magic in Atlantic City; it's called pick-pocketing," Gerard mumbled slowly and sarcastically.

"No. I mean *real* magic, asshole. Heal people. I'm going. Fuck you all. You can stay in this shit storm. Now, who's got the cash? Empty your pockets."

Janice pulled out the pockets of her jeans. It wasn't fast enough. Natasha yanked out the pockets of all three of them, patting them down like airport security. She then pointed the gun at Gerard. "I know you hiding it. Where is it? Shoe?"

Defending her husband, Janice quickly said, "We have nothing."

"Bullshit!"

Gerard sighed. He pulled off his shoe. A wad of cash fell to the floor. A wad that Janice knew nothing about. Once again, her spouse held a secret. She could feel her jaw sore from grinding her teeth.

Natasha backed away, coughing more. She ran into the driver's seat and sped off. Her laughter could be heard as she left skid marks on the ground. "See you around, motherfuckers!"

A puff of exhaust blew in their faces, and then their only ride was gone. Nelson frowned. "Guess we're walking the rest of the way."

That bundle of money seemed to be imprinted into Janice's head, like staring into the sun for too long. It just wouldn't go away. Where did he get all that? How long had he been hiding it? What was he planning on doing with it? Why didn't he just tell her?

Gerard grabbed his bushy hair with both hands. "Did we seriously just get robbed by the Attorney General? Really? Are you fucking kidding me?"

Nelson started his trek, climbing over the traffic pile-up. Gerard climbed up after him, on the hood of a Rolls Royce. He offered Janice a hand to lift her. Without flinching, she climbed up by herself. "You okay, babe?" he asked.

She didn't answer. It was her time for the silent treatment.

✧ ✧

It's called the Diplomatic Room. Located on the ground floor of the White House, it had been used as a war room for many years before Franklin D. Roosevelt began to conduct radio addresses in the room. Nelson, like prior Presidents, used it as a backdrop for his weekly video addresses online. He even shook hands with scoundrel world leaders to give the press an exciting shot. He rubbed his fingers together, as though that could get rid of their filth. After all, most of those world leaders just caused an Earth-wide apocalypse.

Since the room faced the South lawn, it didn't receive the brunt of the nuclear mid-air explosion on Doomsday. Nelson bent over and touched the carpet. There was an emblem of all fifty states lining up the rug and it was still in pristine condition. The fireplace had crumbled, and George Washington's artwork above it had gone missing. In fact, most valuables in the White House had gone missing. The monitors in the Situation Room, curtains in the Red Room, and even the silverware in the China Room.

One more glance out the window confirmed Janice and Gerard had listened to his simple two-word instruction. *Stay here.* Gerard checked his watch again. The third time. How peculiar.

Nelson found another laptop, sitting on the round table by the window. Pushing the power button several times didn't make this any easier to face. Another one out of battery. This was hopeless.

"Mr. President?" a female voice said from the door.

Nelson swung around to see a woman in her late fifties. The usual long skirt, which would make it possible to run if she had to, and high heels that seemed loud even on carpet. It was Secretary of State Coffer. She held a briefcase in her hand that she immediately dropped to embrace Nelson. It might've been inappropriate if cameras or staff were around. She even smelled like Victoria.

"I'm so happy you are alive!"

"What are you doing here?" Nelson immediately regretted not

repeating her kind welcome to him. After Victoria's death, he found himself lacking simple thoughtfulness towards women.

"Well, after the riots, I was hoping to collect some of my photos from my office, but the bastards burnt that side of the wing."

"Who?"

"Protestors. Once the power was down, it didn't take long. It got even worse after the Vice President signed the Union treaty."

He had suspected as much. For the first time, Nelson felt relieved he joined Declan on the journey for Servo Clementia. If he had stayed behind at the White House, rioters would've certainly hung him on the North lawn. Must've been how Hussein felt when his own people turned against him. Nelson didn't want that for his future, but he had to focus on the task at hand...getting his family.

"Madame Secretary, I need to find my son Brent. He was arrested." He hated the sound of his own voice. So professional.

"Yes," she wiped away a hair in her face, "I vaguely remember hearing that news. Vice President Emerson mentioned it. Marcel authorized a transfer." Coffer opened her briefcase and searched through what Nelson felt was a surprisingly huge amount of paperwork. "Here it is. The Vice President wanted to brag about the new Union logo on memos, so he showed me a copy."

Nelson's eyes scanned the paper. There was a logo of a black dolphin with a white background. Marcel always had a thing for dolphins. Quite silly. It made the memo look like an executive order from SeaWorld. Sure enough, Marcel had signed a request to have Brent transferred in 72 hours. He folded up the paper and stuck it in his pocket.

"I saw him two weeks ago. Marcel."

"Good," Nelson said maybe a little too cold and not sure why he shouldn't be more thrilled. He never tried hard enough with Marcel. Maybe because it was too easy. His oldest son wanted to be a carbon copy of him. Perfection turned to dullness. "How is he?"

"He's...different? I mean, call me crazy, but it's almost like he's hypnotizing people. The Union is an awful idea. It's just riddled with eventual problems. I mean, it could be worse than Communism. But every world leader rushed to sign it. Even the ones that hated him seemed to suddenly...love him. I have to leave office. No offense, but I can't work for your son. He scares me."

"None taken."

No one could replace Victoria...ever. But Secretary of State Coffer had the same style and look. Auburn hair that curled around to her neck, strong chin, and the perfect weight between too fat or too thin. Nelson wondered how she could look so good in a time like this. Where did she find shampoo and conditioner? How were her legs shaved? Was that perfume?

In order to seem friendly (but not overly friendly), Nelson had an idea. "Why don't you come with us? Get out of here? The nation's capital is lost."

"Oh, I would. But I'm going to Jersey's shore to see the witnesses. They were here a couple days ago. Everybody left with them. Have you heard of them?"

"Not until the last hour. Now it'll be the second time."

Coffer's shoulders sagged like she was about to give the bad news that someone died. From her briefcase, she pulled out a manila envelope and handed it to Nelson. "Before you open that, it's authentic. Remember Warren Hughes? It's more...perplexing."

Warren Hughes was a death row inmate for almost twenty years. Because he couldn't die. Electric chair only put him to sleep, lethal injection just made him itch like a bad rash, and gas chamber just made him sneeze a lot. In that time, every President carried the same amount of skepticism. How was this possible? Kept entirely secret from the public, Warren Hughes had his sentence changed to life imprisonment. Some things had no explanation. It reminded Nelson of what Declan told him before the hunt for Servo Clementia targets. Every target had a supernatural ability. Marcel was on this list, with the ability to heal quickly. But what else could he do?

Nelson glanced at the envelope. He pulled a stack of photographs, created with a Polaroid camera. More incredible than the fact Coffer found a Polaroid camera were the photographs themselves. Outside the ruins of a fallen Washington Monument were hundreds of people crowded around a couple. The next picture showed a woman's hand with a ball of light hovering above it. Nelson stared for over a minute at it. Adobe Photoshop couldn't alter a Polaroid picture. "It isn't a light exposure –"

"It's authentic," Coffer interrupted. Nelson believed her. She never lied in all eight years of his presidency as his Secretary of State.

Another picture showcased a woman making water move like a worm in mid-air. Nelson's eyes widened. Even more shocking was the woman in the picture. "Is that..." he whispered. The next photo showed a man with the angelic woman.

Nelson recognized them both.

Coffer must've caught onto that reaction. She asked, "Do you know them?"

Since the moment he'd interviewed her for the position of Secretary of State, he'd been honest. This would have to be the first dishonest moment. "No," he said, "I don't know them."

There was a commotion outside. It was Gerard. "Just get in the car," he pled, "Marcel will take care of us!"

Nelson peeked out one side of the curtain. Six suited men surrounded a limousine. All eyes were focused on Janice. The back door was open with Gerard standing next to it. His daughter's arms were crossed, like the time she refused to leave Disneyland. Nelson didn't recognize the suited men. They weren't Secret Service or capital police. But they had that familiar look. The look that didn't *ask* to come with them, but *told* to come with them. He noticed the hump of a gun inside each of the men's jackets.

"How did they find us?" Nelson said.

His face must've seemed suspicious. Coffer immediately stated, "I didn't call them."

Trust wasn't an attribute of the White House before Doomsday, certainly not afterwards. So Nelson lied again. "I believe you."

"They won't hurt her. Just take her to the Union's temporary headquarters. It's the Hyatt Regency in East Brunswick."

Coffer's words didn't comfort him. This all felt strange. Like being dragged away by the Bodysnatchers. This had been the most freedom he had in over twenty years of politics. His daughter felt the same. They were more of a family now.

Janice turned and met his eyes through the window. She seemed worried. Nelson didn't know what to do if *she* didn't. Should he go with her? Keep her safe? Or run? Would they chase after him? Force him to join their cause? Janice answered the confusion in his eyes. She mouthed, "Find Brent." With that, his daughter climbed into the limousine.

"I'll distract them," Coffer instructed and handed him a set of keys. "Take the escape route to the parking garage. I'm the only car down there. Full tank of gas."

"What about you?"

She grabbed his arm and led him to the fireplace. With a flick of the switch on the mantle, the fireplace opened up to reveal an escape patch to the lower level. "Let's just hope I was wrong about him and that he can't hypnotize us." It should've sounded funny, but it didn't.

Nelson nodded and climbed into the escape patch. Coffer closed it behind him.

CHAPTER EIGHTEEN

Willie's Power Workshop. 10211 Essington Ave.

Adam's target could've made up an alias, at least. And what a plain business name for an electrician. It sounded like a positive life coaching class. With such an obvious location, supposedly Servo Clementia couldn't find this man. Or didn't want to...

He looked at the pamphlet one more time – the pamphlet he was lucky to find stapled to a telephone pole. Since Declan abandoned him to find Willie Cooper alone, the search turned from finding a needle in a haystack to finding a needle in a stack of needles. Sure, Philadelphia's population had dropped drastically. But that didn't mean the target would be easier to find. It was a big city. An unfamiliar city. Showing the photograph Declan gave him got no leads. Just some shrugs here and there. One man said he would give him a clue for a dollar. After Adam paid the man, the clue was, "He's somewhere in this city," followed by a burst of laughter. Finding this pamphlet changed everything.

If what Declan told him was true, Adam's visions were from the future. Which essentially meant all this already happened. And it meant he was supposed to find this location of Willie's hideout. The only thing that remained unclear...kill or not kill the target? Declan prepared him for this, but why did the thought of killing a man give Adam a painful knot in his stomach? After all, his precognition was quite vivid. He'd become a tough killing machine. This would be his first moment to test this. Willie Cooper had to die. It was Servo Clementia's plan to save the future.

Stuffing the address in his back pocket, he made his way past the road of abandoned cars and onto the business side of the street. He had a plan. Brent always said when Adam *had a plan*, thirty minutes later it was followed by *this plan sucked*.

A cat scattered away; even those damn things survived a nuclear blast. The shop had glass windows with metal bars, like some sort of pawn shop. He couldn't see inside. Why didn't he wait until daylight? Was Willie even here?

Be tough. That would be Declan's only two words to him now. Adam took a few steps back and attempted to kick the door. Instead, his foot shattered through the glass. "Son of a bitch!" he screamed. So much for keeping quiet. The cat meowed; it almost sounded like laughter. Adam tried to dislodge his foot without falling backwards. It didn't work. He slipped and fell on the icy sidewalk. The cat meowed even louder.

Idiot. That would be Declan's only word to him now.

Adam reached through the hole in the glass and unlocked the door. Not so stupid. The cat didn't make a sound. He walked in and shut the door behind him.

Willie's shop looked like a thrift store. Cardboard boxes were filled with plugs, outlets, and wires that Adam didn't even know existed anymore. Was this a cord for a VHS player? And a Laser Disc player? Adam scoffed. What he would give to even have any working tech right now. No movies to watch on his iPod or books to read on his Kindle. Life had been kinda boring lately.

Everything was covered in dust, even though a massive nuclear missile with 350 mph winds had hit just six miles up the road. This didn't seem like the business of a man who could destroy the world. Adam began to doubt the authenticity of the list. The list that came with him. From the future.

Behind the counter was the cash register. Empty, of course. Wouldn't matter anyway since cash had become moot years ago. There was a picture on the wall. Adam recognized Willie. He didn't seem like an adversary the organization couldn't take down. The chubby belly poked through his NJ Jets sweater. A backwards green cap to hide the receding hairline. The picture was with some fluffy mascot Adam didn't recognize. He hated sports. Maybe because he couldn't figure out the excitement of cheering men that were better than him.

Who were these other two in the picture? A black kid? Cute, but very close to Willie. Nephew maybe? And the man next to him seemed familiar. Adam had to think far back. It was a Hispanic man with a glass eyeball. Then the thought struck him. The man in the photo was an assassin for the Servo Clementia. Adam flipped the picture and saw the date on it. Sure enough, this happened *after* the assassin was sent for Willie. Rumor had been that Willie killed this man. Apparently not the case. The assassin must've gone rogue, just to be with Willie? But why?

Headlights swung behind Adam as someone drove up. He ducked quickly. Someone was outside, parking a vehicle.

"Just wait in the car. It won't take long." Thick city accent. Even the way he said *car.*

Adam dashed down to the basement. There were lights on; he flipped them off with a shaky hand. The floor had nearly six inches of water from a busted pipe. His feet touched the cold water and then climbed onto the top of a furnace. It was the darkest corner of the wide basement. Brent had taught him when the time came to assassinate a target, darkness seemed to mask him better. From his hooded sweatshirt, Adam pulled out two long blades. He found them in an abandoned antique shop four blocks from here.

Now was the time to fulfill his future. Become the killer he envisioned when thousands of people marched to the door of the Union. Adam had to embrace everything the Servo Clementia taught him.

Upstairs, he could hear the front door open.

His target had arrived.

✦ ✦

Four years ago, New Year's Eve was spent in a basement no different than this. Something stunk like a dead wet animal. The air tasted like cigarettes, though no one smoked. Christmas lights still hung around the outline of the basement. A total of five people were there. Declan, Brent, Adam, and two men that would later become AWOL from the Servo Clementia. Most members couldn't stay focused doing the job of a hitman when it was for an organization such as this. Adam grew up in it. He had no other home. Brent had been fascinating; it was their first meeting. Though Adam spoke the whole time. Declan even said he needed more beer to drown out the constant talking. But Brent didn't seem annoyed. Every once in a while he would nod or laugh. His eyes stayed locked on Adam, a clear sign they were becoming quick friends. Then he'd asked a question that made the room silent. He had asked what it felt like before killing a target. Declan answered that his heart would beat slow. Brent said his heart didn't seem to beat at all.

Now, sitting in this basement and hearing Willie Cooper upstairs...Adam realized both friends were wrong. His heart was beating out of his chest. Was he having a heart attack? Maybe he should go to an emergency room. Then he remembered there were no emergency rooms. That made his heart race even more. It sounded like horses galloping across the field. Adam held his chest, begging it to calm down.

His target made it to the basement door. Just then, Adam realized he left it wide open when it had been closed. A clear indication he wasn't meant to be an assassin. Brent always said to leave things the way they were or else the target will become suspicious. And that he did. Willie called out, "Hello?"

Adam thought about responding. Saying he was sorry for breaking in. And that he meant to kill him for the Servo Clementia cause. Then dash out the door and never come back. Sure, a man who could control electricity would just let him walk away from that. No. Adam had to kill Willie. There were no other options.

His victims entered the dark basement, feeling the walls for guidance. "I know someone is there."

No use in hiding. In a quiet, deep voice, Adam recited the Servo Clementia pledge. "You are chosen by the future that you will help destroy."

After a deep breath, Willie exhaled even slower than he inhaled. "You people. I mean, what the fuck? Leave me alone. Connor kept me safe from you all. He saw the truth."

What truth? No time to think about it. Adam slowly grasped the blades. He wouldn't let go of them until his target's blood soaked them.

Willie found the light switch and flipped it on. Adam dashed in. He flung the blade. It stuck into the wall next to Willie. Good shot. But not good enough. He swung the other blade. Willie ducked and slipped in the water on the ground. Adam wrestled him to the ground. He held the blade over his neck; Willie pushed back. Neither of them had the strength. Adam used to be in great shape. Now he was already out of breath. Malnutrition took the best out of him. Willie shoved him away. Adam splashed into the water. It tasted like a stagnant pond. He grabbed Willie from behind and tried to break his neck, but instead spun him around in a circle. *You can't even break someone's neck! Pathetic!*

His target ran through a back door to another end of the basement. Adam didn't even know the basement extended. He could hear Declan's voice screaming at him. *I told you to always survey your area before a kill!* He got up and yanked the other blade out of the wall. Hopefully the next attempt will work. He hurried after Willie.

Adam paused at the door. It was a large room with a few workshop tables. Willie seemed trapped, huddled to one corner. But for someone who had nowhere to go, his target didn't seem concerned. He had his back to the wall, catching his breath. "I don't want to hurt you, brother. But I will to protect myself."

No weapons were around that Adam could see. He took a step closer. Willie's breath calmed to a slow pace. "Alright. I warned you."

Willie Cooper yanked off a wall socket and grasped the

electric wires. No time. Adam jumped on top of a table. The electricity flowed through Willie into the flood below him. He looked like some human tesla coil. Besides his singed clothes, his target remained unhurt by the surge of power running through him. The wooden table could keep him safe for now. But Adam had to figure out a way to take Willie down. He leapt and landed on the other wooden table. Getting closer.

Willie let go of the wires, but the electricity still flowed around him. He backed away and grasped an aluminum baseball bat from the counter. "Back off, bro. I'm telling you. Let me outta here and no one gets hurt."

That wasn't an option. Adam jumped onto a closer table. Electric currents clung to Willie and his bat, like he was caught in a spider's web. Even the slightest touch could send Adam into unconsciousness. *Stop toying around and get it over with,* Declan would say. Adam flung the first blade. Willie hit it with the bat. He obviously had taken a few swings with that thing before. The second blade Adam threw didn't even come close to Willie. He could see an axe at the far corner of the room. Gruesome, but it would get the job done. Adam flipped and landed on another table. He couldn't reach the axe. Maybe if he climbed up. There was a ceiling pipe above him that he could use like monkey bars. Adam grasped it. The pipe broke almost immediately, spewing out even more water. *You idiot!*

Water exploded out of the slit. It caused some sort of chain reaction. All the other pipes burst open and gallons of water filled the room. Adam looked down. The mere foot of water that had been there was quickly escalating. Coils of electricity surged on the surface. It sounded like snakes. Adam could feel the hairs on his body rise. He had to get out of here. But he was too far from the door now. Willie's face seemed concerned. He put down the bat. "I can't stop the energy once it's started. It has to fizzle out. Let me get out the door –"

"No, you're not going anywhere!" Adam screamed. "I'm finishing my mission!" The axe was in reach and he grabbed it.

What would Brent do? He was athletic enough to practically

climb walls. What would Declan do? He wouldn't have put himself in this situation in the first place.

This plan sucked.

The table began to lift and float. His heartbeat sped up even more. Adam dropped the axe then grasped the table. He wanted to cry. Like that time he wanted to create a baking soda volcano in third grade science, but somehow ended up causing a class fire.

But was that class fire fate? Adam was an embryo from the future, grown in a test tube. That meant all this had already had happened. Wouldn't that mean he was essentially immortal? If there was any test of this theory, now had to be the time. Adam looked at his reflection in the electric water. Of course he couldn't die, because then he'd never exist in the first place. He glanced at Willie.

Willie's eyes widened. "Bro? You seriously about to jump in there?"

Adam didn't bother to take a deep breath. If it didn't work...he would be dead. He dove headfirst into the water.

Then his heart stopped.

✧   ✧

There was nothing.

Then there was everything.

Adam gasped. He turned his head and puked what felt like a gallon of water.

"See, I done told you that it was about timing." A female voice said, "Why you got all bent out of shape? Calm down. We should've just left him dead, anyways."

A callused hand patted Adam's back. He coughed so much. His lungs felt like they were on fire with bronchitis. Mucus flowed out of his nose. Adam swallowed back a big chunk of ice cold water. His vision began to clear. Willie hovered, maybe a little too close. "You lucky, boss. She's better at CPR than me. Thought we lost you. You alright?"

Even managing a nod took all Adam's strength. He backed up

and collapsed on the van wheel behind him.

The female with him was in the van. "Where them zip ties? I don't trust him."

"Glove compartment," Willie called to her. He then turned to Adam, his baseball cap dripping water from the lid. "You crazy, brother. That's all I gotta say. I was waiting for you to chicken out, you know what I'm saying? Then you jump in? How'd you know you would survive?"

A hunch. Adam wasn't ready to admit to a complete stranger that he had the power to see the future. Especially someone he targeted to kill. Being immortal suddenly gave him a sense of confidence. He couldn't die. The future already told him that.

"That was brave," Willie nudged him.

"Huh?"

"Brave. I said that was brave."

Brave? Adam had never been called brave. He nodded easily this time. "Yeah, guess I am, huh?"

The female returned and placed a zip tie handcuff around Adam's wrist. He recognized her immediately. "Royal!"

She grabbed him by the wet collar and pulled him closer. "Who the hell are you? How you know my name?"

Adam winced and turned away. To avoid a black eye from bullies, it was better to turn and get a bruise on his head. So much for bravery. Women were more terrifying than the Tanner brothers that used to chase him every day from the school bus stop.

Willie pulled Royal back. "Leave him alone – he just died, yo. Give him a minute."

"Why was he trying to kill you?" Royal shouted at Willie now. "I want answers and I ain't gonna ask again."

It was amazing seeing her. The same ponytail in his visions, threaded through a hat like she was that woman from *The Terminator*. Did she work out? Her calves were bigger than his arms. Royal's nails weren't painted or primed. Makeup never touched that face. Women who used a ton of makeup tended to look tired without it. Royal didn't look tired. She looked almost *too* awake. Ready to run a marathon.

"I'm Servo Clementia," Adam said, curling up on the concrete ground. Those three words answered just almost everything. Royal didn't even need to ask anymore.

"You son of a bitch! I say we toss him back in that water. Let the rats feed off him."

"No, please!" Adam's voice squeaked. He suddenly tasted tuna fish. Which of them gave him mouth-to-mouth?

Willie held his palms out. "Let's all calm down. Listen, I dealt with this before. He —"

"So have I," Royal said crossing her arms. That made both Adam and Willie pause for a moment. What did she mean? Their perplexed faces made Royal roll her eyes and continue. "I'm on that stupid list of theirs too. That's why Daddy try to put an end to the organization."

No, it wasn't right. Couldn't be right. Wasn't right. Adam had seen that list a hundred times. Royal was never on it. Unless. Unless Declan hid it. Removed her. It all made sense. His sudden agenda to end the United States division of Servo Clementia. Brent and Adam continued their endeavor even without Declan's approval.

She continued, "And you, pip squeak, better not tell me we all supposed to die from that list. I argued with Daddy all the time about those targets. That ain't a kill list; it's a recruit list, dummy. I bet my left arm on it."

President Celest suggested the same thing. But how? The targets were all dangerous individuals. Or were they? Willie didn't seem dangerous at all. Maybe they were all innocent. But what about Marcel Celest? He's on the list. So did that mean he's supposed to be *recruited*? And what would've caused the confusion in the first place? From his understanding, the list had been made from individuals in his precognitions. A dozen targets have died because of Servo Clementia. For what? It didn't matter anymore. Adam was at the mercy of these two. The zip ties tightened with every movement. The irony that a thousand miles away, his best friend Brent must've been shackled too.

"What's your name, boy?" she said. She must've been the same age as him. Kind of odd to be called *boy*.

"I'm Adam. We haven't met yet. Well, I mean we have met now, but not yet like in the future. I mean like in the past. Which is kinda the past now, but it's like the future."

If his hands weren't tied behind his back, he may have slapped himself. Their confused faces reminded Adam of when he read his valedictorian speech. People literally scratched their heads at the end.

"What the hell are you talking about? Okay, you know what...never mind." She checked her watch. "We have only twelve minutes to get to town square and fourteen minutes to put up flyers." Now with her hands on her hips, Royal asked Willie, "So what you thinking? You wanna keep a terrorist with us?"

It was surreal seeing her in front of him, and not in one of his horrific precognitions. In the future, she died. Adam couldn't remember where. His visions often became unclear after time. It was outdoors somewhere. Marcel Celest had been able to conjure a tornado of wind with his mind and attack hundreds of people. Royal was one of them. She would be impaled by a light post. Graphic. But should he tell her? Could he change the future?

Willie rubbed the back of his neck. "Listen. The last assassin that came for me ended up becoming the most important man in my life. I don't feel right about leaving this one either."

"You want us to keep a killer –"

Adam interrupted. He better, because Royal seemed to get her way. And her way meant he would be drowned in electric water. "Actually, I'm not. Your father tried to train me for this. I mostly stuck with the computers and building gadgets. He was my first target. And I blew it."

Willie's eyes met Royal. "You see what I mean? He's good with computers! We got our help right here."

Several college girls used him for his brains. They paid him with flashes of their boobs. It made him pursue the technology further. He doubted Royal would flash him, but she might keep him alive. His head perked up. "Help with what? I can help! I'm really awesome at computers!"

Her hand started at the top of her head then rolled down, trying to wipe the stress away. "You gots to be kidding."

Willie knelt down to Adam's level. His breath smelled like tuna fish. "We got a ton of office equipment. I can get the electricity working, but we don't know how to get the networking shit done. You know what I'm saying?"

"Networking? That's it? Yes! Is it a LAN or WAN? If its LAN, is it implemented on a single IP subnet? It could also be a cluster area network. What kind of gateway are we working with here?"

Blank faces stared back at Adam. Willie muttered, "Uh, I think I understood about half of that."

Royal muttered even lower, "I didn't understand *any* of it." She sighed. "Okay, fine. We will catch up with Sirius later. Just toss him in the van and let's go."

Without another word, Royal stepped into the driver seat. She was even stiff like that Terminator chick.

"Sorry, buddy, we gotta keep you tied up until we learn to trust you," Willie said, lifting Adam over his shoulder.

The man he was about to murder gently placed him in the backseat of the van. To make Adam feel even more like a putz, Willie pulled out a sandwich from a lunchbox and began to feed him. Between ravaged bites, Adam mumbled, "Hey...Sorry...I was just trying to do...what was right. Or...what I...*thought* was right." The sandwich was gone by the end of the sentence.

"Conner said the same thing."

Conner. That was that assassin's name. The last one sent to kill Willie. But somehow ended up going into hiding and befriending his target. "What happened between you two?"

"Maybe one day I'll tell you," Willie said, even though Adam sensed it was a lie.

In the driver's seat, Royal peered at him through the rearview mirror. Her eyebrows seemed to be permanently crossed and angry. "Where's my daddy?"

"Honestly...I don't know."

CHAPTER NINETEEN

Durham was the type of town that if someone stopped for directions, the choice would be either *turn left up there* or *turn right up there*. One billboard stood tall near the entrance of the town. A poster for a drive-thru movie theater. Showing *Titanic*. Was that really the last movie they played here?

Declan grunted and leaned against the billboard post. He yanked a water canteen out of his backpack. After guzzling half the bottle, he poured the other half on his head. His double chin was gone. He hadn't weighed this much, a still-slightly-plump 200 pounds, since his last tour of duty in Iraq.

What irony. In Iraq, he and his comrades had a mission to infiltrate a warehouse for weapons of mass destruction. Now in Durham, the butt-fucking-poor area of Pennsylvania, he was about to infiltrate another warehouse. Except there weren't any comrades to help him. And the weapon of mass destruction was an Arabian dirt-bag that had the supernatural ability to make guns with his bare hands. The Forger was no serious threat. He didn't even have a name, just a reputation. Being an incredible gunsmith had kept him alive, supplying the United States' allies with armory. If he hadn't been so useful, Declan would've put a bullet in his head years ago.

Besides, there had been worse Servo Clementia targets. One had skin as thick as Kevlar. After studying where the thinnest part of skin was, Declan sliced his eyelids and hung that target from a ceiling until he bled to death. Good riddance.

The warehouse wasn't far, two more blocks away. Even though this town hadn't suffered a direct attack, it looked empty as a town that had. Every building had that same cream-color awning and brown wooden door. It reminded Declan of warm mashed potatoes and thick gravy.

As he started his walk to the warehouse, he pictured the Forger dressed in a suit and snacking on a plate of warm chestnuts. Barking orders at his subordinates like their lives didn't matter. Because they didn't. Only his mattered. The Forger probably wore several gold rings and a few necklaces, because the Arabians liked to sparkle. Everyone would bow when he entered the room and not look up until spoken to. What Declan would've done to have that respect at the Pentagon. Instead, all he got was counter-arguments to every order he gave.

Adam was probably no closer to ending his target. One of three things happened, he was sure. He died along the journey from a bee sting—the pathetic boy's allergic to just about everything. Willie Cooper killed him instead, the most plausible. Or he chickened out and didn't kill him, also very plausible. But on the other hand, Declan didn't chicken out. Ever.

When his strike team went in the Iraqi warehouse, they came from the front door. In most situations, it was the least guarded door. Mainly because the amount of people traffic. Declan decided that might be the best case here.

No one was around. He expected at least some civilians. Not even homeless. The town had a population of 82. Should be someone around. It was dinnertime – the one restaurant should be full. His stomach grumbled. Across the ways, he could see the town's diner and smell the mashed potatoes from two blocks away. Or was that his imagination? He hadn't eaten in two days.

Focus.

He knelt low and crept to the shadows. There was someone on the roof. An AK-47 swung around the guard's shoulder, no doubt made by the devious Forger. The stupid guard wasn't even paying attention. He sat on his butt and his nose was stuck in a book.

People reading instead of playing with their cellphones...the apocalypse had its merits. Declan studied the ground, making a path to avoid stepping on glass bottles or hard ground. When the guard turned away, Declan dashed towards the entrance. He hadn't run this fast since college track team. It was exhilarating. He slid and landed just below the window next to the front door.

The establishment had tinted windows, but the military had trained Declan to see the number of shadows to estimate the opponents. One, two, four, six. Six men, not bad at all. Should be easy. The Forger, according to CIA intelligence, always stayed below grounds with the burners. Declan had two choices: quietly pass the guards to the basement or quietly break each of their necks.

Breaking their necks sounded more fun.

Unlike in Iraq, Declan wasn't armed. He could remember holding his AR-15. It was hot that day, but the semi-automatic rifle had a cold trigger. All he had were decades of martial arts skill. And the nanobots that surged through his body when his adrenaline rose, a technology reserved for the wealthiest of people and those who had access to government funds. Such as Declan. Thank you, defense money.

He waited next to a trashcan overflowing with foam to-go cases. On his other side was a dead dog. Flies buzzed around it, feeding off its insides. Lucky flies. The dog's intestinal track looked like a string of Italian sausages. Declan wondered what it would taste like.

Focus.

The sun was setting. Without electricity, these men had to work in darkness. Perhaps flashlights or candles would light the room. But that would be easy as pie to get past.

That familiar void of light filled the clouds. His sinuses tightened and throat got scratchy. No telling the amount of allergens in the air with a lack of light. There was no viewing the sunset in an atmosphere like this, but the clouds would fade into darkness. If only Declan knew one day sunsets would be a thing of the past. He may have stared at them every day.

Crickets began to sound. Still not a single person in this town. Maybe the militia scared the locals away. The Forger was an incredible asset to have. He deserved his own town. Declan pictured the asshole demanding the townspeople be exiled. This was his home now.

Two of the guards spoke in Swedish. Countries traded the Forger like a neighborhood traded a weed eater. *Sure I'm not using it*, became *When you bringing it back?* The Swedes were predictable. This would be too easy. He peeked through the window. None of them were even watching the door, conversing at the end of an aisle of shelves.

He quickly opened the door and slipped inside and closed it. Not even one sound. That took eight weeks to master opening any door silently. A faucet spewed water in the porta-potty on his right. How could he have forgotten someone could be in there? Inside the guard was washing his hands. Being hygienic in a non-hygienic world would be this man's death. Declan's heart began to race. The nanobots activated in Declan's blood and the perception of time was altered. Slowed to almost a crawl.

The porta-potty door opened. Declan swooped over, broke the guard's neck, and spun him back into the porta-potty. He closed the door and the guard's dead body tumbled on the toilet. One down, five to go. It was like having a chocolate brownie without a glass of milk. Sure it tasted good, but was unsatisfying.

Two guards were in the catwalks. One snored. The other was playing with a shoe string tied in a loop. Declan hadn't seen someone playing with strings since middle school. No tablets to play Candy Crush on. He climbed up the ladder and crept onto the catwalk. Years of skill kept his movements quiet. Declan was behind him now. He reached over and grabbed the shoe string, then tied it around the guard's neck. The guard choked for air, flinging his arms for help. These chumps didn't get visitors often, none were paying attention. In a few minutes, the guard's body went limp. Declan placed his hand over the dead guard's mouth.

He checked for breathing. Didn't hurt to check. He once had a man fake it and come back to life. This time, the victim was dead. His skin was already freezing. The lifeless body landed on the catwalk.

Declan patted the body down. In his holster was an old fashioned handgun with no finger-print scan. These men were amateur and pathetic. Bottom of the barrel armed guards. He placed the gun in his belt. Too loud for now, but just in case.

Now the sleeping guard. His snores had slowed. Not good. He may be waking up. Declan walked toward him, making a step with every snore and standing still when it was quiet. When finally standing above the easiest kill this night, he wondered how he should murder him. Tear out his windpipe? Rip out his eyeballs and throw them down his throat, letting him choke on them? Then he noticed a razor sharp knife in the guard's belt. Could cut open a cow with that thing. Or a human. That was it. He would slice open his intestines and see if it looked like Italian sausage too.

Then Declan's stomach grumbled. The sound echoed. So much for being stealth.

The guard opened his eyes. Before Declan could reach for the knife, the guard flipped backwards and his foot smacked Declan's mouth. A tooth must've shattered because something was crunchy in his mouth. The guard kicked several times; Declan only blocked half of them. Finally, a challenge. He hadn't gotten a challenge since sparring with Brent Celest.

He grabbed the guard's arm and bent it backwards. Feeling that strength in him, that part of him that loved to maim had extraordinary muscle. The guard screamed in pain and for help. Declan punched him in the face three times. Then four times. Five. Until the guard's nose became flat.

The other guards entered the area. Bullets ricochet next to Declan. He hid behind an air conditioning unit. The nanobots slowed time. He could hear them fluttering in his ears. Good thing he grabbed that gun. He checked the chamber. Four bullets. Three guards left. Something came to him. Something his daughter Royal showed him at a shooting range. She was fantastic aim. *It's all about timing, Daddy.*

Timing.

Declan turned and aimed through the sights of the gun. He pulled the trigger. A bullet landed in a guard's left lung. The next bullet whizzed across the air and went into the second guard's mouth. When it exited the back of his head, it left a trail of blood that looked like Twizzlers. The last bullet entered the last guard's throat.

The nanobots calmed and time returned to normal. Declan listened to one guard choke on his blood and another one covering the hole in his chest as blood spurted out. He walked casually down the catwalk. Even the greatest assassin Servo Clementia had, Brent Celest, would've applauded that moment.

He stood above the fallen guards. They didn't even wear uniforms. Just some white shirts with yellow stains on their underarms. Declan watched them die, wondering if he could see them float away into Heaven. What would it be like?

All this still was not satisfying. Not until he put the last bullet through the Forger's skull. Declan found a door to the basement and opened it carefully.

The heat was unbearable. It felt like the time Declan left on Air Force One from frigid, shithole Alaska then arrived in smoldering, shithole Florida. The change of weather threw his equilibrium in a brief spiral. How on earth did the Forger work and live down here?

He took a few steps on the metal stairs downwards. There was no use in being quiet. The Forger must've heard the gunfire. He pictured the ruthless criminal prepared with semi-automatic rifles and a cigar hanging from his mouth. Like Al Pacino in *Scarface*. Declan had the gun pointed forward and ready. One shot was all it would take.

A mixture of molten steel and ash filled his nostrils. His forehead was already dripping with sweat; his clothes stuck to his body. After months of cold weather, Declan felt a little relieved to feel warmth. But this was drastic. He already wished he hadn't wasted the last of his water, dumping it over his head.

Then the sound of clanking. And more clanking. Like a hammer. A big hammer.

Declan moved slowly toward the noise. Sure enough, the Forger was working. Forming what looked like a bayonet. He watched in shock as the Forger stopped hammering and used his bare hands to mold the red hot steel into a sharp edge. "Which one are you?" he said without turning around. His voice echoed off the metal kilns surrounding him. "Which government has bought or stolen me now? Japan? Russia? Maybe Australia? I've always wanted to go there. I hear it's beautiful. My country was boring." The Forger's thick accent couldn't pronounce the word *boring* without rolling the R.

Just about to pull the trigger, Declan stopped. He noticed the arms and legs of the Forger. They were shackled. His wrists and ankles had red scabs. He had yellow and brown stains on his trousers. The man had been using the bathroom on himself for what looked like years. The Forger was no warlord...but a war prisoner.

"I came to kill you," Declan said putting the gun down.

The Forger's head perked up. He turned slowly. His right eye was swollen shut. Maybe for disobeying orders. "You're Servo Clementia?"

Declan nodded.

"My God. It's been too long since the organization has hunted me. May I finish? I do enjoy making the bayonet."

"Go ahead."

He watched the man slide his finger across the glowing red and orange steel. "My first question to Allah will be why he gave me this gift. I never actually enjoyed making weapons. It started as a stupid job making glass vases. I spilled a bucket of molten, by accident, on my hand. It didn't scar. The word got out. Everyone knew. Then I was held in a prison. That's when the shackles started. Fifteen years ago. One government to the next.

Building weapons. Once, I tried to drown myself in the metal. I didn't die. And it didn't even hurt either."

Declan knew how it felt to have shackles, but not in literal terms. He could've changed the United States as Secretary of Defense. Done some actual good. That had been his intent. When he found his own daughter on the assassin's list, Servo Clementia had to be shut down. His role in the White House was supposed to fulfill his yearning for a brighter future. It didn't. But he had another plan. Another plan that wouldn't involve assassinating more innocent people. Especially Royal.

"Where's the stockpile?" Declan asked.

The Forger never looked up from his work, mesmerized by the glow. "To your left, on the shelves."

Declan searched for only a minute before he found the crates. He used a nearby crowbar to pry them open. Guns. Dozens of guns. Any gun imaginable.

Relief made him take a deep breath. Finally, an arsenal for his plan. Declan looked at the Forger. His bayonet was only half-complete. "I don't have time for this," he muttered. He pointed and shot the last bullet in his handgun. The Forger's head exploded all over the floor.

There it was again. That empty feeling. Like sex with a hooker. It didn't mean anything, but somehow it was needed. Declan looked at the Forger's brains scattered on the cement floor. It looked like a plate of apple pie had spilled.

He turned and began to gather all the guns.

CHAPTER TWENTY

The fire crackled again. Most nights, Marcel didn't even need any other lights besides the fireplace. The element loved him.

You don't seem yourself.

He wasn't. He should've been thrilled, asking staff to ready Janice's room with plenty of lilac flowers. She adored them. His father ran, but hope wasn't gone just yet. Gerard would join his team. Nothing but great news. And Marcel couldn't crack a smile.

Six full-sized photographs were all he had. At first when he received them, he flipped through them quickly. Then he slowed down to stare longer. He then placed them on the coffee table, in a perfect straight line. Long periods of gawking hadn't changed the images. He rubbed one of pictures. It wasn't dirt. Was it a smudge on the camera lens? Too much light exposure? Trick photography? Adobe Photoshop?

Marcel felt numb, like the day his mother died. He couldn't pull out a single thought from the swirling of emotions in his head. He looked at the clock. Thirty minutes had passed since the envelope, with the word *confidential* written in Chinese, was dropped off at his hotel suite.

The landline rang. It rang five times before Marcel picked up. That's right, no voicemail or answering machine. How primitive the lack of technology made him feel. "Hello?"

"Hello, Sir," General Vanderbilt said. No use in stating who he was, the flat voice became familiar. "Ask your questions."

"Well, do we know their names?" he asked, even though it didn't matter.

"No last names. The male is Lloyd. The female is Nina. Facial recognition databases are still down. That's the best we can come up with."

Behind Nina were the remnants of Union Market, just east of the White House. Marcel remembered going there when his father was just a Senator. Mom liked to shop for apples there, nowhere else.

"Sir?" Vanderbilt mumbled.

Marcel cleared his throat. "Does your informant have a rough estimate of how many followers were there?"

"Roughly ten thousand."

Or was it pears that she used to buy at the Union Market? Marcel couldn't recall. It must've been pears. What would ten thousand pears look like?

"Sir?"

Vanderbilt broke Marcel's spell again. He said, "Yeah I'm here. Do we know where the followers are located now?"

"Gone."

"Yes, but where?"

"My informant said one moment they were there and the next minute...gone."

"Ten thousand people just vanished?"

"His English is poor. He kept saying the phrase 'la luz', which means –"

Marcel closed his eyes. "The light." He gathered the photographs quickly and stuffed them in the manila envelope. Like somehow that would make them go away. Lloyd and Nina. "Vanderbilt, I'm going to need a favor."

"Anything, Sir."

Even without the use of hypnosis, the general became his most loyal ally. It made Marcel finally smile. "Until our Union Head of Security arrives," he imagined Gerard's surprise when he would offer him the job, "I will need you to lead my security team."

"Of course, Sir."

"First order of business...I need the rooftop secured."

Vanderbilt said nothing. It was an odd request. There should have been some questions. But this must've been what loyalty was like. He pictured the general sitting there with a notepad and pencil, just awaiting further instruction. Marcel continued, "Make sure all cameras and audio devices are removed in the next hour. Lock all doors and make sure I'm not disturbed for fifteen minutes."

"Yes, Sir." He hung up.

Marcel placed the phone down. Fire lit up.

You are going to talk to him, aren't you? Don't trust him.

"I need answers. And he's the only one who can give them to me."

✧ ✧

Clouds shrouded the full moon. This was unacceptable. Marcel whispered, "Clear the sky." Nothing answered back besides a cool breeze. Air didn't like his demanding tone. He was pressed for time. The roof had been cleared and cameras were off. Now Marcel wouldn't look like a fool talking to himself. He spoke louder, "I said 'clear the sky.' I need the moon."

You ever heard of the word "please"?, the wind answered back.

"I'm in control, do you understand? I will use the darkness if I have to."

Okay! There's no reason to be a bully.

Bully? Marcel felt like the one being bullied. Besides fire, every element was defiant.

After a minute, the clouds began to spread open. The moon lit up the rooftop like a spotlight had been turned on. Marcel turned. Besides the air conditioner whirring on and off, there weren't any sounds. "Come on, Gabe. I know you're there. We need to talk. We're alone, I promise."

Twinkles of light formed around a stack above the rooftop. The moonlight made them shine brighter. Suddenly they fused together, forming a human. A man Marcel had known for years. He was dressed in a ragged brown jacket, torn white shirt, flip-flops, and jeans two sizes too big. The exact outfit he wore the first day they met. Still unshaven and with matted hair, Gabe smiled. "Hello, young man."

"What's the point of a disguise anymore? I already know your true identity."

"Okay," Gabe said. What looked like white fabrics swung out of his back and wrapped him like a cocoon. The cloak became blinding white then changed his appearance. Gabe was now dressed as some type of knight that Marcel didn't recognize, armored cream-colored plating and a skirt perhaps just too high. "This was how I dressed when I taught Merlin how to control his powers. What do you think?"

"You look like you're going to a costume party," Marcel mumbled.

Gabe's right cheek twisted in a way to show he was thinking. "How about this?" Again, the cloak of light changed his outfit. Now he was a businessman, with a pin-striped suit worn in the 1930s.

"You look like a Manhattan gangster. Which of my predecessors did you teach when you wore that? Jimmy Hoffa?"

"I'll have you know, this was the style back then. Bloody hell, a suit like this would cost 100 pounds! And no, it wasn't Jimmy Hoffa. Actually, it was Hitler."

Marcel snorted, finding that hard to believe. "Adolf Hitler was a chosen one too?"

"His path would've been quite different actually, if he followed my guidance and not, well, the guidance of *you-know-who*."

"Lucifer," Marcel said. "Okay, just put something on that isn't distracting." His tone sounded more agitated.

Gabe nodded and transformed once again. This time he was dressed as a woman. He looked like Scarlett from *Gone with the Wind*. Even the same red lipstick and rosy cheeks. Marcel bit his bottom lip to keep from laughing. With a playful southern accent, Gabe twisted in circles. "Oh, how do I look? Am I ready for our talk now? The moon is perfect tonight. Wouldn't you agree?" Covering his mouth with his hand, Marcel hid his smile. Gabe kept instigating. "Shall we dance? How about a kiss?" He squeezed his lips together.

Marcel burst into laughter, so hard he felt his eyes water. Gabe morphed back into his regular homeless outfit. He had a large grin on his face. "There it is, my dear boy. It's so beautiful."

"What is?"

"Your light."

Marcel cleared his throat and wiped away his smile. "We have to talk." He'd known this man for years before the truth came out. Gabe wasn't a man at all.

"I'm thrilled you reached out to me. Truth be told, I never expected to hear from you after –"

"It was revealed you were an archangel and had lied to me all that time? Yeah, I didn't plan on talking to you again. But I need answers."

Gabe hopped off the stack and sat on top of pallets of concrete blocks. His feet dangled. Marcel crossed his arms and said, "Who are they?"

"*They* are your opposites. Chosen by the Light. But much more powerful than you."

Uncrossing his arms and placing them in his pockets, Marcel took a deep breath. "Why?"

Meeting his eyes, Gabe said, "Because there is something in the Light that you cannot find in the Darkness." He paused, then said the word as if it explaining a glorious painting in one word. "Hope."

"Hope?"

"It is the most powerful entity in the universe. More vigorous than you. It can change *everything*."

This was bad news. Very bad. "I was told I'm the only one without a fate. That I can alter the future. Was it a lie?"

"No. Not a lie. Even though it came from the mouth of the master of lies. Before you journeyed through the cosmos with *him*, you were full of hope. But you chose the Darkness. That hope turned into something else." Now Gabe spoke like he had only one word to describe an eerie painting. "Obsession. Clawing away in the dark trying to find something that can't be found. That's the opposite of hope."

Marcel turned his back. Was he obsessed? No. Driven. Not obsessed. He closed his eyes. Thousands of thoughts swirled in his head.

Gabe whispered, "Come sit down, dear boy. Rest your mind."

Dragging his feet, he sat on the pallet of concrete blocks. "I can't hear them. The elements."

"Oh, they cower around me. The elements were born from chaos. They are hard to be controlled, as I'm sure you've encountered. But they listen to the powers of light and dark, which I believe you are discovering."

The sound was nice. Complete silence. Just the cool breeze. The moon looked brighter than usual. "Do you..." Marcel searched for the right thing to say. "Do you hate me, Gabe?"

"Bollocks! I'd never *hate* you. I admire you. You took a deal with the purest form of evil to bring peace to this world. I may disagree, but not hate."

"I should end this deal with Lucifer. I can at any time. Right?"

"Of course! Our powers are drawn from your spirits. We must mold to humanity. But I know you. You won't break this deal. The power is too great. And you are...in your terms...close to peace."

He was right. Marcel couldn't. They both leaned back on the pallets and stared up at the blank night sky.

Gabe added, "Do you know what peace is?"

Only the vision of Marcel's mother came to his head. Her gentle shoulder. Her thoughtful words. Her warm embraces. "My mom. She *was* peace. When *nothing* can bother you. That's peace."

After a slight nod, Gabe sat silent for almost a minute. Even though Marcel was on a timeframe, it didn't matter. This was like old times. Before the Union. Before the apocalypse. Before Lucifer. Just Marcel and Gabe staring at the night sky. He was the father Marcel wished he had. Though there was much to say, nothing escaped either of their lips.

A knock on the door. Vanderbilt's bored voice came from behind the steel exit door. "You told me to let you know when it's been an hour."

Had it been an hour already? Marcel jumped off the pallet while Gabe sat up. He asked, "What do I do about my adversaries? Lloyd and Nina?"

After a short shrug, the archangel answered, "Maybe there's a truce. That's what peace is about, isn't it?"

The knock on the door was louder. Marcel had one last question. "I sense that no one believes I can do this. Create world peace. Do *you* believe I can do it?" Not waiting for an answer, he ranted, "No one believes in me. I can see it in their *souls*. They don't think peace is possible. Even if it was, I can't do it."

Gabe never got to respond. Vanderbilt burst through the roof door with a gun pointed forward. "Are you okay, Sir?" He swung in every direction, surveying the area.

Marcel saw his friend had vanished into little sparkles of light. "Stand down, General. I'm fine."

"Do you have a plan for the resistance, Sir?"

It seemed odd to hear that from Vanderbilt. He hadn't been so nosy before. But there wasn't any harm in giving orders. "I need you to find the location of Lloyd and Nina. Then I want to meet them face-to-face."

CHAPTER TWENTY-ONE

Sirius had no scars, no hangnails, no eye circles, and no split ends. Every angle of the four mirrors looked amazing. She spun one more time. No smudge on the mirrors and no smudge on her skin. The dress was fabulous, black with pink trim along it. It held tight against her body and revealed those natural hip curves. "I'll take it!"

Behind the counter, the store clerk clasped her hands together. "You look amazing. Like a goddess!" Next to the register was a matching pink Fendi handbag, Louis Vuitton sunglasses, and a pair of Yves Saint Laurent high heels. Sirius handed her a credit card. Her smile was so wide, it made her cheeks sore. The clerk rang up the items and the cash register began to print out a receipt.

The paper receipt sounded loud and distracting. It just kept printing and printing. Sirius' smile faded. The receipt fell to the floor and continued going. Making that deafening buzzing noise.

Buzzzzz....buzzzz....

Sirius snorted and sat up. Another dream. Third one this week. Last time she was having coffee with Domenico Dolce at Cinemug on Broad Street. They talked about nothing except shoes.

Buzzzz....buzzz...

That sound again. She got off the couch in the employee break room, wiping saliva from the side of her mouth. Still feeling sore cheeks from smiling. Mumbled something about Prada. Then stumbled into the main lobby of the Office Depot store.

Buzzzz...

It was the printers. Sirius rubbed her eyes to make sure it wasn't another dream. Behind one of the computers, a young man sat. Someone she didn't recognize. A permanent cow lick made his hair messier. And his beard had discombobulated patches of hair, like only certain parts of a lawn got watered with the sprinklers.

He gave an awkward wave. "Hi. I'm Adam. You're Sirius. Brent talked about you aaaalllll the time."

Before she could reach for a crowbar to swing at the intruder, Willie appeared from below the counter. "He's with us!"

"What's going on here?" Sirius peered down at Adam's wrist. They were strung together with zip ties. "Where's Royal?"

"She took the first stack. Said we were already behind schedule. Want some coffee? I found some. Not from the trash can this time."

"Willie, what are you talking about? How are the printers working? What stack?"

Adam held up a printed document. The flyer she had created on the computer, but then no one could get them printed. The visitor said, "It was just a simple IP address config. Piece of cake. I'm a friend of Brent." Adam showed his bound wrists. "You know...a *friend* of Brent."

Servo Clementia. Sirius had done several stories of these assassins. It was strange to see one in the same room. He seemed a little too timid to be a killer. "Where is he?"

"Last I heard, Brent got arrested the night of Doomsday. He went after Marcel Celest again. Failed obviously." Adam tried to load up another printer with paper; the zip ties made it a clumsy attempt.

Sirius looked at Willie. "Take those zip ties off please. If he was like *really* a trained assassin, we'd be dead by now. And I could use some coffee." She always felt groggy after being awoken from such a pleasant slumber. Then thrilled to see her flyers being printed. Then groggy again to hear Brent was in prison.

"I'll grab scissors, bro. Stay there."

"No need." Adam twisted the zip ties and bashed them three times against his knee. The zip ties snapped off. "A trick Brent taught me actually."

After a muffled *hmph* from Willie, he turned to make some coffee.

Adam held up a flyer. It looked better on the computer screen than actually printed. The brown borders that were supposed to look like a doorway turned out to look like rulers. "Is that your slogan? *Let's knock on Marcel's Door?*"

"We had a mutual agreement Marcel Celest must be held responsible for Doomsday. The nations were at each other's throats because of his Union treaty."

"I'm no marketing expert. Especially for a revolution. But *knock* just doesn't seem like the right word."

"Well, too late now. Adam, was it? We could use some more of your help. Grab a stack. We'll split up and put the flyers everywhere. Now's the time to see if anyone is interested in getting our voice heard."

So what if Brent abandoned her? Obviously he had. Finding out why didn't change the fact. Sirius battled the thoughts in her head. Stapling one of the flyers to the light post made a deafening echo on the street. She searched around, immediately regretting her decision to do this alone. Brent would've protected her. *Could've* protected her. If he hadn't chose to leave her in that medical tent, just to go after Marcel Celest. He could have done that at any time. Why did he leave?

Her reflection glimmered in a puddle on the ground. Scarred from the nightmare of Doomsday, she stepped on the puddle so the ripples would erase the image. Who was she kidding? Brent liked sexy girls, not girls with cuts over half their face. If he saw her, he'd turn and run. He'd get the townspeople to chase her with pitchforks and torches. *Kill the monster!*

On the other hand, if Brent had killed Marcel Celest the first time...then none of this would've happened. Instead of stapling posters that begged for a meeting of revolutionaries, she could've been enjoying a pumpkin spice latte at Starbucks.

"Hey!"

Sirius jumped and grasped her heart before it popped out. Behind her, five men crowded the corner three blocks away. They were African-American, each one tall enough to play pro basketball. Maybe they were pro basketball players. The nukes didn't veer away from celebrities or wealthy people.

"Hey!" one of them screamed, his hands cupped around his mouth.

Who knew what they wanted. Money? Clothes? Sexual satisfaction? Her first instinct, as a petite woman raised in the slums of Philly, was to dash for a crowded area. Unfortunately there wasn't any. Sirius grasped her flyers and hurried to an alleyway. Footsteps echoed on the street, running for her. Their feet must've been massive. Maybe they just wanted to stomp her to death. People were getting crazy nowadays. Some committed murder just to have something to do.

Immediately she regretted the decision to go down an alleyway. There was a chain link fence blocking her exit.

"Hey!"

The hooligans blocked the other way out. She had to climb. Sirius dropped the flyers and broke a nail trying to haul herself up. They made it seem so simple on television. But climbing only three feet already made her arms weak. When was the last time she ate?

"We ain't gonna hurt you, goddamn!"

Nearly at the top, Sirius turned. The chasers had stopped to catch their breath. Definitely not pro basketball players if they couldn't run three blocks.

One of them held up the flyer. "You didn't put the date on these."

Feeling foolish and yet cautious, Sirius stayed clung to the fence. "Oh." Royal was so adamant about placing the time everywhere on the poster that the date was neglected. "Um. Tonight."

They all spoke at once.

"You spelled *convenient* wrong."

"I would've used stock paper so the rain don't ruin it."

"Why did you put a door on it?" one of the men asked, squinting at the paper.

This was growing beyond awkward. She had worked with smart proofreaders at the newspaper, but didn't expect these men to excel at it. "We were going for an analogy. Like knocking on a door to get Marcel Celest to answer." Sirius wobbled on the fence. "It wasn't my idea," she lied.

"How many people can go?"

Of all the odd questions so far, that stood out like selling DVDs at a jewelry store. "Um. How many friends you got?"

Expecting to hear maybe nine or ten as a number, Sirius nearly lost her grip when she heard the answer.

"About three hundred."

✧   ✧

"How hard can it be?" Adam swallowed.

He and Willie both stared up the radio tower. They always seemed so tiny from a distance. Now that Adam was standing at the foot of it, he suddenly didn't feel so brave. Willie twisted a knob on his handheld radio. There was nothing but static.

"You said you could do this, brother."

"I know. I know. I just didn't expect it to be like thousands of feet up." Adam wiped his sweaty palms on his jeans. "Where's it at?"

Willie pointed. A tire sat in place, all the way at the top of the radio tower. It was barely visible. "It's blocking the signal. Sirius' speech needs to be heard over the radio, you know what I'm saying?"

"You go up there and get it down."

"You're the super bad ass Servo Clementia, remember?"

There wasn't even a ladder. How the hell would he get up there in the first place? He wasn't Spider-Man. The sun was setting. Pretty soon a few hundred people would show up to hear the voice of the rebellion. Willie was right. This was important.

Just like when he did the 100 meter dash in college, Adam bounced up and down to warm his legs. He ended up second-to-last. Brent, always trying to boost his spirits, had said at least he didn't technically lose.

"What in Sam Hill is going on here?"

Both men rolled their eyes as Royal approached. "We got people showing up already. I need help organizing the stage, dangit."

"Listen, doll, we got debris in the way," Willie nodded at the top of the radio tower. He fiddled with the knob some more. Still static.

"So, get it down. We got 19 minutes until the speech starts." It was the only words she had said to him all day.

Adam thought what it would be like growing up in the Declan household. Who was more bossy? Royal or her father? He seemed thankful to have been raised in foster homes. "That's high. You get it down," Adam spat out.

"You know what...I will." Royal circled and looked at the tire from every angle. Adam pictured her being that bully at the playground, pushing past the boys on monkey bars.

It was his time to bully. "You can't make it up there."

"Who said anything about going up there?"

Royal grabbed a rock, no bigger than her palm. She took a deep breath and looked up. Adam crossed his arms, thinking how funny her reaction will be. Was she seriously going to try to get the debris out with a rock? Royal flung the rock. It hit the railing. Bounced. Slid down. The momentum caught it back up to speed. Bounced again, even higher. Hit one end. Hit the other end. Ricocheted so fast that Adam lost track of it, until it bumped the tire. The tire wiggled then fell. When the tire hit the ground, it popped back up and knocked Adam in the back. He fell flat in the dirt.

The radio buzzed to life. No more static. Willie exclaimed, "Holy shit! Damn, doll, you got some crazy aim!"

"It's not about the aim; it's about the timing," she said, wiping the dirt off her hands.

Adam stood up, covered in more dirt than his hands could wipe away. That was amazing. But he certainly wouldn't admit that aloud. "So that's your ability. Everyone on that list has something."

"Got me plenty of extra cash playing darts at the bars. Now, get yourself cleaned up. We got a show to put on, cowboy."

Before this night, Sirius hadn't seen such an enormous crowd in sixteen years. Miley Cyrus sang her heart out. Drunks puked their guts out. Amplifiers boomed. Girls in those tad-too-tight shorts danced on their boyfriends' shoulders. Beer cans were tossed on the floor next to the trash cans. But everyone had a blast.

This crowd was dull. Two hundred had been an under estimate. Sirius could see three, maybe four times that amount, awaiting her speech. It looked like a mosaic. Tents were set up. Food was being shared. But very few conversations went on. Most eyes stared at the stage. Was this what Eva Peron felt like? A rebellion at her doorstep and unsure of herself?

She stared out the window as Royal continued her rant about Willie. Peering every so often around her shoulder to make sure no one could hear. Royal was like those women that gossiped next to the water fountain at CNN. This was how her friend coped with stress. Changing one subject to another, like it somehow made the other one go away. First it was about tonight's speech, now somehow about the mysterious Willie Cooper.

"I'm telling you, none of this is making any sense. First, we find him with some black kid in the stadium. Some dead black kid. I mean, what's that about? And then I hear him talking about someone named Conner with that goofball Adam. Who's Conner? Why didn't he mention him before? And now we gotta worry about Adam. That boy is a goddang terrorist."

Sirius rested her forehead against the window. It wasn't cold. All these people around added some much needed warmth. "Can we please not talk about this now? I'm seeing close to a thousand people out there now."

"Just read the speech we practiced," Royal said like this was routine somehow. "You reported to millions on CNN."

"But I didn't actually see them."

"And don't forget to mention how the petroleum chemical empire is forcing us to use prescription drugs."

"Yeah, I got it in the speech," Sirius mumbled, closing her eyes to calm her nerves. It was making her even more antsy that the crowd was so quiet.

"And don't forget about the corporate bullshit that even got the nukes made in the first place. Greedy fuckers ain't thinking about us small folk."

"Yeah, I got it, Royal! Jesus!" Sirius suddenly understood how Brent felt in his tantrums. So much frustration bottled up and ready to explode.

"Well who peed in your Wheaties, missy?" Royal snapped back.

"I'm just like so sick of the complaining. And I'm sure all those people are too. Is that all this is? Just a place to come and grumble about government issues? Look how far that got the Occupy movement."

"You gotta better idea?"

Sirius didn't answer. Royal scoffed and walked away. This had been their first argument. A true argument. Not about what to eat or where to sleep. Royal had passion, but hers was more aggressive. Something in Sirius' stomach couldn't shake the feeling that this speech was all wrong.

"You okay?" Willie's voice came from behind her.

Sirius finally looked away from the window. She leaned against the wall and slid down. Her butt slammed the floor. "I can't do this, Willie."

"What are you feeling right now?"

"Fear." Sirius nodded and said it again. "Yeah. Fear."

Willie took off his cap and took a deep breath. He pulled up a chair and sat next to her. Sirius curled up her legs to her body.

"Remember when you found me at the stadium? Under all that rubble?"

How could Sirius forget? They were originally trying to find a food stand. Instead they found someone still alive. Willie had been grasping the corpse of a child like he was afraid it would float away. To this day, he avoided every question about it. Seems like sometimes Sirius didn't need to pressure someone to admit a story. Sometimes the story came to her. "Yeah, I remember."

"On Doomsday...it was me, my husband Conner, and our little boy Kamal were at the Giants stadium."

Husband? Sirius would've never guessed.

Willie continued, "Fitzpatrick just handed the ball to Ivory. The path was completely clear. Ivory hustled. The crowd went wild. 56 yard run. Touchdown!" He threw his hands in the air, then they settled down slowly. "No one could hear the first missile strike. When it happened, we didn't know what was happening. Instinct just made us wanna cower. Hide. Whatever. Knowing what I do now, the first blast of wind from the nuke created this...whatcha call it? That whirlwind thing?"

"Vortex."

"Yeah that. Vortex." He said it as though he muttered the name of a murderer at a criminal trial. "Conner disappeared into the vortex. No goodbye. No final words. No last smile. Never saw him again. His body could be in the rubble or splattered on the stadium wall. I'll never know." A tear began to form in his right eye. "I was lucky enough to be holding my son's hand at the time. I didn't let go. I held it harder than Ivory held that football."

Willie's lip quivered. He cleared his throat. "As we spun in circles, I brought my son in closer and held him so damn tight. We landed...I dunno...somewhere. Under so much stuff that we couldn't move. My boy never stopped crying. He was so pressed against me that I could feel his little heart racing. His heart never sped like that."

Willie beat his chest, imitating the heartbeat. *Thump, thump, thump, thump.* "Then the second wave of air hit. My ear drums popped. His heart started to slow." His heartbeat imitation slowed. Finally that tear escaped and rolled down his cheek. It landed on his knee. "Then the final blast hit. His heart just kept slowing until it...stopped. I couldn't give CPR. I mean, I couldn't even move, am I right? All that rubble. Skin fades quick when you die. He went pale in less than a minute. And faded to white in a few hours."

Another tear slipped past Willie's nose. He tried to suck it in and cough. His lip quivered more. "I checked every part of my kid's body. No scratch or excessive bleeding or impaled by anything. His heart just...didn't wanna go on, you know what I'm saying? Would you believe, I tried to get my heart to do that too? Stuck under all that shit, there was no way out. My man was dead. My boy was dead. I wasn't going to survive anyway. But yet, I couldn't get my damn heart to stop."

Sirius looked away as she felt a tear build up. She wiped it then faced Willie.

His eyes looked directly into hers, for the first time since this story began. "Fear? You have fear? We all faced *Fear* that day. Fear that could stop a healthy boy's heart. We're starving every day, struggling for electricity, wiping our asses with cardstock paper. But all this...ain't nothing. We all faced Fear that day and *we* survived. Going out and giving a speech? That's not fear. Not even close."

It took a minute before Sirius could compose herself. She wiped away what was left of her tears and stood up. After a polite kiss on Willie's cheek, she muttered, "Thank you."

With head held high, Sirius walked to the front door and opened it.

✧ ✧

The warm air blew on her face. Sirius didn't think she should wave. It was inappropriate. Waving was for politicians and celebrities. Neither fit her role. She was a leader of an uprising.

There were a few whispers. *That* questions could be heard. *That's her? That woman will start a rebellion? That the girl from CNN? That's who we heard about?* None sounded too optimistic.

Spotlight shined on her and the crowd quieted to hear her aria. Huffs of frozen mists shot out her nostrils rapidly. She reminded herself to calm down then approached the microphone. It hissed then settled to life.

The notepad was in front of her, nestled on the podium. There was enough light to see the words, but yet she couldn't read it. Because she didn't want to. The words no longer made sense to her. Sirius remembered all the politicians she met with their rehearsed speeches. If they could do it, so could she. But then again, Sirius *wasn't* a politician.

"We had like this whole entire speech that took like a month to write. And I don't even feel like it's right to say it. You all are familiar with Royal Declan and her talks on public radio." More than a few heads nodded. Royal would be proud to see fans. "She's right, there's a lot of stuff wrong in the world. We all know about the corporate bullshit and government control. I guess I just got tired of hearing about the problem...I wanna hear the solution."

That garnered the attention of every eyeball. Even children. The word *solution*. She added, "I remember, when I was with friends, we'd play this drinking game. We would turn on C-SPAN and take a shot every time a politician said the word 'fundamental'. Drunk in no time." A few giggles, lots of smiles. The crowd loosened up. "It's all just so routine. Promise after promise after promise. I realize now why it doesn't work. Behind this podium, you all are looking at one person you think will save the country – when really *I'm* looking at a thousand that can save the country."

Applause. She looked behind her. Willie was clapping through a small window in the store. Beside him, with arms crossed,

Royal looked the other direction like she was about to cry. Apparently the girl's thick skin could be penetrated. Sirius returned back to the crowd.

She continued, leaning against the podium. "I was with CNN, making a story about a protest against population control. We all sat outside and tried to disrupt the flow of Washington traffic into congress. But they just stepped over us, like we weren't there. We sat on top of their cars, but they just took taxis home instead. On taxpayers' money, of course. Then we went to sixteen different homes and knocked on their doors. I wanted to know why they just ignored the concerned voices of Americans. No one answered the doors. Sixteen men and women. We knocked and knocked, but not one cared. It was then I realized they will never answer the door unless it involves them. They'll get their paychecks and payoffs. Our voice meant nothing. But what if *something* stopped those paychecks?"

Behind her, Willie pulled up the stool he had been sitting on. Sirius sat on it, moving away from the podium. She kept her eyes to the floor and pretended like these were all friends reminiscing old times.

"It was Senator Wiles that we tested. He owned 85% of a local business selling shoes. We gathered over 100,000 signatures to boycott the store. And we did it, boycotted every store. His revenue dropped. A month later...he answered the door."

After a deep breath, Sirius brought the microphone closer to her mouth. "I would like *love* to have that moment to knock on Marcel Celest's door and ask why did we need a Union? Why? Why make the government stronger and the people weaker? You know? There's a difference between *wanting* and *needing*. And we don't *want* the Union. And we don't *need* the Union."

A clap. Then another clap. The applause sounded like a wave crashing on the shore. It grew and deafened her ears. A surge of excitement started in her stomach and rushed to her lungs. Sirius shouted, "You want a solution? That's our solution! If we are going to stop the government abuse, then we have to ignore them the way they ignored us! Without taxes, there is no government!

Don't shop at stores, don't go to hospitals, don't pay your bills, don't contribute anything to the government. Don't take their food! Or their money! Or their medicines! Or their health care! Or their education systems! Or their population control! We don't *need* them!"

The crowd was roaring so loud, Sirius almost couldn't breathe. She finally whispered into the microphone, "Then we will knock on Marcel Celest's door, and I promise you...he will answer."

Fists rose to the air. Hands clasped in triumph. A chant started.

"We don't need them! We don't need them! We don't need them!"

Royal quickly closed the window blinds when Sirius walked into the store. She pretended to be cleaning, as though she wasn't hanging on every word of Sirius' speech. The chanting made it hard to hear the words in her head. And she loved every minute of it.

"We don't need them!"

Sirius didn't need to give specifics; chatter could be heard and ideas spewing from everyone's mouth already. A boycott to everything the government represented would certainly end this conflict. Willie patted her on the back and gave a quick hug. "I knew you could do it." He walked away.

Adam was in the back of the store. He gave two big thumbs up in approval. Sirius smiled back. She turned to Royal, who had been wiping down the same spot on the window blinds the entire time. "Did you like it?" she asked.

Her friend shrugged and looked the other way. The crowd was cheering so loudly that Sirius could feel the vibrations in the ground. Royal pretended to wipe another part of the window. This had been the first cleaning done in this store since they moved in. "We should take them out to the forests," Royal murmured. "That way the Union don't know about us. Better that they clueless so no one get hurt. Government don't take kindly to boycotts."

"That's a great idea." Sirius' voice was even lower.

They were quiet for a moment, listening to the rebellions. Then at the same moment they whispered, "I'm sorry."

The family that's created together can be much

more powerful than the family that's born together.

-Victoria Celest

CHAPTER TWENTY-TWO

Potholes riddled the road, making the bus ride bumpy. Just to make Brent's prison transfer agonizing, the driver made sure to hit every one with determination. In the back of the bus, he would bounce and the driver would give a cackle under his breath.

Driving through Massachusetts lately looked like the drive through Arizona. Besides an occasional tumbleweed or clan of coyotes feasting off a dead vulture, there wasn't much to see. Just dirt. And more dirt.

All those anger management steps were out the window and floating away in those dirt devils. Brent had nothing left, just like the great state of Massachusetts.

His jaw was sore from the constant grinding to control his wrath. Devious thoughts had grown more frequent. Darkness was everywhere. Unescapable like a prison cell. Which was what Brent needed. The transfer had been rigorous and annoying. Tons of paperwork and tons of guards. Now it was just him, that driver who had been chewing on the same toothpick for two hours, and another guard. The guard looked like a human version of Snidely Whiplash. A long, ugly snot and a permanent evil green with a pencil-thin mustache, planning his next attempt at ridding the world of Dudley Do-Right.

He shined his shotgun with a brown cloth for the third time, playing a staring contest with Brent. Brent would always look away first. He'd stare up at the sky, hoping for a glimpse of some stars. The clouds hid them. But they were there. So was Jupiter. He couldn't get the image from the digital prison out of his head. The vision was surreal. Maybe he should've taken the deal and lived in that farce life. Brent quickly shook the thought away.

No one else occupied the bus. Three possibilities came to mind. Either the prisoners were scared to ride the transfer bus with him, the warden was scared to put prisoners around Brent, or no one received their requested transfers. Which made Brent Celest a very special case indeed.

The headache returned. It kept coming and going. This throbbing pain in the center of his eyebrows. He tried to rub it away, but the zip ties around his wrists made it impossible. They were leaving red marks on his skin. The guard enjoyed tightening them. His eyebrows were crunched, like the sun was in his eyes when the sun hadn't shined in weeks. He did this when he was irritated. His mom used to say they would stick like that someday. Maybe that's what was causing the headache, his doom to look pissed off for the rest of his life.

He was six rows behind the gate that kept the guard safe from him. They whispered something and laughed, the guard holding his tongue out like he was mimicking a dog. Whatever the joke was, Brent could be certain it was at his expense. Was he strong enough to rip the human tongue from the skull?

Then Brent heard Sirius. She was on the radio. His eyebrows softened and his ears perked.

"There's a difference between wanting and needing. And we don't *want* the Union. And we don't *need* the Union!" Sirius' voice thundered through the radio. Immediately it became drowned out by the applause. Brent sat up. This was it. What Adam envisioned. A rebellion.

The driver spat out his toothpick and put in another. "Who is this bitch anyway?" He turned up the radio.

"No one knows," the guard shrugged. "Just another crazy ass protestor."

This was good news. Sirius needed to remain hidden. No

telling what Marcel would do to her. Brent saw firsthand the power his brother had gained in his coma. A supernatural ability to control elements. He pictured Marcel lifting Sirius in the air and stealing the wind from her lungs. No. She needed to remain safe.

As if on cue, his brother's voice was heard on the radio. The guard finally turned away from his staring contest to listen closer to the radio. Marcel had this polite and gentle voice. Very well practiced. "This is silly. People absolutely need the help of the Union. We are only here to aide those in turmoil. This isn't a Communist regime. We aren't attacking innocent people. There will be no blood on my hands. Peace is the ultimate goal."

Brent sucked his teeth. *No blood on his hands.* What a joke.

The headache returned.

The guard must've heard his snicker because he returned to the staring contest. "How you like that? Huh? How's it feel for your brother to be the most popular man in the world? And you just some lowlife criminal?"

Ignoring him, Brent imagined Sirius' puffy cheeks giving that slight blush below her eyes. Her eyelids squinting just slightly to hide her adorable shyness. And those pearly white teeth twinkling through a wide smile, biting her lower lip to suppress an even larger smile. She always did this slight hop every time she giggled.

Trying again to poke Brent's ego, the guard blurted, "I never thought there'd be the day I would be guarding the President's son. Shit, especially never thought I'd guard a Christian terrorist. You guys were just myths. You know...my church got persecuted for all you assholes."

Servo Clementia never branded themselves Christian terrorists. The media did that. But Brent wasn't going to waste his breath. The headache was back. Thinking of Sirius was the only cure. The only thing that kept him sane. And he left her. Left her to fend for herself. What would happen if the Union did find her and he was stuck behind a prison cell? The will to die was immediately replaced with the will to live. She was the water that doused his internal wretched flame. He had to be with her.

Which meant getting off this prison bus.

As a kid, while his brother snored on the bottom bunk, Brent used to have this game he played. Simply called Launch. He imagined himself in the cockpit of a shuttle, facing the sky and preparing to exit Earth's atmosphere. Holding onto a pretend steering wheel, he'd go through the checklist in his head. All types of procedures were needed to enter the endless allure of space. Meters, launch codes, handles, and knobs had to be done in a flawless sequence.

Brent found himself playing this game, as his eyes darted around the bus. First - the zip ties around his wrist. That'd be easy to break. Second - taking the guard out. That might be difficult. An easy taunt could make the guard open the metal mesh. But the bastard had a USMC tattoo; those guys were trained in martial arts. He'd have to die quickly. A neck break should do it. Third - taking the driver out. That might not be an option, because someone needed to drive the bus. Holding that guard's shotgun to the driver's head would surely get him to listen. Fourth - timing. Brent could see out the side window. They were approaching a steep mountain, next to a tall mesa. Perfect. Climbing a steep mountain side would be ideal. The driver would have to stay on the tight winding road, because pulling over could mean the bus would roll back and lose control. Not a good idea for either of them.

There was a car behind the bus, honking and flashing its lights. The driver extended a middle finger in the side mirror. Whoever was behind them paid no attention and continued flashing their lights. Not only was it strange behavior, but also strange to see anyone else on this road. Brent took this opportunity to fiddle with his zip ties. This scheme would either launch spectacularly or crash spectacularly.

The guard poked his head up. "What are you doing over there? You better not be jacking off!"

With a sly grin, Brent replied, "I'm thinking about your wife."

The guard's lip curled up. Brent pushed further, "Or maybe your daughter too. I like them young."

"This fucking punk," the guard mumbled. He fumbled for his keys and unlocked the gate. Gripping his shotgun like a shovel that he was going to smack Brent with. His eyes looked down.

Brent's zip ties were broken. *Here goes nothing.* The move was so swift, the guard had no time to react. Brent kicked and the shotgun flew out of the guard's hands then landed into his own. He pointed it, but the driver swung the bus at the sound of the disturbance. The guard swung around and grasped the butt of the shotgun into Brent's stomach. He pointed it at his face. Quickly, Brent grabbed the head of the weapon and the bullet blasted through the side window.

The driver jumped and swerved the bus by accident again. He's staring in the rearview mirror, not paying attention. "What do I do?" he yelled.

"Keep driving, fucktard!" the guard bellowed.

Brent flipped around the guard and was about to fire the gun again. This time the bullet fired and hit the driver in the back of the head then shattered the front window. The driver's brains splashed everywhere.

So much for the plan. *Houston, we have a problem.*

The bus flipped and smacked into the side of the mountain. They were at the mercy of physics, being thrown to every edge of the bus like ragdolls. The guard and Brent fought for possession of the shotgun. Then the bus careened off the road onto the desert, smashing through cacti and dips in the sand. It was heading towards that mesa, landing on its side and sliding down another road. The shotgun flew out of reach for both men. Brent used his legs to put the guard into a headlock. He looked out the window. The bus skidded toward the edge of the cliff. He ran for the back of the bus. Too late. The bus fell off the cliff. Brent floated in mid-air. Then slammed against the floor. Something stopped their fall.

Everything quieted for only a moment. Then the noise of the

chassis bending could be heard.

Brent's nose was broken, but it had been through worse. He slowly stood. Outside, they were like on a teeter-totter and slowly rocking back-and-forth. They must've landed on some rock formation. But from his view, the drop was still steep.

The guard was on the other side of the bus. He stood up. Blood poured from his nose, much worse than Brent. Good.

They both eyed the shotgun, centered in the bus. The guard walked slowly toward it, but the vehicle began to sway backward. He quickly backed up and everything leveled again. Brent tried to move, but it was the same. Their balance kept the bus steady. One wrong move could send them plummeting to their deaths.

Behind Brent, the fire escape door banged open and close. With every open view, the ground seemed even further down. It was at least a thousand foot drop. In front of him, he could see behind the guard. The driver window was shattered enough to jump through. Too bad the guard had been in the way. But there might be a chance. Another idea came to him. Hopefully this time, things would go according to plan. His day had already been shit. If there was a God, Brent really needed this plan to work.

Brent taunted his adversary in this Mexican standoff. This wasn't part of the plan. It was just for fun. "You don't have the guts, do you?" he said.

The guard curled his upper lip again.

Brent shrugged. "...but I do."

Brent leapt backwards and grasped the bottom edge of the open door. The entire bus tipped toward him. The guard fell. The shotgun slid. Brent climbed back in. Though it was seconds, everything happened in perfect sync. The shotgun slid right into Brent's hands. He shot the tumbling guard in the chest. Dashing up the slope of the bus, the guard's body flew past him and out of the back door. Brent ran up the descending vehicle, his quads already on fire. The bus was almost at a vertical stance, so he used the seats to bounce up and gain further momentum. Like some frog climbing a tree. He lunged through the mesh gate then burst through the front window as the bus fell behind him.

The momentum felt like a hand of God. Brent's legs and arms swung at the side of the cliff. He grasped anything he could. A few fingernails broke. His shoes slid. Finally, his descent slowed and he clung onto the side of a rock. Below, the bus exploded and sent a plume of fire upwards. He shielded his eyes for a moment until the heat evaporated, leaving a stingy burnt smell of asshole correctional guards.

The relief to be alive felt brief. How the hell was he going to get out of here? Brent only had two options: up or down. Up could be a hundred feet of rock climbing and praying he wouldn't slip. Down meant being stuck in some ravine with nowhere to go.

This was the way luck worked for Brent. Grand for a while, then slammed into a solid wall. In literal terms this time. He thought of Sirius. Instead of wallowing in self-pity, she would see it as a blessing. Brent had survived. For now, anyway. He could only perch himself on this rock for so long, though.

Up was the only choice. His arms vibrated and his legs burned; he'd need rest first.

"Hey!" a voice came from above. Brent looked up. Though hard to articulate, he could see the shape of a man waving his arms. "Hey! You're alive!"

Squinting his eyes seemed to help. Brent could make out the figure. Was that the man in that car, swerving and tailgating them?

"Hey! Brent!"

The stranger knew his name. Brent stared harder, trying to make out the face under the dark clouds.

It couldn't be.

Impossible.

Brent muttered, "Dad?"

✧ ✧

Nelson thought he lost his son on several occasions in just a matter of months. He thought he lost him during the nuclear attack. He thought he lost him when he was arrested. He thought he lost him when he saw the prison bus flip over the edge of a cliff. And he thought he lost him on that last pull up.

Using a rope he had been lucky to have in the car, Nelson yanked Brent up and onto solid ground. Both men collapsed and looked up to the sky. While they caught their breath, Nelson was suddenly reminded of a similar moment. They used to sit on the roof like this and a young Brent would name each of the known stars in the sky...in alphabetical order.

"I'm happy to see you, Son." Nelson said, trying to remember the last time he said those words to Brent.

"I'm happy to see you too, Dad." It sounded more like a question than a statement.

Nelson stood and wiped the dirt off his back, realizing after a second that there was no point.

"How..." Brent started then shook his head. "What..." He tried again. "I don't..."

"I didn't exactly have a plan. When I found the bus, I was just going to somehow get you out of it."

Brent sighed, "Not exactly a good plan."

"And what was your plan of getting off the bus?"

Brent's face twisted and he bit his lower lip. Nelson knew that face well. "Okay," Brent said, "so we're not good at making plans."

"Maybe we can come up with one together. We have to get your sister. Union officials took her and Gerard. They are with Marcel by now." Nelson started winding up the rope. No telling if they'd need that again. Hopefully, his son wouldn't be jumping off any cliffs soon.

"What about the revolution? It's starting."

Nelson heard the radio broadcast too. He recognized the girl's voice, but couldn't place her. Very powerful and yet gentle. Much like his wife's voice. "I may know the location of where this is beginning, but we are low on fuel. We might make it halfway there. At least the car can make it to Marcel and Janice." He placed the rope in the trunk. Time to get going before the snow started. Snow flurries were already dancing in the air.

"Dad, there's no way we can get to Janice. Not while Marcel is around. He's *different*."

"I know about his rapid healing, Declan —"

"No. He's *different*. No human on Earth can do what he can do. Our last encounter, he could...this is going to sound crazy...he could conjure...fire."

First the pictures of those witnesses performing feats that no human can accomplish. Now this. "You mean like a magic trick?"

"Not a trick. His coma awoke something in him. You have to believe me."

"I believe you."

Brent's eyes widened. How long had it been since Nelson told his son those three words?

Brent continued, "Going near him would be suicide. We have to find this rebellion and with their help, we can get him."

"It's a good point. Besides, Adam's vision had us joining the rebellion."

To hear his best friend's name made him smile. Brent said, "I'm glad Adam is still alive. *We* were in his vision."

Nelson paused for a moment. It never occurred to him until now that Adam hadn't mentioned Brent in that brutal fight toward Marcel's castle. "Actually, he never mentioned you in particular."

After a pause, Brent nodded and mumbled, "Oh. Okay."

"Then what about Janice?"

Crossing his arms, Brent stood a little taller. Just showing Nelson's ability to listen made a difference. Perhaps they could learn much from each other.

Brent said, "I wouldn't worry about her. She's smart. Marcel won't get in her head. Her fate isn't in our hands; it's in hers now."

A steady nod, then Nelson replied, "Okay. We will head out east."

He climbed into the front seat. Brent sank into the passenger seat. He twiddled his fingers on his lap then said, "I love you,

Dad."

Nelson closed his eyes and soaked in those words. "I love you too, Son."

CHAPTER TWENTY-THREE

It had been a week. A week of passing each other in the hotel hallway without a word. A week of eating breakfast, lunch, and dinner in separate rooms. A week of keeping the hotel room door locked. Some family. Then again, Janice and Marcel weren't technically family. The Celests may have raised her, but they didn't own her.

Janice finished her morning bath, wrapping herself in the fluffy bathrobe. She wiped the condensation from the bathroom mirror. Feeling grateful after months of forgoing baths, she cleaned her ears with a cotton swab. It was like heaven.

The Ritz-Carlton logo sewn precisely on the top of her left breast. Maybe men did these designs so they can have an excuse to eye her cleavage. She hadn't noticed until now that there was a misprint. Ritz was spelled with an S. Rits-Carlton. That's a big mistake.

A knock on the front door. Janice pulled her hair back and tied it with a bun. Since leaving the slum life, her hair began to phase from dirty blonde to just blonde.

Another knock. Janice rolled her eyes. "Gerard, answer that please!" That unintentional tone again. Starting off the sentence with a command but adding *please* to not sound like a total bitch.

Third knock.

Janice slammed her brush and walked out of the bathroom. Gerard was nowhere to be found in the suite. Typical. She swung the door open. It was Marcel. He immediately looked to the ground and placed his hands behind his back. "Sorry, I was looking for —"

"I don't know where he is. Seems to be happening to our family a lot lately." Sarcasm was an easy way of showing disappointment. And it worked.

Marcel's shoulders sunk. "I'm sorry. But we haven't found Dad yet."

She noted that he didn't attempt to apologize for practically kidnapping her and Gerard. Sure, the policeman had politely requested she come with them. But *no* didn't seem like a viable response. "What about Brent?"

"Like you requested, we were going to have him transferred here. Unfortunately we lost contact last night. He may have escaped."

Hearing the word *escape* made Janice brighten up. Maybe she should think about it.

Marcel shook his head. "I wouldn't."

"Wouldn't what?" Janice caught herself locked on Marcel's eyes.

"You'll be fine here."

How did he know she was contemplating an escape in her head? Coincidence. Maybe. Janice crossed her arms. "Yeah, well, why did you need Gerard?"

"He promised me he would join me for coloring."

Janice repeated the word to make sure she heard correctly. "Coloring?"

"Japan's President gave us these therapeutic books and...You know what? Why don't you come join me? I'll show you."

His eyes were locked on hers again. Suddenly the idea of hanging out with her brother seemed thrilling. Something came over Janice. She craved being around Marcel. She wanted to stare more into those wide pupils of his. "Sure, that would be fun." That bitter tone was gone.

"You should probably get dressed. Meet me in Room 309." Marcel smiled. "And I'll have them fix that misspelling on your robe."

Janice should've felt violated. Her brother had just noticed a misspelling near her cleavage. But instead, all she could think about was spending time with Marcel.

She made Marcel wait. Janice put on the least revealing outfit she could find, a turtle neck sweater and long blue jeans. Without makeup and without deodorant, she marched the hallway toward the room. It was a strange sensation. She had no interest in talking to Marcel after all that happened lately. But she felt compelled to.

Some of the faces in the hallways looked familiar. Being the President's daughter had its perks. Janice could know politicians without them acknowledging her. Japan's President, with too many pearls around her neck, strolled by. Two Senators from the state of Mississippi chatted by the water fountain; must've been nice being the only state not attacked. All these two-faced individuals were crowding the rooms and gathering friends. Gerard had explained to her about the election for approaching. A third seat position in the Union, a sort of *tie-breaker.*

Room 309 didn't even have a number on it. It sat between 308 and 310. Janice opened it and entered. Enriching music played, a steady drumbeat and a melody using a harp. In the middle of the room was a table with incense burning. Marcel was dressed in a kimono that might have been too big. Using colored pencils, he filled in the blanks of a portrait on his sheet. He wasn't kidding; it was a coloring book. A leather-bound and large coloring book.

"This is a joke, right?"

Marcel smiled, "No. It actually helps." It was good to see her brother smile.

After a long sigh, she sat down at the table. He had a second book waiting for her. On the hard cover was a picture of a lilac flower.

"Your favorite. Right?" Marcel asked. He had bought her a dozen lilac flowers every birthday since he joined the Celest family. That's nineteen years. She never got sick of the attention – no one gave it to Janice, even her husband. Always invisible like some ghost.

Drawing around the shape with her finger, she replied, "Of course, silly." She looked up to see him staring at her with those odd tiny pupils. He gave this pumpkin Halloween smile. Cute yet creepy too.

The room was getting stuffier than a crowded elevator. Janice opened the coloring book to relieve this tense silence. She began flipping through the pages. The drawings seemed too complicated for children. These designs were meant for adults. She wondered if the baby would like drawing.

Marcel dropped his pencil. "You're pregnant?"

Her body froze. He had done it again, said something that had been in her head. It wasn't possible. "How did you know that, Marcel?" She wanted to slap herself. Lying would've been a more sane response to this. Tell him she couldn't possibly be pregnant. *The government has to remove the uterus clip for women to get pregnant, remember?*

Searching the room for an answer, Marcel stumbled through his speech. "I...well...I mean...you look...pregnant. Flush. Thicker belly. Yeah."

She had to believe him. There was no other possible explanation. Typically, she'd want an opinion if the child would be aborted when someone found out she was pregnant. Instead, Janice took this opportunity to lie since she already lost the chance earlier. "It's not yours."

After a hard swallow and a biting of his lip, Marcel blurted, "Yeah. Of course. But...wasn't it like four months ago we fooled around –"

"It's not yours, Marcel. I told you. That night we were drunk and being stupid. I'm married."

Her brother's shoulders sank. He continued coloring, scribbling at a faster rate.

She blurted in the same tone Marcel just had. "Try to stay in those lines, you. Don't want to make a mess of the drawing.

Then you can't fix it."

He said nothing.

His drawing made her squirm. She once read that the color red symbolized disgruntlement. There was a lot of red in his artwork. After clearing her throat, Janice flipped through a few more pages. There was an outline of all the numbers from one to nine, scrambled in this intriguing design. She said, "Look. It says to color your favorite number. You have one?"

He said nothing.

"I like the number three. Think about it. There's three to everything. Yes, no, maybe. Hot, cold, normal. Rich, poor, middle class. Black, white –"

"Gray," Marcel said it as though he discovered something. He stopped drawing. "Violence, apathy...and peace."

"That's right."

He blurted, "Do you believe in the Union?"

She shut the book closed. Whatever made her want to come to this room was over. "No. You can't create peace with a union of countries. It's impossible."

His voice rose. "Why...does...*no one* believe I can do this? I have to force people to think I can accomplish it! It's my life's work! I know what I'm doing! I slave for 17 hours a day to tie every end. It's not like I'm killing people to get this accomplished. There's no blood on my hands. I'm not some crazed dictator that wants to murder innocent people! Not some psychopath like Brent."

"Brent's not a psychopath. What has gotten into you?"

"He is psycho! You mean to tell me he put a goddamn bullet in my head and you just simply forgive him? Maybe you should've fucked him in that cave instead of me!"

Janice's hand reached out and slapped Marcel against the face. His cheek went immediately red. She got up to leave.

He cried out, "I'm sorry! Don't leave. Please. I've just...I'm really exhausted. And I just wanted to relax and..." He stared off into his artwork. Janice had to admit, his eyes were almost swollen shut from fatigue. "Don't hate me. Please. I just want *us* to be fixed. We can still be fixed. Right?" he begged.

Exhaustion caused some of her worse behaviors. She would've been a hypocrite to not show some sympathy. "Just as long as you stay inside the lines." Janice turned and exited the room.

CHAPTER TWENTY-FOUR

Intelligent, crafty, strong and best of all...amazing in the sack. For whatever reason, Adam couldn't get Janice off his mind. Their fling lasted only a few months. But that was the longest a woman tolerated him. It must've meant something. Janice's face when he last saw her said it all. She hated him. Hated him for lying to her.

He drew those eyes on his notepad. Round like a kitten, but narrow like a tiger. Her grin conveyed strength and yet sadness. What he would do to be with her again. What he would do to be with her brother. Brent would probably condone his crush on his sister. *Probably.*

Adam took a break and swayed on the hammock. He had never relaxed in one before. There was something this apocalypse created – a connection to this world. The only connections he had before were to his laptop, iPod, and television at the same time.

When working together, hundreds of people can get a lot accomplished. Hammocks had been constructed in the tallest trees. At first, he was concerned about rain. But the leaves were large enough to protect them. He was on the bottom bunk, wishing sleep could be an option tonight. Unfortunately, Adam was on night duty. Like anything exciting ever happened around here. Visitors were scarce. Threats were even more scarce.

Hacking and coughing came from a few people. Adam covered his face. A flu seemed to be spreading. An awful flu.

Something he'd never seen before. No telling what this contaminated air had been brewing up.

Adam flipped through his new sketch book, since his old sketch book must've melted away in the ashes with the rest of the world on Doomsday. Drawing all the things he remembered from his past precognitions hadn't been easy. Starting from page one, he penciled in what he recalled of Marcel Celest. There was no memory of when or where, but the politician would soon attack a group of innocent people. Marcel Celest's frightening ability to control the weather will come soon or it had already. He traced the lightning bolt in the politician's hand.

The next page was Royal with a metal pipe impaled through her stomach. Mr. Declan, along with the so-called scientists from Servo Clementia, instilled the same message in Adam's head...never tell anyone about what he can do. The outcome would be dreadful. Thousands would flock to know their future when that's not what Adam could do. He could only foresee certain moments that his future-self decided to let him see. Which meant...was he supposed to save Royal from dying? Or was he supposed to let her die? Not that she was mean and deserved it. Well, she was mean – but didn't deserve it. No one deserved death anymore. But how could he alter the future when he didn't even remember when this would happen? He struggled to recall the precognition where she would die. Nothing came to him.

More hacking from the hammock above him. It sounded like his lungs were about to fall out of his mouth. Adam made a mental note to request face masks from the scavenging team. People had agreed on jobs. But not the hurry-up-and-get-it-over-with kind of jobs. These trades were something certain people *wanted* to do.

"Excuse me?"

The voice startled Adam so bad, he jumped up and the hammock flipped around. His face smashed into the ground. After a brief sound of pain, Adam stood up. Someone was here. A visitor!

Even with pale skin, the stranger couldn't hide his Hispanic origin. His accent was a dead giveaway too. "I look to speak someone I know."

"Who?"

"Cyrus."

"Don't know any Cyrus."

"She leader. She speaking on radio."

Adam squinted his eyes. "You mean...Sirius?"

The foreigner nodded quickly. Adam walked over and frisked him for weapons, though he had no idea what he was doing. It's not like he's ever checked someone for weapons. "What's your name? Cómo te llamas?" That was the only sentence Adam remembered from Spanish class.

"Pedro."

He was young, maybe early 30s like Sirius. Handsome too. For someone who had survived the apocalypse, his teeth sure looked great. Adam couldn't put a finger on what exactly made this man so odd. Maybe his demeanor. It was just too chipper. His hands were intertwined and he seemed to be humming, even rocking slightly, to a song in his head.

No weapons. He looked harmless. Adam led him toward the building.

✧ ✧

Adam never understood girls. A week ago, Royal and Sirius were arguing about the speech. The next day they were best pals. The day after that they argued about how to setup the camps. Then the next day, completely back to giggling. Another argument. And now, they were at a campfire – roasting marshmallows and laughing hysterically. Janice, at least, made sense to him.

Pedro followed a few steps behind him when they approached the two. The walking iPhone calendar named Royal looked down at her watch.

"Your shift ain't over," she said being more polite than usual. Usually addressing Adam ended with the word *idiot*, *dummy*, or *ignoramus*. Which was technically not even a word.

Adam replied, "I know.... I gotta visitor wants to see you, Sirius."

"And you just let him in?" Royal barked. "Do you even understand how important she is to this cause?"

Sirius placed her hand on Royal's knee and patted gently. "Oh my God, it's fine. Stop being mean to him." She turned to Adam. The stranger came out from behind him. Pedro didn't look like he knew where to put his hands. He placed them on his hips then crossed them then decided on putting them in his jeans.

"Hello, Cyrus."

Sirius' branch of roasting marshmallows just flopped out of her hand into the fire. Her mouth was half-opened and eyes wide. "Holy... Pedro? It can't be."

He stared at her in the fire for a while. "What happen to...What happen...to your cara?" Pedro asked, motioning a hand over his face, since he only knew the Spanish word for it.

Sirius pretended to not be hurt, brushing her hair downwards in a moot attempt to cover up the scars on her face. Adam thought about punching the stranger in the mouth. That's what Brent would've done.

"Oh," she waved, "you know. Accidents happen, right?"

If these two were friends, a handshake or a hug should've been in order by now. Just before Adam was about to be nosy and ask about their relationship, Royal beat him to it.

"Who that?" she said to Sirius without acknowledging Pedro.

"A co-worker. We worked on CNN together. He was my cameraman."

Pedro said, "I come to send message. We hear radio. I remember voice. I know it you. Lloyd ask me for you to come with me."

"Go where?" Sirius asked before Royal could open her mouth.

"Atlantic City. You see...um..." Pedro snapped his fingers trying to remember a word. "...magia."

"Magia?" she muttered.

Willie joined the crowd, sipping a cup of his signature sludge coffee. "Yo."

"Willie, you're from Brooklyn. You know any Spanish?" Royal asked being even more polite to Willie than Adam. No fair. Why does he deserve special treatment?

Willie shrugged. "Yeah. Magia means magic."

Magic? Adam paused. Was Pedro referring to Marcel Celest?

"Yes, magic," Pedro blurted. Instead of stumbling over his English, he spoke quickly in Spanish while Willie paid close attention. "Tienes que venir conmigo y visitar la gente de luz."

"De luz?" Willie repeated and Pedro nodded. He interrupted, "He's saying you have to visit the people of light."

That definitely wasn't referring to Marcel Celest.

"Tienen miles de seguidores que necesitan su ayuda. Que pueden hacer milagros. Me fijo."

"They need your help, Sirius. They've got followers. Bunch of them. And he's saying something about they can perform miracles? They fixed him? What's he talking about?"

Sirius was breathing deeply. Her chest puffed up and down. "Pedro, uno momento please?"

The visitor nodded and walked away, humming some unrecognizable tune. Way too upbeat. Adam didn't like him. Now that Pedro was out of hindsight, he planned on voicing his opinion. He never got to put in his say. Now was the time. "I think –"

Willie interrupted, "That guy is nuts."

"Don't trust him," Royal said of just about every new person they met.

Sirius had her hands up. "Guys, I worked with him for five years. He's not a liar. He can be trusted."

"Sounds like some kinda cult, you know what I'm saying? What's he talking about magic?" Willie downed the rest of his sludge.

"The last time I saw him," Sirius said, sucking in air through her teeth, "it's gonna seem crazy, but he didn't look like that. He had a cleft lip. I saw him the day before the nukes hit. It's not like he went in for cosmetic surgery while 400 mile per hour winds destroyed the city – how do you explain that? I mean, didn't you notice how lively he was. Like, he was so full of..." She couldn't find the word.

"Light," Willie said.

Royal spat out, "So you're saying some miracle workers living in Atlantic City have created a rebellion of their own and now they need you? When I was in N'Orleans and Katrina hit us, people was seeing demons in the marshes. When you starving, you can see some crazy shit."

As crazy as it all sounded, that about summed it up. Finally there was enough silence for Adam to butt in. "You need to go with him!" He didn't mean to shout but Royal was about to open her mouth again.

Sirius looked at Adam for maybe the third time since they've known each other. "Why do you think I should go?"

Adam thought about the river of people in his last precognition. All those people that were unstoppable in their march to Marcel Celest's castle. "Because it's your destiny."

Royal blew a laugh out of her mouth, like she was spitting out rotten berries. "Sirius, don't listen to him –"

"Royal, hush," their leader demanded. "Why do you think it's my destiny, Adam?"

"Don't get me wrong, there's a lot of followers here. But not what I saw –" He stopped himself.

"You...*saw*?"

What choice did he have? They wouldn't believe him unless he said it. Just blurt out what he'd been forbidden to say. What Servo Clementia told him never to utter. Sirius wouldn't believe him unless he told her the whole truth. And it started with just four simple words.

Adam looked down and said, "I'm a time traveler."

CHAPTER TWENTY-FIVE

Time Traveler? Healing light? Marcel Celest will be able to control the weather? All this was too much. Sirius felt so overwhelmed, she kept reminding herself to peddle the bicycle faster. Day two since Adam admitted everything he knew about the future. A lot to grasp. Besides that dumb story about a ghost sighting at Carpenter's Hall, Sirius never done any supernatural investigations.

Pedro peddled his bike next to her, smirking at her. Not even a hint of that cleft lip. According to him, light healed him. Some guy named Lloyd. Kind of a cheesy name for a presumably powerful god.

At least she was able to convince the group to let her travel this alone. But she was already feeling the loneliness. Sure, Pedro kept her company but he barely spoke enough English to hold a conversation. Like all those nights they worked together, driving the streets of Philadelphia for the next story, it eventually turned to few words.

"You look muy beautiful," Pedro smiled. He never grinned at her like that before. But he kept staring at her scars with a slightly curled lip. She never looked at his deformity like that.

"Thanks," Sirius managed to say.

"I look beautiful?"

Unsure if he meant it as a statement or a question, Sirius just decided to nod yes. He had become increasingly handsome. His weight dropped to normal and he seemed well-groomed for a homeless man. So it wasn't a total lie. He combed his hair back with one hand. That gesture became oddly familiar. It occurred to Sirius how she used to do the same thing. Comb her hair constantly, bat her eyes to keep the mascara from clumping, and fix her lipstick in the mirror every thirty minutes. After a long sigh, relief overcame her. None of those things mattered anymore.

"You sleep in my tent there," Pedro offered.

"Uh, no thanks."

His eyes widened. Maybe it had been a while since that line didn't work.

Suddenly fog drowned them. It came subtle, but increased in seconds. "Pedro, let's stop. I can't see."

Then he disappeared from view.

"Pedro?"

His voice answered, but was faint. Far. Great, he had just kept going and left her behind. Sirius stopped peddling and pulled her bike aside. A bottled water fell out of her backpack and rolled into the unknown void on the side of the freeway. "Pedro, wait up. I mean...uno memento?" No answer.

Sirius sighed. This was turning out to be a nightmare. Her curiosity had gotten her in trouble again. Pedro, this man named Lloyd, and if Adam told the truth – she wondered if it was worth the hassle.

Just enough visibility to see four feet in front of her, Sirius sighed again. She needed that water bottle. Being her only source of water, she hunched over and searched the ground. She walked for a few minutes before concern withheld her courage. Behind her, the fog was so thick that her bicycle seemingly disappeared. This may have been a bad idea. Sirius bent down and ran her arms along the road. She was sure the bottled water fell in this direction.

Then a rattling noise grew in the mist. Piercing. Threatening. Sirius stood absolutely still. Before her, the shape of a rattlesnake appeared in the fog. Its head curled upward and stared at her.

She did a story on a rattlesnake scare. They were something to be terrified of. Their venom became increasingly deadly in the last decade. Evolution at its best.

"It's more afraid of you than you are of it," a voice said.

Sirius wanted to scream, but the rattlesnake would strike. She stood absolutely still. Who was talking? That wasn't Pedro's voice.

The voice added, "It should've killed you already."

The snake just kept rattling. Sirius stated with a hint of sarcasm, "Well, that's encouraging."

"You scared it more than it scared you. You *are* impressive, Miss Sirius Dawson."

Slithering its head downwards, the snake quieted and slithered its way back into the fog's shadows. Sirius walked back and stood still. The air had gotten thicker. "I can't see."

"I can help that."

The fog began to lift, drag away like a vacuum sucked it in. In mere seconds, Sirius could see again. Pedro was nowhere to be found. The man who had spoken to her stood a few feet away. He handed her the pink water bottle she had lost.

Reluctant to take it, Sirius stood in her position like the stranger was just as dangerous as that snake. "How did you do that? Make the fog go away?"

His pupils were large. He stared into hers. The man was taller than her, long gray beard almost reaching the collar of his shirt, and a pudgy nose like Santa Claus. His outfit seemed odd. Like he was from the Middle East. But his skin was Caucasian.

"I'm Lloyd," he said, still holding out the water bottle. This couldn't be *the* Lloyd. They were still a day's trip from reaching Atlantic City.

He added, "And the reason the fog went away...is because I asked it to. The elements are our friends."

He opened her water bottle and the water rose out of it. Sirius covered her mouth, for no reason since she couldn't find a word to say or get a scream to escape. The water hovered in mid-air, moving at a slow pace in a circle, before it returned to its home in the bottle.

Sirius contemplated jumping on her bicycle and seeing how fast she could take off. But her body was stiff.

"It's frightening to accept there are things out of the realm of what we call...reality. You'll get used to it, kiddo. Wait until you see what the Light can do." A kind smile emerged from his face.

Finally able to remove her hand from her face, Sirius reached out a stumbling palm. He placed the water bottle in it. She grasped it. "I'm, like, too afraid to drink it now."

Lloyd laughed. "Pedro said you were funny. He was right. You *do* have an amazing light in you. Some people, it's so faint. But yours is almost blinding."

Sirius eyed his outfit again. "Where are you from?"

"Oh, the Moroccans gave it to me. Well, actually, they gave me the djellaba. My wife says it looks like a dress, but it is actually pretty comfy. Then the Saudis gave me the thobe overcoat thingy to keep me warm. Indians made the shoes for me yesterday. Oh, and some really nice Iranians hand wove the scarf." He petted the scarf like it was a cat on his shoulder.

Her voice froze before words could escape, either from the frigid air or nervous tongue. Sirius caught herself holding a breath and closed her eyes to inhale. This was happening too quickly. "Yesterday, you were in India? You know all flights are grounded, right? How do you expect me to believe that? What...don't tell me you can fly too?"

"Well," Lloyd drug out the word *well* while he searched for a reply. "Sort of. It's more like teleportation."

"Oh," Sirius shrugged, "of course. That just makes *way* more sense." Perhaps being sarcastically rude toward a man who can control the wind and water wasn't smart. She decided to take a deeper breath. "I'm sorry. I've faced some of the weirdest stories, but never one that's made me speechless. How are you able to do these things?"

"When nuclear missiles hit us, me and my wife went into another place. A place of light. And we bonded with it."

Sirius had been trained to know a liar. But Lloyd hadn't twitched an eye, scratched his arm, or even bit his lip. "So, you're telling me the light around has what? Like a...soul of its own?"

"Couldn't have said it better myself. Yes. It sort of does."

He moved in toward her. Maybe she could've backed away, but Sirius found herself motionless. Lloyd scanned the scars on her face. He said, "I enjoyed seeing your face on this news. But this face...has done so much more."

"You can fix it?" Sirius asked.

"If you want that. Yes." His voice sounded like he had just been asked to put a jet engine in a Miata. Sure it would work, but was it necessary?

Hesitating, Sirius closed her eyes and imagined those days of flawless skin. Looking in that mirror and moving her head around in every position, just to make sure there were no flaws for the camera. And all that expensive make-up. She had to eat pizza rolls for a week once to pay for them. Then the moisturizers and sunscreen always made her skin so oily. God forbid she got a pimple. She would just call in sick rather than step outside her apartment.

Then there was Pedro. Perfection turned him into an impolite jerk. Was she like that? Only concerned for herself? Sirius touched the side of her cheek and ran her finger through the scars.

Lloyd asked, "Have you ever seen the Rocky Mountains through Colorado?"

"No. Only pictures, I guess." She opened her eyes.

"From afar, they might seem fairly gruesome. But up-close, they are quite breath-taking. They have various heights and long peaks. Earth has changed so much throughout its history that scars *had* to be left behind. They are reminders of that change."

"Don't fix them," Sirius whispered and repeated it to herself. "They are *my* scars."

Lloyd gave a steady nod then turned around. "Where the hell did Pedro go? He must've just kept going. Typical."

"Well, don't you know the way back?"

"The shoes are nice, but not that nice. I'll have a callus by morning if we walk all that. I'm going to need a favor." Lloyd's pupils widened again.

"Oh my God, those eyes are freaky. Is that how you see more light?"

Lloyd gave a smirk and a nod, that same reaction her editor used to make when surprised with her sense of intelligence. "I don't have enough in me to get us both to travel there. You're going to have to boost it, so I can see the strings."

"The what? Okay, you know what, never mind. I probably should just listen. Okay, so how do I boost it or whatever?"

"Think of something that makes you *truly* happy."

"You mean...like Peter Pan?"

Lloyd laughed again. "Heck no. We need to go *much* faster than that."

Closing her eyes, Sirius had the perfect thought to make her happy. A warm bath in some sea salt, with lavender petals for smell and her hair wrapped in a damp towel.

She opened one eye. Nothing happened. "Okay," Sirius cleared her throat. "I know what you are going to tell me. I need to *believe* that this will work, right?"

"Do you know there's a difference between believing in something and knowing it? For instance, do you believe the sun will rise? Or do you *know* it will rise?"

Sirius slowly nodded and closed her eye. After a deep breath, she decided on another happy thought. Brent. They were lying down on the couch, munching on pretzel sticks, laughing at old episodes of the *Simpsons*, and Brent rested his head on her lap. She smiled and held onto that feeling. The feeling of that amazing day.

Everything turned warm. Almost too warm. Sirius felt a drop of sweat build on her forehead. Before she could panic...the warmth was gone. She opened her eyes.

They were somewhere else.

Atop a hill, looking over rows of trees. There was a vast lake surrounded by tents and hammocks. People were everywhere, cooking and cleaning.

Lloyd said, "Pretty radical, right? Isn't that what you kids say nowadays? *Radical*?"

Grasping her chest like it was about to explode, Sirius managed to say, "No one has said that since the 90s." She stumbled forward over grass. Actual grass. These people had grown real grass. Bending over, Sirius touched it.

She took off her jacket. It wasn't cold here. How? Why?

Lloyd took in a deep breath. "Welcome to the home for the 'People of Bliss'."

As revenge for accidentally placing nuts in the Christmas brownies and nearly killing the Editor's allergic daughter, Sirius had been sent on the worst assignment. Her insider story was to be about the infamous Scientology. They greeted her with all-white uniforms and freakishly wide eyes.

No one was like that here. Not a sense of farce merriment. Children had somehow made a game using busted rubber tires, hopping between them. Some white guy with long dreadlocks and no shirt lit up a joint. Diversity was clear here, all colors of people mingled. Language didn't seem to be an issue for helping pitch tents and cook food. Sirius could hear several mixes of tongues from African, French, Creole, and even Russian. People waved to her. Eventually she began to wave back. Being from Philadelphia, Sirius wasn't used to friendly waves. Middle fingers and curse words were the usual welcomes. Everyone dressed as they pleased. In fact, a few didn't dress at all, walking around in their birthday suits. She'd covered her eyes only to notice she was alone in her actions. No judgements or barriers here. Odd and yet satisfying. Was this how the hippy phase started? Was this what Marcel Celest preached so much about? Freedom?

It felt like a regular summer in the Northeast out here. Sirius' scarf began to choke her with the stuffiness. She unraveled it and got hit with a brief chilly breeze. The warmth was a welcome blessing.

A child ran up to Lloyd and handed him something. Circular in size and mechanical. Sirius hadn't seen one of those in ages. It was a CD player. They mumbled something to each other. Lloyd reacted like a 12-year old on Christmas morning. He hugged the kid and gave plenty of kisses before the child ran off, laughing.

"What did he give you?"

He examined the CD inside before closing the lid. Lloyd held it close to his heart. "My favorite album. He found it. It's N'Sync. I *love* N'Sync."

One eyebrow rose and her other eye squinted. Sirius said, "Did you just, like, say you loved a boy band?"

He scoffed, "Don't tell me you're a Backstreet Boys kind of girl?"

She shrugged, "I was in love with AJ."

Lloyd put the CD player in his pocket and led her past a series of tents. "Let's go over the rules. There's only one. We help each other."

"Cool beans," Sirius replied.

"No one has said that since the 90s." Lloyd made a quick glance back to reveal his sly grin.

Sirius hid her laugh and it came out as a small snort. Finally, they stopped at a large purple tent, tied to tree branches. He politely opened the flap and gestured for her to enter. "My wife Nina wants to meet you."

"What if I said *no*?"

"God, I don't think I've tried that with her. I don't know what will happen." That sly grin crossed his face. "She's harmless, I promise."

Sirius slid through the tent's door and entered. A dozen colored children hovered around a chair. When they brushed aside, Nina was revealed. Her hair was a mess of braids going in several directions. She smiled, "I'm afraid to look in the mirror. Did they do a good job?"

Lloyd zipped closed the tent door and said, "Yes, honey. You look immaculate."

Nina turned to Sirius, the ugly braids drooped down like a dead plant. "Is my husband lying to me, Sirius Dawson?"

She covered her mouth to not laugh. Then whispered, "Yes."

Nina's eyebrows rose. "An honest woman. I like her already. You see, Lloyd, honesty is the best policy."

"Until the wedding day, my love."

Nina spoke in a foreign language to the kids. Sounded Jamaican. They giggled and began to loosen the braids. She turned to Sirius and her pupils changed drastically.

"God, that freaks me out when you guys do that," Sirius held her chest.

"I don't blame you. It's a lot to comprehend. But we have to be careful. All I'm doing is reading your soul."

There wasn't much to read – Sirius felt confident about that. Her life had been pretty boring. That is, until Brent came around.

"Oh, he's just so handsome," Nina said, "Mr. Brent Celest. Yum."

Lloyd's face scrunched. "The President's kid? He's a terrorist."

Nina scoffed, "So are we in the Union's eyes. Our leader here is in love with him. I can see it."

Changing the subject would make Sirius feel a lot more comfortable. "I'm no leader."

"Your light says different," Nina said as the young girls finally loosened her hair. It plopped down and they began to comb it. "She'd be about your age right now."

"Who?"

"Our daughter," Lloyd answered.

"Where is she?" Only after the question did Sirius remember how nosy she could be sometimes. The sad faces on Lloyd and Nina answered the question.

"Gone," Nina answered. Her change in subject was as blunt as Sirius'. "How many followers you have?"

"A lot. Probably a thousand."

Nina sighed. "The both of us don't have enough light to transport that many."

Lloyd cleared his throat. "Well, me and Sirius did a neat trick earlier. I used her luminance. So I have an idea how to get more of it. We're going to need the help of the People of Bliss."

✧ ✧

Church was boring. Raised a Catholic, Sirius often fell asleep. Something about being *told* what to believe bothered her. But for some reason, Lloyd's preaching made more sense.

Night had already settled in, but the cold hadn't. Sirius would've checked the temperature on her iPhone if it worked. If she was to guess, it must've been a warm 70 degrees outside. Completely strange since almost every night had been in the 20s. These people had warmth. A lot of it.

Everyone sat on the grass, wearing shorts and T-shirts. It had been months since she'd seen someone in shorts. Sirius placed herself all the way in the back. A reporter was an observer before an advocate. Until she learned to trust these people, Sirius would remain that way.

"Our bodies are bioluminescence," Lloyd continued his teaching. "Science has proven we give off a faint light, so faint that the human eye cannot focus on it. But it's there. During embryogenesis, the ovum and the sperm cell ignite in a spark. A spark. That spark...is you. It's in you."

Someone came and perched himself next to Sirius. Perhaps too close. It was Pedro. He waved.

Sirius whispered, "Where were you? You abandoned me."

Pedro shrugged, "Sorry. You disappear. I go. I'm okay though."

She noted that Pedro never asked if she was okay. Most of the people here had language barriers, but communicated with actions. Pedro's actions, so far, hadn't been polite. They turned to listen to Lloyd. Sirius slowly moved aside to get more breathing room.

"Close your eyes. Don't pray. Just calm your mind and your soul for a moment. Then listen closely to what I have to say to you."

Everyone did as Lloyd requested, without hesitation. Even Pedro. Sirius hated this part in church. She pictured that when everyone would close their eyes, the ushers went around and pick-pocketed the congregation. She chose to keep her eyes open then...and also now.

Then Lloyd spoke to the people with a soft, solemn voice. "We are at a crucible. There will be life...and there will be death. You can either wallow in the darkness...or bask in the light. Self-control will be difficult as two entities fight for your soul. As the shadows close in on you, remember there is a candle in the palm of your hand. It will always be there, no matter how much the blackness tries to devour it. That little wick can ignite when you need it the most. And what it took was simply *confidence* in yourself. Take the moment in your life that meant the most to you. Focus on it. Sink into it. Become it. Relive it."

Silence filled the masses. As much as she enjoyed meditation, this felt different. More quiet. Sirius couldn't even hear wind. The air stopped. Behind Lloyd, the lake stopped moving. What was happening? As much as she enjoyed his words, how was this related to his plan to bring her followers over here?

"You all *are* powerful, beyond belief. Now, open your eyes and witness how powerful you all are."

The crowd opened their eyes. Sirius' hands cupped over her mouth in shock. Suddenly each of them gave off a red glow, like a powerful flashlight was below their skin. Most of them gasped, staring at their hands with wonder. It was the bioluminescence of the human body that was now visible. Even Pedro glowed. He giggled. Sirius wished she had meditated now. The light was amazing.

Lloyd's voice echoed, "Now, my friends, I need your help. With your power – we have more followers to bring here."

CHAPTER TWENTY-SIX

Marcel could almost smell Janice's perfume from across the banquet hall. It was called L'Occitane en Provence, an enriching lilac scent. He lied about setting up this dance to establish relationships between the political leaders. Instead, this night was for Janice.

The chandelier reflected the lighting while the band played a mellow tempo. Tonight's attire was formal. Politicians seemed pleased to pull out those old tuxedos and clad dresses. It had been months since the snobs got the chance to expose their money.

Janice's gown outdid them all. Marcel had it handmade for her. Then sent it to her room with an invitation; he was nervous she wouldn't come. But there she was, looking confident in her long silk dress that opened up at the thigh. Gerard was next to her and the luckiest man alive. Getting inside either of their heads was difficult. Either because it didn't feel right to use his powers against his own family or because they both prevailed at hiding their thoughts. But every so often he had the chance to plant ideas in their heads. Ideas that could bring their marriage to an end. Then Marcel and Janice could be happy together. Forever.

Gerard abandoned her, aiming for the open bar and the variety of scotch. Sometimes he made it too easy. Even without Marcel's persuasion, their marriage stayed together by the thinnest string. It would have to end. Especially since in Janice's womb was a good possibility of Marcel's child. Last night, he stayed up thinking of baby names.

Janice hadn't noticed Marcel yet; instead she scanned the room. Some politicians approached her and shook her hand. She knew how to handle a crowd with a smile and a stern attitude. Mom taught her that.

Finally, Janice noticed him. Marcel smiled as their eyes met. He walked away from the dull political conversation with President Wen. He hadn't been listening anyway.

She smirked as he approached, "Are you going to ask me to dance?"

Marcel became so entwined in her beauty that he didn't answer. Diamond earrings sparkled in his eyes. Janice snapped her fingers, like a hypnotist counting to ten. "Sorry," Marcel blushed. "Sure, let's dance."

Being raised in a political family taught many talents at a young age. They danced softly to the music, in tune with its deep, slow rhythm.

"So, you know what I'm going to ask."

Marcel nodded. "The latest news. Well, the prison bus crashed but Brent's body wasn't found. It's safe to assume he survived. There's tire tracks from the vehicle Dad had. It's safe to assume they're together. We lost track of them in the woods. They are heading east toward the rebellion."

Janice gave a slight nod and a slight sigh. She looked up at the ceiling. The chandelier's lights reflected on her smooth skin. She said, "Remember when you asked me to dance at the Prom because Gerard passed out in the bathroom?"

"Yeah and he only had one glass of scotch that night."

"That's right! He did!" Janice giggled. Then rolled her eyes. "It'll probably take more than one glass tonight."

Next to the open bar, Gerard raised his glass like a toast to Marcel. It was as if he knew he was being talked about. They nodded to each other.

Marcel couldn't deny the friendship of his brother-in-law.

They'd known each other since high school. "I think Gerard deserves a drink tonight. He's celebrating his new position."

"Position?"

"US Forces Supervisor? For our new security team, sort of like a mix of military and Secret Service. We're still working on a name. Didn't he tell you?"

Janice cleared her throat then purposely turned them so she faced away from Gerard.

Marcel added, "I'd like to offer you a position in the Union too. *Education Liaison*." He said it like he was Bob Barker opening the doors to a new car. Except Janice didn't hop up and down. In fact, she didn't react at all. Maybe she hadn't understood. "You would be in charge of enacting new education policies. This is your chance to make a difference! Remember when you told me that saying? About the fish climbing a tree? Albert Einstein, I think."

Janice recited in an uneventful tone. "'Everybody is a genius. But if you judge a fish by its ability to climb a tree, it will live its whole life believing that it is stupid.' And yes, that was Albert Einstein."

She was about to say no. Marcel could sense it without even looking into her soul. He hadn't pictured a negative response, so he wasn't prepared for a rebuttal. Instead he thought about the night with Gabe. And then uttered his words. "You can change everything."

"It's not that simple, Marcel. In order to change something, you need a resistance. We're just recycling old government. It's the power of that resistance that will alter the world."

He couldn't believe it. She had the nerve to bring up the rebellion. His smile faded. The night ruined. *Resistance.* Just one simple word made his stomach boil. The room became stuffy like an elevator with too many people. "So you heard the bitch's speech?"

Janice's neck twisted at the curse word. "That's a rush to judgement. Whoever that woman was, her words were powerful."

"So are mine!" Marcel said through tight teeth.

Janice glanced back to the open bar. Gerard was gone. Was she looking for an out to this conversation? Like he was annoying her? Marcel had become the most powerful man in the world, figuratively and physically. And she had the audacity to glance away when he was talking?

"It doesn't matter what you think of these fucking protestors. They'll be gone soon anyways."

"What?" Janice finally showed some reaction to shocking news tonight. "What do you mean?"

"We've got their location."

His sister stopped dancing and took a step back. "Marcel. Please. Tell me what you plan on doing to those people."

After a snort, Marcel answered, "They're going to be arrested for treason. All of them."

"There's got to be over a thousand people there."

He shrugged silently. That was the only response. "So? We got the prison room. Most inmates died when the nukes landed. Who cares? If it makes you feel better, most of them probably will fight back and get shot in the process. Less people to worry about."

She swallowed hard and shook her head. "Are you insane?"

Darkness seemed to grow and pulse. *Insane?* Marcel forgot to breathe, he became so enraged. The air settled. His pupils grew wildly.

"Don't do it," a familiar voice said behind him. Gabe. The devious archangel again tried to calm Marcel. "Calm yourself, dear boy. You don't want to hurt her. I know you don't. You're in control."

He returned to breathing and felt the blood rush back to his head. The darkness settled. The air returned to his lungs. Gabe had succeeded, as always, at creating focus in Marcel's mind.

Janice gently placed her hand on his chest. "This is how it started. As a simple dislike. Then it turned into a genocide of Jews. Then...a world war. Please. Don't turn into that...monster."

"Enough with the name-calling, Janice." Now he took a step

back, tossing her hand away.

"Your eyes are so different."

Marcel raised his eyebrows. Had she noticed his pupils? His power?

Janice whispered, "Your eyes have changed since that coma. They used to be filled with fun, laughter, and contentment. Now, they are filled with demand. You know why you were so special back then? Before the nukes hit? Because you didn't need to *tell* anyone what to do. They did it for you, because they adored you. But not anymore."

With that, his sister turned and left the gala. Marcel wanted to will the ground to open up and swallow this night's evening into a sinkhole. Slaughter everyone into the molten lava under the Earth's surface. Watch them all burn. Watch Janice burn. Just like all his hopes and dreams had been tossed into the fire.

"Try listening to her," Gabe said behind him.

Marcel said nothing to the archangel or else he would look insane talking to himself.

Gabriel continued, "You cannot make her love you as anything more than a sibling."

Marcel smiled and whispered, "That's where you are wrong. Oh yes, I can."

He stormed out of the banquet hall toward Janice. She had dipped into the empty hallway toward her room. Marcel spoke up. "Janice, I'm not done talking to you. You don't walk away from me."

Janice opened the door and closed it quickly. Marcel held out his hand. He commanded the wind to unlock the door.

Anything you want, the air element muttered frighteningly.

The door unlocked and burst open. Janice screamed, holding her chest. "How did you —"

Marcel's pupils grew and he stared into Janice's eyes. She relaxed. Her arms dangled at her side. Locked onto the sexual impulses in her soul, he whispered, "I want you to get undressed and lie on the bed."

After a dreamily stare at the floor, she nodded. Janice started by removing her necklace. Marcel felt aroused immediately. That perfume became potent to the point he could taste it. She removed her earrings and laid them on the nightstand next to the bed.

Something he'd never seen before of someone under his trance – Janice began to turn flush. Forehead, cheeks, and neck all turned the color red. Suddenly, she spat out vomit and rushed to the bathroom. In one swoop, Janice lifted the toilet seat and vomited profusely.

After catching her breath, she mumbled, "The baby's never done that before. Made me that sick."

The baby. Marcel had nearly forgotten a child grew in her. He backed away. The darkness returned to normal. His pupils returned to normal. He felt disgusted with himself. Clenching his head with one hand, Marcel tried to comprehend what he had almost done. He almost raped his adopted sister.

Janice stared at the floor like it knew more about what just happened then she did. "How did... Why did I...have such a desire for you like that? Marcel? What just happened?" Her eyes became glazed and bulged.

Too many emotions flooded his head. In events like this, reassurance was often the only response. Politics taught him that. "It will never happen again."

Marcel backed away and held the door. Again, he didn't have to read her mind. The reassurance wasn't enough for her. She lost trust. Something Janice rarely gave anyone. If reassurance wasn't enough, dominance would have to be. He said, "Think about joining the Union with me. When we find Dad, I'll offer him a job. Even Brent can join me. It'll be better if you did too." He left, slowly closing the door behind him.

Marcel hadn't slept. What had come over him? Before his coma, deciding between right and wrong was simple. Now, not so much. Treating Janice like some whore in a Spanish novela just seemed out of place. Unlike him.

He grabbed the biggest coffee cup he could find in the kitchen cabinet. Pouring as much of the black Columbian brew into the cup as possible, his hip vibrated. It was the damn pager again. Cellphone towers were weak for normal phone calls, but pagers worked just fine. Unfortunate for him because his hip buzzed practically all day. He read the message: FNANCE ADVSOR GOLDMAN AT YOUR OFFCE. Great. Talking about money would surely wake him up this morning. He had to skip on the creamer because there was none and loaded up the cup with sugar.

Who would've thought something as simple as creamer became difficult in a post-apocalyptic world? Most dairy plants couldn't produce enough product to make up for the loss in downed facilities. And the dairy needs refrigeration. Roughly only 50-something reefer trucks even remained to transport.

Another buzz on his hip. It read: DONT FORGET-DOC WANTS TO UPDATE YOUR NANOBOTS THS MORNNG 11AM. He really had to remind that secretary to fix the "I" key on the keyboard. Marcel just wished the damn cellphones were working.

He sipped coffee like it was an ice-cold Gatorade. The heat never hurt him. Even hot showers felt chilly. His body subtly mutated in some way, practically every day. Marcel just didn't feel *normal* anymore.

Maybe he should've calmed all the vexation after his coma, instead of letting it build into a world war. He could've made a few phone calls and saved the world from annihilation. Grains of sugar melted between his teeth as he stared at the kitchen counter. This had been the longest he'd let himself debate the issue in his head. The issue of whether or not he could've stopped this nuclear attack. Plain as day, the answer was yes.

Another buzz on his hip. It read: GOLDMAN CANT WAT MUCH LONGER.

Marcel sighed and walked out of the kitchen area. He crossed the lobby. It wasn't until he got to the elevator did he realize people had greeted him *Morning!* And he had just ignored them.

The elevator zipped up to the third floor.

The hall reminded him of right before his coma. That creepy, dark night. Right before an assassin had leapt out of the shadows to attack him. Right before he had been beaten to a pulp. Right before he received a bullet to his head. Right before he entered the realm with Lucifer.

"Hello?" someone said.

Marcel had just been standing at the open elevator door, blocking that someone from exiting. "Oh, sorry!" he said, moving aside.

He entered his office and sunk into the chair without even shaking the visitor's hand in the front of his desk. Goldman, some wealthy 76 year old that spent over 40 years in the financial market, just sifted through some paperwork in his lap.

"What can I do for you?" Marcel mumbled. He went to take another sip of coffee but found the cup was empty. Not even a slight memory of guzzling it.

"I'm just going over this provision again in the Union contract." He shook his head and rolled his eyes. Goldman tossed the paper on the desk. It almost felt like he had just flung Bible sheets all over the ground. Just a little disrespectful. "I can't believe you got them to sign this."

"I'm sorry?" Marcel said even though he heard him clearly.

"So," he began, "let's get straight to the point. When I was nine years old, I began completing my parents' tax forms. At fourteen, I began prerequisite courses for Stanford. At twenty-two, I owned a tax firm. At thirty-two, I sold that tax firm for $583 million. At forty-five, President Obama hired me to become the Treasury Secretary. To this day, I'm still a master of the financial market. So – I know what I'm doing. I'm not one of these amateurs that will lie to you to avoid your disappointment."

Marcel didn't ask for an autobiography from this guy, but pretended to be intrigued. "Quite a career."

"The Union *is* and *will continue* to be a financial failure."

Marcel was at a loss for words; the air around him had left the room and he couldn't breathe. He wondered how that was possible. Maybe he misunderstood. The Union was flawless, after all. "Are you saying we're broke? That can't be. We have money."

"No, Sir," he interrupted with a confident wave, "you have I...O...U.'s. There's a difference. The idea of the Union was to bring together one currency, similar to the bitcoin, and use that currency for bartering purposes. But several countries depended on the United States Dollar, which is now useless. Therefore most of the globe is broke. And to make matters worse, most areas don't even have Internet to process the electronic currency you have in mind. Which means you need a physical currency for the time being."

This was all confusing and irritating. Without money, the future of Marcel's goal was in jeopardy. "A physical currency? Well, how do we make more money? Just print more?"

"That's the thing. We can't just print more. It's not that simple."

He opened up his briefcase and pulled out a folder. Then handed it to Marcel. It was diagrams, numbers, and graphs he didn't understand. Economics wasn't his specialty.

Goldman could see the confusion. "Let me put it in an easy summary for you. Nations make money through *taxes*." He said it speaking like he was hosting a children's program. "Ben Franklin wasn't exaggerating with the saying that death and taxes are inevitabilities."

"But aren't we collecting taxes through product sales? Homes? All that stuff?"

"Sure. To the businesses that are still running. And to the people that are still alive."

Without saying another word, Marcel sensed what Goldman was implying. There weren't many businesses running and not many people alive. "So there's no one left to tax. And you're saying...it's not enough?" He meant it to sound like a statement but it came out like a question.

"We estimate only thirty-four percent of the United States population survived the Doomsday. Most are able to return to work in the rural areas and taxing their income hasn't been an

issue. They buy foods at local grocers and fill up their tanks with regular gas. But that's only a third of what this country used to have. A *third*. And...that number is dropping."

Marcel rubbed his forehead. "What? The number is dropping? Why?"

"Because of someone's powerful call for a boycott of the Union."

After a deep breath, Marcel still didn't feel better. That damn woman on the radio had started a rebellion. And then there was that couple, Lloyd and Nina, with the power of Light behind them. He had to diminish them quickly before the Union fell apart. No power Lucifer supplied could change the human lust for money. No one would certainly work for free. And Marcel's persuasion ability could only last for so long. He needed old-fashioned belief in him again. The American people had to root for Marcel Celest once more.

Goldman gathered up his paperwork. "I just don't understand how you got these world leaders to sign this treaty for a Union. I, seriously, cannot comprehend their ignorance. But whatever you did to convince them...use it on that Anti-Union movement." He left and slammed the door behind him.

Gabe had mentioned a word to Marcel early that struck him at that moment. Hope. Hope was a characteristic of the Light. All he had to do was crush that hope.

CHAPTER TWENTY-SEVEN

'MAANALAISEEN BUNKKERIIN 100 ASKELTA POHJOISEEN.'

Brent stared at the bent sign. "What the fuck?" he whispered.

'MAANALAISEEN BUNKKERIIN 100 ASKELTA POHJOISEEN.'

Out of breath as usual, Nelson approached him and stopped to look at the sign. "Holy shit."

"What?"

His father hastily wiped the dirt off the sign. It was plain white with stamped black letters.

Brent repeated louder. He hated being ignored. "What?" This had been the majority of their conversation for the last twenty or thirty miles. Short and emphatic. In fact, that was always their conversations.

"It's directions to a missile silo. The signs were written in Finnish, in the hopes that if Russia did invade that it wouldn't be found because it's their least used language."

"You mean one of the nukes fired off from here?" After saying it, he realized how naive the question was. The entire area was a flat land. Any type of plant or tree that attempted to grow here had been scorched from the missile's launch.

No answer came from his father, who instead focused on trying to find another sign. A surreal feeling came over Brent. From this spot, a nuclear weapon launched from this very spot. How frantic the situation must've been for the staff that had no control over the weapon of mass destruction.

Brent's stomach grumbled. An underground missile silo could mean rations. He'd been on tours with his father in these facilities. They were practically a town underground. Even more important, there was clean water. Water had been a task for the last 24 hours. Their canteens were dry and throats even drier. Brent couldn't produce any saliva.

"I don't know their language completely. But seeing there's '100' written on it, we could assume 100 feet is the entrance." Perhaps it was the thirst that gave Nelson such an attitude in his voice. Brent decided to brush it off. One thing therapy taught him was he made rash judgements on just the tone of someone's voice. "Let's split up. Search everything. The doors are hidden well. Probably below some type of marker."

Always so bossy. Brent walked away before the better of him lost control. What he would give to see just a stagnant puddle. Water infested with mosquitos was a cut above no water.

Night was peeking in. The North Star hid behind a bombardment of black clouds. They had been using that star all week to guide them. Brent threw his backpack off. It clanked with all that junk camping gear they'd collected. The handle of the pan snapped off. He bent over and attempted to screw the handle back on. Now the cooking supplies were broken. Brent kicked the bag as hard as he could. Everything scattered over the ground. He fell over and smashed his head against the tree trunk – even that little outburst made him weak. Lightheadedness overcame him. Blood trickled down his forehead. His tongue stuck to the top of his mouth; it felt like sandpaper.

One star peeked out behind a cloud then disappeared again. He wondered, for the hundredth time, if there were other worlds out there. Did they suffer the way humanity suffered? Turning weapons against each other? It was all because of an internal fury. A fury that even lived inside him.

He thought about the prison simulation on Jupiter's moon. Europa. He closed his eyes and envisioned it. This was what he did every night to help him fall asleep. Imagining a place where he could be alone gave him comfort. But, as always, he reminded himself there would be no Sirius. Life without her didn't seem to mean much anymore.

"You really do love her," a gentle old voice said.

Brent opened his eyes. A man stood above him, dressed in an odd Arabian outfit. Before he could ask, the stranger answered, "I'm Lloyd. Pleasure to meet you."

On their walk today, Brent and his father talked about the supernatural. Dad had spoken briefly about the pictures he saw of Lloyd's miraculous abilities. Brent spoke about what he saw Marcel do in their last battle, causing fire to attack in mid-air. Though neither man had words to say afterwards, it certainly didn't mean they were skeptical.

Brent tried to stand. Lloyd shook his head. "Don't get up. I can see you are weak. Here..."

The stranger closed his eyes and took a slow breath. Then he lifted his hands slowly. In sync with the movement, the ground sunk in a six-foot-wide circle. At the same time, water rose and filled the new hole. Brent didn't ask how or why. He ran over and began to swallow the crystal water. The reflection showed peeled lips and his beard had gotten out of control. Facial dirt had seeped into his pores causing discoloration in his skin. The blood from his head wound dripped down and landed in the puddle.

"Looks deep," Lloyd said. "Have you ever heard of cytosine base?"

Brent shook his head. Science wasn't his thing. He spent more time in gym class than a lab.

Lloyd explained, "UV rays kill bacteria by breaking up the cytosine base and causing infections to die. The heat cauterizes the wound and ends the pain. So, in essence, light heals. Do you believe the Light can heal you? After what I've just stated to you?"

Brent shrugged, "I guess."

Lloyd looked him in the eye the same way Coach used to. *Are you going to make that home run or not?* After a long inhale and finally feeling hydrated again, Brent corrected himself. "Yes. I believe the Light can heal."

Then Brent had to squint to see, because a light appeared like a cop's flashlight pointed at his face. As quickly as it appeared...it was gone.

Peering into the water's reflection again, Brent saw the cut and blood were gone. He doubted Marcel would ever use his powers for good like that.

The stranger said, "There's no need to say it. I'm not the one to thank. *You* did it. I'm only a bridge between you and the luminous power." Lloyd crouched down and grunted as he sat on the grass. As if the miracle wasn't enough, the mystical man did something even more surprising. He pulled out a marijuana joint. "You have a lighter?"

"Is this a joke?"

"What? It calms my head. A lot of things do. As long as it doesn't hurt you or anyone else, where's the harm in it? Unless you know where to find a Starbucks caramel macchiato instead?"

Brent searched his pockets for the lighter. After a moment, he grew peeved. He couldn't find it. He turned his pockets inside out. "What the fuck? I *just* had it." His breathing deepened, the spell of content instantly broken.

He opened up his backpack, tossing things out. "What the fuck did I do with it? God..damn..it!" He continued throwing things aside. "It's red and has a picture of Marilyn Monroe on it. What the fuck?! I lost it!"

Lloyd casually picked up an object in the grass. It was the lighter. He lit the joint, taking in the dense smoke of the marijuana. Brent could feel his breathing returning to normal. Now came the part where he felt moronic for losing control over something so simple.

"You know," the man said calmly, "just because something is lost, doesn't mean it's gone. What is it? This thing you've lost and assume can't be found, that makes you lose control?"

Brent had lost several meaningful items in his life. His job. His home. His reputation. But he decided to mention the deepest and most sincere missing aspect. "My mom. I lost my mom."

"Just because you couldn't find the lighter, did that mean it wasn't there?"

Brent felt a chill up his spine. Then it felt like a cold hand touching his shoulder. He swung around. No one was there. Could it have been his mother?

"Hello, Lloyd," a solemn voice said. Nelson stood next to a tree, arms crossed.

Lloyd lifted his head in disbelief. After a pleasant smile, he replied, "Hello, Nelson."

Calling each other on a first-name basis didn't trigger a shock in Brent, but the fact they both smiled did. The way old friends smiled. "You know each other?" Brent asked.

Both men cleared their throats simultaneously. They shook hands. Lloyd muttered, "Good to see you. Where is..."

"Janice is with Marcel."

"Oh," Lloyd spoke so low that it sounded more like an exhale than a word.

Nelson walked over and took a few sips of the water. "I found the entrance to an underground bunker. Would be a good hiding place. It's big. *Really* big."

"I'll keep that in mind," Lloyd nodded.

His father finished one long last sip then said, "We were on our way to find you."

"I know," the stranger said, "I felt it. That's why I came looking for you. You were *only* eighteen miles off track."

Eighteen miles? Brent wanted to pull his hair out. Instead, he thought about what Lloyd had said. Hope hadn't been lost like that lighter. Hope stood before them. He asked, "Can you lead us the right way?"

After a snort, Lloyd said, "Hell. I can do better than that. I can take you right to our camp."

"How long will it take?" Brent asked, picturing Sirius in his arms.

"That'll depend on you two," Lloyd said. "I'm going to need you guys to...think of happy thoughts." A big grin slid up his face.

CHAPTER TWENTY-EIGHT

First agenda: creating a war. *Sure, no problem.* Gerard loved the new job, but hated the first assignment. Marcel didn't call it "creating a war". His exact words had been "securing an opposition". Same thing. Gerard had no idea how to eliminate such an enormous amount of people. Of course, Marcel wouldn't call it "eliminating" either; he would say "reasoning with".

Suits and weapons were definitely needed. Gerard started off last week with a prototype suit. Since the internet went from excellent to mediocre (just like his marriage), the uniform wasn't an easy task. But he managed. Making a plan always seemed second nature to him. Sticking to it was where it becomes complicated.

His office was cramped with stacks of paperwork. He used two fingers to type on an old typewriter. Gerard wondered how many people were starving and yet the Union didn't have any qualms with providing a 100% pure cherry wood desk. Then there was a knock on the door. "Yeah?" he said not looking up.

A man cleared his throat. "I wanted to give a proper introduction. I'm General Vanderbilt. Marcel has appointed me in charge of military services."

Gerard didn't bother to look up. Typing took concentration. He hated computers. "Okay. That's great. Would you mind closing the door when you leave?"

"Hmm. Well. I actually would like a moment with you," Vanderbilt said. The guy talked slow. Gerard bet he could teach a sloth to talk and have a faster conversation than this.

"Goddamnit, you made me hit the Z instead of the X!" Gerard yanked the paper out of the typewriter and crumbled it up. "The stupid IT department can't find me a printer, so I gotta use this piece of junk to print stuff out."

He finally looked up at the bald-headed freak. The man wasn't proportioned right, like he skipped leg day at the gym. Gerard tossed the crumbled paper at a trash can and missed again. It collapsed on the floor with the other paper balls. The General snorted and handed a manila folder to him.

"What's that?" Gerard said with his hands behind his back.

"Plans for a uniform."

"Uh no, Mr. Clean. That's *my* job to make the uniform."

Vanderbilt's lip curled. "I came up with an idea that you might like – "

Before he could finish his sentence, Gerard responded, "Yeah, I hate it."

"But you haven't even opened up the envelope."

"Okay, fine." Gerard opened up the manila folder and crumbled it into a paper ball. "Yeah, I hate it." He tossed it and this time made it perfectly in the trash can.

Now was the time where his superior would pretend he had the power to fire him. Gerard had no superior. He always made sure his employment didn't rest in the hands of one person. The only man with the authority to send Gerard home packing was Marcel. His brother-in-law didn't have the guts. Vanderbilt muttered, "You may be the leader of US Union forces, but as a General, *I'm* a step above. I control the actions of the Union military."

"*Keepers*," Gerard held up a finger, "Union *Keepers*. Marcel doesn't like the word *military* or *army*. Scares people away. So I came up with the term: Union Keepers. He loves it." Actually, he hadn't even told Marcel the title for the new security team. "As for the guns, we'll be using rubber bullets. No need to hurt innocent people, right?"

Vanderbilt laughed. Kind of an odd giggle, but yet genuine. After the cackle turned into a snort, he said, "*Innocent* people? May I ask you something? Do you have any idea what we are about to face tomorrow night, Mr. Collins?"

Gerard waved his hands like a magician willing a rabbit out of a hat. "Oh, you mean the *magical* Lloyd and Nina. I'll believe it when I see it."

"Maybe it's true, maybe it's not. But that married couple aren't the real threat, even if they can perform convincing parlor tricks. No. I mean the rebellion. They are much more powerful."

After a deep breath, Vanderbilt took a seat across from Gerard. His breathing had exhilarated and eyes widened. The Frankenstein-wannabe had a strange reaction to his own interpretation of the opposition. His right hand began to rattle like he was holding a maraca. Gerard was a detective long before writing letters on a rickety typewriter, so he knew actions spoke louder than words. General Vanderbilt was a coward hidden under a military mask. He put down his shaky hand so Gerard wouldn't see it. Too late.

"I want to show you something," the general said undoing his neck tie.

"Look. I'm flattered. And I get this a lot. But I don't swing *that* way. I mean, I had a crush on Brad Pitt, but what straight guy doesn't?"

Unamused, Vanderbilt yanked out a necklace from underneath his tie. In the glass charm was a peculiar item. He held it up for Gerard to investigate. Brown in color, dehydrated and crusty. Circular with a slit through the center.

"Do you know what this?"

"I dunno," Gerard shrugged. "A miniaturized vagina?"

"It's a vocal cord," Vanderbilt said, massaging the area of his throat where the vocal cord resides.

"Is it yours? Did you lose it gagging on Marcel's dick?"

Again, no smile from Vanderbilt's lips. "If it were mine, we wouldn't be having a conversation."

This guy's sense of humor was drier than that organ around his neck. Gerard sighed, "I can never be so lucky. So tell me why do you carry body parts around your neck? I have a feeling it's going to be a long, boring story." He leaned back and rolled his eyes underneath close lids.

"When I was stationed in Syria, we were sent to train rebel armies. The first rendezvous was a town named Sadad. It reeked of dead bodies and feces. I had to remind myself that I could lose my job if I shot a child out of mercy, to free them from that ridiculous way of life. I met a man there that was so thirsty he would drink his own urine every morning. Then there was this mother who breast fed her children because there was no food, even her 16-year-old son.

"Then there was this prison, basically a motel with locks on the doors, where the captured opposition were held. They were tortured in the most inhumane ways, like lacing their food with Comet cleaner just to make them puke and suffer in hunger. The 'warden' would, as with every new capture, have their vocal cords cut out. You are probably wondering why."

Actually, Gerard was curious but didn't want Vanderbilt to know that. So he gave a slight shrug.

"Because he said he couldn't sleep when prisoners were screaming through their torture. You may be thinking: Why were these opposition soldiers being punished in the first place?"

"Not really."

"Well, I'll tell you anyway so you understand the lesson. They weren't being tortured to gather information about the opposition or being held for ransom. Nope. They were being tortured because the rebels were 'bored'. And worst of all, *we* were on their side. That's why I keep this vocal cord, to remind me of the grotesque yearnings of rebels. Do you really not fear an uprising? Do you really want to be held in a cage waiting to be tortured to death, without any chance of pleading your freedom?"

It took approximately three minutes before Gerard decided if he liked someone or not. Only two minutes later had he made up his mind. Vanderbilt was annoying. "Give me a break, Vandy. Look at Occupy Wall Street. They weren't cutting off brokers' balls or anything. Kinda wish they had."

"That's because they didn't have a leader. No one to organize them."

Gerard squirmed in his seat. He clicked his nails against the desk, thinking. The asshole had a point. He hated when someone had a point. That meant someone was smarter than him. Rebels, in fact, needed organization. Or else they would just fall apart. Gerard hated disorganization. But what to do about it?

"I'll leave you to your thoughts, Mr. Collins." Vanderbilt got up.

Gerald hated this guy. He wondered if the general was a robot. He talked like one, stood like one, and even blinked like one. Maybe he should punch him in the nose. Then see if blood comes out...or motor oil. "Later, Vandy."

Smoke rose and collected in the air. Dangled for three seconds. Then fell apart. Three seconds felt as long as the three weeks Janice had been here. She tried everything she could to save her relationships. The relationship to her husband. And the relationship with her brother. The hotel had all there was needed to relax. But there was still that itch. An itch to get away from this life with the Union. Run, if possible. Run as fast as she could.

Another inhale of the marijuana cigarette and then a slow exhale. It didn't leave behind any sense of calm. Sort of like drinking decaf coffee. There were times Janice only needed one cigarette to escape her surroundings. Three cigarettes later...nothing. Only the memories of sharing one of these with Adam. She smiled to herself.

She hadn't turned the light on. The living room felt better that way. And the darkness grew as the day got older. Gerard still hadn't come home. Supposed to be home three hours ago. The hotel room stunk like cigarettes. Good. Gerard hated the smell of pot.

It all came down to trust. Such a complicated emotion, Janice created an entire lesson surrounding its evolutionary impact on the world. The Dean, of course, said to stick to the University's approved curriculum. Humans required trust to survive from the moment of birth. Without a parent, a baby couldn't make a bottle of milk or change its diaper. Dependence was key. But why, as humans age, does that trust become less dependable?

The front door opened. Her husband walked in with his tie undone and shoulders sagged. "Babe, what are you doing smoking weed?" Gerard waved the air in front of him like it helped. "It's bad for the –"

He paused when he saw the suitcase by the coffee table. Then he looked over at the suitcase on the other side of the table. Confused, he squinted at her. Then his face drooped and his shoulders sagged even lower. "Baby? Why? I'm not cheating."

"True," Janice mumbled. "I've known you for almost twenty years. I've learned to become a human lie detector, examining your respiratory rate. Want to test it?"

Gerard held his breath.

Janice continued, "I was thinking about that day at the White House, when the police found us and took us away. How did they know where we were? Unless someone tipped them of our location. Was that someone...you?"

"No."

After a long sigh, she said, "False."

Sweat began to form above Gerard's upper lip. "Honey, I did it because we are safer with Marcel and –"

"What's your plan here?"

Gerard's shoulders straightened, "I am here to serve the Union."

Janice grunted, "False." She wondered what his plan had been to come here. Knowing she wouldn't get an answer, she asked something else. "Are you guys planning on arresting those liberators tomorrow?"

"No."

Rolling her eyes, Janice said, "False. Do you know who their leader is?"

"No."

"Hmm. That's true."

"Do you?" Gerard quickly spat out.

Janice smiled, "I don't need to lie. Yes. Yes, I do recognize her voice. Am I going to tell you? Nope."

Her husband stared at the two bags of luggage. "Why two?"

"One for me. And one if you decide to leave with me."

"I can't."

Janice nodded, "True." She put out the cigarette in an ash tray and stood up. Before she could grab the purple luggage bag, Gerard gently touched her shoulder.

"Marcel has changed. We have to change with him. He can get inside your head. I've seen it."

"I've experienced it," she muttered.

"You have to just give in. You don't have to trust me, but trust him. He wants what is best...for everyone."

Nodding her head, Janice sighed. "I have to catch the bus in fifteen minutes."

"No," Gerard spat out. It was the first time she'd seen his eyes water in years. "I can get you a car. It's got plenty of gas." He searched through a drawer in the kitchen and yanked out a set of keys.

She took them then stared into his eyes. "There's a tracker on the car, huh?"

"No."

"False." Janice looked down at the keys. "It doesn't matter. You know where I'm going anyway."

"You won't make it there before we do. We've got choppers. I've already instructed the team that your father and brother don't get arrested."

"I know. I'm just hoping to get to them and then...I don't know what. But I'll feel more at home sleeping in a tent with them than sleeping here." She kissed him. She shouldn't have, but did. All these years together still meant something. But time apart would mean more. He hugged her tight.

Light poured in when she opened the door to leave, rolling her luggage behind her. Gerard said, "When you are ready...and when *I'm* ready...I'll come find you."

Janice smirked and said her last word to her husband. "True." Then walked away, closing the door.

CHAPTER TWENTY-NINE

"It feels like...sitting in a tanning booth."

Adam didn't feel any better. Especially since he had no idea what it was like sitting in a tanning booth. But at least Sirius stayed behind with him.

He watched out the window. Another group of those weird glowing people gathered some of Sirius' followers. Sixteen teleports later and they still creeped him out.

One of the lit people came to the door. Pedro. He herded the next group outside the store. They all remained silent as they followed the shepherds' instructions. The radiant Pedro stepped into the store where Adam and Sirius stayed at the window. "Come," he said. Even a single word like *come* sounded like a struggle in his Spanish tongue. In the internal light, all the organs could be seen. Adam watched his chin wiggle. "Ew," he whispered.

Their fearless leader Sirius stepped up to the door. "Are you, like, going this time, Adam?"

"No." He stumbled through his lie, "I'm staying behind...to...watch over...stuff. Make sure no one causes trouble...or something. Yeah."

She giggled and kissed him on the cheek. He could see why Brent loved her so much. Sirius was the right amount of empathy, hilarity, and sympathy.

Out the window, he watched as Pedro pulled out a boutique of dried flowers. He held it out for Sirius. "You? Me? Date?"

Sweet. But also this man was worse with talking to women than Adam. This wasn't the time nor the place to ask someone out. Sirius gave that all-too-familiar forced smile and whispered something in Pedro's ear. Probably the words: *it's complicated.* The words that seemed more complicated to men than women. Then followed by that all-too-familiar pat on the back. Sirius walked away.

"Friend-zone sucks," Adam said to himself.

Adam watched closely in amazement. Pedro's bright light began to pulse with each of his rapid breaths. With each huff of his chest, the light's color began to fade. In minutes the light disappeared to reveal the normal Pedro. Sirius had already made her way down with the group. Her companion stormed away into the forest.

From behind Adam, Royal appeared. The tomboy wouldn't admit she held back too. She put on a pair of sunglasses and handed a pair to Adam. "It helps," she mumbled. They both stared out the window like people in line at a rollercoaster, with no choice but to ride soon. Pedro was gone. Approximately a hundred people smushed themselves into a roped-off circular section of the street in front of Office Depot. Sirius joined them.

Adam put the sunglasses on. Those illuminated people from Lloyd and Nina's group held their hands together as they created a circle around Sirius and her followers. They closed their eyes in sync. Suddenly the light from those glowers became blinding. The sunglasses didn't help much. One nano-second, over a hundred people stood in the circle...the next – no one.

With her arms crossed, Royal muttered, "We could just drive there and meet them. There's only like fifty of us left."

"Fifty people don't fit in Willie's van." Adam took this opportunity to make him look like the tough one. It seemed to work with bullies. "Stop being such a wimp. It doesn't hurt."

"I know that!" Royal's pigtail flung around like an iguana's tail. "Whatever. If I can gut a pig with a pair of scissors, then I can go through one of them portal things."

Adam would rather have gutted the pig. He stepped outside into the warm air. Today had been the first summer day this summer. One of those glowers made his way to Adam. From a closer point-of-view, he could see their veins. A nurse wouldn't have a problem drawing blood from this one. "Hello, are you ready?" Staring long enough at him, Adam could see the form of his skull. Such an odd sight but yet more comforting the closer he got. The light source in them seemed to be coming from their bones. Or maybe something even deeper? Adam reached his hand out and poked the man in his forehead. The skull moved.

"Yuck," Adam mumbled.

"Um, thanks."

The glowers led them to the inner circle. "Hold your horses!" Royal squealed and got close behind Adam. The right side of his mouth grinned. He could feel Royal's warm breaths on his arm.

The glowers connected hands. It started getting bright. He felt someone embrace his arm and put her head in his shoulder. Royal, no doubt. She trembled as the light grew.

It got hot. Very hot. Then...back to normal. Adam had expected a spectacle of lights to shoot past them. Instead, they just ended up somewhere else. He wondered if teleporting was that boring in Star Trek.

He opened his eyes. Royal let go of his arm quickly. "Well, that wasn't so bad. I'm going to find Sirius." She stormed off as though she knew where she was going. Which she didn't.

While the others marveled at the miracle and shook hands with the new followers, Adam's mind couldn't get away from Royal. She reminded him of his third foster mother. Rude as hell to neighbors but when it had come time for Christmas, she would place wreaths on all their doors. Then play dumb when they asked where they came from. Royal was like that. Like an avocado, hardened shell and all soft inside. And according to one of his visions, Royal was doomed to die in an attack by Marcel Celest. He stayed up most nights trying to remember where or when. If only he had his previous dream diary.

Then his other precognition came to his mind. About a flood

of ravaged men and women, fighting through a mob of Union military. Breaking skulls with baseball bats. Firing guns until they were empty then smashing them in the faces of SWAT. Setting policemen on fire. It was going to be one hell of a protest. And Adam had to question the authenticity of yet another dream of the future. Where were the people in that dream?

Certainly the numbers were correct; there must've been thousands here...but the mood wasn't. These were a bunch of hippies. One woman even had a crown of purple petals on her head. Doesn't get more 1970s Woodstock than that. Though the welcome was a much needed welcome, Adam wanted out of this group. He separated and found himself standing in front of tall older man with a white beard like Gandalf.

"Looks like we made it just on time. Hi, I'm Lloyd. You're Adam, right?" He didn't wait for an answer. "I got a birthday surprise for you."

"It's not my birthday."

"Well, consider this the best present you'll ever receive. He's been asking about you since he heard you were arriving." Lloyd lifted out his hand and presented a man facing a tree in the distance.

Adam didn't recognize right away who it was. Two men stood by the tree. One turned to reveal Nelson. Adam's mouth dropped. He immediately knew who was next to him. His best friend. The guy who took him around the world to chase the prettiest girls. The guy that went to every movie with him. The guy who stayed up to watch the *Star Wars* marathon with him, dressed as a Jedi.

"Brent?"

Brent turned and his mouth dropped. Adam ran. He hopped on Brent and they both fell to the ground. Nelson stepped back like the bromance would just splatter all over him. After finally out of breath from laughing, both men got up. Nelson reached out a hand to shake. Adam hadn't noticed until after he embraced the President. He noted that Nelson never hugged back. If it had been any other reunion, it might've been awkward. But Adam didn't care. His friends were here.

"Dude, where's Sirius?" Adam asked.

Brent looked around. "I haven't found her. What if...she don't want to see me? I mean, I abandoned her. She probably hates me. I'm..."

All their years together and Adam had never seen Brent nervous about a woman. He smiled. "She's going to be thrilled."

The tent was enormous, enough to sleep thirty people. But Lloyd and Nina had insisted that it become Sirius' new home. Much too humble to accept such a gift, she declined. Nina had responded: it was either this tent or sleep on the dock. Sirius made the choice. Now, she wandered around her tent wondering what to do with all this room.

In one corner was a lonely house plant. She knew nothing about plants. Even a bonsai tree had died in Sirius' care. Her green thumb was more black.

One corner had a queen-sized mattress. *For a Queen*, the kids had said earlier to her. She had to admire the attention. Even if it felt more luck than skill that got her here.

Against the longest side wall was a very wide and large bulletin board. It had been held up poorly by two metal legs; the entire board leaned to the side. On the corkboard surface were some pin-ups. Six different maps showed the surrounding areas with circles drawn around certain sections. What those sections meant, Sirius was unsure. Maybe districts to recruit more followers? Next to it, a *Time* magazine cover had been pinned up with a picture of Marcel Celest. The tack had been placed right in his forehead. Someone scribbled "Enemy!" over his perfect blue suit. Sirius remembered when this article came out. At that time, she too believed Marcel Celest deserved the "Person of the Year". Perhaps...he still did. And next to that photo, someone pinned up her flyer. The flyer that started this all. She smiled. *We need to knock on Marcel Celest's door!* Now that she thought about it...that was a cheesy tagline.

On her bed, Sirius began to unpack. Her entire life had been consumed into one tied off Target bag. This wouldn't take long.

Behind her, the door unzipped. She had been promised privacy, so it came as a surprise.

It was Brent.

Sirius dropped her shampoo bottle. The liquid leaked onto the ground. It was the only shampoo that didn't fry her hair and became difficult to find during an apocalypse. But that didn't seem so important at the moment.

Brent stood at the doorway, his chest heaving up and down. He looked thin and tired. Circles below his eyes made them seem even more sad. That's what had attracted her so much the first time they met so many years ago. Those eyes. The same blue as the bottom of the ocean, and just as lonely.

He said nothing. She couldn't read his expression. Was it the same look of disgust as Pedro when he gazed upon her disfigured face?

She touched the ridges the glass had made in her cheek. "God, I must look awful. Um. I...like...wasn't ever expecting to see you again. I would've at least dolled myself up or something." Her giggle sounded so dumb. "Maybe if..."

There was nothing left to say, so the words just drifted into the air.

Brent had caught his breath. He rushed up to her. His lips locked onto hers. Sirius felt the warmth in her cheeks travel down to her heart. He held her close, the way a hysterical mother would hold a lost child. Never let them out of sight again. Finally releasing his lips, he took a break and stared into her eyes. If she had the ability to freeze time, she would do it here. A tear bobbled on the edge of his eyelid. "I'm so sorry I left you."

"Oh that. Yeah, it was fine."

A dimple appeared on the right side of his cheek. "Really? Because Royal just told me you called me a –"

Sirius leaned in and kissed him again before he could continue. After what felt like an eternity, she removed her lips from his. Eternity wasn't long enough. He brushed a little hair from her face. She wrapped her arms around his chest tighter. Then leaned her head on his shoulder. Brent rested his cheek on her hair. This was peace.

The world seemed to quiet for just them. She used her hand and touched the side of his face. "I want you," her voice whispered lower than expected. He kissed her again. Their breaths synced up. Becoming more and more rapid. She brought him back to where the mattress was. Picturing them falling seductively onto the bed didn't become a reality. They basically tripped and fell on top of each other. That didn't stop the moment. Brent kissed her neck on the right side, then the left side. He gasped for air in her ear. She loved that sound. It had been a while since she felt this turned on by someone so turned on. Brent held Sirius tighter by the waist. She moaned, but not with ecstasy.

"You alright?" He stopped, his eyebrows raised.

"God, sorry," she said straightening her back. "It's just this stupid back. It's been sore for weeks. Try going from a Tempur-Pedic mattress to Sanibel-tiled floor." She reached in and kissed Brent some more.

Brent's stomach grumbled. "Sorry. I haven't eaten in three days." He continued locking her lips.

"Ouch, ouch, ouch," Sirius said through tightened teeth. "I think I got some brown recluse spider bite on my leg." She moved around to be on top of Brent.

He sucked air in through his teeth. "Shit, I think it's got frost bite on my left big toe."

"Okay," Sirius said backing off, her hair discombobulated in her face. "I tell you what. Let's make a deal. We will save the love-making for when we're both in better shape. Deal?"

"Deal."

Sirius pulled her sleeve back up. Brent closed up his torn shirt. She didn't remember tearing it. Also didn't remember how much strength she had when in a lustful situation.

At the tent door, Brent reached to unzip it. Sirius reached around him and closed it. "Oh, who am I kidding? Let's do it!"

She hopped on Brent. They both giggled as they fell to the ground.

It felt like the first day of college all over again. Adam didn't know anybody. The only friend he had was locked away with a foxy girl and probably getting laid. And here he was, standing with his hands in his pockets, waiting for something exciting to happen. Crowds of people had walked by, gathering at the lake. Maybe something exciting might happen soon.

He strolled over to see a familiar van. Still covered in a light layer of soot over the words "Willie's Power Workshop". The tires didn't match, neither did the rims. It was supposed to be white but looked gray. Willie climbed out from underneath it carrying a wrench and hammer. He wiped grease on his trousers. "What's up, boss?"

Adam didn't have anything prepared to say, so he just mumbled, "What's up?" Somehow his voice cracked. It hadn't cracked since fifth grade.

After a steady nod, Willie said, "So." At least he found a word to say. "Any idea why people meeting up at the lake?"

"Swimming!" a little girl screamed as she ran by.

Willie snickered, "What? Mad crazy? That water's gotta be thirty degrees."

Adam nodded. But found himself curious too. He turned and strolled down the hill. The curiosity had spread because he saw Willie following. "You hear that? Swear that's a helicopter," he said peering up at the sky.

"Must be hearing things."

They made it to the edge of the lake where thousands had gathered. The expanse looked endless and quiet. It didn't stir. Adam found himself overwhelmed. It had been ages since he spent time near the waters. He remembered days he and Brent would fish on a lake and ponder their purpose with Servo Clementia. People called them terrorists, but on those days they felt like their decisions were to help people – not terrorize them.

Adam still questioned his purpose every night before drifting to sleep.

A long dock led out onto nearly the center of the lake. Lloyd stood alone, staring at nothing. Maybe he was sharing the same thoughts. What's right? What's wrong? What's...the purpose?

The crowd quieted as a wind picked up. Everyone's eyes focused on Lloyd. Willie shook and whispered, "Just gotta chill."

"Yeah, me too."

Adam's ears popped as the air pressure changed. He wiggled his right ear. Then his mouth dropped.

The clouds parted away almost instantly. They revealed a sky that had been hiding since nuclear weapons struck the United States months ago. The artist in Adam had to take a step back to emerge himself in this. He didn't know the color blue had so many shades. Reds mixed with oranges as the sun settled into the horizon. Adam's lip quivered. For the first time in ages, he felt alive. Like all this world around him didn't exist. It was just him...and the Light. He closed his eyes. It held him with the warmth of a mother's bosom. Then said it was worth living. That life only got better. The future may be dark clouds, but hope hid behind it.

He opened his eyes and a tear streamed down his cheek. It dried in the hot sun. As the ball of fire in the sky fell out of sight, Adam was reminded of that time his first foster parents abandoned him. Leaving him with the neighbors like some used furniture they no longer needed. The door closed slowly behind them the way the sun set.

Lloyd's outfit, a cloth djellaba, fluttered in the wind. He turned around. And though there were thousands standing around Adam, it seemed like he stared right at him. "You can change the future or....lead it."

His arms opened up and impurities from the lake floated up. Brown and green specks of dust were washed away by the wind, leaving behind only the purest form of water.

The People of Bliss stripped off their clothes and ran into the lake. Adam smiled at the naked bodies diving into the waters.

"There's no way I'm skinny dipping –"

Before he could continue, an unclad Willie ran past him with his arms in the air. Adam watched all the flabby parts of Willie jiggle as he ran. He swallowed back hard. Then said, "Okay, fuck it."

Adam tore off his clothes and dashed toward the lake. He leapt in the water. In there, everything was silent. He held his breath and let his body float for a moment, listening to the body of liquid wobble around.

He came up for air. Willie wasn't far, giving him a thumbs up. "Woo hoo!" he hollered and dove back in. Who knew how long it had been since they'd been this clean.

A few feet away, a familiar face giggled with some other girls. Royal. Adam swam up to her. She immediately covered her breasts. With a red cheek, Adam pretended to smell the air around her. "Is that pheromones I smell?"

She scoffed and gave him a quick slap to the face. Adam rubbed his cheek. "Ouch! Do you even know what pheromones are?"

"No, but it sounds gross," Royal said. "And you keep them eyes to yourself, you hear?"

"I will," Adam lied. Men had the ability to see all over the place while keeping their eyes straight. Royal obviously wasn't aware of this. She turned her face, doing a terrible job of hiding a smirk.

"Dude!" Willie called out to him. "I'm not crazy! It's helicopters!" He pointed up.

Sure enough, the balls of light in the sky revealed themselves to not be stars. Instead, they were searchlights. Adam could see a sense of worry cross Lloyd's face.

"Adam!" a voice called out to him from the shore. It was Nelson. "Adam! Come here! You too, Willie!"

He swam fast. Those looks of worry crossed more and more people.

Nelson threw a pair of jeans that landed on Adam's head. "Get dressed! I need you now!"

He felt humbled and concerned at the same time. The helicopter got louder. "What can I do for you, Mr. President?"

"Stop calling me that, damnit. I need both you guys to help. We're doing an evacuation."

Willie appeared behind him, "What you need?"

Nelson pointed, "That's your van, right?" He didn't wait for an answer. "Help me get Sirius out of here before the choppers land. The worse thing that this movement needs is their leader to be apprehended."

"You got it, boss." Willie ran off.

Nelson pointed at Adam, "I'm putting you in charge of getting Lloyd and Nina out of here."

"What's going on?"

"Adam, it's the Union."

The Union. The word made Adam's heart stop. He looked up. An emblem of a dolphin could be seen on the side of the circling helicopters. Dozens more people ran out of the water to cover up. Others tried to steady their tents from flying away. Anger started showing its ugliness as some of the followers began booing and tossing beer bottles at the choppers.

Running and squeezing his jeans on at the same time, Adam made it onto the dock where Lloyd and Nina were staring up at the sky.

Catching his breath, Adam managed to say, "Mr. President...I mean...Nelson...says...we need...evacuation...now..."

After clearing his throat, Lloyd muttered, "Good idea. Get Sirius far from here. She's the face of the rebellion and so far they don't know who she is. Let's keep it that way."

"But," Adam said, "he told me to get you guys out of here."

The couple didn't seem to listen. Nina whispered to Lloyd, "He's here. I can feel him. Can you?"

Lloyd nodded. "Yes, I can feel the darkness. Marcel Celest is here."

Adam didn't fully understand any of it, but knew his instructions. "We *have* to go now."

Nina said calmly, "We're not going anywhere."

Lloyd nodded and glanced ahead of him. "Stick around, Adam, if you *really* want to see what the Light can do."

CHAPTER THIRTY

Marcel felt a palpitation and coughed to clear his throat. It was warm here. Too warm. Sweat began to form on his upper lip. Lloyd and Nina were not far. He didn't know how he knew, but he knew. Their power clouded his mind like taking a sleeping pill but not falling asleep. Marcel definitely learned to focus in those situations.

The helicopter he was on began to land. It took longer than expected to find a clearance. No telling who could've gotten away at this point. It didn't matter. His true agenda was Lloyd and Nina. The Light had to be weakened. Or destroyed.

Him and Gerard stared out the window. Another larger helicopter flew in next to them. Below it, a highly armored SUV detached and clunked on the ground.

"Neat," Gerard mumbled into the headset.

Marcel smirked, "I've never known you to be a fan of technology. You still used flip phones, while everyone else switched over to smartphones."

"Yeah, and don't you dare let Vanderbilt know I called his vehicles 'neat'."

Same old Gerard. Always had to be jealous of someone's accomplishments. Even though he had done so much already. He joined the Union while Janice ran. As though Gerard sensed what was on Marcel's mind, he said, "Janice isn't here, right?"

"No. Her vehicle is still a ways."

Nothing more was said. They already hadn't spoken much about Janice's abandonment. Marcel preferred it that way. Staying focused on today's task was enough. Then he could refocus on bringing the Celest family into a safe environment...with him, of course.

The helicopter landed with a steady bump. In unison, they both removed their headsets and ran out of the chopper. Union Keepers led them to the SUV that had just been placed down. Inside, General Vanderbilt opened the door and let them both in. Shutting the door quickly, he began to speak. "We lost contact with our informant, but the last news was that all followers have been combined into this spot."

"Brilliant plan having them mesh together with the female's followers." Marcel could see Gerard cross his arms when he said *brilliant plan*. That's because it was Vanderbilt's plan.

The general nodded, "Lloyd and Nina aren't the true voice of this movement, but our mole swears by their abilities. I say we fire and take no chances."

"I already said that we aren't shooting them." Marcel saw Gerard uncross his arms and snicker. "What kind of authority figure would I be if I just said fire on anyone we don't agree with? That's not how we handle this."

His brother-in-law butted into the conversation. "Haven't you ever seen *Braveheart*, Vandy?"

Vanderbilt shook his head.

Gerard continued. Marcel smiled at the memory of watching the movie together. "It's just like when William Wallace went to face the king in the middle of the battlefield. It's tradition."

"The most effective strategy is to show those people out there that Lloyd and Nina aren't who they seem."

Vanderbilt squinted his eyes. "You mean provoke them? If they attack us, it'll make the movement fall apart."

Marcel grinned. "Exactly."

The general showed some concern, rubbing his head. "Sir, what if they hurt you?"

He hadn't meant to laugh, but he did. This cocky abrupt

cackle. Marcel didn't know what came over him. He cleared his throat. "They won't hurt *me*. I know what I'm doing."

The wind element whispered, *Don't make me have to choose a side.*

Someone started up the vehicle and followed the other fleet of SUVs. The three men wiggled in the back as they ran over every bump on the ground. Gerard broke the silence. "So, General, your mole still won't tell us the identity of the female in charge?"

"For whatever reason, the informant is being silent about that."

"Probably afraid what you'll do to her if we find her," Gerard said.

"Doesn't matter," Vanderbilt shrugged. "Knowing their leader means nothing. Killing their leader means everything."

Marcel objected again with a hand in the air. "I said we don't kill anyone today."

"But, Sir, this is a serious situation."

Gerard rolled his eyes. "Here we go again."

Vanderbilt continued, "We have to deal with this cult in every way possible."

"Cult?" Gerard asked almost at the same time Marcel questioned the word.

"Yes, David Koresh led a cult to their deaths in Waco, Texas. I was there. The Branch Davidians would've done anything to save their cause and their leader. This group is no different. So then what makes a movement turn into a cult?"

"I don't know," Gerard mumbled, "but when I need help falling asleep one night...feel free to tell me then."

Marcel turned to the window to smirk.

They were quickly approaching the compound. The vehicles stopped in a vast open field with no trees or grass lain. It must've been three hundred feet away from them. Sitting on top of a pile of rocks were Lloyd and Nina. Hundreds had gathered around them. His power of persuasion couldn't work on this many at once. Smart move on the part of Lloyd. No wonder the Light chose those two.

Marcel felt his slippery hands rub together. Sweat wouldn't stop pouring. He wiped his forehead. He held the door handle, but hesitated.

"You cried at the end of *Braveheart*," Gerard said. "Remember?"

"No, I didn't," Marcel said quickly.

"Yeah, you did."

"Okay," he admitted, "I may have cried a little."

Gerard snickered while Marcel smiled. "Why did you cry?"

He nodded, understanding where his brother-in-law was going with this. "Because Wallace screamed one single word..." Marcel closed his eyes and hollered out, "...freedom!"

Gerard laughed and patted Marcel on the back.

Once again, but much quieter, he said, "...freedom." Without another word from him or anyone else, Marcel opened the door and stepped out into the warm air.

Marcel's shoe hit a puddle of water. He heard the voice of the element scour, *Don't you dare hurt them.* Whether Lloyd and Nina fought back was their decision. And their fate.

He had never met these two before and yet had this sense of malice toward them. If they weren't three hundred feet apart, Marcel would consider spitting at their feet.

Dozens of his Union Keepers lined up beside him. It didn't sway that look on Lloyd's face. The Witnesses looked as irate as him. Lloyd hung his head low while Nina curled her lip. Marcel took this as an opportunity to make them look like the *bad* people. He searched the faces of the People of Bliss. "We are not here to hurt anyone. We are here to rescue you. Rescue you from what has happened for thousands of years. Oppression masked by a sense of freedom. All with a simple technique called brainwashing. Or in other words...religion."

Before nuclear weapons hit the United States, his father had started a movement of anti-religious rhetoric. Some of the followers raised eyebrows at the word *religion*. He may not have the ability to enter the minds of this many people, but he had the chance to talk sense to them.

"They are trying to confuse you. The Union is not. We can help you get homes, eat, be wealthy again. Don't you miss drinking clean water? Shopping at malls? Chatting on cellphones? Hot water?" Instead of nods, Marcel just received unknowing stares. He continued, "This is a new government. A government that wants to grant equality. That doesn't take years to enact laws. Or argue for decades over political nonsense while the lower class begs for money. We have a van here that can take you to a local shelter and feed you...dress you...make you feel human again."

The van with the Union logo pulled up. At this point, Marcel had imagined scores of people running toward it. He had even suggested more vans, just in case. But now, no one approached the vehicle. Not one. Were they afraid of Lloyd and Nina? That had to be the reason, Marcel convinced himself. The Light couldn't be this powerful in a world full of dark matter. "This is nothing more than a cult. A movement with no real intention but to weaken the government. Lloyd and Nina are lying to you. Eventually, you will all see this. And we will be waiting for your arrival."

"You've got some nerve!" Nina sat up quickly. Even Marcel felt himself take a rapid step back. Something about her aura just sent the hairs on his arm erect.

Lloyd's hand clenched while he said, "Religion has saved countless lives –"

"And killed even more!" Marcel interrupted, looking into their eyes for the first time. Their pupils were the opposites of his, soaking in the light everywhere. More than just these mere mortals had become involved here. He sensed both sides of this argument growing from within their souls.

Nina intruded, "My husband wasn't done talking!"

"But I'm done listening!" Marcel screamed.

The crowd went silent like the opening pitch of a baseball game.

You cannot defeat them, the water laughed.

"Wrong, I got the upper hand here," Marcel said aloud.

Gerard glanced back and forth. "You talking to me, Marcel?"

Without answering, Marcel said to the water element, "Because I have something they don't have. Technology."

Nanobots surged through his blood rapidly as his adrenaline kicked in. Time slowed. His muscles tightened. Darkness gathered from the clouds above. His pupils opened up to accept the power all around him. Thunder pounded so hard that the Union Keepers all stood back.

Gerard said, "Woah!"

Lloyd flung his thobe overcoat back as he took a step down from the rocks, "I suggest everyone stand back!"

A slim tornado formed immediately from the clouds and crashed into the ground. Lloyd controlled it with a wave of his right hand. It tore up ground and dirt as it headed straight for Marcel.

The Union Keepers ran behind vehicles, some tumbled over each other. Marcel held up his hand and the wind halted the tornado's path at them. The air element whimpered, *I'm sorry! They made me do it!*

The tornado spun between this tug-of-war between Lloyd and Marcel. Just as hope lied in the power of white matter, fear lied in the realm of dark matter. Fear would have to become Marcel's tool. He conjured up a hostility in him, with the thoughts of everyone who'd ever hurt his ambitions. Janice. Brent. Dad. Gabe.

With gritted teeth, Marcel pushed the tornado forward. It split into several pieces. The People of Bliss scattered like the ants that they were. Lloyd tried to control the uncontrollable spirals of air. One of them spun Nina in the air. She held her hands with pointed fingers, concentrating on calming the wind. Eventually it slowed and dropped her. She was talented with the elements, but clumsy as well. Marcel tossed a gust of wind at her. She flew into the air, possibly hundreds of feet. Nina bellowed backwards then smashed into the lake.

Lloyd, seeing his wife injured, grew even angrier. His eyes glowed white. Then a bolt of lightning crashed onto the ground before him. Another bolt zipped around Lloyd and flew toward Marcel.

Marcel ducked and raised his forearm. The now-loyal wind element created a solid barrier with the ground. The bolt bounced off the barrier.

Lloyd shot another bolt; it moved around toward the Union Keepers. Marcel raised another ground barrier, protecting his troops. The nerve of the Witnesses to attack his men put him at an even grander ire. The wind picked up, surging his wrath. The cult members had scattered everywhere, holding onto anything to keep them to the ground. Lloyd held to the rocks, barely able to stand. He created a barrier of light around him, slowing the wind just barely. The air element had chosen the winner of tug-of-war.

Marcel looked back and grasped at a tree in the distance. The tree lifted out of its root. It hovered in the air for only a moment before springing forward at Lloyd. The feeble man from the Light lifted his palm and the tree cut in half, from top to bottom. Nice trick, but Marcel had a better one. It was only a decoy. Another tree smashed Lloyd from the side. He flew backwards and landed on another set of rocks.

As the wind slowed down, Marcel thought he was done. But then he heard a familiar voice. The voice of the water element. *I told you to leave them alone!*

From the lake, Nina rose. Her lips curled and blood trickled down her nose. Two enormous streams of water rose toward the sky, like a water fountain. Marcel stepped back. There was only so much wind could do.

Master!

It was the fire element talking. But from where? Marcel searched around.

Master! I can help!

As Nina's hands rose, so did two water spouts from the lake behind her. The spouts flew into the sky like snakes, commanded by their charmer.

The first spout circled around; Marcel never took his eye off it.

Wind controlled the temperature, so he might stand a chance. As it got closer, it lunged for him. Grasping his hand at it, the temperature got cold immediately. The first spout's head turned to ice. The ice continued to its entire body, creating a magnificent frozen worm in the sky. The spout fell to the ground, smashing into ice cubes.

The second water spout backed off to create a greater distance, maybe planning for a running start at Marcel.

Master! Ignite me!

He looked around for any clue of where the fire element spoke from. The second spout sped toward him.

Master!

Marcel turned. The voice was coming from the utility belt of a Union Keeper. The grenade! He snatched it and pulled the pin. Like a pitcher at a baseball game, he threw it at the head of the spout. It blew up into a wall of fire. The Union Keepers ran for cover into the woods. In seconds, the second spout had disintegrated in the flames.

Fire slithered around Marcel, giving him warmth and protecting his well-being. Becoming his only friend in this entire planet. He grinned. It felt empowering. The elements finally in fear of him and obedient. Is that what peace will be like? When millions of people crowd around him to keep him warm?

Suddenly, the ground began to sink. Water rose from the bottom of the ground. It collected so quickly, Marcel had no time to react.

Master? What do I do?, the flame cried out.

The liquid extinguished the fire wall immediately. Assuming it was Nina controlling the water, Marcel shot out a burst of wind. The wind lifted the docked and it smacked on top of Nina.

But it wasn't her. Lloyd, struggling to sit up on his elbow, sneered. He waved his hand.

The water shot Marcel up into the air. Before he could scream and beg for help from the wind element, he fell hundreds of feet. The last sound Marcel heard was his bones crushing against a solid tree.

✧ ✧

One eye opened then closed. The other eye didn't respond.
Marcel just laid still. Not that he had a choice. His body was
numb. Just like before his coma, beaten to a pulp.

Voices spawned above him.

"Is he alive?"

"Hell if I know!"

"Did you see that shit? I mean, what the fuck!"

"I think I shit my pants."

"So what, he's like a wizard or some shit?"

"I think wizards use wands."

"How we gonna get out of here? The team abandoned us."

"There's a chopper."

"Yeah, up in the tree. What good is that? Did you see that shit?
I mean, really? Seriously, guys, tell me if I'm losing my fucking
mind? Did you see that shit? Did you?"

"Dude, I really shit my pants. I'm not kidding."

"We should move him."

"I ain't touching him."

"Me neither."

"He's some alien or some shit."

Finally a voice Marcel recognized. Gerard. He sounded spent,
like after running up a hill. "Jesus Christ! Is he still alive? Please
tell me he's alive!"

"We haven't checked."

"What if he zaps us with lightning or something if we touch
him?"

"What the hell is wrong with you guys?" Gerard knelt down
and listened for breathing, then checked for a pulse. "There's a
building nearby. Mountain Rescue Squad. There's probably
medical supplies there."

"We ain't got no chopper. It's in the damn tree."

"Then we walk. Help me pick him up."

Silence.

A minute passed.

More silence.

"This is Marcel. He's our friend, remember?" Gerard spat.

Even more silence.

After a loud grunt, Gerard lifted Marcel over his shoulder. "You guys are a bunch of assholes."

Then the silence turned to sleep.

Both eyes opened.

Warmth, such warmth that Marcel woke up covered in sweat. He opened his eyes. An inferno from a candle danced next to him, swaying to and fro in a hypnotic movement. The element celebrated when Marcel wasn't sure what to be celebrating. His chest was bandaged, head half covered in gauzes. Surely several bones were broken. Didn't seem like a time to be happy. Suddenly the flame disappeared. Like it had been scared away. Everything hurt when Marcel moved to look around. He was lying on a cot. The facility looked like he'd expect from a mountain rescue team. One corner had shelves of medical books, the other had medical supplies. Sitting on top of a surgical table was the reason for fire's hurried escape. Lucifer.

The boy demon just stared with wide eyes. It wasn't until this moment did Marcel realized the creature never blinked. Lucifer had that look his father used to give him, trying to find the words to express his disappointment.

"What?" Marcel said. The same thing he would tell Dad.

"Do you have any idea of the massive hysteria you've bestowed on humanity? *Magic* has been kept secret for centuries because of its ruination on the human psyche. Witch hunts, false gods, and the enumeration continues...all attributed to supernatural abilities. I told you three simple rules, do you not recall?"

Marcel sat up from his cot. His back cracked, but it created relief instead of pain. He sighed and huffed. "Yeah, I remember. Don't let anyone know about our deal, don't harm anyone, and don't show them my powers."

"*Our* powers, Marcel. This is a bond between us. I'm trusting you."

"And I know what I'm doing!" he spat out. The last thing he needed now was another disbeliever of his intentions.

The door swung open and Lucifer vanished. At the entrance, Gerard stood there dumbfounded. "You're awake. Great. How you feel?"

"Good," Marcel said, standing up. He saw a pack of cigarettes and a lighter on the table.

"One of the guys must've left that here," Gerard said.

His brother-in-law's tone seemed cautious. Marcel noticed his breathing had escalated. All this stress lately, he deserved to cheat on his quest to become smoke-free. He grabbed a cigarette and lit the end. The fire element gave a moan of ecstasy as he inhaled.

He lifted his shirt to see the gauze taped on with duct tape. "No doctor here, huh?"

"Nah, sorry. I had to do my best. You heal quickly though. Did you know that? I mean, from the time we put you on the chopper to the time we got here...stopped bleeding."

Marcel's healing had always been rapid, but not that rapid. It must have been the dark energy surrounding him. Healing him and protecting him. Otherwise, he should've been dead. He could've broken Lucifer's first rule and told Gerard the truth that a demonic treaty brought him closer to the darkest realm, but it didn't seem proper. "Just lucky, I guess."

Gerard said, "Let me wrap it up again, supposed to keep a fresh gauze on it every hour." He opened up a first aid kit while Marcel slowly peeled off the bandage. "I didn't even know you were awake yet. Thought I heard you talking to someone."

"Just a dream."

"Oh," Gerard said.

Marcel unpeeled the gauze to find the slightest hint of a cut. His healing had improved. The stitching was a mess though. From the first aid kit, he pulled out a pair of scissors to clean up the cross tie.

Gerard pulled out masking tape, "Sorry, out of duct tape." He grinned. It was good to see someone grin. "So, um, have you always been able to do that?"

"Stitch? No." The cigarette's ashes wiggled at the end when he spoke.

"No, Marcel. I meant...you know...*that*. The whole...magical stuff."

The way he said *that* made Marcel realize that perhaps Lucifer was right. It was said with a sense of fear. And Gerard had never been the type to be afraid. Marcel lowered his tone. "I'd never hurt you or our family; you know that right?"

His brother-in-law stared at him for a long time before answering, "Yeah...I mean. Yeah. I know. Just hard to wrap my head around."

"It happened after the coma. The...magical stuff." It wasn't the complete truth but at least some of it.

After a few minutes of rewrapping the cut on his chest, Gerard said, "Of course, people want answers. There's already a manhunt out for you."

"Manhunt?" That sounded similar to a witch hunt. Marcel swallowed.

"The thing is, it's all hearsay because there's no video or anything, but trust me...all the people that saw it are spreading the news like wildfire. Even all the way up to the Union members. President Wen just said on the radio that he's questioning the visual accounts from the Union Keepers about what happened. He's calling for your confinement."

"Confinement?" That sounded similar to a prison.

"You need something to calm people down. Make them sure, like you just made me, that they are safe around you."

Marcel finished the cigarette with one last inhale and slow exhale. It had already made it to the cigarette butt by the time he was done. He asked, "Any suggestions?"

"I don't know. Maybe like...a peace rally or something."

Marcel grinned. "That's an excellent idea. A rally."

CHAPTER THIRTY-ONE

Getting stuck in Washington DC traffic would make the average citizen pray for everyone to just leave town. But now that the city was empty, Declan felt even emptier inside. His days of grumbling in rush hour, an hour late to the Defense meeting, had been replaced with grumbling in a barren street. He trudged along, wheeling behind him a trash can usually picked up by the city garbage men. Sleeping in trash compactors and now hauling trash cans. The position of Secretary of Defense didn't seem so awful after all.

But inside the can wasn't waste. It was the solution to the problem called government. Guns. Lots of guns. The Forger had quite an arsenal. Uzis, hand cannons, pistols, semi-automatic, and even a Gatling. Storing all of the Forger's weapons had been unsuccessful at first. Declan originally used a dumpster to lug it all. Seemed okay for a while until the dumpster rolled down a hill and live ammunition tumbled like clothes in a dryer. He had no choice but to give up some of the weapons on the side of the road. No matter. For Declan's plan to work, he only needed enough to carry underneath clothing. But how it broke his heart to abandon the Gatling gun. That would've been fun.

He should've felt a sense of accomplishment making it this far. No one had mugged him for the weapons. Worse yet, no one had recognized him as the President's cabinet member. Judging by the vacancy of Washington, people lost hope in the nation's capital and paved way for the Union. Tumbleweeds slid across New York Avenue. There wasn't ever going to be a sense of accomplishment, not until the Union collapsed. Soon. Very soon.

The Safeway grocery store wasn't far. He removed his shirt. Looking down at his body used to be tough. It still was. Except instead of rolls of fat, there were lines of bones. He could even see his rib cage. Declan wiped sweat from his face and sat down in front of the Safeway.

"Don't bother." A childish voice. "It's ransacked too."

Some boy, no older than 10, sat near the wall and bounced a tennis ball against it.

"Not even any water left?"

"Nope," the kid laughed, "that was the first thing they looted."

From his backpack, the youngster pulled out a bottled water and tossed it to Declan. Declan caught it, opened it, guzzled it in less than thirty seconds. "Thanks," he forced himself to say. There was no denying children made him uncomfortable. Even when Royal was a baby, Declan never wanted to hold her. Kids just didn't like him. And vice versa. Like the way no one likes cockroaches; they aren't dangerous – it's just an instinct to be disgusted by them.

"What's in the trash can?" the boy said trying to balance the tennis ball on one finger.

"A solution to the Union problem."

"You too? Why is everyone whining about the Union? It won't be so bad. They got food supplies coming in a few days. And get this. No more cars. That's right; the radio said all cities will only do public transit. Which is cool because I already have a bus pass. But they said something about there'll be no more traffic jams and stuff. And free bikes for everyone. Which is cool too because my bike landed on top of the Lincoln Memorial somewhere. Why you think the Union is bad? Radio says it's cool."

He sounded like a young Adam, full of dumb questions and talking too much nonsense. Declan already felt a headache coming. "Because look around, stupid. Government caused all this shit. We need to get rid of it, not redefine it. *I* need to get rid of it. It's up to me now."

After a long silence, the boy said, "You said the S-word."

From his backpack, Declan pulled out a small bottle of whiskey. Even though it was plainly empty, he opened it and hung it up over his head. Hopefully one drop would hit his tongue. But nothing.

"Daddy said drinking is bad for you. It leads to divorce, hookers, and kidney stones."

"That's the least of my worries," Declan replied solemnly. "You think there's drinking in Heaven?"

The boy shrugged. "I guess so. Jesus drank. Didn't he?"

"I imagine there's a lot of partying there. Because the opposite would be really boring. It be like a bash with all your friends and everyone just trying to have a good time. Hopefully they've got a bottle of Macallan whiskey waiting for me."

Declan got up to go inside Safeway. The kid followed even though he wasn't invited. Just like Adam, Declan made an attempt at being a father figure. Father figures gave lessons about the things mothers were too timid to speak about. "You heard about this woman on the radio that started a boycott?"

"Yeah, why?" The kid seemed surprised Declan talked to him.

"Because she started something that I'm going to finish. A rebellion." Declan made his way through the shelves of the grocery store. The boy was being honest – the place had been emptied by looters. Even stealing all the mouthwashes. He would've loved to get this bitter and rotten taste from his mouth. One of his teeth had rotted and another bled from the gum every day.

"Rebellion? You mean like in *Star Wars*? Cool!"

Declan ignored him and looked around the store, trying to remember the layout. It had been years since he'd been here. "No, it's not cool, idiot. A lot of people are going to die."

"But, you don't mean...people around here? What about the Maitlans? Or the Smiths? Or that old creepy guy in the tent outside my house? He's got an awesome dog though. Are you saying they are going to die because they are rebels? Why?"

Declan didn't answer. Kids were naïve, thinking this world was like some sort of movie with a happy ending. There would be no happy ending. Not for the role of Charles Declan, anyway.

Without an answer, the child rambled on. "So Mr. Treble's class talked about the American Revolution and stuff. He said it's called a revolution only when it becomes a successful rebellion. I don't know, though. I like history class. It's better than geometry. Geometry sucks. Why do I need it? I don't plan on becoming a landscaper or something."

That had been the fifth time he'd said *why*. The rest of the boy's speech turned into a long drowned-out mumble as Declan concentrated on his surroundings. This was one of the times geometry became essential. He had to remember where he planted the bomb. The layout had changed. Declan found himself wandering while his tail continued babbling about video games or something.

Then he found it. The wall with a broken thermostat. It was his idea to use the thermostat. People never messed with them. Especially if it wasn't digital. Analog dials scared most nosy people away. He clicked it over the knob until it reached 54 degrees exactly. He turned around. "Hey, boy, count to eighteen."

"Why?"

Exactly something Adam would say. "Stop with the why questions. Just do as you're told. I'm about to tell you why you shouldn't trust the government."

That caught the boy's attention. "Okay." He closed his eyes and stood quietly for several seconds.

"Not in your head, stupid. Out loud."

"Oh! Ok. One one-thousand, two one-thousand..."

While he counted, Declan held down the thermostat knob. At number eighteen, he let go. Suddenly the entire box slid open like a safety deposit box. There was a key code on the side. 1776, the easiest code to remember. The year America built a government. Declan typed it in. The box popped open.

Inside was an aluminum cylinder about the same shape as a

corn on the cob.

"Oooh. What's that?"

Declan snorted. "With a flick of this tiny switch on the side, three liquids inside combine to create an atomic bomb."

The boy stepped back like the cylinder might bite him if provoked.

Declan continued. "Fifteen years ago when a nuclear weapon facility had been attacked by terrorists, our government secretly placed decoys in the facilities and the real weapons in the most unsuspecting places. Imagine every time you came grocery shopping here with your mommy and daddy, there was a bomb next to you powerful enough to level a city. That's your precious and safe government putting your best interests in mind."

He put it away safely in his pocket. The boy said nothing for a while then muttered, "Shit."

"You got people you care about around here? Get them out of here in the next 72 hours."

"Why?" That would be the seventh *why* from this kid. But Declan would be happy to answer this one.

"Because I'm going to put an end to Marcel Celest and his new government."

CHAPTER THIRTY-TWO

Finding a group of three thousand people seemed harder than Janice had expected. It was even harder to stop and ask directions when no one was around to answer them. She had enough gas to last a solid trip around Atlantic City. But eventually she had to find the People of Bliss. Maybe a rebellion wouldn't be in such plain sight. She had to admit that walking might be the best course of action.

Pulling alongside the road, she saw an endless array of dying trees in pain. Cracked and bent beyond their capabilities, if trees could talk they would beg for a bulldozer. Beyond that was a pathway. Perhaps the rebellion would hide amongst the area no Union police dared to go. It looked like something out of a horror movie. The branches of trees looked like claws reaching for her.

Bravery was something Brent taught her. He also taught her how to use a switchblade. Concealed, but ready for a quick yank if needed, the switchblade was secured in her back pocket. It only took about a hundred yards of walking before Janice realized something was stirring. Not out in the woods, but inside her. She grasped her belly like she'd been shot. Was that the baby? Did it just kick? Before she told herself it was just her imagination, it happened again.

Twenty minutes of walking seemed to be going nowhere. There was no wildlife so the forest seemed too quiet. Janice noticed something and paused for a second. "Can't be," she mumbled to herself.

Sure enough, growing out the side of a tree trunk, was a plant. Not just any plant. A very green plant. Alive and thriving. Janice knelt down and took a closer look. It was a Swedish Ivy. They usually grow in darkness, but it still made her feel hope again. Hope that life finds a way to thrive. She had a jar of cotton swabs in her backpack. She emptied them and scooped the plant into the jar.

How old was the child in her? Four months? Five months? Would it be too late for an abortion? Or could she really go through with raising a child in this world? But if the plant can survive, so could a child.

"Who are you?"

Janice spun around at the sound of the female voice; the switchblade nearly bent in her hand from the grasp. She stopped. It was just a teenage girl. Probably no older than 15. He wore a harness that put the children of *Lord of the Flies* to shame. Knives, grenades, bullets. Janice's switchblade seemed pointless. "I said, 'Who are you?'" This time with more sass and attitude.

Instead of learning how to drive and flirt with the neighborhood boys, this teenager looked like she wanted to learn how to cut and murder the neighborhood boys. This didn't seem right. Women had an understanding amongst each other. Doomsday may have melted away some of that understanding, but it was worth a shot. Janice put the switchblade away. "My name is Janice. I'm looking for the People of Bliss."

The girl snorted. "Your one of them Union people, aren't you?"

"No." It felt strange saying that since she'd spent weeks with Marcel at the center of the Union.

"Well, I'm not supposed to tell you that I know where they are."

The girl pierced her lips after saying that, realizing that she just revealed she knew the location. Janice remembered that awkward face since she'd made it several times herself. Especially the first day of her adoption with the Celests. Those crossed arms were supposed to say she's tough; the cocked eyebrow meant she's smart too.

Janice took one glance over the girl. There was more brown on those jeans than blue. Instead of make-up, dirt covered her face. Her shoes were different and so were her socks. This was no way for a teenage girl to be happy. Will this be how Janice would have to raise a child? To live in filth?

"Please help me," Janice asked, "I need to find them."

"Our leader is banning visitors. For now anyways. Witnesses got hurt. They are barely alive. It really sucks. Just...go somewhere else. Leave us alone."

Janice tried a different approach. Trust. "I know the leader."

"You do?"

"Yes. Her name is Sirius Dawson." In fact, Janice had always known since the first moment she heard the speech on the radio. But didn't feel right about telling Marcel, Gerard, or anyone about it. Every time Gerard would rack his brain trying to recognize the voice, Janice would say he's being silly. It was better to keep Sirius' identity a secret. Especially now.

The girl seemed shocked by this knowledge. "How did you...But no one...It's..."

"I just need to see my family. I tell you what. Go tell her that Janice Celest is here. I'll wait." She sat down and placed more dirt over the Swedish Ivy.

Uncrossing her arms, the teenager nodded. "Yeah, fine. That's what I was going to say. You stay here. Yeah. Okay. I'll be back."

✧ ✧

A lot could be done without a television and game system. Adam had finished three notebooks filled with drawings. After the first pencil withered away, he started using a black marker. Sitting up in a tree, the quietest place in the area, he finished the last drawing for tonight. It was Lloyd and Nina. It broke his heart to see them. So battered up mentally and physically. On cots next to each other, Adam captured them facing one another. It wasn't their bandages or scars that he wanted to draw, but their love. In their eyes there was something Adam had never seen. No ink or pencil could sketch it, but he tried anyway. There was no telling how long they would live. The doctor said they both were bleeding internally. That was never good.

Adam heard a noise. It had been so quiet a sneeze would've sounded like thunder. The noise seemed like talking. Then from one of the tents, Brent appeared dashing past Adam. Before he could ask what was the matter, the talking became louder. Brent was hugging someone. A very hard hug. Adam was about to jump down until he caught a glimpse of who it was. Janice. He climbed higher up the tree, not wanting to be seen. The embarrassment was turning his cheeks into plump tomatoes. Janice Celest. His professor. His idol. His infatuation. His affair. How was she here? What would he say to her? Which one would kill him faster when they found out he had sexual relations with her? Brent? Nelson? Gerard? All of the above?

They approached the encampment and Adam clung to the tree, bringing his head back like he had been launched in a shuttle. They didn't see him. They kept walking and chattering. Nelson appeared and embraced her tightly. And there it was again. Love. It thrived in peoples' eyes. The Celests truly were a family. Adam pondered what that must be like. None of his foster parents ever ran out to greet him. Declan only gave handshakes. What was it like to hug a father figure?

Nelson stayed behind as Brent led Janice through the area for possibly a tour. Adam peeked over one more time to see if that pleased look still lived in Nelson's eyes.

The tree branch snapped. Adam hit one branch then another then heard something snap, which he hoped wasn't his back. As soon as he hit the ground, he could only groan. "Owww," he moaned.

"Damnit you nearly gave me a heartattack!" Nelson said helping Adam off the ground. "You alright, son?"

Did he just call him son? "Yeah," Adam replied.

Nelson brushed off the leaves from Adam's back. "My

daughter is here."

"I noticed."

"Oh that's right, she was your professor. I forgot," Nelson said scratching his head. "Listen, Adam. I need a favor. An assignment. It's important."

An assignment from the President of the United States? Adam couldn't be more excited if he'd been given an iPad. Besides it gave him something to do. "Sure! Anything!"

Nelson looked down at Adam with a stern face. The kind he gave at his Inauguration. "I want you to make sure Janice doesn't see Lloyd and Nina."

That was an odd request. "Huh? Why? How?"

"I don't care how. Just make sure she doesn't step into their tent. Do you understand?"

Whatever Nelson was thinking came off as desperate, anxious, and blunt.

"Yes, Mr. President," Adam said proudly. Though he didn't have a clue how he'd do it. Not without confronting her. He gave a long sigh. Why did he want her to stay hidden?

"Oh, that be so lovely," the weird old botanist said. "May I?"

Janice had simply just showed the ivy plant she found, but the woman acted like it was a newborn. Her tent had all types of plants that grew some tasty vegetables and fruits. The taste of cherry tomato still clung to Janice's tongue and it was impressive.

Her name was Matley. Raised in New Orleans, the botanist's thick creole accent became a little difficult to understand at times. Matley inspected the plant for what seemed to be too long. Her eyes looked magnified behind coke-bottle glasses. "This be a miracle plant. Made by the fingertips of Mother Earth to show us the hope." She searched through a box under the crates of carrots. "I've got just the food this little guy be needing. It be incredible he survived." Matley sprinkled coffee grinds on it then glanced up at Janice. "I know you. You're Janice Celest, right? The President's adopted girl?"

Janice would've preferred just being called *the President's girl*. People always added that unnecessary adjective. "Yes, that's me."

After tying her long strains of gray hair into a ponytail, the botanist said, "I didn't hear you was pregnant, child."

It was the first time Janice noticed how big her stomach had gotten. Seemed to have happened overnight. Time slips by so rapidly. She rubbed it for a second. Would it be too late to abort it? "Yeah."

"Two miracles in my tent today. This be the greatest day in months."

The baby conversation made her feel awkward. She searched around for something to change the subject. The tent was riddled with hanging veins and shelves of various plants. Janice saw an abundance of aloe vera growing. "That many people get hurt around here?"

"Oh! The aloe? I be using it for the Witnesses. They be banged up pretty bad. Not sure if they are going to make it."

"The...who?"

"Witnesses. Don't tell me you haven't heard about them."

Janice hadn't. They sounded like a rock band. She shrugged. "No."

"They perform the magic. They be representing the Light."

One glance around at the borderline voodoo witch's collection answered Janice's question. There was an array of mushrooms. Perhaps Matley had been eating too many of them and hallucinating. "Um. Okay."

Matley brushed her dreadlocks aside and looked out the mesh window. "There be that pacing boy. What's his name again?"

Janice blushed. "Adam. He thinks I don't know he's been following me." Memories flooded her mind. Standing at the college podium while her top student smiled and stared. None of her students had struck her the way Adam did. Twelve years younger than her, but they felt the same age.

The botanist handed the plant back delicately. It wobbled slightly in its glass jar. Janice nodded, "Thanks. I'll take good care of it."

"Now, go take care of that boy. He's just as helpless as that ivy."

She was right. Janice sighed and walked out. Adam dove behind a bush. "It's been an hour. You're not going to talk to me?"

Adam poked his head out. "Oh my God. Miss Celest? Is that you?" He deserved a Razzie award for Worst Acting Performance.

"Please don't call me that. Janice. Call me Janice."

Standing up, he wiped off the twigs. "Sure, yeah. No problem. So. Um. I'm thrilled...I mean... happy...yeah...to see you. Sure, yep. Happy. No, I mean like...it's good to see you alive."

Janice nodded. "Ditto."

He peered down at her stomach. "I thought you didn't qualify for pregnancy?"

"I didn't."

"So...then...um...how are you...you know...I mean, you are pregnant, right? Unless you're getting fat. Which, I mean, isn't a bad thing...I'm just..."

"I'm pregnant," Janice interrupted Adam's tumble down the stairs of words. "I didn't qualify. It just...happened."

He blinked several times like he was giving Morse code. "Um...how?"

"It...I'm...just it was...I don't..." Now Janice couldn't complete sentences. She took a deep breath. "It might be yours."

Adam took a step back, like she was a grenade. He stared for what felt like several minutes. Then he took a step forward. "Wow."

"I should have it aborted, huh?"

"That's your decision," Adam said with a straight, unemotional face. The same damn answer she always got when asking that question.

Frustrated and feeling unsure of herself, Janice walked away. "I gotta go find Dad."

"Wait!" Adam chased after her. "Don't go in the orange tent. That's where he is."

"Huh?"

"I mean...that's *not* where he is. In fact...um...no one is there...yeah, it's empty."

In the distance, Janice could see the large orange tent. Several people hung around it. They looked sad, worried, and in prayer. "Who's in the orange tent?"

"Um...well...I can't tell you."

That made Janice even more curious. She turned and walked toward the tent.

"No, wait. You can't go in there!" Adam said.

"Why?" she asked, her former student and lover scurrying behind her.

"I don't know. But your dad said you can't."

"Oh, he did?" That made her walk even faster.

She flipped open the door to the tent. A few people hung around something, lined up in a circle. Nelson was there and his eyes widened. "Goddamnit, Adam. I told you not to let her see this!"

The circle parted to reveal a man and woman, badly injured and lying on cots. She recognized them. Janice dropped the glass jar of her ivy plant. It shattered into hundreds of pieces. Her hands cupped her face. Tears came to her eyes.

Holding her breath for perhaps too long, Janice finally opened her mouth to say something. But words couldn't escape. She stared at the two familiar faces. Lloyd and Nina. Their eyes met and they were just as shocked as Janice. After a short breath, Janice asked, "Mom? Dad?"

CHAPTER THIRTY-THREE

Adam spent the next day contemplating the issues lying before him. Since discovering Lloyd and Nina, Janice refused to speak to him, Nelson, or anyone actually. It was expected. It was also a welcome distraction. Adam needed this time to figure out his future.

As a child, he understood his future. He wanted to build trains. Unfortunately that had never happened or will. So the future could change. But could his precognitions change? If so, then his battle on the bridge to the forces of the Union would somehow include a baby. Adam had a difficult time imagining carrying a bat in one hand and an infant in the other. If not, then that meant that Janice would make the decision to not have the child. That made him squirm a little.

Not that Adam was ready to be a father. In fact, he still had some growing up to do before he could take on such a task. But the idea of a kid with Janice made him feel like a family was possible. And that kind of future seemed pretty cool.

"You going to pass it?" someone asked.

Adam had been holding a hookah pipe in his hand for perhaps too long. The six other people, surrounding the hookah, waiting patiently for their turn to inhale the...whatever blend the botanist Matley concocted. "Oh," he said. "Sorry."

After a long inhale, Adam held it in his lungs then tasted it. It might've been marijuana. Might've been mushrooms. Whatever it was, the group promised him it would relax him. So far, it worked. Maybe too well. He exhaled a long stream of smoke, and then handed the pipe to Willie.

Willie took a long hacking cough before grabbing the pipe. This had been the sixth person today with that awful cough. His nose was red and eyes bulged. Ever since Lloyd and Nina had been incapacitated, Adam noticed an increase in illness around the camp. It also had been colder. He could see Willie struggling to breathe in short breaths before taking a steady inhale of the pipe. Whatever was in that smoke calmed his hacking and his satisfied shoulders fell down.

The future. Would it be with Janice? A baby? Or maybe with Royal? Royal did seem to be wearing more perfume than usual around him. But she was going to die. When? He couldn't remember that dream. That fury of magical powers unleashed by Marcel Celest on an innocent crowd of people would happen soon. And Royal would be impaled by flying debris. Would telling her the future change it? Could it all be changed? His precognitions?

"Dude, pass it along." Another voice.

Somehow the pipe had ended up in his hands again. It made it full circle without any recollection. Adam smiled. Whatever it was in the center of that hookah giving them smoke fumes...was working. He took another puff. It tasted like cranberries. Or strawberries. Or raspberries. He already forgot what had been on his mind. "Where's Royal?" he said aloud, meaning only to say it in his head.

"The rally," Willie answered.

After a long pause, Adam repeated the word. "Rally?"

"Yeah," Willie said between coughs. "Marcel Celest...is doing...a rally in...the square."

A picture began to form in Adam's head. The precognition. Marcel Celest standing on a platform with a bolt of lightning swirling in his hand. "Rally?" Adam whispered.

"Um, yeah, bro," Willie said, squinting his eyes at him.

The picture in his head began to move. Marcel Celest

controlling the weather. Making a whirlwind of anger. Tossing debris. Royal screaming. Adam hanging on.

He grasped the sides of his head. "Rally?" Adam screamed a little louder.

"Uh. You alright, boss?"

Adam stood up. The moving picture in his head showed a pipe landing through Royal's gut. Behind her, dozens of people crying out. A stage. Some type of stage.

"Rally!" Adam yelled louder.

"Dude, chill."

The moving picture cleared up. Adam's pulse sped up. In his mind, Marcel Celest's eyes bared down at him. The sign behind him said the word: Union Rally.

"Rally!!" Adam screamed.

He stumbled and ran off. It was all clear now. Royal was about to die. He tripped over someone's tent and dashed toward the hill.

Someone behind him said, "That kid's even weirder when he's high."

It was getting hard to breathe as Adam ran through the hills. Maybe it was lack of food, the clogged air, that weird flu virus, or the desperation of the situation.

The memory of his vision was still cloudy. Besides that Royal was about to die, the rest seemed convoluted. Something triggered Marcel Celest to attack this group of people. But Adam had no clue what it was.

He tripped and tumbled down the hill, landing on what smelled like dog feces. Without hesitating, he got up and dashed toward the city square. Lights could already be seen from the stage. Marcel Celest's voice sounded professional, kind, and apologetic. Just like in the precognition several months ago.

Now Adam slowed his pace from either fear of the politician or the realization he had no plan of saving Royal. Or both. He squeezed through the crowd, looking for that familiar baseball cap and blonde ponytail.

People began to give some strong audible rejections to Marcel.

"He's evil! Don't trust him!"

"He's the devil!"

"You killed our people!"

"If you are that powerful, than why didn't you stop this from happening to us?"

"Coward! You could have saved all of us from the nukes!"

Thunder echoed. The wind picked up, sharply. Marcel's perfectly parted hair began to whip with each gust. He calmly spoke into the microphone, not looking at the crowd. "I've tried and tried with you people. You won't listen. I'm not evil. I'm not a murderer. Things got out of hand. We can help Lloyd and Nina. Bring them to us –"

Louder boos.

"No fucking way!" a masculine female voice hollered.

Royal! Adam searched around for only a moment before he saw her. As he pushed through the crowd, he realized that most of these people were about to die. Faces peered at Marcel with such disdain; Adam noticed the People of Bliss were no more. Lloyd and Nina had been injured beyond repair. And those faces wanted to make sure the mystical politician paid for it. They all screamed objections at the same time, to the point it made no sense what was being said.

The politician's prepared speech began to sound jumbled. "I didn't mean...I don't want them...it was an overwhelming moment. I'm not a killer. I can bring peace without blood on my hands. We want to help them."

"Liar!"

He grabbed Royal by the arm, tighter than he intended, and whispered, "We have to go. Now."

"What?" She tried to speak louder over the crowd, but it was useless.

"Demon!" an outburst came.

"He's an alien!"

Adam remembered that word. *Alien*. It wasn't what would

trigger the politician's fury. But it was another word. What was it? Adam didn't have time to think about it. He kept yanking on Royal, but she just pulled back with this look of how-dare-you on her face.

Marcel Celest's patience was running thin. "People, calm down! I'm trying to explain –"

Adam pulled on Royal's arm, but she wasn't moving. "Let go of my arm!"

"He's going to attack us, Royal. Let's get out of here."

"What?"

"I said, 'He's going to attack us.' Goddamnit, Royal. Stop pulling away from me. Let's go!"

"We aren't afraid of him!"

"You need to be," Adam whispered.

"What?" Royal couldn't hear Adam over the uprising.

"You need to be!" Adam screamed in frustration.

"What?" Royal yelled with her hand cupped over her ear.

The crowd was so loud, Adam couldn't hear himself think. He finally blurted out, nearly echoing. "Royal, listen to me! He's the Antichrist!"

As if someone muted the volume on a television, it suddenly became pitch quiet. Adam closed his eyes, realizing his costly mistake. *Antichrist.* That was the word that would begin Marcel Celest's attack. He turned slowly towards the stage. The politician eyed him with widened pupils and gritted teeth.

"I am not the Antichrist!" Marcel shouted.

Marcel flung his hand out and the mass of people flew into the sky. Adam slammed into the windshield of a car. Another car flew in the air toward him. He leapt off and the car smashed down, only inches from his head.

People began to cry out in fear and scatter like ants seeing a foot about to stomp on them. If the witnesses couldn't defeat Marcel, this crowd of degenerates was certainly below par. Lightning strikes came down, aiming for them. Some got hit. Others escaped into the woods.

Royal crashed into a set of bushes, struggling to get up from the impact. He'd never seen her panicked.

Marcel Celest controlled the wind to float him off the ground. The stage began to break apart. Not until now did Adam realize who was on that stage behind Marcel. Janice's husband. Gerard was shielding his eyes from the wind and pleading with Marcel. "Marcel, stop! Control it! Don't hurt these people!"

There was no talking sense into this magical being. Adam saw the movie *Carrie*. That much power clouded a sense of judgment. There was no stopping Marcel Celest. Gerard flew back by the wind.

The stage's scaffolding broke apart. Scaffolding! A pipe! Royal was about to get hit with a pipe! Adam dashed toward her and then grabbed her leg. He yanked her backwards and her head thumped a tree. "Ow, you idiot!" she screamed. The pipe that would've ended her life embedded into the ground like an arrow hitting its target. Royal paused for a moment. She stared at the pipe with widened eyes. "How did you know..."

"Let's go!" Adam yanked her arm.

They tried to run but tumbled on each other in the wind. He got up to see a dead body on the ground. Then another. And another. Adam had to do something. Something to stop Marcel Celest, for good. Before more people died. If Royal's life had been saved, then the future could be changed. That also meant Adam couldn't die. Or how else would the future become true?

He turned toward the politician. "Marcel Celest!"

"What are you doing?" Royal said, this time yanking on Adam's arm.

"Go," Adam instructed her. He turned and stormed toward the leader of the Union. The eventual leader of the world. The demon in sheep's clothing. "Marcel Celest!"

Marcel turned. A bolt of lightning landed in his hand and swirled into the shape of a ball. Adam's feet stopped. Suddenly all the courage he had a moment ago disappeared. Thunder loudened. Wind popped his ear drums. Even though he shouldn't hear him, Adam heard Marcel speak softly. "I wish it was that easy to stop me. I really, really do."

Adam thought of running. But how would someone outrun lightning? He felt a stream of urine flow down his pants. Maybe he could be killed.

Then Marcel flew backwards. An unseen force flung him like a rock in a slingshot. The politician disappeared into the distance of the city until he was only just a sparkle.

It was instantly solemn. The wind died down and the lightning storm dispersed. As much as Adam wished he'd done that, he had to admit telekinesis wasn't on his palette of talents. Something pulled Marcel away. But what?

CHAPTER THIRTY-FOUR

On the list of Marcel's possible abilities, flying hadn't come to mind. Yet here he was. Flying at a rapid pace. Unfortunately not under his control. Something had pushed him. No, not pushed...shoved him. Marcel flew backwards for maybe a quarter of a mile before smashing through something. A window. Glass penetrated his skin and he tumbled several times on a concrete floor. When his body stopped spinning, his head continued to spin for almost a minute.

Lucifer's voice broke as he screamed in that childish voice. "Have you lost your mind, imbecile?"

Even though his hand had been covered in shards, he placed it down to lift himself off the ground. The adrenaline in him surged so fast. Anger boiled inside like lava escaping a mountain. "How dare you? You little fucking twerp! Our agreement was you had no control over me. Who the hell do you think you are? I know what I'm doing! Why doesn't anyone ever believe in me? Why!"

Through tightened teeth, Lucifer said, "Who am I?" He strolled toward Marcel. "I am the one who has bonded with the blackened matter throughout this universe!" His steps grew louder. The floor vibrated. Marcel stepped backward. "I am the one it has bowed to. It too thought an agreement had been made. No agreement had been made! I've encountered thousands of beings that thought they could control me! And all have failed!" Lucifer's skin tore, his clothes expanded. The true monster in him arose. Wings crackled and released themselves. "You think you are the one to defy me? I am the god, not you!"

Marcel panicked and fell onto the floor. He lifted his hands to thrust wind. But the wind element didn't answer.

You're on your own with this foe.

The monster grew so big, Marcel had to look up to meet with Lucifer's eyes. "Please! I'm sorry! I didn't mean it!" His voice sounded pathetic and desperate. It wasn't enough. Lucifer's horns morphed his face into the true Devil. What looked like lava flowed where his veins should be along his skin; when he screamed, instead of saliva...lava spat out in droplets. Marcel tried to run, but he was grabbed by the foot. Lucifer threw him through the plywood wall of a building and back onto the street. He slammed into a statue in the middle of a city park. The bones cracking were the least of Marcel's problems. He dashed but tripped again. "Lucifer, please! I wasn't thinking!" he begged.

Before he could escape, the creature punched him in the back. It felt like a crate of barbells had fell on his spine. Just when Marcel was going to begin to cry, he was flung like a Frisbee. His face fell flat into a lawn. The grass tasted horrid mixed with a mouthful of blood. He couldn't hear any of the elements around him. Water retreated, Fire hid, and Wind stood still to watch Marcel's inevitable demise. He didn't even bother to get up as he heard the footsteps sound like thunder behind him. The world's savior, Marcel Celest, was at the mercy of an invisible being.

Then the footsteps stopped. He expected a slam of some kind, maybe Lucifer's final smash of frustration. But nothing happened. Marcel lifted his head.

Someone stood above him. A homeless man that had kept Marcel company through his darkest days and brightest moments. Gabe.

The archangel's eyes remained locked on Lucifer, not even a moment to glance at Marcel. He'd never seen Gabe this irate. In fact, he'd never seen him irate at all. Gabe took a few steps toward the Devil. Lucifer took one step back.

Gabe spoke with the authority of a king to his minion. "Don't you dare...lay another finger...on him!" His shout shook the air. Gabe threw his arms out and his light shot out like a cape in every which direction. Lucifer covered his eyes and stepped further back. The cape of light swallowed back into Gabe, leaving him glowing and only slightly easier to see now than a second ago.

Lucifer's skin looked burned. Singed down to the black fluid in his body. Gabe's light had done it. It seemed even the supernatural had weaknesses. Lucifer could be harmed. But as quickly as the scar came, it began to heal. Molecules of dark matter in the air healed the skin, making it new. Lucifer grinned. "Gabriel? I should've known you would interfere with my prodigy. Do you sincerely wish to challenge me in a world of darkness, Archangel?"

Gabe turned around slowly and faced Marcel. "Gabe. No. Please don't. Please. I need you."

Inevitability had a strange face. It became even noticeable on Gabe's face. A slow smile. A slow nod. "You were wrong earlier, my dear boy. Not everyone doubts you. In fact...I believe in you."

Through watery eyes, Marcel took a final look at his only friend. Gabe turned and charged toward Lucifer.

So many millennia had passed that the angel Gabriel retained little memory of when he first laid eyes on pure evil. Evil that hid under the guise of innocence. Lucifer had been such a unique creation from the light matter in the universe because he seemed to expel something the other beings of light hadn't seen. He expelled emotions, thoughts, and eventually skepticism. Gabriel could feel nothing but joy during those times. Now they felt something that could only be described as...fear. Fear that this being would execute all the light in the universe. Only until the Light created this creature did he and the others feel compelled to destroy it. It was that moment, when the angels beat Lucifer, did the universe change. Once nothing but endless white colors –

the universe began to turn to gray. Black bubbles of dark matter exploded out of Lucifer instead of blood. Then an explosion. An explosion so loud, the energy mutilated their energies. Gabriel watched in horror as his body burst into flurries of light. He smiled because death was euphoric like that moment before falling into a deep slumber. More millennia had passed or perhaps very little — Gabriel never took the time to remember these moments — then he somehow formed back together. His atoms of light fused together and allowed him to learn the ability to control his form. The first moment he eyed the new universe was something he did remember perfectly. Because even though it had mostly been taken over by dark matter, it was still quite beautiful. He floated cosmos after cosmos, in search of his fellow beings of light. It took millions of years for them to finally combine. They all agreed this new universe was disorderly, ungovernable, and wild. The previous universe had been quaint, controllable, and rich. Their hunt for Lucifer took them to the farthest of galaxies. Darkness had to be destroyed for Light to thrive. Lucifer had been so strong when they found him in the depths of what would eventually be known as the Milky Way. Their battle lasted thousands of years, both sides growing weak at some moments and brute at others. Gabriel had watched many of his companions beheaded in those days. Lucifer enjoyed it. Actually enjoyed ending the existence of Light. Gabriel and the last of his fellow angels cast Lucifer into a planet newly forming in the galaxy...Earth. The opposer hadn't been heard from for millions of years.

Not until he began to meddle with humanity.

Gabriel found humans as intriguing as the demon had. Humans had the ability to actually create darkness and light matter. No other concoction of molecules in the universe had such an incredible power. While Lucifer tried to manipulate them, Gabriel took the opposite approach. He wanted to befriend them.

Just the way he befriended Marcel Celest.

In his first years, Gabriel watched him from a distance. Taking forms that Marcel Celest would only see. The imaginary friend that his father would laugh about. The coach that taught him how to toss a ball. The arms that he'd cry in when his brother bullied him. Gabriel enjoyed every moment. That feeling reminded him of the universe when it was constructed of just light.

Now, Lucifer had the nerve to attack Marcel Celest.

Frustration, something the angel had never felt, exploded in Gabriel. He dashed at Lucifer, the master of lies. All he could think of was to see the demon's end. Doubt became reality almost immediately. Gabriel could not win this fight. But sometimes it wasn't about winning.

Gabriel's cloak blew out and wrapped itself around Lucifer's neck. He flew up, dragging the dark leader with him. They launched into the sky. Gabriel needed more light, just past the clouds. Lucifer screamed in pain then clawed at the angel as he struggled to get out of the choke. Gabriel's cloak grew as the sunlight approached. His cloak released Lucifer's neck and formed into a large blade. It embedded into the demon's shoulder. Lucifer's cry echoed throughout the universe. Gabriel punched, hitting wherever he could. Their ascent grew faster. Through the stratosphere then into the mesosphere. Gabriel felt stronger. This had been the closest he'd been to the sun in hundreds of years. Lucifer must've known the angel's plan because the claws began to sharpen as they scraped away at him. Then, just within the sun's reach, Lucifer grasped Gabriel by the neck. They descended so rapidly that the angel couldn't muster enough light to bring them back up. Lucifer's fists smashed into Gabriel's face repeatedly and broke his concentration. His light decreased while the darkness increased. The universe began to turn black around him. Demise, as an angel would see it, was coming. All he could do was make sure Marcel saw. Make sure Marcel understood.

Gabriel steered their descent while Lucifer continued punching him and cackling loudly. They fell toward the ground. Back to where they started this fight. Gabriel could see Marcel.

The angel closed his eyes, feeling that familiar euphoria. It was time to slumber.

Maybe it was the nanobots in his blood, or the shock, but Marcel watched in slow motion as Gabe and Lucifer fell to the ground. The devious creature smashed the angelic mentor into solid earth. Like he'd fell into a field of feathers, Gabe's body burst. Twinkles of light hit Marcel's face.

He immediately thought of the first moment he met Gabe, a homeless man outside of the United Nations. Mom had died, Dad didn't return phone calls, Brent rolled his eyes anytime he saw him, and Janice locked herself in the basement. Marcel had no one. Anytime he'd speak of his sorrow, people would respond with the typical rehearsed lines given to any sufferer. *Oh, I'm sorry for your loss. I have the number for a therapist.* Gabe didn't have a number, only advice. And it hadn't come to fruition until now. That day, Marcel sat outside of the United Nations building and fed the pigeons – a good thirty minutes late to his meeting. Gabe appeared, seemingly from nowhere, to simply say hello. "I don't have any cash on me, sorry," Marcel had said. Gabe replied, "I don't need money. I need someone to talk to, mate. Gets lonely around here, am I right? Why are you out here instead of in there?" Marcel answered, "Because I don't see the use in going into this meeting. They aren't going to listen. I won't get what I want." Gabe laughed, "Don't be silly, dear boy. Do you think everyone who runs a race is there to win? It isn't about winning. It's about learning to endure."

Learning to endure.

Lucifer formed back into the small, familiar child. Marcel just stared, with no emotion to show. But as he hid his emotion, the demon hadn't. Lucifer turned from eventful, to regretful, to sorrowful. His eyes widened. "I...sometimes..." The creature stumbled over his words. "There's an interminable history between the archangel and myself. Vexation is my weakness. I've lost supremacy and deserve punishment. I shall give you the option, Marcel. Say the words and banish me from this world. Undo our agreement. Undo your powers. Undo this future. Say it, and I shall obey."

Could Marcel go through with such a thing? On one hand, the planet would be left without a powerful entity to lead it and Marcel would become nothing but another politician with just his mouth to change issues. On the other hand, the power Lucifer had was essential. How else would the Union survive without the ability of persuasion?

Learning to endure.

Lucifer's chest heaved up and down, his tantrum subsiding. His eyes began to water and a tear of lava sputtered down his cheek. Marcel was silent, still in disbelief at the death of his friend. Several thoughts ran through his head, but he couldn't make sense of any of his feelings. Could Lucifer be trusted? Something strange had happened beforehand; Lucifer controlled Marcel's body and powers. He attacked Marcel, like he was suddenly part of this world. But it was impossible. How could Lucifer do this?

"I can comprehend your skepticism," Lucifer mumbled. "You want the covenant broken. I shouldn't have intervened as I did. I should have trusted your actions."

Marcel could sense the sincerity in Lucifer's tone. He watched as the Devil began to fade. The bond between them began to break.

Learning to endure.

Then Marcel felt panicked. His dream of the Union would fail if he didn't endure this. "Wait!" Marcel pled. "Don't leave!"

Lucifer's fading stopped. He began to immerse himself back into Marcel's mind, re-entering the world in full color.

With some effort, Marcel was able to stand up now. He groaned from the pain in his ribs. Before, the dark matter used to take days to fix him. Now, the matter began healing him instantly. It meant Marcel had become closer to that dimension than ever before. Then he took a deep breath of air, no longer feeling the pain of broken ribs.

He crept toward Lucifer and fell to his knees. His eyes were at the same level. "World peace. It's almost there. Right?" Marcel's voice quivered.

"Yes," Lucifer said sounding the most authentic since their first encounter.

"Then don't leave me."

CHAPTER THIRTY-FIVE

Awakening from a nightmare was always the same. A sticky sweat soaking the pillow. A rapid sequence of quick eye movements to make sure the nightmare had ended. Then the sad realization that the world around him hadn't changed. That it was still on the brink of destruction under the dictatorship of his brother. Brent almost wished he could fall back asleep into his nightmare.

Lying next to him in an even bigger puddle of sweat was Sirius. "Dreaming about Neptune's moon again?" she said through a hoarse voice.

"Jupiter's moon," Brent corrected her. "And no. It was somewhere else. Somewhere...weird...I don't know. Not like that digital prison."

After a long series of coughs, Sirius mumbled, "Why did you leave that digital prison? Much better than this flu-infested place."

"Because it wasn't a utopia without you in it."

For the first time in a while, he saw Sirius' smile so wide that her dimples poked in. "Aw, so cheesy."

After a brief smile, Brent tried to remember his dream. "I was here. In the forest. Right between Lloyd and Marcel. They were about to fight again. I felt...I dunno..."

"Scared?"

He could never admit such a thing. Servo Clementia taught

him being afraid wasn't an option. Brent just said, "Seems like both sides have their tempers, huh?"

"Yeah. It wasn't the magic that freaked me out as much. It was, like...you know, Nina's eyes."

Seeing anger like that made Brent realize his tantrums were minuscule. "I don't think they had control of themselves." He said it confidently, speaking from experience.

After brushing the wet hair from her forehead, Sirius said, "Did you know they were Janice's parents?"

"Not a clue. Dad's been acting weird about it. Not used to seeing him so high-strung."

Sirius nodded. "God, this headache," she rubbed her temples. "That purple mix from the botanist didn't do anything. How are you not feeling sick?"

"Because I got the cure of love sleeping next to me."

"Aw, more cheesy stuff. Keep it coming. I miss watching my soap operas." Sirius sat up to drink from a jug of water. It was half full. Brent had filled it before they fell asleep. He noticed the scars along her back. Glass had shredded more than just her face on Doomsday. He ran his fingers down her naked back. "I wish I could've protected you that day," he whispered more to himself than her.

"You can't be everywhere, silly. I can take care of myself. Look at these puppies." Sirius flexed her frail right arm, "That's called 'Zumba'. You're free to touch it."

Playfully placing his hand over a fake racing heart, Brent gasped, "May I?" He squeezed the arm in several places like he was checking the ripeness of a cantaloupe. Then ran his hand under her arm to tickle her. Sirius burst into laughter.

Suddenly the tent flap swung open. Sirius immediately covered her naked body with the rest of the blanket, leaving Brent exposed. It was Adam at the entrance.

"Adam," she scowled, "can't you knock!"

His best friend ripped off his scarf, sweating more than an Olympic marathon runner. "You guys won't believe...knock where? There's no door...you won't believe what...it just

happened...Jesus Christ, Brent, put some pants on...I changed
the future...Like Marty McFly...or maybe Doc Brown?...I mean,
who really changed the future?...But my precognition came
true...Marcel did this...God, Brent, there's a towel only a few feet
from you...Royal!...She's safe now...And lightning!...lightning is
his hand...like a baseball...maybe bigger, like a bowling ball...no,
that's too big...Brent, cover up please, it's getting
awkward...Sirius! Sirius, we have to tell Nelson...and
Janice...now! Witnesses got to know too! You got to tell them!"

Both Brent and Sirius blinked several times. She finally said,
"Tell them what? I don't understand anything you just said."

"Royal! She almost died."

An unknown force caused by extreme concern shot Sirius up
from the cot. "Is she okay? Where is she?"

"Just some scratches...she's with the plant chick...God, what's
her name anyways?...We have to...Brent, I changed the future!"

Holding his hands out, Brent spoke slowly. "Adam, take a
breath. Tell us everything that just happened."

The room sounded like Janice's classroom before the lesson
started. She fought the instinct to say, "Class, let's get started."
There was nothing to teach this group of people anyway. Sirius'
eyes stayed peeled to Adam's story. Brent remained unemotional
with not even a sign of anger. His head just kept down to the
ground. Declan's daughter Royal nodded to every insane chapter
of Adam's tale. And Nelson sat in a stool chewing on his nails.
Her father never chewed on his nails. She only remembered him
doing that before his first inauguration.

"And then he flew away!" Adam exclaimed. His voice echoed
in the increasingly crowded tent. Only an hour ago, it had been
just Janice and her birth parents.

Sirius blew her nose into another tissue, "Wait, what? Did he,
like, turn around and shoot up like Superman or something?"

"No! Something pulled him away. I mean, he must've been
doing a crazy amount of miles per hour. He was just...gone.

Then the weather calmed down."

Royal nodded rapidly, "It's true! I saw it. You'd think after what we done saw between Lloyd and Marcel that we'd be used to it. But my dang hand won't stop shaking."

Janice just shook her head as she removed Nina's head towel. It was warm. Very warm. The fever was getting out of control. She sunk it in a bucket of cold water and placed it back on Nina's forehead. Her birth mother didn't even flinch. Whatever dreams filled that head, it kept her alive for the moment. What Janice would do for some more powerful meds. Even a few capsules of Tylenol could do the trick.

"What pulled him away?" Brent asked, the first thing he'd said the entire conversation.

Adam shrugged, "Dude, I don't know. But whatever it was – saved us."

After numerous reminders to the group to hush while her birth parents slept and already giving her skepticism of this story so far, Janice decided to keep silent. The idea of so-called *magical powers* or whatever just seemed too far-fetched. There was probably some scientific explanation for what had been happening lately. Maybe hallucinogenic toxins had entered the atmosphere, but that seemed just as far-fetched. And the fact that innocent Marcel would attack anyone just seemed out of his character. Then again, she couldn't argue the sensations he left her with in her brief stay at the Ritz.

Nelson looked again in her direction and began to chew his nails more. Did he even have nails left? He was nervous. But in a time of so many things to be nervous about, Janice couldn't pinpoint what.

While her eyes peered at her adopted father, her real father awoke in a long moan. Nelson's eyes diverted back to the conversation, pretending to be concerned like when anti-abortion lobbyists used to speak to him.

Lloyd asked in a whisper, "Hey, Janny. Is there something to drink around here?"

Janice gave him a sip from a bottle. "It's this mixture of leaves

I got, so it will taste funny."

"My only question is...is it gluten-free?"

Even on the verge of death, Lloyd still had a sense of humor. Janice giggled as he drank from the bottle.

After a few sips and a satisfying sigh, Lloyd said, "You've got that same giggle, just like when we used to watch *SpongeBob*. I'm glad I got to see you one last time."

One last time? Janice objected, "Dad, don't talk like that."

"Just call me Lloyd. It doesn't bother me. Nelson is your dad. He deserves that title more than I do. It takes more than blood to combine a family. I have thousands of followers here. And they're my family too."

Before Janice could utter another objection, Lloyd dozed off. She looked back to see Nelson staring. He immediately turned his head.

The group's conversation seemed to be going nowhere. "Trust me, it's not safe here. Not for us. Not for anyone," Royal said, fiddling with the gauze wrapped around her bicep.

"There's a ton of people here. Where would we go?" Sirius asked.

Nelson spoke up, his voice low and drained. "There's a missile silo. Brent and I saw it on the way here. It could easily hold all these people and then some. We just need help finding the entrance."

Brent perked up. "Can't believe I forgot about that place. Yes. Dad's right. We could go there."

With a show of hope, the group seemed to sit up straight in unison. Royal said, "Well ain't that the best news we'd heard all day. Sirius, we gotta tell the others. Come on." Without asking, Royal dragged Sirius by the arm out of the tent.

"How long are we going to have to hide?" Adam asked. It was like the good news had no effect on him. "We're being hunted. I mean, this isn't how it was in my vision. We fought back."

Nelson flipped his head toward Adam. "And what are you suggesting? You suggesting I go to war with Marcel? For God's sake, boy, this is my son we're talking about. I won't condone any brutal action against him."

Adam looked at Brent. "Dude, don't tell me you don't agree with me. We planned this a long –"

"I'm tired of fighting," Brent said. And Janice had never been more proud of those words escaping his mouth.

Exactly as she expected, Adam turned to her. "Janice? You were with him. Don't you understand? We have to start a rebellion against him. He's going to destroy everything."

Janice didn't bother to look up.

"What's with you guys? Are you blind?" Adam asked.

"He's my son," Nelson whispered.

"But, Sir, you saw what he can do."

"He's my son," Nelson repeated a little louder.

"We have to kill him –"

Nelson shouted, "He's my son!"

The tent quieted. Adam finally kept his mouth shut and placed his hands in his pockets. Going toward the door flap, he paused for a moment. "I'm sorry, but you all need to hear this: Marcel Celest died in that coma. Something else is living inside him. What is it going to take for you guys to realize he's become a monster?" With that, Adam left.

Janice said, "Looks like he's not the only one changing. In fact, I think the day those missiles hit...changed us all."

A moment passed and Nelson finally spoke. This time directly to Brent. "Do you remember where it is?"

"Yeah, Dad."

"Take them there."

"Aren't you coming?"

Nelson shook his head. "Lloyd and Nina are too ill to move. I'll stay here with Janice. We'll nurse them back to health. Then we'll meet you guys there."

The Celest family gave an agreement to the plan without saying a word. Just simple nods sufficed. Brent left the tent and Nelson slumped into the table.

✧ ✧

Nine hours it took for the entire camp to be evacuated. And Janice hadn't moved much, besides to replace Nina's bandages and change Lloyd's towels, which seemed damper from the infection-fighting sweat. Reading helped pass the time. Though Nelson tried to keep her occupied with mild talk, he eventually fell into a deep snooze. The books of Charles Dickens, Anne Rice, and Michael Crichton kept Janice's eyes moving and mind occupied. She couldn't fathom the idea of napping when her birth parents floated on the thin line between life and death. It had been the same when Marcel fell into the coma. Endless nights of watching and waiting for...whatever fate decided would happen.

She watched her dad's nostrils expand with every slow breath. Nelson was definitely asleep. But Janice never knew him to sleep with his eyes slightly open. She waved her hands in front of his face.

"He used to do that when he got back from the Afgan War," Lloyd whispered, trying to sit up. Before Janice could object to him moving out of bed, he was already lying back down and groaning. "That bastard got us good."

"How are you feeling?"

He didn't answer. Instead, he apologized. "We were just trying to help."

"I'm sure your followers understand."

"No. I meant when we abandoned you. At the orphanage. We were just trying to help." The word *help* had a distinct tone of regret.

Over twenty years since that memory of being left at a quaint Catholic orphanage, and it still seemed so clear. She said, "I had so many questions about that day. But can't think of a single one right now."

Lloyd closed his eyes for so long that Janice began to panic. Then he replied, "Servo Clementia. They hunted us to the point we couldn't care for you. My old friend had an idea."

"Who?"

Lloyd motioned his head toward Nelson. "God," he said, "still sleeping with his eyes slightly open. Used to creep me out when I came to the dorm room late at night."

Janice tried to smile at the joke but couldn't muster it. "I thought those Christian terrorists only came after people with special abilities." Her voiced sounded more sarcastic with every word of that sentence.

"We can feel the future. The emotions anyway."

The right side of her face curled into a cynical smirk. "Yes. Okay. Sure. I thought it was maybe all that weather tricks you guys did, I heard."

Lloyd whimpered as he turned to his side. He stared at Janice as though it was the first time he'd seen her. "I still remember when you were nine years old. Before bed one night, we watched *Jurassic Park*. Of all the silly things in that film, you objected to the whole dinosaur DNA in an amber fossil."

That time, Janice found her smirk genuine. "Time would've decayed a 66-million-year-old specimen."

He continued speaking with a growing smile, "Yes, some things are far-fetched. But you know what else was far-fetched a long time ago? That the world was round."

Though she understood where he was going with this, Janice ignored it. Sanity was all she had left and might as well focus on it.

A groan behind her made Janice turn. Nina had awoken. "You know what else is far-fetched?"

"What?"

"That a woman who had been surgically clipped to not be pregnant now has a baby growing in her?"

Janice touched her belly. "How did you know?" she said, hoping Nina wouldn't say she had another silly ability.

"Oh, please. That pale look of about to vomit, rubbing your feet constantly because of the water weight, and no longer able to hide the tummy." Her birth mother gave a huge grin, "I knew the minute I saw you that I'm going to be a grandmother."

It was that assumption that always broke Janice up. That assumption that she wouldn't have an abortion soon. "I...I just don't know if I should have this baby. I keep asking people and everyone says the same rhetoric. 'Oh, you're a woman and that's your decision.' It's what politics trained us to mimic in those awkward conversations."

"I remember that feeling too. Janice, hon, have the baby."

Finally, someone to help her indecisive mind. Janice felt a little thrown back. Nina continued, "I did much snooping about you over the years. Evolutions Professor at Baltimore University? I was so relieved. Because you have always been obsessed with the process of evolution. Plants, animals...people. Janice, you are now a part of that process. More than the power to feel the emotions of someone's future is the power to create the future. Growing inside that womb is the next step of human evolution. Don't let it slip you by."

Piercing her lips, Janice managed to still smile. "Thank you." Doubt left her mind and possible names for her child entered. "I needed to hear that."

Nina swallowed back hard. "Remember, wherever there is light, we will be there."

Maybe the fever was affecting Nina. Janice squinted her eyes. "Say again?"

"Can you get us some water to drink?"

Janice nodded. She stood up quickly. Her dad hadn't even moved, leaned back in his chair and head cocked to the side. At this point, she realized how lucky she was. While most struggled for any family, like Adam, she almost had too much. Too much love. It made her feel important, what every man and woman wanted.

After pouring a glass of water from a jug, something suddenly didn't seem right. The room was quieter somehow. Janice turned slowly.

Still holding hands, Lloyd and Nina stared into each other's eyes. But their stare never broke. Their eyes never closed. Their smiles never faded.

Janice walked a little more forward before halting in front of their cots. "Mom? Dad?"

No answer. Their faces began to grow pale almost immediately.

Janice cupped her hand over her mouth. Tears dribbled past her knuckles onto the floor. Lloyd and Nina were gone. Again. Ripped from her life before she could enjoy their presence. She cried like the day she'd been left at the orphanage. Janice used the back of her hand to wipe her eyes. Both mothers had changed her life forever. Made her stronger. Even though one father was gone, Janice had one left. She turned to Nelson.

"Daddy?" she said, wobbling him awake.

Nelson's eyes blinked for a moment. "Yes, pumpkin?" he mumbled.

"I love you."

He seemed surprised to hear that. Had it been that long since she'd said it? Janice made a vow to remind him every day so as to never see that reaction again. "I love you so much."

She leaned in and placed her head on Nelson's shoulder. Then he rested his head on hers.

CHAPTER THIRTY-SIX

The helicopter's blades were deafening. Which came as a relief to Gerard since he had no desire in speaking to the man in the helicopter with him. He would've sat with anyone else in the world but General Vanderbilt. A bucket full of snakes, a jukebox that played "Don't Worry, Be Happy" on repeat, even a ringing alarm clock that couldn't be shut off...any of those could've been better company than this man. What sounded like a boring audiobook read by a sleepy Orson Welles, the general drudged on about his war experience.

Below, the forest looked the same as it did yesterday. And the day before. This mission seemed a waste of time. Marcel was nowhere to be found. The People of Bliss were just as elusive. How could this many people suddenly disappear? Sure, the forest was dense, but the fact that sunlight had barely cut through the clouds made it difficult to see. Without simple night vision goggles or heat signature equipment, Gerard felt useless. He stared at the clouds for some more. From up there, the particles of dirt had been more visible. It looked like that murky gunk in the Everglades when the water sat still for too long.

"Mr. Collins, are you listening?"

He answered politely, "Nope."

"I said that scientists have an idea of how to get the cloud seeds to deactivate and finally get some sunshine back."

Just when Gerard's interest got piqued, Vanderbilt added, "I remember when I was stationed in Iraq and the sand storms made it black outside for eight days."

Gerard immediately lost interest while Vanderbilt mumbled on. He looked through binoculars. If a deer had sped by, he'd be excited to see some indication of life around here. The clock was ticking. Who knew how long Marcel could survive without food or water?

Something stirred in the trees below. No use in getting excited, though. The last time, it had been birds feasting on a dead body and Gerard nearly vomited the can of ravioli he had that morning. He zoomed the binoculars in.

The movement became more evident. Definitely something bigger than a bird. As the helicopter got closer, the figure moved under a bush. It was a humanlike shape. He zoomed in to the max.

Humans.

Two of them, to be precise. Before he gave an exclamation of joy, Gerard tightened his lips. He recognized the blue torn jeans and purple blouse. The figures hid further into the bush as the helicopter flew by.

It was Janice.

Covering her as best as he could was Nelson.

"Mr. Collins, are you listening?"

After a roll of his eyes and a long sigh, "What, Vandy belt?"

"Did you see something?"

Though their facial expressions were blurry, Gerard could sense desperation on Janice. Maybe something even worse. Fear? Sadness?

"No," Gerard mumbled, "nothing's there. Keep going."

The helicopter whizzed by. His wife slowly faded out of view. The thought passed his mind a while ago, having to listen to Vanderbilt's story about his first Medal of Honor, to use the parachute and jump out of this helicopter. But now the feeling escalated when he knew his wife and father-in-law were down there. Where were they going? There didn't seem to be much out here besides trees and more trees.

Underneath the seat was a packet of maps. Even in an area where wind constantly entered and exited, the packet had a layer of dust on it. Gerard pulled out the laminated papers. Thanks to technology, people rarely used reference books. He scanned the maps of the area. Then stumbled upon one that showed abandoned military establishments. Instead of screaming *Eureka!* Gerard held the outburst in. Sure enough, there was a missile silo nearby.

As with all good information, Gerard took a moment to reflect if sharing this knowledge would benefit him. There was no Marcel to kiss up to, so a pat on the back from Vanderbilt didn't seem very rewarding. Perhaps a promotion for this finding? But the money system had become so convoluted that a raise didn't seem that important to him. Besides, no wife or kids...not even a pet...it's not like it took a better paycheck to feed himself hotdogs and ramen noodles every day. So then what about this fear of a rebellion that the general tried to dig into his brain? Okay, so what if all the followers were found and arrested? That meant his loved ones would be arrested too. Seeing Janice behind bars gave no comfort to him. And Nelson was the father Gerard never had. So putting him in harm's way of the Union's punishments didn't seem satisfying.

"Why are you looking at those old maps?" Vanderbilt asked.

Placing them back under the seat, Gerard answered half-heartedly, "I was looking for a good place to bury your body if you don't stop talking."

"Such the kidder. One of these days, Mr. Collins, I'm going to think all this joking is actually being serious."

Gerard grumbled. Maybe the pilots wouldn't notice if he opened the door and shoved Vanderbilt out of the helicopter.

The microphone chirped. An unfamiliar voice spoke, "General, we have eyes on Willow."

Willow. That was the codename for Marcel. He sat up straight. Before the general could answer, Gerard pressed the button on his mic, "Where is he?"

✧ ✧

Gambling had never been his thing. Gerard stood outside of the mostly crumbled casino. Vanderbilt stood behind them.

"He's in there," the general said, even though that had already been established by radio calls. But yet neither of them could move.

In all the years Gerard called Marcel a friend, he'd never seen a temper like that explode out of him. He thought of the whirlwind of innocent protesters and lightning strikes he aimed at them. Brent was the Celest with the outbursts, not Marcel. It occurred to Gerard that maybe this had been a poor decision to come here. Maybe Marcel wasn't himself anymore. Of all the slots, blackjack tables, and rolling dice games in that building - was Gerard about to take the biggest risk out of all them? With just his mind, Marcel could destroy this building and all of them in it.

Vanderbilt must've been thinking the same thing, because his feet didn't move. "We've got several men inside with automatic weapons, ready to fire if Mr. Celest shows any sign of...you know."

"Okay. So. What now?"

"There's an SUV ready to transport him to a holding cell in DC. Steel walls, soundproof, windproof, there's no escape for him in there."

"Why not use the chopper?" Gerard asked, just buying time for his hand to stop shaking.

"The only people aware of what Marcel can do...were the people who actually saw it. The Union isn't making any statements about eyewitness accounts. That means we keep it secret until Marcel learns to control whatever he just did. Until he is no longer a liability."

Gerard took a deep breath and sighed. "I'm assuming it's going to be *my* job to get him out of there."

Vanderbilt didn't bother to answer the obvious question. It had become Gerard's duty now. He guessed he deserved it, since everyone knew he'd been the biggest kiss-ass to Marcel.

Finally, his feet started moving. He entered through the shattered front door. "Did Marcel do this to the building?"

"He got upset when Union Keepers chased him in here," Vanderbilt said from a distance.

Apparently, the general had no intention of coming inside. Good. Gerard didn't need the distraction. He followed the path of the main hallway, stepping on shards of glass with his thick leather boots. After a room of slot machines, he climbed over a large Keno wheel to enter an even more vast room filled with card tables. In the center were what looked like mannequins. Mannequins that wore the uniforms of Union Keepers. Not until Gerard approached closer did he see one of them breathing. They weren't mannequins, but actual men. So still that their only choice of movement was their lungs. The men surrounded and pointed their rifles at the same target.

Marcel.

Gerard approached at a slower pace, finding the uniform seemed particularly hot from the amount of sweat building on his body. Marcel had his head hung low, looking at the ground. Red dots from their rifles looked like a disco ball hung above Marcel. All the Union Keepers kept their eye through the gun's sight as Gerard approached.

"Let me through," he instructed. But no one adhered. There was just too much tension in the room. He resorted to bending down and squeezing through the wall of armed men until he was hovering over Marcel.

"Hey...it's me...Gerard."

His friend said nothing, just keeping his head down. Gerard realized he didn't exactly have a plan in place for this situation. Improvising wasn't his style. "So...um...we're here to arrest you."

"I know," Marcel whispered. One of the Union Keepers stepped backward when Marcel spoke. Gerard held his fist up. No one needed to move.

"Everyone is just a little scared here —"

"I know."

A moment of silence passed. "Do we...um...need to be?"

Before Marcel answered, he shook his head slowly. "I...don't know."

Not the reply Gerard wanted. He took a deep breath. "Okay...well...can you look up at me?"

Slowly, almost at a snail's pace, Marcel raised his head. His eyes were closed tightly.

"Why are you closing your eyes?"

He answered, "Because that's how the power in me works. Through the eyes."

Gerard's breathing began to settle. At least Marcel attempted to keep peace in this room. "Alright...well...let me see..." He looked around the room, then at his uniform. In one swoop, Gerard tore off a long piece of cloth. "I'll tie this around your eyes. How about that?"

"Thank you."

With surprisingly calm hands, Gerard wrapped the cloth around Marcel's head and covered the eyes. His friend whispered, "I'm sorry. I really am."

Gerard answered with a slight smirk, "I know." He tied off the cloth tightly. Then the part he imagined for Brent was now happening to Marcel. Gerard yanked out a pair of handcuffs and secured them softly around Marcel's wrists. "That too tight?"

"No."

"I'm going to drive you in the SUV outside. The other guys are...you know...intimidated."

Marcel nodded, "You sure you want to take such a gamble with me? What if I lose control again?"

"Well, buddy, I guess I'm just feeling kinda lucky today. Let's go."

When he stood, the Union Keepers backed away in unison. The red dots followed both Marcel and Gerard as they made their way to the exit.

CHAPTER THIRTY-SEVEN

After a long gulp of the ginger hot tea that Matley made, Sirius' throat felt a little better. She took a deep breath and exhaled slowly.

"You okay, darling?" Royal whispered with a tone a nurse would give a child stricken with cancer.

They sat at a table next to the usual setup of microphones, wires, and antennas. It looked more like a lab to find extraterrestrial signals from space than a radio station. Without answering, Sirius moved the microphone closer to her mouth. "You need to wear that mask I gave you."

Royal scoffed, "I ain't scared of that flu."

She should've been. Sirius remembered the fate of so many people infected with unknown viruses. CNN had sent her to one of the victims of Zeka a decade ago; the woman died the next day even though she seemed hopeful.

On the table was Sirius' speech for the week. She looked it over briefly. It was always a good idea to proofread Royal's writing; her best friend's grammar was harder to swallow than Matley's natural flu medications.

"Royal, this speech sounds just...angry."

"We can't get more followers by being all mushy."

Sirius coughed for a moment then said, "We've agreed that we're not like *them*. This is CNN, Fox News, all of them...I don't want to be like that. We don't address rumors."

"Rumors? Marcel is the devil. He flung us all around like rag dolls −" Royal stopped herself. Reliving the memory of the rally must've been too hard. Sirius put her hands in her lap.

"I know you're upset about what happened. But painting Marcel Celest as the quote-unquote-bad guy...that's not what I want us to represent."

"You don't believe he's evil?"

Pausing for a moment, Sirius thought long about this. Was Marcel Celest the bad guy? Certainly, he had a difference of view. His path to world peace may be extreme, but to label him a *villain* didn't sit well in her stomach. "We don't know him. This is what I hated about working for the news. A lot of, like, assumptions get made. It's not fair. He has a temper. Just like everyone −"

"But look what he did at the lake."

"And from the point-of-view of a Union Keeper, Lloyd and Nina were the villains. Right? Didn't they start it? These are the kind of questions you need to, like, ask yourself. Is there really such a thing as a 'bad guy'? I don't agree with the Union and I just want our followers to feel the same way. And when we're strong enough, we will knock on Marcel Celest's door to ask for a different type of government. The government that doesn't seek to control us, just...I don't know...help us."

Royal chewed on her lip in defeat. "You know the news ain't even reporting about Marcel Celest's powers? Not a single word." Royal crumbled back into her seat. "It's all just rumors. It's not right."

"It's too unbelievable. A politician who can control the weather with his mind? Even the *National Enquirer* wouldn't print that. This was how we chose stories at CNN: we chose the stories that people could, like, *actually* believe."

She cleared her throat and felt a glob of hot mucus trickle down her throat. Fever began to make her sweat again, even in such a cold tent. Sirius wasn't used to being sick. Before Doomsday, she practiced yoga every Sunday and Wednesday. She would eat only organic. And sit in salt rooms to practice proper breathing.

Without another word, Sirius grabbed a black marker and began to edit some of the speech. Usually at times like this, Sirius would take Royal's negative speech to Lloyd who would help turn it into a positive speech. The option was no longer there. For now anyways. "Let's skip this week's speech."

"You're right," Royal said as her shoulders shrunk, "It'll be better we let you get some rest."

Rest had been tough. The People of Bliss were getting very ill from this flu. Sirius worried if she fell asleep...she may not wake up and instead drift into a dreamily death. When she faced it, wasn't death inevitable for all of them? The bitter cold slipped through her sweater and reminded her the darkness was winning. Lloyd and Nina's light diminished every day and so did the hope. The hope of the People of Bliss. Doing a speech wouldn't change that. Hope needed more than words. And Sirius couldn't think of a thing to bring it back.

CHAPTER THIRTY-EIGHT

Before becoming Secretary of Defense, Declan had quite a list of accomplishments. But his accomplishments all shared the same theme: ends. In high school, he put an end to the cafeteria's use of high fructose corn syrup products with a petition. In college, he put an end to co-ed dormitories by using his voice as a weapon. Hell, he even put an end to the secret organization Servo Clementia in the United States.

After becoming Secretary of Defense, his egotistical and controlling attitude diminished. Thanks to politics. The bully had met an even bigger bully. And there was no backing down. Government controlled everything.

But today would be his final accomplishment. He'd put an end to governments. And an end to the Union.

Standing outside the Capitol building, Declan began to feel the weight of his outfit. That kid outside the grocery store built a pretty tough bulletproof shield underneath this trench coat, but it was also damn heavy. He climbed a few steps before a familiar voice exclaimed behind him.

"Is that...my goodness...is that Charles Declan? My word. It surely is."

He turned to see the southern mistress, a congresswoman for the state of Alabama. Her name eluded him and his expression must've showed it.

"Oh my, it is you! Charlie, it's me. Miranda." She covered her nose, "Oof. I'd hug you but...let's just say...you've definitely been one of the refugees sleeping in the garbage. Ugh, I usually throw dollars at them to shush them away. So smelly and icky."

Declan had once checked the background of Miranda. She wasn't even from a southern state. The accent was completely fake just to get votes and become a congresswoman. Her cleavage was too perky, her lipstick too bright, and her teeth too white. She was one of the sexual deviants in congress and not afraid to show it.

"Well," she said, "surely you must be here to join us inside. This is the big day! The Third Seat is going to be voted on." Miranda climbed the stairs; her tight blue dress left little for Declan's imagination. "Now, I ain't supposed to say anything, but I already know I'm gonna win. We got politicians from around the world. And I've gotten them on my side. Except you, of course. I didn't know you'd be here. Honestly, I didn't even know you were still alive. Thought the papers said you was good as dead. We are going to have to get you a change of clothes. I mean, the whole *trench coat* look went out in the 1930s, silly. And I'm pretty sure that's some kind of cum stain on your sleeve. Follow me. There's wardrobe inside."

While Miranda babbled on about how spectacular her chances were at winning the vote today, Declan took a closer look at the Capitol building. It stood up well against the blast of the nuclear weapon in the sky. The nuclear weapon that didn't get to land, thanks to the sacrifice of the Air Force pilots in the air. Sacrifice. Declan reminded himself again about this.

At the entrance were two metal detector booths. The guard was under dressed, under the weather, and definitely looked under paid. Miranda scratched her head when they made it to the booth. There was so much hairspray that it looked like a helmet. "Well, it looks like the Union spared no expense at guarding the place. Do you even speak English, Mr. Security Man? Ugh, don't answer. I already know you don't. My name is Miranda...Hopkins. It's on your list thingy."

The guard curled his lip and waved a wand over her. "Go

ahead," he groaned.

Declan scanned his surroundings. No one was around. Seemed so quiet for such a special day. "Where's Marcel Celest?"

Miranda held her chest and giggled. "My God, Charlie, I guess you have been sleeping under a rock lately, huh?"

Whatever that meant, Declan grew tired of her. He stepped through the metal detector. A red light came on. The guard approached with the wand. "I have to scan you, Mr. Secretary. Please hold your hands out."

Miranda giggled. "Oh please. Charlie is too chicken to carry a gun around. He ain't from the Deep South like myself." She approached him slowly, seductively then whispered, "The only big gun I heard you carry around is in that crotch of yours. How about it, Charlie? I heard you like it rough. What can I do for you to get that vote? How about you show me what you're hiding in those pants?"

Declan shrugged. He pulled out an AP revolver from his pants and fired a single shot through Miranda's perfect forehead. The top of her head flew onto the pavement floor, along with that stiff mash of hair. Before there could be a reaction, Declan faced the revolver at the guard's head and shot. Brain matter stained the perfectly waxed floor.

And then there it was. Quiet. Two dead bodies on the floor and Declan still felt no sympathy. He frowned. Maybe killing Marcel would make him feel better. Where was Marcel Celest? Surely, he would be here. Declan walked through the front double doors, making sure to step on Miranda's scalp.

The Capitol building used to be such a bustling place. Congressmen dashing one way; visitors dashing the other way. Now, no one seemed to care that Declan had murdered two people at the entrance. He closed the double doors behind him. The vaulted ceilings echoed the clank of the doors shutting. Without even taking the time to remember, Declan slid the gate shut over the doors and pressed a number in the keypad. The gate locked. His keycode still worked. Typical. Security hadn't even gotten the authorization yet to remove his number. This was going to be too easy.

He stared up at the circular ceiling and then circled around until he became dizzy. The first time he stepped into this building twelve years ago, he did the same thing. Now, sadly, it would be the last time.

"Mr. Secretary?" someone said.

Declan looked to see a security guard exiting the bathroom. He paused. The guard looked at the locked gates, then down. Until Declan turned, he didn't understand the curiosity on the floor. Blood seeped through the slit on the bottom. Miranda's blood matched the color of her lipstick. Even in death, the bitch had to have style. Declan turned to the guard.

Then the man's hand slid toward his gun holster. Declan whipped out a shotgun from inside his trench coat and pulled the trigger. The guard flew backwards when the shot hit him, his blood now staining the floor. A shotgun's blast wasn't usually this gruesome, but Declan sawed off the end. Not that a regular shotgun bullet wouldn't do the job. It was just that a sawed-off end gave such a nastier kill.

With a trembling bloody hand, the guard reached for the radio that had fallen off his belt. Declan blasted the guard's hand into just a mess of what looked like dropped fruit salad. The guard screamed. It was such an annoying scream that Declan decided to take out the guard's vocal chords. He aimed and shot.

Finally, the area was quiet again.

Then footsteps. And more footsteps. Six guards ran down the far hallway. Declan pulled out a grenade and threw it. One of the guards must've been confused because he caught it like it was a baseball. The grenade exploded. Declan covered his face as shrapnel flew everywhere. The Forger had made quiet an arsenal. Laughter escaped Declan's throat as he thought about the stupid guard that caught the grenade.

A shot fired from the group of guards. It smacked Declan's shoulder and made a *ping* sound. He looked at the hole created in his trench coat; the steel armor had a scoff mark on it. But otherwise intact. That smart kid created an excellent suit.

Then another shot fired and hit Declan's chest. That one hurt. He took a step back, feeling a surge of adrenaline slow his perception of time. The nanobots in his blood gave him keen eyesight. He saw one more shot come at him. Declan raised both his arms and the bullets pinged off his steel gauntlets. The stings from the impacts began to hurt more, but he found himself more annoyed than despaired. Eventually it would be time to reload.

He backed up and hid behind a pillar. In one swoop, he ripped off the remains of the trench coat. Every part of him that wasn't covered in armor plating had guns and grenades. He reached for a flash bang grenade and threw it at his opposers.

The guards wailed as it hit, making them blind and their hearing just as useless. He came out with a semi-automatic pistol; the shotgun had gotten boring. Without hesitating, he shot three guards in the head. The other three were hiding.

Declan listened closely. Thanks to the technology of internal nanobots, his sense of hearing peaked. Then there was the clanking of someone trying to reload a gun...poorly. He went toward the sound. Actually wasting his time hiding behind a trash can, the young guard must've been straight out of high school and wetting his pants like he'd left middle school. The guard didn't even know how to reload the gun and kept fumbling with it. Declan saved him the trouble of embarrassing himself. It's not like the kid had a future anyways. He fired a shot through the guard's chest, aiming for the heart so he'd die quickly.

Two more guards were left. Declan walked slowly, stepping on debris from the grenade's explosion. One of the guards appeared from behind a planter. He dashed towards the door instead of being a true hero and dashing toward the enemy. The guard tried to wiggle the door open. Declan yanked out a four inch blade and tossed it. The blade landed in the back of the guard's neck.

One more was hiding somewhere. Was this all the Union could afford to watch the front? Declan found himself infuriated.

World leaders were housed in this building. This was the best army they had to secure them? Then the last guard appeared and jumped on top of Declan. They both fell to the floor. Then he felt a sharp pain in his rib. He kicked the guard off. There was a blade sticking out of Declan's right rib cage. He looked to see the guard had taken the blade from the last dead guard's neck. Clever. And there was just enough room between his chest plate inseam to fit the weapon. Declan didn't pull it out; there was no point. Before the clever guard could stand on his feet, Declan shot off the right side of his face. It was only fair since the guard injured Declan's right side too.

Now that his opposition was dead, he stood to his feet. The blade in his side barely hurt anymore; nanobots soothed the wound with natural painkillers.

Declan looked up at the ceiling, smiled, and circled one more time as he laughed.

For all those years, one side of congress had been up his ass and the other side down his throat. Eventually, they met in the middle and stole his soul. Today they would pay.

Spike grenades caused an extreme amount of damage. That's why Declan enjoyed them so much. The problem was, though, the user couldn't be around when they went off. Spikes flew out from every angle. So in order for this plan to work, Declan would have to use them in closed rooms.

He walked up the stairs and pulled out three spike grenades from his knee pack. Having to use messy nail polish, Declan had already written names on each one. The first door he came to was marked REPRESENTATIVE HAROLD MARKS. In his hand was the spike grenade with the word *Harold* written on it.

Declan swung open the door. The bastard was hiding behind a chair, his gray toupee falling off the side of his head. "I heard gun shots. Senator Declan? Is that you?" Harold asked. He never even had the decency to accept Declan's promotion and still called him *Senator.*

He threw the spike grenade inside the room and closed the door. The house representative screeched. The grenade shot out 48 spikes, three of which nearly broke through the door. Declan listened to the sound of Harold's body hitting the floor and then he flicked the edge of the spike poking out of the door. It made a nice-sounding ping. He closed his eyes, hoping to feel satisfied. But nothing.

Declan went to the next door. Then threw in a grenade marked *Carol*. The woman in the room screamed. Her scream gargled when the spikes exploded out and probably landed in her throat. No satisfaction though. And that bitch led a team to cut his defense budget last year.

The next door might be a chance of feeling a sense of fun from murdering one of these assholes. On it was a silver plated name: CHRISTIAN MANSFIELD. His name was actually *Christopher*, but he went by *Christian* just to get religious voters. Declan shook his head. These people were unreal. He opened the door.

"What's all that noise downstairs?" the grumpy senator complained.

Declan tossed in the grenade and shut the door. Spikes covered every inch of that tax-payer remodeled office. He opened the door and saw the senator's bloody carcass on the floor. Blood soaked his bear skin rug. Fucker mocked him on Fox News. Declan wished he had killed him a better way. That was too quick. Perhaps he needed a slower kill to feel satisfied.

Representative Sanders' office wasn't far. Perhaps that coward would accept a slow death. Before Declan made it to his office, he heard hollering. Representative Sanders, in that overpriced suit, ran for a window. "You're not taking me alive!" Then he jumped out the window three floors to his death. Declan's shoulder sank. Damnit.

Two women dashed out of the cafeteria, obviously forgetting about their high heels. One of them tripped while the other kept running. With an Uzi, Declan unloaded four shots through the one woman on the floor. The other woman hadn't made it far down the hallway before he emptied the magazine into her back.

He climbed a spiral set of stairs. All this walking made him tired. But it was almost over.

Screaming could be heard. Lots of voices spoke at once.

"He's got a gun!"

"He's killing everyone!"

"Call 911!"

911 might've worked if Declan's hadn't cut the land lines this morning. And good luck finding a cellphone signal. Besides, who would pick up the phone on the other line? He laughed to himself. It sounded more maniacal than he anticipated.

At the top of the spiral stares was Vice President Emerson. His hands were up in surrender. Surrender wasn't an option today. Always the one who thought he could calm any maniac down, Emerson spoke slowly. "Secretary Declan, I know you're angry but –"

"Open your mouth one more time and it'll be your last," Declan warned.

Only able to keep it closed for three seconds, the Vice President opened his mouth to speak again. Declan shot a chamber from his gun into the man's throat. Emerson grasped his throat then fell halfway down the spiral stairs. "All your accomplishments are so half-assed, even falling down the stairs," Declan sighed. He shoved him until the Vice President tumbled again, this time descended several flights of the spiral case. Fun to watch, but not indulging. With sagged shoulders, Declan opened the door and went onto the third floor.

To his left was the men's restroom. The knob didn't turn. Locking it would be a waste of time when there was a gunman with this arsenal. Declan whipped out his shotgun again. He blasted the knob off and kicked the door down. Cowering in the corner, in plain clothes, was the Pope. He'd never looked so dull and boring. The Pope held up his hand, which had been intertwined with a set of rosaries.

"Please, my son. I am a man of God."

Declan snickered, "Yeah, you're also a man who molested

sixteen children."

Shaking his head slightly, the Pope said, "*Allegedly.*"

Even in his final moments the man still lied. Declan pointed at the Pope's genitals and fired. The Pope bellowed at the top of his throat. Blood spurted out in all directions. Leaving, Declan made sure to close the door. It helped to mute the sound.

After a brief stop to indulge in cold water from the water fountain, Declan made his way casually to the next set of doors. He laid the empty shotgun down; it was already out of ammo. Such a shame because he enjoyed the echo of its blast.

Behind the doors, he could hear the sounds of several congressmen trying to push desks in front of it. Retards didn't even realize the door opened outwards. Declan swung it open then emptied out his automatic rifle. This was why he hated politicians. They were glorified stupid a-holes. Each shot blew the congressmen's heads backwards. These kills were just too clean and rapid. None of them really suffered the way Declan had in this building for over a decade of political service.

He was about to walk away until he heard whimpering. Still staring at the floor, Declan pulled out another Uzi and shot at the bodies on the floor. But a moment later, still whimpering. Then sniffles. Someone was hiding.

After one good shove, the mess of desks fell over and Declan climbed into the board room. He stopped to listen. Then he could hear yells outside. Through the window, he saw several people downstairs trying to push through the metal gates that Declan locked. They were literally crushing each other to death.

"Someone open up the gates!"

"Help!"

"There's a madman inside!"

Madman? Declan was the only sane one in the building, he felt.

The whimper again. He turned in a circle. There was a closet in the back of the room. Without much ammo left, Declan decided to use just a pistol as he continued his search for the perfect kill. The kill that would gratify that demon in him. He slid open the closet door.

President Wen.

The Chinese President shook his head quickly, begging without saying words. Declan shot a bullet through the man's leg. He screamed and shouted some obscenities in Chinese. The president clung onto the bloody wound. "Please! Mr. Secretary! Don't do this! I have a family!"

"So did the rest of us before nukes killed them all."

"Please! Mr. Secretary! I'm sorry for what I did!"

With a perplexed eyebrow up, Declan asked, "Sorry? For what?"

"Isn't that why you came here? For me?"

Well, there were several reasons why Declan was here. Murder politicians. Destroy the Union. End Marcel Celest. Get some satisfaction. But he had no clue what Wen meant. What could've *he* done? Instead of continuing to look perplexed, Declan tried a different technique. A tactic he used when torturing targets of Servo Clementia. "Admit what you did and I'll let you go."

"Okay, fine!" Wen's voice squeaked. "I did it. I caused Doomsday. Iran only meant to make a threat of nuclear attack, but behind closed doors...my men pulled the triggers. It was the only way to make the Union a reality. I didn't know there were other worldwide attacks going to happen because of it. And I live with that every day! Now, would you please let me go! Please!"

It took a moment for the words from Wen's terrified, whiny voice to make sense. Declan had to process all of this. In that last five months, so much had happened. Nuclear weapons devastated over 90 locations nationwide and sent the electrical grid into obsolete status. Scientifically-modified locusts killed millions in Africa. A government-created virus spread like a wildfire through several European countries. All this – set off by this one simple man? Adding his action to the world leaders was like placing a brick on top of a house of cards. Everything came tumbling down.

Declan pointed his firearm and shot Wen three more times. Twice in one leg. Once in the shoulder. Wen's screams echoed throughout the rooms.

Then it hit him. Satisfaction. Declan took a big inhale like being under water for too long. Killing Wen, hearing those screams, was going to fulfill that need in Declan's gut. The need to feel all this was necessary. A sacrifice well worth the journey.

"You...told me...you would...let me go!" Wen cried.

"I'm a mass murderer, dumbass. It's your fault for believing me."

With a careful, slow hand he pulled out the nuclear device from his belt. The device hidden in a grocery store. Strange to think such a small item could flatten a city. That the atoms swam around in there, begging to be split. Declan looked down at Wen. "Where's Marcel Celest?"

After a brief smile, Wen said, "Marcel Celest isn't...Wait a minute. Haven't you heard?"

Again, Declan gave a blank stare at yet another person asking if he'd heard the news. What news?

Wen giggled, but his giggles slowly turned into sobs. After a moment, he composed himself after a deep breath. "Is that why you did all this? You are here to put an end to the Union? Like some sort of...redemption?"

No need to lie. Declan answered, "Yes. But Marcel Celest needs to be here. Where is he?"

With a shaky hand, the former president of China wiped away a tear. He spoke to himself, "Redemption. Yes. Redemption. That's sometimes necessary."

"Where's Marcel, goddamnit? Tell me!"

Wen sighed then said. "He's upstairs. Do it, Mr. Secretary. Take out the entire Union. End the lives of all the politicians left in this world."

Finally some verification. Marcel was in the building. The Union was about to be over. Declan looked down at the bomb in his hand. He asked Wen, "There's a place in Heaven for people like us, right?" With watery eyes and tears soaking his face,

Declan asked one more time desperately. "Right?"
    Then he pressed the device's trigger.

CHAPTER THIRTY-NINE

Today was the day. In a million years, Marcel would've never thought the power of persuasion led him to this fate. Instead of shaking the hands of Union members in the Capitol building as they voted for the Third Seat position, he was in handcuffs ready to be locked away. In a billion years, he would've never seen that end for him.

There was this awkward silence from everyone, even from the usual chatty Gerard. Everyone feared him. Suddenly, Marcel felt this approach may have not been the best. He liked genuine respect, the kind that is earned and not forced. That's what he craved. It all came from simply trust. But how? After all that had happened?

From the driver's seat, Gerard spoke. Marcel looked in the direction even though his eyes were blindfolded to see. "Why did you attack those rally people? And that couple, Lloyd and Nina?"

Then came the familiar bumps on the road of Washington DC. He couldn't tell if it was from the nuke that exploded in mid-air or just the usual potholes.

Marcel chose his words carefully. His brother-in-law had been a genuine ally so far and there was no point in losing his trust as well. "I wasn't trying to hurt them...but save them. The elements have gotten out of control. I'm trying to put a leash on them."

Even I'm impressed with that lie, the Wind element said sounding smug. *Now instead of a 50/50 chance of being locked away forever, it's a*

60/40.

Water must've been around somewhere, because Marcel could hear its voice too. Even a simple bottled water in the vehicle, with all the shaking, was enough for the rebellious attitude to begin. *Sure, blame us. Typical Marcel Celest. Not taking responsibility for your own actions.*

Gerard didn't smoke, but for some reason he lit up a cigarette. Marcel smelled the fine tobacco. It must've been freshly rolled. Before he could ask why Gerard ignited the cigarette, he felt the warm flame and potent smell approach his face. His brother-in-law was offering a puff from the stick. "Go ahead. You're still shaky."

Fire from the cigarette hissed gleefully. *It was a marvelous idea, Master. Now he trusts you.*

Then there came the sound of an explosion. Coming from the direction of the Capitol building. Almost like the rattle before an earthquake. Before Marcel could ask what it was, the SUV flipped several times. They crashed into a light pole. Hanging upside-down, blood dripped downward out of Marcel's nose. The blindfold slipped off his head. Outside, the wind picked up.

His mouth dropped. A mile away, where the Capitol building once stood, was an enormous cloud in the shape of a mushroom. Only familiar from those apocalyptic movies, Marcel knew what it was. A nuclear explosion. Growing at a slow rate. But growing, nonetheless. Hundreds of people ran into the streets and stared with the same gaping mouth Marcel had. All eyes clung to the incoming nuclear mushroom.

Marcel glanced quickly at Gerard. In the driver's seat, his gaze was stuck on the explosion. Never until this moment had he seen him that frightened.

"Gerard! Free me! I can stop it!"

His friend ogled at the mushroom cloud. He tried again, "Gerard! Please!"

Like awakening from a dream, Gerard slowly looked in Marcel's direction. "What?"

"Take off the cuffs! Gerard! Now! I got the power to stop the cloud! Please!"

Without hesitating, Gerard yanked keys off his belt and released Marcel's handcuffs.

The Wind whispered, *If you really believe we can stop that, than you're more of a fool that I thought.*

"You don't have a choice!" Marcel screamed aloud as he ran out of the vehicle and onto the main street. Directly in front of him, he got a clear view of the nuclear cloud nearly a mile away and closing in. People on the streets fell to the ground, hopeless to the incoming death.

Darkness increased all around him as Marcel's pupils shrunk. He lifted both hands toward the nuke and pressed against it like an invisible wall. Wind picked up rapidly, blowing debris of newspapers and tumbleweeds in the direction of the explosion. Marcel felt it. The fission of nuclear activity. Split atoms began to dart his way. Only a few at first, then more by the seconds. The wind wasn't stopping them.

Like taking the element by the throat, Marcel used darkness to overpower Water. Fire hydrants exploded upwards with mass amounts of the liquid. He used it all to create a wall of water. The split atoms cooled at the touch.

Then came the heat. Massive amounts of it. People scuttled into the buildings, screaming. Marcel coughed and blood shot out of his mouth then streamed across his cheeks. He pushed harder.

Fire seemed panicked. *I'm trying to stop it, Master!*

Marcel lurched forward, each step making the elements battle this devastating, manmade energy. The cloud finally stopped expanding. Controlling all this took every bit of Marcel's physical and mental strength. Darkness, fire, water, and wind kept pushing against this explosion.

Then the mushroom began to implode slowly. Marcel hollered, conjuring up any bit of vigor left in him. People watched him with wide open eyes.

The mushroom collapsed into only a puff left at the center of where the Capitol building used to be. And the madness ended.

Marcel fell to his knees. The air calmed. Water splashed onto the street. Fire dwindled.

His hands were shaking uncontrollably. He looked down to see they had been burned by the nuclear fallout. Even his clothes gave off a smoky singe. Without a single word said, Marcel collapsed onto the ground.

Then the sounds of footsteps ran toward him. In seconds, citizens of the once-overpopulated city gathered.

"Is he dead?"

"Oh God, I hope he's not dead."

"He saved us."

"I can't believe he did it."

"I've said it from the beginning that Marcel wasn't the enemy."

"He's still breathing."

"I can feel a pulse."

"We have to get a doctor, right away."

"He's already healing! Look!"

"God, I hope he's okay."

"Please be okay."

Barely able to open his eyes, Marcel reached out a hand. It seemed like dozens of hands grabbed for it at once. Trust. Marcel gave a gentle smile and felt the warm hands touching him.

"You're going to be okay."

"Help is on the way."

"Thank you."

"You really are a blessing to us."

"You saved us all."

Genuine respect. Marcel finally earned it. This was his moment of redemption. And it was worth every scar.

CHAPTER FORTY

The mixture was cold to the touch as Matley rubbed it on Janice's belly. "What's in it?" she asked.

In that distinct creole accent, Matley answered, "A sweet blend of the apricot seeds, cocoa beans, and the oils of the lavender. It's going to help remove those stretch marks, child, before they begin."

With a slight smile, Janice said, "Lavender. It's my favorite flower."

Drip.

Though thankful the community agreed to let Janice have her own room in the massive underground silo, she wished it had been one without a constant ceiling drip. The water bead hit the bucket that she found herself emptying twice a day now.

She also found herself staring at the belly that seemed to grow twice a day. Matley's mixture of plants, leaves, and vegetables seemed to make it shine. "How far along do you think I am?"

"Maybe five months, maybe seven."

Five months was good; that meant Adam could be the father. Seven months was bad; that meant Marcel could be the father.

Matley continued, "Don't you worry. We will be ready when the baby be ready." After finishing, she wiped her hands on a hand towel. "You ready to say goodbye tonight?"

"I'll be there," Janice said thinking this would be the second time a mother would be buried. The despondency remained the same.

"I think that boy be outside pacing again," Matley said, pronouncing the *th* like a *d*.

"Adam. Yeah probably."

Matley gathered her towels and glass jars. "Okay, sweet child, I'll leave the door open."

"Thanks again, Matley."

Drip.

Janice put her shirt back on and walked up to the mirror on the wall. This room must've been a bathroom at one time, because it seemed to be the only room on this floor that had a mirror. Thankfully, her father decided on the next room over and Brent was down the hall. It somehow made it feel more homey and less terrifying to be eight stories underground.

The mirror reflected someone so different. Her dirty blonde hair actually had become dirty. Circles enclosed around her eyes like a California sinkhole. So much had changed. Just a few months ago, she had a closet full of clothing but yet nothing to wear. Now, she literally had nothing to wear. Her old clothes, stuffed in the bottom of a backpack, didn't fit. The local women did what they could to sew her new clothing, but even that clothing seemed too small.

"Hey," Adam whispered from the open door. "Are you –"

"I'm fine," Janice said, sick of hearing *Are you okay?* "Come in."

He closed the door behind him. "Smells like catfish in here."

"The cafeteria is downstairs."

"Oh."

While Janice washed her face with the ice cold water that didn't seem to have a hot water option, Adam sat on the carpet that probably hadn't been changed since the 1940s. "So, this place probably as nice as the Union was, huh?"

"Not by a long shot."

"What was it like staying there?"

Janice shrugged, "Just like staying at any hotel."

Adam used his nail to scrape at what was probably gum in the carpet. "What was your brother like? Did he show any of his...abilities?"

The supernatural was just foolish. Until a ghost spoke to her, Janice didn't believe in the afterlife. Until a spaceship zapped her into their craft, Janice didn't believe in UFOs. And until Marcel controlled the weather with just a wave of his hand...Janice couldn't believe it. "Nothing weird, I noticed," she said not mentioning the submissive behavior Marcel seemed to lure her into. Like some sort of hypnotizing behavior. Perhaps she just had too much to drink that night. But thinking of that night still made butterflies stir in her stomach. Something was a little off with Marcel, though supernatural actions seemed implausible.

Next to Janice was a rack of dresses. Without hesitating, she undressed to her bra and panties and then tried on the first dress.

"Um, should I leave the room?"

"This isn't the first time you've seen me without my clothes on."

Adam cleared his throat. "Yeah, but if your dad found out about us...or if Brent found out about us...I mean, there's a lot of places to bury me around here."

The dress seemed to fit her okay, but it was floral style. Not something proper to wear to her birth parents' funeral. She ripped it off and tried on the second dress. "Adam, zip me up please?"

He cleared his throat again and stood up. His fidgety hands worked diligently to raise the zipper.

Janice smiled, "You really aren't that good with zippers, huh? Remember when you tried to help me get undressed at that party and you ripped up the entire back of my outfit?"

Adam's hands seemed to relax. "Oh yeah. Wow. I do remember that night. What were we doing that night? PCP, I think. I was so fucked up, I thought there were two zippers on that."

"That's right! Oh my God." Janice paused for a moment, "Where was that party at?"

It should've been an easy question to answer. In her younger years of joining the Celest family, Janice paid attention to how

Victoria would reminisce with political colleagues at parties. No one ever had been hesitant of remembering details. But now, here was Janice and her younger student Adam trying to remember a single party. Yet, neither of them could answer such a simple question.

"Um," Adam stammered, "I...um...maybe it was that frat house? No. No, it was a club...I think? Sorry, I don't remember."

"Hmm." Janice sighed after looking at her slumping body figure in the mirror. This dress looked terrible too. And it was black. Wearing black at a funeral just seemed too stereotypical. "Unzip me please," she said holding her hair up.

Adam obliged. He looked through the dresses piled on top of each other, probably getting wrinkled. "What about this one? Reminds me of that pink one you wore that one time."

She put it on, yanking it over her enlarged stomach. "When did you see me in a pink dress?"

"That one time when we...um...I think we tried ecstasy that night? We made out in that movie theater, remember? No one was in it. God, what movie was playing?"

Janice thought long and hard before honestly answering, "I don't remember any of that."

Partying with Adam was like riding a rollercoaster without brakes. It may be fun the first few times, but after a while...reality would sink in.

"All those nights together. We had fun, right?" Adam said, sounding like the question was more for himself than for her.

"Well," she replied, "maybe we can start focusing on bringing the best out of us, not the worst?"

Adam nodded, agreeing too quickly maybe. It had been on his mind too.

Neither spoke as Janice tried on another dress. This one a dark brown color made of loose fabric that didn't leave her feeling choked. She looked in the mirror. It looked like the same dress she wore to Victoria's wedding. An elegant attire that made her look years older. Janice rubbed her plump belly.

"I can help raise the baby," Adam said. "I always thought I'd make a good dad. Since I never had one, that means I'd have to start from scratch. Which is a good thing, I guess. It needs to be my responsibility. I'm the baby's dad, right?"

Choosing not to say *yes* with a sense of doubt in her voice, Janice stayed quiet.

Drip.

Then a knock on the door. It sounded loud against the steel walls in this establishment. Janice would have to get used to that. Behind the door, Matley said, "The service is about to start."

"Thank you, mad lady," Adam said.

Janice whispered, "Her name is *Matley.*"

Adam covered his mouth like when a naughty word comes out of a child. "Oops." He started to do this silent laugh, a combination of snorts and snickers. Janice joined in and found herself giggling. A much needed giggle.

As if one funeral wasn't enough, watching the nation's favorite First Lady Victoria Celest be lowered into the ground, Janice now had to endure another. When surrounded by so much death there is no other choice but to accept it. Janice hadn't said much besides an occasional *thank you* to the usual *sorry for your loss*. It was better than listening to *drip*.

Having no security made everyone feel a little on edge. Men, trying to act tough in front of the ladies, would scan the skies for any signs of Union choppers. But nothing. A part of Janice wanted to believe that her husband called off the search tonight for the People of Bliss. Would Gerard do such a thing?

Brent and Nelson joined her. Everyone was in either black suits or black dresses. Why did she choose this brown dress?

People parted ways, making a path toward the lake. The lake that started the whole movement. Bobbling on the smooth water surface was a casket made from tree branches, like an eagle's nest. Sunflowers filled each open hole, crevasse, and slit. Before Janice could ask the significance of the bright flower, Sirius stepped up with a boutique of them. "This is what they wanted.

A flower for each person lost in this catastrophe."

When something so devastating occurs, it's often overlooked. That's the brain's way of coping. Janice hadn't realized that she wasn't alone here. Everyone here had lost. The casket didn't seem to have room for the two sunflowers she grabbed.

Approaching at a slower pace than she wanted, Janice stared at the dead bodies of her parents Lloyd and Nina. Victoria Celest had been cremated and fused with the seed of a tree, quite a different experience; Janice didn't have to face the dead body. Nothing could prepare her.

Their eyes were closed, hands cupped on their chests, and dressed in tailored clothing. Janice choked on her tears. She had accepted the death of the man and woman who brought her into this world. That wasn't what made her choke. It was their look of peace. No makeup could create those smiles on their faces. They were finally at peace. And Janice found herself slightly jealous. Marcel and his Union couldn't possibly create peace. Not like the one on the expressions of her parents' faces.

Scientifically, several things happened at this point in death. The CO_2 in their bodies were at the stages of creating enzymes that destroyed cells and spawned bacteria. Those millions of bacteria were liquefying muscles and tissues at this point. Janice could almost smell the benzene and carbon tetrachloride gases. In 1902, Dr. Duncan MacDougall conducted studies on dying patients that found a common missing weight of 21 grams disappearing at the point of death. The studies had been discredited but also accredited. This was the issue of education, having to look at both sides. But if it were true...what happened to that proposed 21 grams? Was that the soul? Where were her parents, Lloyd and Nina, at now? Floating amongst them? Watching this funeral? Could they hear her thoughts? See her accomplishments? See her lies?

Nina looked gorgeous. Her hair had been tied up in a bun; the grays glowed under the moonlight. The cheeks were a bright red and the lips even brighter. Lloyd wore a white suit with a silver tie. His hair had been combed over; she preferred it rustled and discombobulated. This made him look too conservative. Which he definitely was not.

Janice placed one sunflower on each of their chests. Being gentle. She immediately went to nervously straightening her hair with her hands. Brent put his arm around her and Janice sunk her head into his shoulder. This brotherly love was something she'd missed around Marcel lately.

With his pants rolled up, Nelson went into the shore of the lake and pushed the flowery grave. It drifted toward the center of the hushed water.

Several minutes passed. Then something strange happened. So strange that Janice questioned if this had been a dream. The casket rose. Only a few inches at first, but then to several feet. A rogue wave? No, that's not plausible in a lake. A maelstrom? Maybe, a whirlpool would be plausible in a lake. Janice walked toward it, not caring that her feet got wet at the shore.

The casket sat still in this platform of water. No one said anything. Then the platform began to spin, swallowing up the casket. What should've seemed barbaric...wasn't. It was calm. Like slipping into a warm, fluffy bed in the chills of the winter season. Lloyd and Nina's bodies sank into the water and its platform gently flowed flat again.

Then came a burst of light. Within the surface, blue pebbles of light flew in every direction. After only seconds, they flowed naturally like part of the liquid. Janice dipped her shaky hand down into the lake and grabbed a handful of water. Little dots reflected the moon's light in her hands, like someone had sprinkled millions of pounds of glitter into the lake.

Behind her, footsteps climbed into the shore. Adam's voice said softly next to her, "We told you it was real."

Janice stared longer at patches of light in the liquid. "There have been studies of a bioluminescence phenomenon on shores of certain oceans which found micro marine creatures secrete –"

Adam placed his hands over hers. "Janice. It's real. There's a power of light all around us. That we can become a part of. Just the way Lloyd and Nina were."

She looked into the eyes of perhaps one of her most intelligent students, who seemed to be enduring his most unintelligent times. Because all the books in the world couldn't teach him how to find a strength in himself. Then again, Janice hadn't been so different. She could solve equations for the Hodge Conjecture and Riemann Hypothesis, but yet couldn't answer why she'd rather wallow in discontent than exceed in content.

"Victoria once told me: 'Perhaps you need to learn acceptance, because that is where peace really is.' I didn't understand that until now. If logic can't explain it, then there's no other choice but to accept it."

"I agree."

Then Janice reached in and kissed Adam on the lips.

The People of Bliss hadn't returned to this lake, in fear of being spotted. But for this purpose, capture was a risk worth taking. Lloyd and Nina's bodies had been laid upon a large flat surface built of twigs and leaves. There were four corners of branch handles and four men to lift them. A few people had brought torches to help see in the night sky. The evil clouds had backed away, in fear of the human entities of light, to reveal a full moon.

Brent helped lift the bodies, facing the lake. No one spoke. No one coughed. No one even shed a tear. Brent had never seen such respect for a man and his wife in all his years of political funerals. In politics, people were reminded how powerless they were, but for Lloyd and Nina they were taught how powerful they were. The People of Bliss weren't treated like workers, but as warriors that can defeat anything.

They walked toward the water. Brent barely knew the couple while they were on Earth, but like everyone else he was fascinated to see that there was more to the world than what our eyes could see.

They reached a high enough level in the waters to lay the bodies down to float. One of the men helping carry was Nelson. Brent wasn't sure of the past of his father and the Witnesses. But judging by the sadness in his eyes, they were close to his heart. Brent had seen Nelson at many political and military funerals, but his evening Nelson had a genuine face of disbelief.

Janice was handed a torch. Its flame crackled, making the only sound in the forest. Even the elements bowed their head in admiration for the fallen cocoons of light. Janice lit the bed of twigs, watching Lloyd and Nina's body ignite. The bed floated away on the gentle water. The fire element embodied their souls and the water element helped them drift into the center of the lake.

Then there were sparks of light from their bodies. And what looked like hundreds of butterflies floated into the sky. Though an unseen phenomenon, no one was frightened. The sparks drifted into the air, carried away by the wind element.

Though they were gone from human eyes, Lloyd and Nina were not gone. They were in the air the people breathed. They were in the water they drank. And they were in the flames that warmed them.

CHAPTER FORTY-ONE

Adam awoke to the sound of bacon frying and the smell of eggs. Must've been a dream. Janice's kiss must've been a dream too. It wasn't until he opened his eyes did he realize neither were.

She'd already been up, but didn't look like she slept. Her eyes focused on the mirror's reflection again, glancing down at the enormous hump over her stomach. "You're still sexy," Adam said.

Without looking behind her, she said, "Do you think it's a boy?"

"Hope so. That way I can teach him how to be a man in this world."

"Funny. I was just hoping it would be a girl so I could teach her how to be a woman in this world."

After a deep breath and long exhale, he stood up and stretched. Cuddling with Janice had been the best sleep of his life. His chin was high, back straight, and a smile lit up his face.

"Life is just so awesome!" Adam hollered and kissed Janice on the cheek. He held her from behind as they looked in the mirror. "Is that bacon and eggs I smell?"

"Cafeteria has acquired electricity and storage for food. So maybe we can have a decent meal."

"You've gotta be starving, right? You got two mouths to feed now. I'll go get us some breakfast. I bet they got cereal! Oh my God, if they have Frosted Flakes..." Adam rushed to put some jeans on.

Janice smirked, "Thank you, but I'm not hungry right now. I think I'll try to get some more sleep."

"Okay!" He gave her a peck on the lips and headed to the door.

In the hallway, it felt like a hotel. And Adam had spent plenty of time in hotels growing up. His third foster family had lost their home in the 2008 economic crash. A few doors would open and close with children rushing down to the cafeteria. "No running," Adam said trying to sound like a responsible parent. But instead he sounded like a bellhop on his first day. His squeaky voice got ignored by the kids.

He made his way to the main center of the silo, a large empty circle that went thirty floors up and two floors down. If he stared up long enough, dizziness would settle in. The facility was so big. How many people did it take to run a nuclear weapon that just sat there? Well...*did* just sit there. Now, it was gone. A strong image tried to break down Adam's wall of happiness. The image that a missile used to sit here several months ago collecting dust and had suddenly been hacked then fired. Probably killing over a million. Where had this missile hit? Detroit? Philadelphia? Was this the one that got destroyed over Washington DC? He shook off the depression. Life moves forward. And with Janice, this life had a bright light at the end of the tunnel.

Downstairs, he could hear the sizzling sound of bacon. Dozens had already started a line to the cafeteria. Adam walked briskly toward the staircase.

But it was blocked by someone crying. Royal. She sat right in the middle of the staircase with a radio on. The volume was so low, Adam couldn't hear it. He could only hear the sobs of Royal.

"Oh, hey, Royal," he said, unable to think of anything else to say. Already poor at talking to women, Adam was even worse at talking to crying women. "So what's with the waterfalls? I mean...waterworks? I can't remember the saying now."

She ignored him, her head down and buried in her arms. If Adam could pass Calculus, he could pass this conundrum. After a moment he solved the equation. "Oh, I know what this about. Okay," he took a deep breath, "I'm really sorry. I know you liked me."

Royal slowly looked up, tears soaking both her cheeks. She looked like she fell in a barrel of cut onions. "What?"

"I know you liked me. And I chose Janice. But you have to understand...me and Janice were meant to be together. You and me...I just don't think we would've worked as a couple."

After blinking several times, Royal said, "What in God's name are you talking about? I'm not crying over you, jackass."

"Oh," Adam said placing this moment in his top ten foot-in-mouth situations. "What's the problem then? I gotta get past you before breakfast gets cold."

Royal reached over to the radio and raised the volume slowly.

The radio announcer's voice sounded desperate, shocked, and overwhelmed at the same time. *"Never in all my decades of reporting have I faced such an awful issue. Is there no doubts that the gunman was Secretary of Defense Charles Declan?"*

Adam's knees got weak. He sat down closer to the radio.

The other radio announcer replied in an even more nervous voice, *"It has been confirmed by several eyewitnesses that called in the attack before the explosion. Charles Declan has never shown a history of mental illness, sadly, until this day. He opened fire on several politicians before igniting the nuclear device. If it hadn't been for Marcel Celest, thousands more could've died in the city."*

"How many have been confirmed dead?"

"We don't have an exact number, as of yet, but it's confirmed that all Union Members were present except for Marcel Celest, of course. And that Secretary Declan was killed in the explosion."

"Devastating, just devastating."

A hand reached over and clicked the radio off. It was Nelson. His hand shaky. Just months ago, it had been him, Adam, and Declan traveling alone. Adam's wall of happiness crashed to the ground like the Berlin Wall. No chance for it to ever be resurrected. He slid down and his butt hit the cold, steel staircase. "Mr. Declan's dead?"

Royal sunk her face back into her arms. What she must've been feeling to know her father had done such a terrible thing, Adam couldn't imagine. Though Declan had been his only father figure, it was nothing like the feeling of a real father. He glanced up at Nelson. The President's best friend had caused a massacre and his glazed eyes showed the blow. "Jesus Christ, Charles, how could you do such a thing?" he asked to the sky above.

Now all Adam could hear was Royal's sobs; the sound of sizzling bacon disappeared. He no longer felt hungry. Instead, he felt nauseous. Why couldn't he have had a precognition of this moment; stopped Declan before this travesty?

"You know what this means, don't you?" Nelson asked.

It looked odd to see concerned, wide eyes from a President. Presidents only showed strength. Nelson was no longer an example of strength in this moment.

"What?" Adam replied.

Nelson whispered, "It means my son is the only Union member still alive."

Trying to get past the news of Declan's death was already enough. Now, Adam had to understand what Declan's actions meant. Then it sunk in. "Oh crap. It means Marcel Celest is in charge of...everything."

To Gerard, this felt like prep school all over again. A few people sitting at a conference waiting on the student council president to show up fashionably late. But instead of a student council, it was the Union's czars. And instead of some silly unimportant class president, it was the president of...essentially the world. Marcel sure had moved up the ladder.

Gerard didn't know a majority of the people in this room and the awkward silence meant they didn't know each other either. The only familiar face was the slow-babbler General Vanderbilt. And he enjoyed the silence from that idiot.

On the conference table, he'd been given a black folder with the Union logo of a dolphin. Until now, Gerard hadn't bothered to open it, but there was nothing else to do while Marcel made his way to the meeting. The folder contained some maps and stuff that Gerard ignored. He found a memo with the header "Czars". That must've been the people sitting next to him.

Feeling immediately humble, Gerard saw his name with the title "Security Czar" first on the list. Six spots above "Military Czar - General Peter Vanderbilt." The guy at the end of the table, wearing a yamaka, must've been the Financial Czar Goldman. An older lady with one of those haircut-too-short-for-a-woman looks cleared her throat. She must've been the Health Czar because women were better at that health stuff. And she was the only woman in the room. Sitting next to her was a man that picked his nose. Yuck. Gerard wondered where he was going to put that booger.

The door opened. Marcel, balancing himself on a cane, stood at the doorway. Everyone stood. Gerard shrugged and stood up too. He didn't remember doing this in student council.

"Thank you, all," Marcel said as he walked into the room. For a man that just subjected himself to a nuclear mushroom cloud, he was in relatively great shape. Besides that walking cane. But it somehow made Marcel look more distinguished than crippled. "Take a seat. We should get started."

The first person to talk was some overweight man in a wheelchair that may have been young, but his too-lazy-to-shave face made him look older. "I'd like to start by saying that we are glad to see you have recovered nicely, Mr. Celest."

Recovered nicely. Gerard had heard those words said to Marcel so frequently that it meant little. Obviously his supernatural abilities included rapid healing. Even Marcel seemed sick of hearing those words too. "Thank you."

"The Press is overwhelmed with rumors," Nose-picker said. "It makes for a good story: a sorcerer saves the nation's capital. But so far, it's all been rumors. No proof. We should make an audio address soon."

"No," Marcel said, "not yet. I'm still regaining trust. Especially from the terrorists."

Nose-picker jotted some notes down. "Are we sure we should use the word *terrorists*?"

Vanderbilt interrupted, "But they are terrorists."

"Terrorists are people who instill terror," Nose-picker said. "I don't see the People of Bliss as people causing terror."

Gerard scoffed, "Tell that to all the people that got their head blasted off by Secretary Declan."

"But Declan wasn't a member of the People of Bliss," Nose-picker said, wiping his nose.

Before Vanderbilt could throw in an objection too, Marcel said, "I agree. They aren't terrorists. Maybe...extremists?"

"Extremists makes for a better headline," Nose-picker jotted down more notes.

Too-lazy-to-shave interrupted, "We aren't ready yet for a national audio address. Cellular towers are still down, which means we are going to have to rely on old radio towers that haven't been used in decades to relay an audio address. The technology isn't there yet."

"How long would it take?" Marcel asked, leaning back in his chair.

Too-lazy-to-shave snorted, "I don't know. A decade? We switched everything to digital signals ages ago; analog is a dated tech. I wouldn't even know where to begin. There's no way to triangulate on analog towers."

"What about heavily populated areas? That's all we really need to be working. My message would be for them, not the refugees."

"I guess we could make that happen," Too-lazy-to-shave said, wheeling his wheelchair up to the table to make notes on his pad.

"And where would we get the money for this?" Yamaka-head asked.

Marcel shrugged, "Continue with IOUs until I authorize more financial resources."

"We need to speak about health issues worldwide here, Mr. Celest," Haircut-too-short-for-a-woman said. "We used to have the aide of the World Health Organization, but most facilities didn't survive the blasts. A serious flu virus is spreading in water sources. In all my years, I've never seen such a thing."

For a while, Marcel thought this through. "How long until we find a vaccination?"

"We haven't even started the research."

Marcel looked at Nose-picker. "Let's put out a press release to every news outlet possible. Just because someone doesn't work directly for the Union, doesn't mean the work can't be done. Anyone that can figure out a vaccination for the flu will be compensated well."

The Yamaka-head raised his hand, but it got ignored. Marcel said to a man in the back of the room chewing on his nails, "We need to speak about political elections."

Nail-chewer uttered, "There's nobody left to elect, Sir."

"Then set up a voting system, sooner the better. The Union is not a dictatorship. People decide leadership, not me. I'm not changing anything about the Union's regulations."

Too-lazy-to-shave said, "We don't have a computer system to cast votes at −"

"Neither did American citizens for over two centuries," Marcel replied. "If we have to use punch cards...use them. I want the two of you to implement a new voting system."

"But, Sir −"

Marcel didn't have time for objections. "Look. I'm well aware that Secretary Charles Declan opened fire on innocent world leaders and tried to destroy the nation's capital. I'm well aware I'm the only elected politician in the Union, leaving me in charge of 143 countries. And I'm well aware that the people need to vote immediately for Second and Third Seat positions. Again, this is a democracy."

Nail-chewer said, "Actually we are not 100% positive all elected officials are dead. Russia's president is still unaccounted for, also...well, your father's location is still a mystery."

Marcel rubbed his chin. Gerard hadn't thought of this either. If his father-in-law was still alive, Nelson could technically run world politics with Marcel by his side. The thought lit up Marcel's face.

Vanderbilt had to break the silence, of course. "Actually it isn't a mystery. We know President...excuse me, *former* President Celest...is camping out with those hooligans. My informant has returned some pictures from the movements. Apparently, rumors are true that Lloyd and Nina Jacobs suffered fatal injuries during your *battle*."

His smile faded immediately. Marcel took shallow breaths. "They're dead? Oh God. I didn't mean to..."

The general interjected. "It doesn't make you a murderer, Sir. If they had sought proper treatment at one of our hospitals, they surely would've survived."

Nose-picker made some more notes, "We'll make sure to issue that statement on the newspapers."

"Yes," Marcel nodded, "I want everyone to be aware I will have no blood on my hands."

Vanderbilt handed Marcel a folder of pictures. "Here's some of the shots, Sir. These people are all stubborn and would rather continue in their primeval ways. They remind me of the filthy Kurdish forces. Something needs to be done immediately."

Unable to not be nosy, Gerard leaned over to glance. Then Marcel didn't hesitate to share the photographs with him. "Look at this one," he whispered to Gerard. "Is that –"

"Yep, that's Brent, alright," Gerard whispered. There wasn't even a flash on the camera, maybe so that the informant wouldn't be noticed taking pictures. It seemed to be at some kind of funeral by the lake.

After flipping through a few of the pictures, Marcel asked Vanderbilt, "What about my father?"

"We believe that's him," the general said pointing at one of the photographs. "In the gray tie."

Marcel squinted his eyes. Gerard looked closer over his shoulder. With one quick glance up, it confirmed Gerard's suspicion that Vanderbilt was slightly jealous of Marcel's visible kinship to Gerard. "Yep, that's your dad. He's got a beard, but it's definitely him."

"Haven't seen him in a beard since Mom died," Marcel

commented.

Hearing a sense of melancholy in his voice, Gerard decided to give a friendly pat on Marcel's shoulder. He then smiled at Vanderbilt's envious smirk. The general reached over and pulled out another photograph from his folder. "Oh, how could I forget?" He said it in this fake concerned tone. "We found your sister Janice."

Both Marcel and Gerard grabbed for the picture at the same time, but Vanderbilt took care of sliding it on the table for both to see.

It was definitely Janice. And it was definitely her kissing another man. Gerard felt weak; he slid back into his seat. There were suspicions of his wife's infidelity. But just that...suspicions. And often suspicions were easier to deal with than truths. He felt sick, his stomach knotted like a pretzel. How could she? Why? With their child in her womb?

"Oh my goodness," Vanderbilt said in that Oscar-worthy performance of sympathy, "I forgot, Gerard. That's your wife, isn't it? Such a shame."

Janice was kissing Adam, that college kid he had hunted before the missiles hit. Some sap that had been involved with Servo Clementia. Gerard imagined what he would do to Adam if he'd been in the room. Maybe set him on fire, punch him several times, then piss on him...in that order.

Marcel stared at the photograph longer than Gerard had.

Vanderbilt said, "Our informant is finally ready to turn over the leader of these *People of Bliss*. When we capture her, we can get the information on the location of your father and make her an example of the Union's intolerance for this movement. We can kill two birds with one stone."

Gerard grumbled, "Did you know animal murder is a sign of a serial killer?"

Vanderbilt smirked at him then turned to Marcel. "Sir?"

Marcel said nothing, just kept staring at the photograph.

"Sir? We need authorization," the general said.

Marcel still said nothing.

"Sir?"

Then Marcel shook like he'd just been awoken. "A capture?"

The sense of hesitation was enough for Gerard to pounce in. Anything to take the opposite side of the general. "It's crazy. That would be a direct attack on her freedom of speech. It's not a message the Union should be sending out after just taking down Lloyd and Nina."

"I agree," Marcel nodded. "Gerard's right."

Hearing *Gerard's right* sent a shiver up his spine. Vanderbilt didn't appreciate the opposition. "Well, I'm sorry to hear that," he muttered. "Sirius Dawson would've been an easy catch."

Marcel sat up. "Her name is Sirius Dawson? Who is she? What do you know about her?"

Even Gerard was taken aback by the news of the leader's name that been held secret since her first radio address. "Marcel, you know who she is? Remember the CNN reporter? The red head with the big knockers?"

After rubbing his chin for a moment, Marcel said, "Oh...her."

"Brent had the hots for her. Remember? He's crazy about her. The last thing I recall was she and him were an item. Very *close* item," Gerard said.

Marcel stared at the photograph of Brent in the woods. Gerard wished he could read his mind. A plan was forming in there; he could tell because Marcel liked to chew his lip deviously. "Okay, General, you have my authorization to capture the known-terrorist Sirius Dawson." Before Gerard could blurt out an objection, Marcel intervened. "I've made my decision. Make sure the People of Bliss know we have her. Especially my brother. Make sure he's the first to find out."

Vanderbilt smiled widely, "Yes, Sir."

"We have to make Sirius' voice even stronger," Brent said.

Nelson batted away some tree branches in his way with one foot. He'd had these types of conversations while on walks around the White House. A political voice could be powerful, but not enough to downplay a world leader. Especially one in the position of Marcel. "Rhetoric can only go so far, son."

"Yes, until it reaches the point of a war."

Their stroll in the woods stopped. Nelson turned slowly to Brent. "You too? For God's sakes, Brent, this is your brother we're talking about."

"Maybe Adam is right. We need to have a war against the Union. But we need more followers."

"Sirius is too ill to continue her weekly radio addresses."

Brent grumbled. It might've been out-of-line to bring up such a delicate subject. His son loved that girl. True love that he hadn't sensed ever from Brent. "I'm sorry. We should just concentrate on taking care of each other. And then..."

"Then what?" Brent's hands went up in the air. "Hide forever? We've got no clear plan here, Dad. Sirius is just continuing the vocal animosity against the Union, but how long will people wait before there's action? Maybe Declan did a good thing. The Union has definitely shrunk. They're weak as hell now."

"Murdering a bunch of innocent people is never a good thing."

They stayed quiet. Father-son quarrels like this never ended with a resolution. Not with Brent anyways. Nelson couldn't say the same for his other boy. Marcel always found a resolution between them. How was it possible he brought two completely different individuals into this world? Victoria would be at odds about whose side to take, just as much as Nelson was.

Then there was the sound of whimpering. It echoed throughout the dark overhead trees. Nelson didn't even realize how far they had ventured into the forest. Brent even seemed concerned. "Shit, I forgot which way we were heading."

While Brent searched the clouded night sky for the North Star, Nelson searched for the source of the whimpering sound. "Hello?" The sound stopped. "Someone up there?" Nelson said to the crowded batch of trees. It was so dark his eyes couldn't focus up there. Tree branches twined around each other tightly. Only after a moment did the shapes start to make some sense.

There was a structure caught up in the trees. "Hello?" he asked again.

"Go away," a familiar voice said. It was Adam. That man climbed more trees than a monkey.

"Adam, I can't see. Where are you?" Nelson demanded.

Then the structure started to make more sense. It was a vehicle. Nelson could see wheels. A van? A car? No. Something bigger. He could see long blades with vines wrapped around it. "Is that...is that a helicopter?"

Brent squinted. "Holy shit. It's a chopper."

"Yeah," Adam whined from the inside of the vehicle. "This is nothing. I found a Starbucks sign in the westside trees and a Hummer in those southend trees."

With arms crossed, Brent said, "Dad, you think it still works?"

"Maybe," Nelson replied optimistically.

"We could get it down. Let me get some more guys out here. I know the way back."

Now they were agreeing on a plan. "Good idea. I'll climb up there."

Nelson hadn't climbed a tree since junior high school. But it should've been like riding a bike. After the first ten feet of ascent, he quickly realized it wasn't. He clung on to a branch wondering where to go next.

"Step on that branch by your left foot," Adam said above. Even though it was pitch black outside, the kid still had great vision. Nelson listened as Adam walked him through every step of the climb. When he was finally inside the chopper, he collapsed in the backseat. His arms began that tingling, weak feeling that men his age get after a vigorous workout.

"Good job, Mr. President," Adam whispered from the passenger seat. His legs were curled up to his chest.

After catching his breath, Nelson climbed into the pilot's seat. It felt like it had been just as long of a time climbing into the pilot's seat as it had been climbing that tree. A refreshing boost of power came over Nelson. The memories of flying flooded his head like a movie montage. A pleasant movie.

"You used to fly, huh? In the Air Force?" Adam whimpered.

"Yep." Nelson smiled, touching the wheel and throttle. He glanced over at Adam, whose cheeks glimmered wet even in the darkness. "Why were you crying?"

"Crying? Crying! Nope, you're mistaken. I was humming a song."

Nelson only wished politicians lied as poorly as Adam; then his job as President would've been a cinch. "Is it about Charlie?"

Adam looked out the window. "You guys were friends for a long time, right? Doesn't it seem just...weird that Mr. Declan did that?"

"Not in these times."

"Are you sad he's gone?"

Nelson didn't know how to answer that. His and Declan's last conversation hadn't gone well. And the man he knew had turned into a madman when nuclear weapons destroyed the United States. In fact, every man had turned into a madman. Though he didn't condone Declan's actions, he did somehow understand the frustrations the government put many people through. "Yes, Adam. I am. But I like to focus on the good memories. It helps. Try it."

Adam wiped his nose with a tissue. "Well, there was that one time Mr. Declan went to my Judo competition when I was seventeen. I remember there was this one guy from the audience who laughed at me when I tripped onto the fight mat. He shouted out, 'Pussy kid!' I saw Mr. Declan grasp the guy by the arm and take him to the back alleyway of the gym. After the competition, when we left, I seen the guy with cotton balls in his nose to stop the bleeding. Mr. Declan had beat the shit out of him! That was the first time he felt like a dad to me. He was the only one who seemed to *try* to act like a father."

"A proper father doesn't raise his kid to be so violent. A proper father teaches his kid how to handle situations with words first."

Adam nodded. "Yeah, I guess so. I wouldn't know. I've been on my own for so long." He shrugged and tried to wipe his nose again, using a little edge of the mucus-soaked tissue.

Been on his own. Nelson suddenly felt overwhelmingly miserable for Adam. Always surrounded by family, Nelson couldn't relate to the loneliness. Besides Brent and Declan, Adam had no one else. No one that knew of his existence anyway. What would that be like?

From his back pocket, Nelson pulled out a handkerchief. "Better clean up those tears before Brent shows up with some of the other guys."

"Yes...Sir."

The way Adam called him *Sir* sounded like the way Marcel called him *Sir*. Did Adam see him as a father? Like some kind of leadership presence that he badly needed?

He handed Adam the handkerchief. "Thanks."

Nelson twiddled his fingers, only noticing at that moment that Adam was twiddling his fingers too. They sat in silence for so long that Nelson wished Brent would hurry back with that crew of guys to bring down the chopper from the trees. "Listen, Adam. Just...you know...don't make it...weird."

"I understand," Adam spat out quickly.

"If you want...when we get this thing down...maybe I can show you how to fly it."

"Sure!" Adam spat out quickly again.

They both twiddled fingers for even longer. Minutes passed, but it felt like hours. Nelson scrunched up his face. As President, he set an example for as many people as possible. There's no reason those actions should cease. Adam needed a father image in his life.

He sighed. "Okay. Fine. You can call me *it*."

Adam reached quickly past the helicopter controls and gave Nelson a tight bear hug around the chest. He had to admit, it was a welcome hug.

"Thanks, *Dad*," Adam whispered.

Destiny isn't determined by what emotions you

create, but by what emotions you leave behind.

-*Victoria Celest*

CHAPTER FORTY-TWO

Sweat. The kind that not only stuck to the skin but also just made her feel more disgusting. Sirius awoke in a bed of it. She had suffered flus, but nothing like this. A regular flu virus didn't want its host dead. This one did. Years of being a reporter told her to trust her instinct. And there it was. The great Sirius Dawson would succumb to a head cold. "Goddamnit," she sighed.

Her bones begged her not to stand up, but she did anyway. It was the middle of the night. The time when even late-nighters were sound asleep. She heard Brent snore gently beside her. There had been so many nights she stared at him while he slept. Some people would think that's creepy, but she just couldn't help it. It was like the first time she went inside the White House and stood in the Oval Office. This fusion of luck and admiration combined into one. That was Brent Celest. How could she be so lucky?

A series of coughs made her throat feel on fire. All this hacking every night must have created immunity in Brent because he continued to snore. Either that or his work last night with getting that helicopter on the ground tired him out.

Why did this virus only attack some but not all? Not that she wanted Brent to get sick, but certainly it didn't seem fair an organism smaller than the tip of a needle would take her down.

The heat resonated from her throat to the rest of her body. She stood and guzzled a liter of water. Her extra-large T-shirt and sweat pants stuck to her body. Maybe a shower would cool her off.

With the slightest steps, she snuck past him and left their room. In the hallway, the lights were dim. The missile silo always made these noises. A *ding* here or a *bang* there. The pipes sounded like someone kept dropping pennies down it. She walked towards the locker area, but suddenly felt like it would be rude to awaken everyone on the floor with a cold shower. But the heat on her body had to be cooled.

The lake. It was one of those thoughts that made sense in so many ways, there was no questioning it. A dip in the lake would be magical. The water must be freezing, which made it all the more inviting.

Removing her flip-flops to not make any more noise, she crept toward the front entrance one story above. There were a few ideas that came to her about how to convince the door watchman to let her outside. Maybe be authority. *I'm Sirius Dawson, and if it wasn't for me there would be no movement, so I demand you open this door!* No, she'd probably cough through most of the speech and the watchman wouldn't understand her. She could show some leg then, like some hitchhiker flirting her way to a free ride. Then Sirius remembered she hadn't shaven her legs in weeks. When she'd cuddle with Brent, there was no telling which leg hair was hers or his.

Lucky for her, the watchman was sleeping. His head was cocked against the stool he's supposed to be sitting on. Drool crept down the side of his beard.

With just a few twists of the enormous knob on the door that looked like it steered a pirate ship, she got the door to swing open. The watchman didn't even wake up either. Sending the men out to haul down a 6,000 pound chopper from the tree was a good idea; it put them all into this baby-like sleep.

She went out into the cold air. It helped cool down her fever, but only a little. That lake was the answer. Sirius walked for what seemed like three hundred feet before seeing a glimpse of the lake. And also sensing this eerie feeling like someone was watching. She stopped and turned around. Maybe it was reporter intuition; whatever the feeling was, she couldn't shake it away. Someone else was out here.

Now that regret settled in. How could she be so stupid to be wandering outside alone?

"Sirius?" someone said.

She gasped and grabbed her chest. It was Willie. "Jesus, you scared me."

"Why you out here, doll?"

She walked toward him. He sat on a rock near the edge of the lake. There were pebbles in his hand. "I had to cool off. Mind if I take a dip?"

He nodded. "Yeah, go ahead. Don't worry about me."

Sirius didn't. She knew Willie's homosexuality made him a safe man to get undressed in front of. Dipping in her toes already felt invigorating. She started to strip off her shirt to reveal her bra. The lake still had those beads of light that Lloyd and Nina left behind. They were mesmerizing. "So, you can't sleep either?"

"I like to toss pebbles at night. Reminds me of the days when me and my man used to go out camping. He taught me how to do this. Watch."

While Sirius got undressed and completely submerged herself into the water, Willie tossed three pebbles at the same time. Each one bounced six times before sinking. "That's so cool."

Sirius paused for a moment. "That's so cool," she repeated. It was her voice. Even Willie noticed it. Her voice was no longer raspy.

She took a deep breath through her nose. No longer was it clogged with mucus or made that weird *wizzy* sound. Her sinuses were clear. Willie stood up. "It's the water. Sirius, check it out!"

All around her, the beads of light were brighter. She could suddenly swallow without tasting some kind of nasty glob. "It's curing the flu," Sirius whispered. "Oh my God. The lake is, like, healing me."

Willie's mouth dropped. "We gotta tell the others."

Sirius hurried out of the lake and threw on her clothes. It was like waking up from the perfect dream and the perfect night of sleep. She felt invigorated. The thought of seeing everyone who was on the verge of flu death rush out here to be cured by stepping into the lake – Sirius couldn't feel more lucky.

She rushed and gave Willie a big hug. He laughed. "It's like the Mets won another World Series!" he screamed triumphantly.

Then Sirius covered her mouth and screamed in fear. Someone was standing in the trees staring at them. Willie turned.

The dark figure had his arms crossed and eyes wide.

"Pedro?" Sirius asked.

It was her ex-cameraman. The poor Hispanic man's language barrier caused him to go so un-noticed, forgotten, and possibly bullied. Pedro's face had a glimmer of the moon's light hitting it. He looked terrified. Slowly, he walked toward them.

No words were said. He reached over to Sirius' left cheek and kissed it gently.

The kiss. A reminder of an old story. A traitor's kiss that sent a Messiah to his grave. Was this that look of betrayal? Kind yet angry. Bitter yet thankful. Sad yet happy. She stared into Pedro's eyes. Her luck had finally ended.

He whispered, "I am...so...sorry."

Flashlights and searchlights lit up the area. Dozens of armed Union Keepers surrounded Sirius and Willie.

"Down on the ground!"

"Hands in the air!"

"No sudden movements!"

Willie panicked; he shoved Sirius behind him in the way of the gun's red lasers. She cried and screamed, burying her face into his shoulders.

Guns pointed at them from every direction. Pedro tripped and fell as he scurried away. "I am sorry!" he exclaimed in a sorrowful tone.

"You're not taking her!" Willie yelled to the armed men. They closed their circle.

Sirius thought of diving into the lake. But where would she go? Union Keepers had the lake surrounded. There was no escape.

Not for her anyway. She wiped her tear on the back of Willie's shirt. "Okay," she whispered to him, "here's what we are going to do. *You* are going back to the silo and telling the followers about the lake."

"By myself?" Willie asked. "Not happening."

The armed men moved closer. "We said hands on the ground, goddamnit!"

Sirius continued, "They won't shoot us or they would've done it already. Marcel Celest knows if we get killed, we become martyrs and he's got a bigger threat on his hands." She took a deep breath. "See the Tasers on their hips? They'll use them if we try to run. Think you can handle the electricity?"

"Yeah, but I'm not leaving you. You're the voice of this rebellion. They'll take us both then."

"Willie, please. If they take us both, the followers won't know about the lake. You have to go to them. The Union only wants me. Just get out of here. *Please*," she whispered into his shoulder. His breaths began to calm down. It was confirmation enough for her. Willie agreed to the plan. "Go!"

She pushed him and he ran. Just as expected, the Union Keepers fired their Tasers at her. Sirius cried in pain as all the nerves in her body seized and she fell to the ground.

Willie made it past a few of the Union Keepers before they fired their Tasers. Miraculously, the bolt traveling through the wires to his skin bounced back and sent the Union Keepers into seizures.

"What the fuck? Take that guy down!"

"It's not working on him!"

"Take him down!"

A few of the Union Keepers ran after Willie while most stayed behind to surround Sirius. "Don't move!" Like she could.

From one of their walkie-talkies, she could hear another Union Keeper. "*I'm telling you, this guy is a fucking ox. He won't stay down.*"

Then another Union Keeper came on the line. "*We lost him! Where did he go!*"

"Fuck him. We got Sirius Dawson."

Sirius took a deep breath. That was right. The Union had finally caught her. Months of hate speech against the Union on radio stations wasn't going to buy Sirius a trip to a day spa. Maybe prison. She prayed just prison.

They threw her in the van. Sirius' head clanked against the wall, leaving her moaning. The doors shut behind her before there was a moment to tell the Union Keepers to go fuck themselves. Her head ached not only from the abuse but also the hundreds of volts of electricity that had been shot through her.

Inside the van was pitch black. Thinking she was alone, Sirius mumbled to herself, "Okay. This sucks."

"That it does," a voice said behind her.

She turned and started flailing her legs to kick. Up sometimes late at night and watching cheesy horror movies, Sirius would question why the girls always kicked. Now in this situation she understood. Confinement makes a woman's mind kick into survival mode. Her attacks and screams, of course, were useless. The attacker laughed, "You are a fighter."

What felt like a bee sting on her arm was a needle. Immediately her head spun and heart rate slowed.

"That should calm you down a bit," the weirdo said. His voice was low even though there was no need to be quiet. "I do recognize you. From the news. What's your name, young heroine?"

"Sirius. Sirius Dawson." Normally she wouldn't have said her name like that. But something in this shot made her feel loopy and unable to control her words. Like some sort of truth serum.

The man's face began to appear thanks to the little moonlight peeking through the window. He was bald, tall, and older with this slight grin. "I'm General Vanderbilt. Nice to finally meet you. You know, I dreamed about you. But you're not what I imagined. I saw you as a flawless blonde incarnation of Chilonis." He slid his finger across her facial scar. As much as she wanted to pull away and bite him, the needle's concoction kept her too weak. "But you aren't flawless. Are you, sweetie?"

Sirius didn't know who Chilonis was. Her face must've showed confusion because Vanderbilt answered.

"You have no idea who she is? Do you? I find history so intriguing. Because it's knowledge that people choose to ignore. If you'd paid attention to past revolutionaries...then maybe you wouldn't have been caught." The general lit up a cigar; the stench immediately stung Sirius' nostrils. "Chilonis led a war against her ex-husband General Cleonymus. Did you know that she wore a noose around her neck as the Spartans began their rebellion? Do you know why?" He gave Sirius a moment, like she actually had the strength to answer the question. Then he said, "Because she would have rather hung herself than return to her ruthless husband's rule. Perhaps, Miss Dawson, you should've worn a noose around your neck, huh?"

Her heart rate tried to escalate but was quickly calmed by the medication. She mumbled because words couldn't escape. Anywhere would've been better than here. Being on top of that building again as a nuclear weapon devastated the world around her would have been a more ideal situation. At least there was a chance of surviving. What were they going to do to her? The Union's biggest threat was now in their hands. And in the hands of possibly the most odd man in the Union.

"Shhh," the general said as he wiped away the sweaty hair from her face, "It's okay. The time to kill yourself already came and gone. Oh! Don't worry...we won't kill you. In 1859, John Brown was hung by the state of Virginia for trying to bring about a liberation of African Americans. It just caused a larger uprising and eventually the Civil War. So, no way will we let you become a martyr. In fact, I tell you what –" He turned and banged on the wall where the driver was. The vehicle stopped and the wobbling through the forest ceased. "How about we give you a chance to end this?"

Sirius' tongue felt swollen. She chewed on the side of her lip. Mucus flowed out of her nose. "End this?" she mumbled.

"Yes, Miss Dawson, end this. You see, we have a problem that's even bigger than you. Any idea what that could be?"

After a deep breath, Sirius forced the words out. "My followers." This serum made truthful words so easy to say.

"That's right. Your followers. How about you save us the trouble? We've been wandering these woods for days and days. Even Pedro couldn't give us any clue. Your men did an excellent job of hiding any tracks. But where did all those thousands go? Where are your followers, Miss Dawson?"

Her eyes widened and head shook. Sirius fought this internal craving to just say it. Just say that there's thousands of people hiding in an underground silo, not even a mile away. But then it would be the end of the movement. The Union would win.

The silence made Vanderbilt give a long frustrated sigh. "Oh, come on now. Don't fight the sodium pentothal. It's so much easier to just give in. Wouldn't it save you so much trouble?"

She bit her tongue. Hard. Blood poured out her mouth. Vanderbilt lazily pulled out a napkin and wiped the blood carefully. "Fine. We have other means of getting the information out of you. Let's make a visit to the building site of the Union castle. I hear there's a basement being built which, ironically, used to be a torture chamber. The workers there tell me you can't even hear a single scream in there." He banged on the wall. The vehicle turned on and rumbled again through the woods.

Through a mouthful of blood, Sirius whispered, "Give it your best shot."

"Oh, I will, Miss Dawson. I will."

CHAPTER FORTY-THREE

Everything made Brent angry. Like all these selfish pricks rushing into the lake to get their magical cure of the flu – instead of being concerned their leader had been taken by Union Keepers. Or the night watchman that fell asleep last night and let Sirius leave the facility unattended. Even Willie abandoning the scene instead of fighting to the death to make sure Sirius hadn't been arrested made Brent want to punch him.

"Brent?"

What were they doing to Sirius? Beating her? Raping her?

"Brent?"

"What?" he mumbled to the voice behind him.

Poor Adam's attempt at not sounding nervous made him sound nervous. "I'm trying to –"

"Trying to *what?* Who left *you* in charge? No one. Because no one trusts an ex-addict who tries to act like he knows what he's doing!"

Immediately, Brent took a deep breath but the regret didn't go away. It lingered like a bruise. Adam just looked down. Making an apology seemed more difficult than the time they climbed Mount Logan. "Listen, Adam, I'm just –"

"Don't bother. I know how you get when you're angry. And this time I think you got the right to be. We let the voice of the rebellion get taken."

They stared at the lake for several minutes. Its water reminded him of the Green Pond in New Jersey. Sometimes he and Adam would go fishing there. They never caught anything, but it was a nice feeling to just have a friend. A friend that understood him and never judged his decisions. In fact, Adam trusted his decisions time and time again. Even something as drastic as Brent's decision to incapacitate his own brother Marcel.

Adam scrunched his face. "You remember when we met?"

"Yeah. A few months after Mom died."

"Mr. Declan was thrilled when you accepted the chance to join the Servo Clementia. I should've been jealous when we met. The President's son, rich boy, entrepreneur, gets ladies whenever he wants...I just *wasn't*. We just understood each other."

"And I appreciate your friendship all these years."

Adam placed his hands in his pockets and used his shoes to kick around a rock on the ground. "Mr. Declan had this whole basic training planned out in the fields. It felt like we were training a quarterback, not an assassin." Adam smiled at the memory. Maybe feeling it was an improper response, he cleared his throat. "Remember how pissed off you were that day? Remember why?"

"Yep. I sat in fucking traffic. Was two hours late. Goddamn retards caused an accident in the tunnel."

"That's right. And I remember you just performed so...I don't know...poorly. You couldn't get the number of pulls-ups high enough. Instead of the six mile run, you did two. The pole vault was a disaster. Shit, I did better than you. And I was just your backup."

"What's the point?" Brent snapped.

"After that day was finished, you still were griping about the damn traffic jam. I mean...you just couldn't let go. The *past* is your problem. You can't fix it...and it pisses you off. It ruins the *present*. You don't think straight."

Children ran into the water next to them. The little brats were laughing and tossing around an inflatable ball. Like this was a time to celebrate or something.

This conversation was a waste of time. Sirius could be hours from here. And they were no closer to a lead. Brent rubbed the spot between his nose and mouth. "Sirius is gone. Can we just stick to what we know?"

"Well, we know she's not dead. Surely, that would've been all over the radios by now to scare us," Adam said, speaking loudly over the children's laughter.

Brent thought of Lloyd and Nina's casket floating on this very lake. It made him cringe. But then he imagined Sirius inside a casket. "We don't know they won't kill her. Maybe they're just buying time. If people hadn't let her out last night –"

Adam snapped. "Focus, brother. There's nothing we can do about the mistakes that were made last night. Nothing. But what we can do is come up with a plan to get her back."

The inflatable ball landed near Brent. He yanked out a blade and popped it. The burst made the kids back up and stop laughing. They had those same innocent looks on their faces like Adam. As though they were doing nothing wrong. And that Brent was the enemy. He hollered, "Get lost, you little fuckers!"

They ran like shots had been fired. Adam scratched the back of his head and watched the deflated ball sink into the lake. "I'll fix that later, I guess."

"It's a goddamn ball, Adam. They can get another one."

"I wasn't talking about the ball. I was talking about the kids."

Whatever that meant, Brent didn't need to hear it. No one was making him feel like the bad guy here. Especially his best friend. He crossed his arms and changed the subject before he said something that would make Adam never talk to him again. "We don't know where she is."

"But there is someone who will."

Hope made Brent's back straighten up and his morale raise. He scanned the horizon. "Pedro. That bastard knows where she is."

"That's right. Maybe we could –" Before Adam could finish the sentence, Brent was already storming back up the hill. "Hey, I tell you what. Let's do this together. Just like old times when we tracked targets."

Brent stopped walking. He thought about this for a moment. They were such a good team, why not get his help? But that feeling in his gut objected. Adam might slow him down, always planning instead of acting. Something like this had to be done aggressively. Brent felt the wrath in him flutter up his spine. It was ready for a kill. It had been so long since he experienced ending a life. A life that so desperately needed to end. And Pedro certainly needed an end. A very brutal end.

"No," Brent said, "I do this alone."

Adam squinted his eyes. "You plan on coming back, right?"

Brent didn't answer and went inside the silo entrance to pack his essentials. A long journey lied ahead of him.

Brent made Adam promise to keep his endeavor a secret. Knowing his best friend, that secret wouldn't stay bottled up for long. It would eventually slip out. So Brent decided to leave the People of Bliss at midnight when everyone was dead asleep, even though he had told Adam he'd leave in the morning. Lies were useful at times like these. Otherwise, Adam would've tried to convince Brent to stay longer.

Snores could be heard down the hallways as he left his room. He peeked through Adam's open door to see him sleeping and cuddling with Janice. It was pleasant to see his sister and best friend in this position. Maybe someday Adam could be his brother-in-law. Would be a much better choice than Gerard, in Brent's opinion. He shut the door quietly.

At the exit of the silo, the damn watchman was asleep again. These people were idiots. He slipped past him and out the door.

Tracking Pedro wasn't going to be difficult. The terrain had been damaged by Doomsday missiles, so there was really only one road here. In or out.

Janice had left a vehicle on the outskirts of the woods. It didn't have much fuel supposedly, but Brent had a plan for that. Used vegetable oil, supplied by the silo's cafeteria, should suffice until he made it to the destination.

Philadelphia is approximately 50 miles. He'd have to drive slowly in order not to burn out the engine with this oldie-but-goodie technique of running a car without gasoline. It would take six hours and maybe an hour to find where he assumed Pedro had gone. Sirius had spoken about her former cameraman several times. Little did she know, the Hispanic prick would eventually betray her. She had mentioned he used to live in a very dangerous part of town. So dangerous, she never liked to visit. It was called Camden. Though, there might not be much of it left – that may work to Brent's advantage. Less places to search meant Pedro should be easy to find.

The further away he went from the silo, the more anxious he became. There was much being left behind. Not only Adam, but Janice and even his dad. Just when it was starting to feel like a family again, this had to happen. Sirius had to be taken. And now the family was apart again.

As he climbed up a large hill toward the road, lugging this heavy backpack and keg full of vegetable oil, he reflected on his family. Suddenly, the thought of Victoria entered his mind. His mother had been haunting him lately. Ever since the funeral for Lloyd and Nina.

On that night, Lloyd had floated with his wife on the still water. Brent realized he'd never seen a dead body. Not for anyone he actually cared about. The day his mother Victoria died, Brent had been the only visitor in the back of the church. A mantle had been set up with a jar of her remains. Everyone waited in line to say a silent prayer for the First Lady. But not Brent. He sat the entire sermon in the furthest seat. That day, Janice came up to him and whispered, "Don't you want to say goodbye?" His answer had been colder than winter morning. He said, "Why bother? I already know she's dead." Janice hadn't talked to him for months afterwards. How could he have been so cruel?

Janice's car was exactly where she left it, covered in a thick layer of ashes from the never-ending barrage of nasty weather. Brent tossed down his backpack and supplies, feeling a large weight lifted from his shoulders.

After catching his breath, he used a towel to begin wiping off the car. Besides the soot, the car was in pretty decent shape. He placed his supplies in the backseat and guzzled the first container of water. The silo's water still had this lead taste to it, but much better than the feces taste of sewer water.

Just as expected, the keys were in the ignition. His sister always had that habit. When they were teenagers, Brent would steal her car all the time and go out drinking. The way he saw it, it was better to wreck her car than his. He was such a shitty brother; how could she love him so much?

After letting the car warm up for a bit, he looked out the side window. He could return back to the silo. Maybe Adam was right and they could do it together. Janice and Nelson would be devastated he left. Why not just bring the entire team along to find Sirius?

Brent laid his head on the steering wheel and took a deep breath. A reporter had once asked him what it was like being the "black sheep" of the Celest family. He keyed the reporter's car later that night. But what was it like? Brent looked back in the direction of the silo. Being the black sheep meant making tough decisions.

He pulled the car onto the road and began his journey to find Pedro.

Nestled between a liquor store and what used to be a Burger King was Pedro's apartment building. It hadn't been hard to figure out. Philadelphia had been practically flattened and so had the neighboring city of Camden. So when Brent had questioned the local refugees if a black Union SUV was traveling here recently, the answers were clear. I-676 no longer had traffic jams and seeing a vehicle driving around was hard to miss. Someone had described a *pescado* on the side of the vehicle. Which translated to a *fish*. Brent quickly realized that it was the dolphin logo on the side of the Union's vehicle. Pedro had hitched a ride. He just had to figure out where the Union Keepers dumped the traitor off at.

And the locals led him here. Pedro was well-known in this city. Some called him the *el soplón*, which meant the snitch. Seemed like a good title. Thank God for those years of lessons in Spanish or else Brent might've not made it this far. Jersey Hispanics always admired a white man that can converse with them so easily.

There was a light on upstairs. His assassin instinct kicked in. It was definitely Pedro up there. Brent secured his gun on his belt. That gun had cost him a trade of the car. And it only had one bullet. Bartering didn't seem fair around here, but Brent only needed one bullet.

It was three stories up to Pedro's apartment. The stairs would be something he'd be watching. So Brent took the easy way up via a fire escape ladder. As he climbed, visions stabbed his mind. Lloyd and Nina's casket floating on the lake. Their closed eyes that would never open again. The sunflowers representing so much death. Brent shook his head. Not the time to think about a funeral.

Dressed in his familiar white black suit for mobility, he climbed up onto the cat walk and kept his steps so light that a crow continued to preen its feathers as though no one was behind it. Pedro's apartment had a broken window; air seeped out of it, making a whistling noise. Brent peered through the window into Pedro's apartment. An assassin would never take such a chance of being caught, but he was out of options.

The Latino prick sat with his back to the window, staring at something on a dinner table. Whatever it was sat in a briefcase next to a bowl of half-eaten spaghetti. By his side, an oscillating fan blew air in all directions. It was ice cold outside – why on earth would Pedro need a fan? Unless he had that uncontrollable sweat. The sweat that even Brent had experienced when stress wreaked havoc on your mind and body.

Brent pulled his hand through the shattered glass and unlocked the window. This took guts. The window could creak when it opened. But thankfully the oscillating fan made enough noise that Pedro didn't even turn.

One foot at a time, Brent entered the apartment. Pedro stood so still, it might've been a mannequin. Tiptoeing kept the floors from making a sound. He reached for the gun and cocked it.

All those sunflowers.

Brent shook his head. Again, Lloyd's casket distracted him. He moved forward and pressed the barrel of the gun to Pedro's skull. Pedro still didn't move.

Brent whispered in Spanish, "Where did they take Sirius?"

Pedro trembled then began to sniffle. "She loved you. *You.* Not me. It didn't matter what I looked like, what I did for her." His Spanish stuttered the more he cried.

Inside the briefcase were stacks of cash. Brent said, "Looks like you did enough."

"All this and I don't know what I'm supposed to do with it. I'm still not happy."

This wasn't a trip to make an episode of *Dr. Phil* with Pedro. He wanted answers. So Brent repeated, "Where is Sirius?"

"A castle. In Far Rockaway."

Of course. The Celest family took a trip there once. Long before they became America's favorite political family. "Why?" Brent asked.

Tears plopped onto the useless dollar bills.

"Why?" Brent repeated, pushing the barrel more into Pedro's head. The Latino didn't seem fazed. Not even scared. Did he welcome death just as much as Brent had?

"They will kill you if you go there."

"I know," Brent admitted. Then he repeated, "Why did they send her there?"

"Torture chamber," Pedro said.

The thought made Brent's lip quiver. He heard imaginary screams of Sirius in pain. What were they doing to her?

"Please do it. Please. If you don't, somebody else will."

It took Brent a moment to realize what Pedro meant. He meant the trigger. All Brent had to do was pull the trigger and end Pedro's suffering. The man was ready to die. And Brent should've been obliged to do it. But why did his finger tremble over the trigger button?

The sunflowers.

So many lives lost. Lloyd, Nina, Declan... People he cared about were gone. Murder didn't seem so odd in a world full of it. It lost the thrill and had been replaced with guilt. Then Brent felt something he hadn't felt before a kill. Sympathy. It didn't seem right to pull the trigger and end Pedro's measly existence. How many times had he been in this position? Watching someone sniffle and beg for forgiveness? Why did this routine get tougher, not easier? He understood why Pedro was so angry and why his anger turned into one of his worst decisions.

Brent placed the gun down gently on the table, next to the bowl of ice cold spaghetti. "There's only one bullet. I'm going to walk downstairs and head out to save Sirius. Either use that bullet for me or for you."

Two men with not much to live for stayed quiet. Brent walked to the front door and opened it. He stepped into the hallway to the smell of pot and booze. The stairs twisted down like a spiral. He walked slow, unsure what fate had decided yet. Was Pedro going to come running after him, firing the weapon? Or was Pedro going to put the barrel in his mouth and fire it? Maybe the third choice could happen...Pedro may do neither and finish his spaghetti.

Brent made it back outside into the bitter cold. The calm crow, preening its feathers, flew away rapidly at the sound of the gun shot. Upstairs, Brent could hear Pedro's dead body crash onto the ground.

He placed his hands in his pockets to keep them warm. So much death. He just had to make sure Sirius didn't die this day too.

CHAPTER FORTY-FOUR

For a news reporter to be shackled with handcuffs to a desk meant that serious lines had been crossed. Sirius had always been a careful reporter in her days on the field chasing stories for CNN. So she never experienced that cold metal restricting her movement. She also never experienced so many cold eyes staring at her, begging her to try an escape so they can have an excuse to shoot her.

It was humid air; the mist outside had snuck through the many unfinished holes of the castle, leaving the situation even more unpleasant. She was on the top floor, before reaching the castle's roof. Sirius was sure of it because she only fought the Union Keepers for five flights of stairs before deciding to become more difficult and let them drag her up four more flights. They gave her the most uncomfortable metal chair, where she had been sitting for nearly three hours she assumed. Time had no meaning when its end was looming. They also never offered food or water.

Many years before, Sirius had done a story on torture in Ukraine. The story had such an impact that the Ukrainian Government backed away from the inhumane practices. But another lesson had been taught by that story – Sirius learned that the first stages of torture mirrored this exact situation she was in. The starvation and dehydration were meant to weaken the body, the constant ticking of the clock were to weaken the mind, and the continuous stares weakened the soul.

A bald man walked in, carrying a briefcase. He had a special uniform, a step up from the other Union-keeper uniforms. He sat down across from Sirius. "I'm General Vanderbilt. And I'm going to get the location of the rebels from you tonight."

"Well, let me think. Um, no way."

Vanderbilt smirked and curved his eyebrows, like being told the Earth was flat. "You familiar with the Oculus software?"

Sirius went numb. Her eyes struggled not to widen. She was familiar with the atrocious program. It was created by a video game company that had made such a realistic game that the government purchased it. The program was being used on inmates to create lifelike environments and situations in their heads. But the software needed loads of computers and RAM to initiate. Sirius wasn't sure how Vanderbilt was planning on using this on her with a simple briefcase.

"Of course you do. What we have is a miniature version of it. It only works in intervals, at my command." Vanderbilt pulled out a halo-looking device, with a red and green light on the front. Sirius didn't have a chance to fight; the Union Keepers held her down. She tried biting Vanderbilt's hands, but they covered her mouth. Vanderbilt connected the halo to her head, securing it down with a twisting lever that made it too tight.

Sirius was released from the grips. She wanted to cry, but didn't. It was heartless to do this to a woman, but she knew the darkness gave little room for light in these men.

Vanderbilt calmly sat back down. "It's a prototype, so I'm sure it's a little uncomfortable. You may be wondering if it's illegal, but see...there is no American government to outlaw the software's use."

Sirius stared at her hands, shackled to the table. "You are a beautiful woman. I used to watch your reports with keen interest in your eyes. They are like diamonds."

Vanderbilt could talk all he wanted, but Sirius was not going to give in to his attempt at kindness. It was another form of torture, to be misled into a friendship and giving that friend vital information.

Supposing he wasn't being listened to, Vanderbilt got immediately upset. From his briefcase, he pulled out a pair of pliers.

The Union Keepers held her down again. "Leave me alone! Please!" Sirius screamed.

Vanderbilt grabbed Sirius' hand and reached for her fingernails. Sirius' mouth was covered, muffling her screams. Vanderbilt used the pliers to slowly pull off one of her fingernails. Even though her mouth was covered, her cry for help still echoed throughout the building. The pain was excruciating, resonating through her hand and arm.

Then the pain was gone.

Sirius looked down to see that Vanderbilt hadn't pulled off her fingernail with pliers. It was all a farce, created by the halo. He just sat there with that smug look again.

"You want to know what's the best form of torture? When the mind doesn't have a clue if what it sees is real or not. I promise you, some of this will be real and some of it not. That's how the Union tortures.

To Sirius, it was amazement at the technology then a sudden fear of it. It was real to her eyes and senses. She had never experienced questioning reality. This was going to be a terrifying ordeal. Sirius thought of just making up a location, keep leading the forces astray. But then she risked not being trusted and therefore becoming a useless tissue that had served its purpose.

"You can avoid it all, you know. Just help us stop this rebellion. People are going to get hurt if it continues to grow. Let me help you. All we will do is imprison them – Marcel doesn't want blood on his hands. He never has."

Even when the nuclear bomb threw her out a high rise building, Sirius had never been this scared. At least Doomsday began and ended quick, giving little time to wrap the mind around what had happened. In this case, Vanderbilt was no doubt going to make this evening an endless affair.

His stood up to cast his shadow over Sirius. "You really want to experience a night of constant pain?"

Sirius copied his matter-of-fact smirk, "Bring it, asshole."

For two flights of stairs, Sirius kicked. Three flights of stairs, she bit. And the last flight of stairs, she gave up. Dehydration had exhausted her. The Union Keepers had tied her up so well that walking was difficult. She fell a few times. Her clumsiness got some good laughs. At least they thought this situation was funny. Because she didn't.

How long had it been since she ate anything? Would she ever taste food again?

Finally, the descent stopped and they threw her against a metal chair. One man secured handcuffs to the chair while the other put a muzzle over her mouth. She guessed the biting was no longer funny to them.

"Damn, you know how long it's been since I been with a lady?" one of them said.

"Don't get weird, man, just follow orders."

That creepy bald guy walked into the room. The two Union Keepers stood at attention. Vanderbilt had a briefcase in his hand. He put it gently on a wooden table. From the far side of the room, he dragged a metal stool across the ground. The sound hurt Sirius' ears. Vanderbilt stopped and sat on the stool right in front of her.

He stared at her for almost too long. Was this some type of technique to intimidate her? If it was, it worked. Sirius began to feel her heart beating like it wanted out of her chest.

Vanderbilt scanned the room and pointed at a device on a brick wall. "You know what that is?"

Whatever it was, it didn't seem so frightening. It was made of thin steel and was about six inches in length. It looked like a very big wrench.

"That's called a Heretic's Fork," Vanderbilt explained. "How it works is you'd place it here," he tapped underneath his chin, "and the other end sits on your breast plate. Anytime you'd talk, the fork would cut into your throat. Quite handy when you want to shut someone up, wouldn't you say?"

Sirius kept her mouth shut.

He pointed to what looked like an oversized cheese grater. "That was used during the Spanish Inquisition. A religious movement, might I add. It's called the Spanish Donkey. The victim would straddle it naked and weights would be applied to their feet until the device sliced them in half."

If there was food in her stomach, she might have vomited.

Vanderbilt pointed to other devices hanging on the walls. "Tongue Tearer. I bet I *don't* have to explain that one. Then there's The Breaking Wheel. The Chinese Water Cell. Scold's Brittle. Excuse me a minute," the general wiped the side of his mouth with a tissue, "I was drooling a little bit. This is nostalgia. I like nostalgia. All my years in the military and I never got to play with any of these exciting toys. But I bet of all these inhumane weapons in here...I know what scares you the most." Vanderbilt smiled, "The torture of not knowing what's in that briefcase I brought in."

Her breaths were becoming jagged. She could hear them against the leather muzzle. The insane man was correct. Whatever was in that briefcase could possibly be much worse.

"How about I show you?" Vanderbilt said like he was about to show a neighbor a new lawnmower. He opened the briefcase with his back to her.

She tried to look at the Union Keepers, hoping to see sympathy. Maybe even some sign of opposition. But they just stood there, arms behind their back and eyes toward the ceiling.

Vanderbilt slowly turned to reveal a metal adjustable ring with a green light pulsing through it.

Sirius immediately seized up and began fighting the restraints. Her wrists bled. She tried to kick but the chains wouldn't let her move. "Please! No! Please!" she pled.

The madman stood there with wide eyes. "Oh, come now. Your boyfriend had to wear this program for weeks. It'll be fun."

She started to scream for help, like anyone was there. The Union Keepers rushed in and held her head still. Their grips were so tight, Sirius prayed they'd stop her air circulation and just kill her now. Get it over with. "Please! Don't!" she pled.

"Everyone who's ever been tortured in this very room had more luck than you. At least they knew what was real and what was fantasy. I'm sorry, dear, but you won't get that chance."

She'd never fought like this before. Even if it meant breaking her wrists or ankles, Sirius had to escape before he put that device on her head. "Please!" She scrambled around with every bit of strength she had.

"We are buried deep underground, where no one can hear your screams," Vanderbilt said as he placed the metal ring over her head.

Then it was like waking up from a long drive, not remembering what had happened the last fifty miles. Sirius blinked several times.

Glasses clanked and the smell of ribeye steak filled her nostrils. The table was covered with a pure white cloth. So pure that it looked like it had been manufactured that morning. Sirius smiled. A bottle of Remy Martin Cognac was displayed in front of her within a white napkin. "Yes, please."

The bottle was corked by the waiter and he filled her glass to the brim with the bubbly liquor. Seeming somewhat familiar, Sirius stared at the bald-headed waiter. He stared back. "Are you enjoying your steak, ma'am?"

"Yes," Sirius said, slicing a piece of the tender meat and placing it in her mouth. It was the perfect temperature.

"Are you sure?"

She looked down at the ribeye steak. It was riddled with maggots and mold. Sirius screamed.

The waiter giggled, "How about I cut it for you?" From his pocket, he extracted a large butcher knife and slammed it down on the table. It hit Sirius' wrist and sliced her left hand off. Her cry echoed in the dining room.

Then she was somewhere else. Somewhere cold that smelled

like dried blood and feces. It was the torture chamber.

Vanderbilt laughed and touched some buttons on his electronic tablet. Sirius' eyes were wide. She looked down at her arm. Her left hand was still there. Just an illusion brought on by the metal ring on her head. She tried to wiggle around, knock it off. The damn thing was tightened as much as possible to her skull.

"Please," Sirius whispered.

Touching some more buttons on the tablet, Vanderbilt never looked up. "This software has loads of scenarios. Hell, if I had this at Guantanamo Bay, we could've gotten lots of information from our prisoners. There's even a molestation scenario. That could be fun." He looked up at the two Union Keepers. One smiled, the other didn't. "Watch this one," Vanderbilt said as though Sirius didn't exist.

He went over to the wall and grabbed what looked like a pair of forceps. Using his sleeve, he shined the metal. "Still blood on this thing. Fascinating. Must be a century old."

Sirius shook her head, "Don't."

Vanderbilt sat back on the stool and grabbed her hand, still secured to the chair. With the forceps, he snatched her index finger. Sirius cried. He yanked. She could feel every tendon snag as he pulled back harder. The skin extended and the bone crackled. Then Vanderbilt did one more hard yank. The finger came clean off, gushing blood onto the floor.

She'd never cried so hard in her life. The pain. The anxiety. The terror. All it flooded her mind. "Stop!"

Then Sirius looked down to see the finger was never torn off. She calmed down as Vanderbilt laughed some more.

"It wasn't real, Miss Dawson," he grinned.

The Union Keeper finally spoke, "Sir, she's just a girl, Sir."

Without turning around, Vanderbilt said, "So was the legendary Succubus." He stared into Sirius' eyes as he placed the forceps torture device in his lap and began to massage her left hand. "This could all end, very easily. Pedro had no qualms with giving you up. Doesn't that mean something? That even in a group of followers like the People of Bliss, there can be deceit. You can't escape it. No one should ever be trusted. So why fight for them? Why stand up against the ideals of a perfect government? We're not the ones causing problems...you are."

Sirius' lip quivered. She wanted to scream that he was right. That she was sorry. Just release her.

From his pocket, he pulled out a portable tape recorder. "So, dear, I had an idea. And you won't even need to tell us the location of your followers. All you'd have to do is record a message. You're good with that, right? I've listened to your weekly rhetoric against the Union for the past couple months. Very charming, by the way. Let's change the message. Instead of telling them to boycott the Union, how about telling them to surrender themselves to the Union? That's it. Tell them to give themselves up and they will be tried only for second-degree treason."

He put the tape recorder close to Sirius' muzzle and turned it on. After a moment, she took a deep breath and then opened her mouth. "Go...fuck...yourself."

Vanderbilt flipped off the tape recorder, not seeming surprised. He touched a few buttons on the tablet then placed it down. One more time, he wiped off the forceps with his sleeve and grabbed Sirius' left hand.

She kept telling herself over and over again that it wasn't real. The device was just signals to her head and turning reality into a program. With wide eyes, Sirius watched Vanderbilt tear off her index finger slowly. She felt every nerve ending scream in pain. Gritting her teeth didn't quiet her screaming. Although useless, her cries for help never stopped.

Sirius closed her eyes tightly. The pain wasn't going away.

It's not real.

She opened her eyes to see both Union Keepers' mouths wide open. The one on the left looked pale enough to vomit. Sirius looked down to see her index finger was still missing and blood dribbled out.

Vanderbilt grinned, "*That* was real, Miss Dawson."

CHAPTER FORTY-FIVE

What sounded like a jackhammer ripping away concrete from a battered street was actually just Adam's snores. Janice woke up again and nudged him. The agonizing melody didn't stop. Gerard never snored. Perhaps because he was too busy to sleep next to her most nights.

Janice nudged Adam again, "Shhh."

A drop of slobber worked its way down Adam's cheek. She stared at him for a long time, wondering to herself what she'd gotten into. Her former student, twelve years younger than her, somehow had won her heart...but not her soul. What was Gerard doing now? Did he even wonder where his wife was?

The jackhammer snore echoed in the room.

"Adam!" Janice snapped.

He sat up. The drop of slobber rolled off and hit the pillow. Janice made a mental note to wash these sheets in the morning.

"Sorry, Miss Celest," he mumbled in a half-sleep trance.

"Please don't call me that," Janice said. "I'm not your teacher anymore, remember?" She had to thank him later for reminding her of their near-decade age difference.

"Oh yeah, sorry...*babe*? Do I call you *babe*?"

It was times like this he seemed so young and immature. *Babe?* She preferred *Miss Celest* if that was the case. Before she could ridicule him for his ignorance, the baby kicked. Janice lay on her back, sighing. Was this going to be her new family? What would wake her up first every night: Adam or the baby?

"At least I have Dad and Brent."

Adam asked, "What was that?"

"Nothing."

Turning to her side didn't help the backache. She tried a few different positions but nothing worked.

"You want me to scratch your back?"

She smiled. Adam knew the technique well. It was something Victoria used to do to her as a kid to help her sleep. "Yes, please."

Adam turned to his side and with just the edges of his nails he ran them over her back. So gentle. Like a very light massage.

"What's been on your mind?"

What hadn't been on her mind? The lack of hot water? How painful was this childbirth going to be without painkillers? Did babies bite when they breastfed? Instead of bothering him with selfish questions, she decided to confront the question that had been on every human's mind in this silo. "I'm wondering why they took Sirius."

"Really? I mean, don't revolutionaries usually get captured by the government?"

"It just doesn't make sense. Marcel isn't like that. He sees fairness. Did you say that when he approached Lloyd and Nina, he tried to recruit the followers? Everyone around here talks about my brother like he's a monster. A monster would've plowed all you down with bullets and missiles."

Adam grunted, "You're still defending him?"

"It's just not *him*. That's all I'm saying. He'd convince people he's right, rather than force them."

Obviously not agreeing, Adam just gave a long *mmm* sound. Janice rubbed her stomach. She said, "Did I ever tell you that Marcel tried to commit suicide?"

Adam's silence meant he was contemplating responding with '*Maybe he should've.*'

Janice continued, "After Mom died, he slit his left wrist down the middle. The bathtub had to be replaced because there was so much blood that got stained. Yet, he never died. Marcel's physical wounds always closed so easily. It's his mental wounds that never heal. He had that same demeanor right before I left. That calm and yet disturbed face."

"Well, whatever he plans with Sirius won't happen. We'll get her back soon."

"Wait a minute. You have a plan to rescue her?"

Adam shrugged. "Sort of. Me and Brent are leaving in the morning to try and track down Pedro. He'll know where she is."

Janice sat up. "What? You mean...Brent agreed to this?"

"Yeah, why?"

"Do I need to remind you about their brotherly quarrels?"

Adam shrugged again. "It's fine. Lay back down, so I can scratch you."

Janice didn't listen. Instead her mind wandered on and on. Something didn't seem right. The pieces of this puzzle didn't fit into place. One thing Nelson taught her about politicians was there's always another agenda. And Marcel deep-down was just another politician. What game was he playing? No matter how much back scratching Adam could do, that question would keep her awake tonight.

She stood up and put on a pair of pants. "I'm talking to Brent." This was what the Celest family, that Victoria had built, did. They leaned on each other for guidance and resolutions.

"Right now? It's like four in the morning."

Adam's objection got ignored as she continued dressing. He sighed as he stood up, showcasing his pair of Scooby-Doo boxers. "Okay," he mumbled, "I'll go with you."

Janice opened the door and walked toward Brent's room. His door had been left slightly ajar. She slowly swung it open, "Brent?"

The room was empty.

Adam seemed to awaken a little at the sight. "Hmph. That's weird. Sirius' room is still empty too. Maybe he's in the bathroom." He scurried toward the restrooms.

Janice knocked on Nelson's door several times before she heard her father's grumpy voice. "What?"

"Daddy, is Brent there with you?"

He opened the door with hair still shaped to the side of a pillow. "No, why?"

Janice turned to see a disappointed look on Adam's face at the end of the hallway. He whispered, "Goddamn watchman fell asleep again."

"Are you saying..." Janice couldn't even continue the question. Adam's face said it all. Brent left.

She touched her chest. It was that cold feeling all over again. The feeling of the Celest family being ripped apart. "Oh God," Janice whispered. Finally, the truth hit her. "This was what Marcel wanted. Don't you see?"

Nelson reached for some clothes and tied on a coat. He obviously understood but Adam didn't.

"See what?"

"Marcel wants Brent to come after Sirius. So he can kill him."

Adam squinted his eyes. "But Marcel Celest keeps saying he doesn't want blood on his hands. How –"

"I'm not talking about Marcel murdering Brent. The other way around."

Finally, Adam's eyes opened wider.

Nelson, dressed in a heavy coat, came out of his room. "I can fly the chopper. Any idea where he would be?"

Janice nodded her head. "The castle."

Adam came out of their room, covering up his boxers with a tight pair of jeans. "Castle?"

"Yes," she elaborated, "the Union is building a castle. It's where their headquarters will be."

"Where?" Nelson asked.

"I'll tell you where, but I'm coming with you. We're family. And family sticks together."

CHAPTER FORTY-SIX

Desk jobs were so dull. Gerard joined the Secret Service to get out of a desk job, only to be assigned to another desk job. Then when he left that job to become Capitol Police, he somehow ended up in a fancy Ritz hotel working for the Union...at a desk job.

He loosened his tie and leaned back in his chair. A photograph of him and Janice hung on the wall. It was set up there as a reminder of what he sacrificed to protect her. Then he thought of the photograph of her kissing Adam. As always, the feeling made him swallow back a gunk of stomach acid. Gerard wondered if she even thought about him anymore. He also wondered if this plan would ever work. The plan to give his child a bright future.

Rather than wallow in self-pity, Gerard had better things to do. Room service was definitely in order for tonight. He put away some paperwork in his briefcase. The stacks were getting too large. A bigger briefcase would have to be ordered soon. Organizing security detail for the most wanted man in the world was going to be difficult. Surely, the amount of attacks on Marcel's life would increase in the coming months. Obtaining a bigger briefcase was going to be a lot easier than obtaining a bigger security detail. Job applications for Union Keepers were far and few between. Did anyone have much hope in the Union?

Two Union Keepers were with Marcel and General

Vanderbilt, so tonight was going to be a night off for Gerard. Whatever happened to Sirius Dawson was out of his hands. Could the voice of the People of Bliss really be silenced tonight? What did this mean for the impending war? He didn't like hovering question marks over his head. Gerard's room service was going to have to include a bottle of wine.

He opened the door to his office and locked up. It must've been the middle of the night and someone else was using an office across the hall. Gerard became curious as to who shared his nightshift biological clock.

It was that czar from the meeting, the one in the wheelchair. His desk had six monitors, three computer towers, two keyboards, and a trash can full of empty Doritos bags.

"You step onto the road, and if you don't keep your feet, there's no knowing where you might be swept off to," the czar said in some kind of silly, deep British accent.

After staring blankly for a minute, Gerard obviously was going to have to ask. "Is that from a movie or something?"

"Book! *Lord of the Rings*. Written by the masterful J.R.R. Tolkien. The movies never did it much justice," the nerd said, his eyes scanning each monitor rapidly.

There weren't many people to talk to around here, but Gerard needed friends. And this man, with more zits on his face than poppies on a poppy seed bagel, was his best shot. "So you're the tech czar?"

"Right-a-mongo. Lester's the name. Come hither and take a seat."

Lester motioned toward a chair behind him. Gerard walked in and removed the pile of comic books on the chair before sitting. "So, what you doing?"

"Playing a game. Duh. MMOs are kind of dull when...you know...billions of people are dead and there's no one to play with."

"What's an MMO?"

"Ugh. Noob. MMO stands for Massively Multiplayer Online. It's a game world."

Lester's video game character was some kind of creature humanoid.

"Is that a Spock?" Gerard asked. The last video game he played was on his cellphone a decade ago. He sure missed those angry birds.

"A...*Spock?* You really are a noob. This, my friend, is called an elf. And what I'm doing right now is creating an army by using a spell called 'dominate mind'."

The video game character was using some kind of magic to make the other characters do things against their will. How well could Marcel do this?

Gerard said, "So, why do you need an army?"

"Because, my friend, we are going to war. Elfen war, that is," Lester said snacking on a donut with one hand and typing on the keyboard with the other.

War? Gerard's curiosity peaked. He watched for a while.

Lester slammed his hand down. "Damnit, it happened again!" He changed the screens to a large map of this fantasy world.

"What did?"

"It just got so disorganized. Look, I've got some of my minions in this land, this one, and then this one. But they're scattered. I can't get this organized because I don't know where my followers are. There's no way to track them."

Where his followers are? Gerard leaned in. "What if there was a way to track them?"

"There isn't."

"But what if there was?"

"Well, now that the game's population is so small, I guess it's possible. I could set up beacons, but I would need to attach a device to each of them." Lester turned in his wheelchair and faced Gerard. "Wait a minute. Are we still talking about the game?"

Stuck in a trance of a new plan formulating, Gerard didn't even hear the question. "Would you be able to build a program to track...people? Organize them?"

"Hmph," Lester mumbled. "I guess we aren't talking about the game anymore. Are we?"

"It's all a game," Gerard smiled.

Lester turned back to the computer and closed the MMO game. He opened several programs showing the maps of various countries. "Few cellular towers are left, but that could also mean stronger signals. With some tweaking, we could plot people using some type of devices. But you're talking something very controversial. You're talking about people's loss of privacy. That's unconstitutional."

"Yeah, when we used to have a Constitution. Now, the Union is in charge. Remember? I'm sure Marcel Celest would like this proposal. And you're smart enough to come up with a program, right?"

"Well," Lester snorted, "of course, I'm smart enough. But we'd still need a device to mark people. Duh. How else would we track them?"

Gerard's child did have a chance at a bright future. The thought made him lock his fingers together to keep from rubbing his hands manically. This impending war may have a shot after all.

"Are you listening to me? I said we need a mark. Duh. I can't track people by their hair color or something," Lester said, finishing his donut but leaving crumbs on his Darth Vader shirt.

Glancing at Lester's desk, Gerard saw a smartphone. He picked it up and glanced it over.

Lester snickered, "Cellphone towers aren't ready for chatting. Just data. And besides...unless you plan on convincing Google to give out four billion Androids for free, it's not going to happen."

"I'm not interested on what's on the outside," Gerard said, placing the smartphone on the ground and smashing it with his foot. The phone separated into several pieces.

With his hands out like Gerard had just ate the last bit of food on a deserted raft, Lester whimpered, "I waited three days in line at Best Buy for that phone."

Not paying attention, Gerard lifted a computer chip from the smartphone remains. A chip so small he was afraid to drop it. He placed it gently on his other hand and held it out.

"It's an FFC chip. So what?"

Gerard said, "Yep, the spawn of the NFC chip. It's crazy tiny, huh? This thing can hold a lot of information though. It can work as a bank account and hold your entire life. The Union could transmit currency to it and subtract currency from it. All wirelessly." He played with it using his index finger. "So small that it could fit inside the palm of your hand."

"You're suggesting we force people to implant these?"

After a deep breath and a roll of his eyes, Gerard leaned back. "Take a look at yourself. You are *exactly* what most of mankind has become addicted to. It's everywhere. And we want it. It goes by the name of *technology*. You think we'll have to force people? No way. It'll give food, shelter, homes, health insurance, transportation...the list goes on and on. People will wait *four* days in line for this thing." He nodded to himself, sensing confidence again. No need for a bottle of wine to put him to sleep tonight. Hope would settle his mind into a deep slumber. "This is what will organize this war."

"What war?"

Gerard leaned in and whispered, "The war between those who have technology...and those who don't."

CHAPTER FORTY-SEVEN

"Ugh...you...look...awful," that familiar raspy voice said.

Sirius looked down. Her sweater had been torn revealing the left side of her bra. Urine had soaked her pants down to the tennis shoes that were two sizes too big and belonged to a boy. Above, her wrists had been shackled to a hook hanging from the ceiling. In front of her, Grandma had her arms crossed and mouth gaping open.

"Didn't I tell you red is for sluts?" Grandma spouted. That expensive set of pearls around her neck shuttered. Her outfit cost more than Sirius' car. "Then why are you wearing a red sweater? Are you a slut?"

"No, Nana." A tear trickled down Sirius' cheek.

Grandma scoffed. From her purse, she pulled out red lipstick. "I think you want to be a slut. Just like your mother. Here –" She grasped Sirius' mouth hard to make her lips pucker.

"Please, Nana. I'm sorry."

Her grandmother took the red lipstick and smeared it over her lips, cheeks, and chin. "There! Now you look like a slut! And would you just look at that eyeliner...it's got clumps. What did I tell you? No clumps! A dignified woman never allows it." She stared down at her figure. "You're getting fat. I'm putting you on a strict diet. Crackers and cheese for one week!"

"But –"

Grandma slapped Sirius across the face. The sting lingered for several seconds as Sirius turned her head. Grandma was gone, replaced by General Vanderbilt. He smirked, "That slap was real. I figured if one side of your face was scarred, then why not the other?" His voice came out muffled. She could sense a drop of blood exiting her ear. No telling what that was from. Memories kept fading. Concentrating became difficult.

Sirius could only feel the pain. Everything hurt. Her wrists, neck, feet, ankles...she had no idea how many fingers were left. The Union Keepers stared at the floor. Somehow it made it easier to watch a petite woman get tortured if they couldn't see it.

Vanderbilt wiped his hands on a towel that might've been white but had turned burgundy. "I don't enjoy this. Honestly. But torture is effective. It's been used for centuries. Eventually you, just like the other men and women who suffered here, will co-operate. That's it. It's not that hard. All you have to do is speak. Haven't you been doing that for months?" He pulled out the tape recorder from his pocket and held it to Sirius' mouth.

She thought about it. This night could end with a few sentences. *This is Sirius Dawson. I'm not sure why we fight this new government, because they care for us. The Union is a blessing. The Union can feed you and dress you. The Union wants only what's best. Please come out of the silo and gather at the steps of the Union Castle to give yourselves up for treason. You all will be shown Marcel Celest's mercy.* Then Vanderbilt could put away the tape recorder, remove the metal computer ring on her head, untie her, give her a warm meal, provide whatever health supplies she needed, and offer her a bed in one of the chambers. She could sleep soundly. And never have to worry again.

But if this new government could get away with this situation, who's to say what *else* they could get away with? Sirius said, "I'm getting bored with these old torture tools."

Vanderbilt smiled. "I agree. I'm getting bored myself. How about something new?" He put away the tape recorder and reached inside a duffel bag to pull out a weapon. It was a foot long silver rod with a handle on one end. "Inside of this rod are little strings that carry a jolt of electricity. When I swing it, the strings touch and increase the charge. The harder I strike, the more the jolts."

"You whore!" Sirius turned to her left. The vision of Grandma had returned with that bitter look of disgust. "I saw that. You groaned at it. In lust. Because you are a whore. I bet you want him to stick that up your pussy, don't you? Why did your parents have to leave a whore at my doorstep?"

Sirius' head snapped to the right as she got hit. Her neck popped. More pain. Pain that may never go away. She looked down. Half her sweater had been torn and she didn't even remember it. Bruises formed around her ribcage. Then Vanderbilt swung the weapon and hit her in the stomach. A mix of saliva, blood, and possibly vomit exited Sirius' mouth.

It could all end by just giving in. Maybe the Union wasn't so bad? Maybe a world leader, with the power to control weather, deserved to be a ruler?

Then came a familiar sound. A rattling noise. It was a memory...with Lloyd. When they first met. A rattle snake had shuttered its tail at her. What was it Lloyd told her as the animal slithered away? *You scared it more than it scared you.*

Sirius looked down. The sound was coming from the weapon in Vanderbilt's hand. Not from the weapon itself, but from his grip. The general's hands were shaking. Shaking so vigorously that the metal rod wobbled. Sirius realized the truth...Vanderbilt was terrified of her. Just like the rattle snake.

From the deepest part of her stomach, Sirius laughed. Then laughed some more. Then it turned from giggles to a snort. Vanderbilt looked embarrassed. He hid his quivering hand behind him. Another smile crossed his face, trying to give an acting performance that William Shakespeare would die for. "Is this amusing, Miss Dawson?"

After a round of laughter, her giggling turned into crying. Tears streamed down her face. She took a deep breath and closed her eyes. "I did it. I *actually* did it. You...the Union...Marcel Celest...you are all scared."

Vanderbilt's upper lip twisted into a frown. "Why would we be scared?"

"Easy," Sirius said, extending her neck closer to Vanderbilt's face. "Because there are more of *us* than *you.*"

Biting his lip, the general's face turned solid red in an uncontrollable fury. He beat her with the metal rod over and over again.

"Sir!" a Union Keeper objected. "Sir! Calm down! General!"

Vanderbilt hollered as he continued to whip the rod over every part of her body. The pain was excruciating. Every inch of her body screamed louder than her in pain.

Then...all at once...the pain stopped.

The castle was much larger than Brent anticipated and much less guarded than he anticipated. When he arrived, it crossed his mind that perhaps he was lost. But Union vans outside erased any suspicions. The basement seemed the most obvious place to search first. He made his way through the scaffoldings, stacks of cement blocks, pallets of concrete mix, and bundles of lumber to get to the stairs in the courtyard. He climbed down for what felt like a mile. How far did this castle go down into the ground?

Spiraling down these steps made his head spin. He finally made it to the bottom to be greeted with a few inches of backup water. It stunk worse than any sewer. The bottom floor was so dark, he had to give his eyes a few minutes to adjust. Minutes he didn't have.

Then a scream. A woman's scream. Sirius.

He dashed forward and slipped into the puddle of water. Without taking a moment to wipe the piss water off his face, he ran forward. The screams stopped. Brent returned to the pitch black hallway with no idea which way the cries came from.

Instead of using his eyes, Declan had taught him to concentrate on another essential sense...his hearing. Brent closed his eyes. Water splashed against the wall from his previous running, but besides that he heard nothing.

"Oh shit," a man whispered. Coming from a door straight

ahead.

Brent moved slowly toward the locked wooden door.

"Unhook her," another man said.

He moved slower. An assassin never dashes into the scene, Declan had taught him.

Another male voice said, "Jesus Christ. She's not breathing."

No time for stealth anymore. Brent dashed toward the door and smashed through it. Two armed Union Keepers never had a moment to reach for their guns. He flipped backwards. His foot smacked the first Union Keeper's chin, knocking him out immediately. Brent spun and kicked the other Union Keeper so hard, he flew backwards into a table. Some bald man with rolled up sleeves and blood on his shirt tried to attack. This man was more skilled. Brent found himself dodging a few punches before he could grasp the offender around the neck.

"I can't breathe," the bald man said, "I can't breathe."

Brent held tighter. The bald man tried to struggle out of the sleeper hold. They were both on the ground. Wrapping his legs around the bald man so he couldn't move, Brent gripped the neck even more. Thirty seconds was all it took to stop oxygen to the brain and put him to sleep.

"I can't breathe. My vocal chord. You're crushing it. I can't breathe. I can't..."

The attacker's body went limp. Brent dashed toward Sirius. Barely recognizable, she was bruised, beaten, and blood poured from her nose. He turned her over so her back laid against the ground. Lifeless eyes stared at him. Listening close to her mouth, he heard no breaths.

Please breathe.

Nothing.

Extending her neck back, he began the CPR maneuver and placed his hands over her chest. He had brought people to life before. Brent felt confident he could do it again.

Four thrusts to her chest.

Brent bent over and gave Sirius two deep breaths. Her chest raised as the air entered her lungs then caved in as it escaped.

Four more thrusts to her chest.

He plugged her nose then gave two long deep breaths.

"Come on, baby, you can do it."

Please breathe.

Four further thrusts to her chest. He stared at her, praying her lips would fade from blue to red. Two long breaths. As a lifeguard, he saved a dozen lives with this procedure. He only needed one more.

Four thrusts. Her eyes stayed open. Brent just needed them to vibrate just slightly. He imagined Sirius taking an enormous gasp of air, embracing him, then saying something funny to lighten the mood like 'I need a phone. I got to tweet that I just died.'

Returning from his imagination, Brent had attempted his sixth routine of blowing air into her lungs. Or seventh? He lost count.

Please breathe.

After his eighteenth try, he was out of breath. He gave two deep breaths then he rested his face against her cheek. It was ice cold. Brent wrapped his hand around hers. There was no use anymore.

Sirius Dawson was dead.

CHAPTER FORTY-EIGHT

Brent refused to let Sirius' body lay amongst the men and tools that had ended her endeavors. He carried her up the five flights of a spiraling defeat to his soul. Then carried her further up until they reached the roof.

Once atop the castle, the night seemed to quiet. The wind swayed in almost rhythmic dismay. Crickets didn't make a sound. Clouds opened up to reveal a starry sky that looked like salt had been sprinkled onto the black atmosphere.

All this openness and Brent felt more alone than he had in a prison cell. Sirius' body began to weigh heavy. Gently, he placed her body on the brick edge of the castle's roof. Those beautiful hazel eyes looked up. That moment returning to his mind when he first met her. Standing outside the White House, while his father spoke to reporters. He caught her eye. She smirked then hid her red cheeks behind that gorgeous hair. Who would've thought he'd enjoy even more than that simple smile? Brent could only reflect on their content moments together because there were no substandard ones. Every kiss, laugh, and conversation filled that empty spot in Brent's heart. Instead of a tear down his cheek, his dimples sunk in with a grin. All those therapists, after his mother's death, finally made sense. Only reflecting on the happier moments made the pain easier to swallow down.

Brent scanned the system of stars. They twinkled back at him.

"There it is," he whispered. Pointing, Brent said, "That's the star Sirius, in the Canis Major constellation. It's the *brightest* star in the night sky. Centuries ago, navigators followed it to keep them from getting lost. Just like I did to you."

He reached down and kissed Sirius' dry lips. Walking away seemed tougher than he expected. He'd never get to touch that soft skin, look in those vibrant eyes, or hear that silly snort. When Brent turned to leave, he stumbled and fell to his knees. A tear rolled down his face. The last time a tear rolled like that was at his mother's funeral. Oxygen seemed to be stolen away and he found it hard to breath. His bottom lip trembled. His mouth gaped open like a scream wanted to exhale, but nothing happened. It seemed so difficult to even talk. Or walk. Or take a whiff of air. All he could do was cry with a gaping wide mouth.

Then Brent grasped his hands on the cement ground and dug his fingernails into it. His furious scream finally escaped. It echoed off the walls into the night air, filling it with ire and despair. He cried more. Crying like the first time a bully picked on him. Crying like the first time he'd broken his arm. Crying like the first time he fell down and couldn't get back up.

"I'm so sorry," a whisper came from behind him. Brent didn't need to look. He knew who it was. Burying his face into his two hands, he listened to his brother approach.

"I didn't mean for them to kill her," Marcel whispered. It sounded genuine. But then again, Marcel had become more than just the master of weather...he'd also become the master of lies.

Then Brent felt Marcel's cold hand touch his shoulder as he knelt down to his level. "Brent, look at me please."

Not listening, he continued to wail into his hands.

"Brent," Marcel continued, "please. You have to do this. I put the love of your life in the hands of a psychopath. I knew the general would kill her, I felt it in his soul that he wanted to. You see? I'm losing my mind. I can't control my emotions. All I feel is...hate."

Slowly, Brent released his hands and stared into the eyes of his brother. The last time they'd been this close had been a duel to the death. Even Marcel seemed saddened; circles darkened his glazed eyes. In his hand was a blade. A blade long enough to pierce deep enough to rip a lung out. "Please," Marcel pled, "you have to do this. You *have* to kill me. I can't do it. It's your destiny. I see it."

Shaking his head didn't stop Marcel's request. He continued, "Here. It's easy. Just aim for my heart so I don't heal. I'll die quickly."

Trying to shove the blade into Brent's hand didn't change his mind. Brent pushed it away still crying. "No."

"Brent, please! I'm pure evil. I made a deal with Lucifer. That's how I got these powers. I don't know what I was thinking. I'm losing control. You have to do this or things will get worse. Do this for the People of Bliss. Do this for our family. Do this for Mom. She wanted peace. This is how you do it. You take this blade and stab me through the heart."

Death hadn't solved any of his problems so far. This was no different. Brent again shoved the blade away.

Marcel clenched his teeth. "Goddamnit, Brent! Why don't you ever listen to me! What do you want? A fight? Is that what you want? A challenge. Fine!"

A harsh wind exploded and Brent was flown off his feet. He landed further down the roof. The floor collapsed. Brent fell through, smashing against a pew. He felt his rib crack. Wind blew in every direction. His eyes opened to his surroundings. It was a church, one story down from the roof.

Marcel floated down. The wind picked up so much, Brent's eyelids flapped. Windows shattered and glass flew in circles. Then dust and cement mix filled the air, making it impossible to see. Brent covered his face.

Then a fist smashed down on his face. Marcel punched him over and over. Brent spat blood. He couldn't see where the punches were coming from. Dust blinded him. It was all a reminder of their first brawl; Marcel being attacked by an unknown assassin in black.

"How's this feel, huh? Being beaten by someone more

powerful than you!" Marcel screamed, appearing from every angle to attack Brent. "What's it like to be weak?"

Without getting up, Brent laid there and took the beatings. The wind flung him against the wall. Glass shards from the church windows cut him several times. Then the wall behind him gave way and opened onto a wide balcony. He fell and tumbled a few times before hitting the balcony's edge. Brent's right eye bled from a glass shard. All this pain didn't outdo the pain in his heart. He'd rather be buried in a coffin of these glass shards than go another day without Sirius.

Marcel stormed toward him. Brent tried to stand. And then a cold steel pierced his stomach. Being stabbed was much worse than a gunshot. His throat filled with a mixture of bile and blood.

The blade stuck out of him; Marcel had stabbed him all the way to the hilt. He looked into his brother's eyes.

"Every species on this planet has one thing in common: purpose," Marcel said with a single finger held up, "and you didn't fulfill yours."

Though his insides felt tight and blood began to dribble out the side of his mouth, Brent still managed to whisper, "Actually...I...did." He grasped Marcel's collar and brought him in closer. "There's...blood on your hands."

The angry, bitter face on Marcel altered. His crunched eyebrows softened. His trembling lower lip stopped. His smile leaned down into a frown. He looked like he'd just been awoken in the middle of the night by lightning. Marcel's breathing sped up. "Oh my God."

Brent collapsed onto the ground; his clothes became wet with his blood. He looked up at the sky. Stars and planets began to twinkle brightly. So bright that he wanted to shut his eyes, but couldn't. Light made every spot in the endless black atmosphere come alive. He could see the magnificent volcanos on Mars. Venus' ice storm flowed by. Saturn's rings followed in alignment. Mercury's valleys were more stunning than any satellite photo could capture. The Moon's surface looked more like bruises than craters. Then Brent could see Jupiter. And then there it was. Jupiter's moon Europa. The *real* Europa. Not some computer-generated prison. But the real one. Brent stared at it and smiled.

Then a kiss warmed his forehead. A familiar kiss. Something he hadn't experienced in many years. He closed his eyes.

It was his mother's kiss.

Brent Celest: *Entrepreneur, People Magazine's Sexiest Man of the Year, The President's Son, Eligible Bachelor, and misguided terrorist*...lay dead before Marcel. While mere seconds passed, it felt like hours. Marcel stared at his bloody hands. He quickly wiped them on his jacket but it just smeared. Guts smeared. Blood smeared. It wasn't like the movies. This moment couldn't be wiped away with one simple swipe on clothes. Marcel Celest: *Business Owner, Time Magazine's Person of the Year, The President's Son, and...murderer*.

Marcel looked at his bloody hands as though he could magically make it disappear. It didn't work. The situation didn't go away. No matter how many times he blinked, his brother's dead body was on the ground. His tears dropped, mixing into Brent's blood. His own brother's blood. What had come over him? How could he possibly end the life of another human with these hands?

Then the wind blew more harshly and it wasn't him in control. Something broke the air. Then the sound echoed around him. It was a helicopter.

The chopper rose into his view, right above him. A blinding searchlight shined down. Marcel just stared with his palms wide open, feeling blood drip off of them onto the floor. Then he could see who was in the helicopter.

His father Nelson stared down at Brent's body with wide eyes. In the back seat, banging her hands against the window and screaming was Janice. Staring down at Brent's body, Janice's face was filled with tears. Her eyes stayed focused on Brent. Marcel had never seen his sister like this. She had never been in so much physical pain. Then, her eyes peered up and locked onto

Marcel's. Her mood changed from anguish to bitter hate. She'd never looked at him this way. No one had. Not one person had ever been so vexed at him. If Janice had been on the balcony with them, she would've grabbed the blade from Brent's stomach and stabbed Marcel.

"Wait," he managed to say, "wait...Janice. I didn't mean to...I...Dad?...Wait."

The helicopter slowly turned and fluttered away from the scene. No matter the angle, Janice's eyes were locked onto Marcel's. If there was any chance of the Celest family reuniting, it flitted away like the helicopter into the distance.

"Oh God," Marcel said to himself.

He stumbled backwards and fell to the ground. Scurrying away from Brent's body just made him feel more scared. Marcel ran back into the church, tripping over the ruins of pews as he hobbled onto the ground.

"Gabe?" Marcel screamed. "Please! Are you there? Gabe!"

There was no answer from the Light, because there was no Light. Only darkness. The still, quiet voice of darkness.

Lucifer appeared, twiddling his thumbs on a chair that faced a painting. The painting depicted a war between angels and demons. "They color me in such distain. Such indignation. Without investigating my true nature. When the universe created us, I was its very introduction to an opposite. A...'black sheep', of sorts. I've spent millennia...feeling reclusive." The way he said *reclusive* made Marcel pay more attention. "Gabe and the paladins of Light were so rebellious. They hunted me throughout the cosmos with no excuse as to why they loathed me so much. Just because...I wasn't alike to them. No assurance. No appreciation. No family. I've experienced your sentiments. In fact, I exist in them." After a moment, Lucifer continued shyly. "I could instruct you. Educate you how to master the desolation."

Marcel approached Lucifer and knelt by him. "*I've* been so rebellious...why do you keep coming back?"

"Because I'm alone," Lucifer said with his head down.

For the first time, Marcel understood this being of dark matter.

What must it be like to endure in sorrow for all eternity? It made him feel selfish to only endure a moment of that. And for the first time, Marcel touched Lucifer. His body quivered but not from the cold.

Then they hugged.

CHAPTER FORTY-NINE

The good son had murdered the bad son. As he flew the chopper toward the missile silo, Nelson found himself lost in more than the clouds in the sky. He was lost in the cloud of depression. Darkness closed in on him.

On the trip back, Adam had snapped his fingers to remind Nelson where he was. He barely heard anything besides the cries of Janice. Buried in Adam's shoulder, she went from cries of sorrow to cries of anger.

All this effort to keep the family together failed. Just like his presidency. If Nelson had been flying alone, he may have contemplated crashing into the fields below. Let it all be over in just a flash. Seeing Marcel's bloody hand over Brent's dead body overshadowed the worst of his memories. Nothing would ever be the same. Four years ago, Nelson lost his wife. Tonight, Nelson Celest lost two sons. Marcel was good as dead to him.

What now? The question plagued him every moment of his descent into the woods next to the silo's entrance. His landing was rough. It hadn't been that sloppy since his first training in the Air Force. He looked down to see his grip wouldn't release from the handle. Adam reached over and caressed his shoulder. "Come on. You can do it."

Nelson nodded. His legs weighed a ton a piece as he climbed out of the chopper. It was this feeling all over again. Hopelessness. Like tying a sack of potatoes to his back, hopelessness made him drag his feet toward the silo's entrance. Underneath several bushes, the door looked like a sewer entrance. With three taps of Adam's foot on the surface, the door was opened by the watchman. They walked in and the door slid closed behind them.

Sleep was all he could think about. Maybe the botanist had medicine to help him sleep even deeper. A slumber so static that he may never wake up. The thought thrilled him.

Sirius' room had been left open. Nelson couldn't walk any further, even though his room was just two more doors down. He slid down against the wall until he hit the ground. If only he could slide lower. Maybe into the depths of Hell to cry amongst the other hopeless souls like him.

Janice and Adam stopped. People were waking up. What time was it? Did it even matter anymore? They seemed concerned, standing in hallways and whispering amongst each other.

Declan's daughter Royal appeared from behind the growing crowd. "Where's Brent? Did you find him?"

Adam seemed to be the only one strong enough to continue standing, because already Janice had sat next to Nelson and put her head on his shoulder. Without saying anything, Adam's glazed eyes answered Royal's question.

"No," Royal whispered. "What about...Sirius?"

Again, Adam said nothing.

Royal covered her mouth as tears rolled down on her eyes. In amazement, Nelson watched as that reaction spread faster than that gruesome flu had. The People of Bliss had different reactions; some clenched their fists furiously while others shed tears mournfully. Though their reactions were different, the idea all remained the same. The same question still on Nelson's mind. What now?

Sirius had been their voice and their leader. Plans had been decided by her and her alone. As much as he should've stepped up to the plate, Nelson didn't have the strength to swing a grand slam for this team. They needed a better leader. One that wouldn't lead them into the nuclear turmoil this world had faded into.

Adam bit his lip. He stormed past Nelson and Janice into Sirius' room. An enormous poster of the earlier propaganda hung on the wall read *We Need to Knock on Marcel Celest's door!* Adam stripped it down and crumbled it. He ripped maps off her wall and instructions for the boycott. With one hand, Adam wiped all the items off Sirius' desk onto the floor. Pencils, papers, office supplies sprung and covered the ground. He grabbed an eraser and cleaned off Sirius' dry erase board. While he scribbled on the board, everyone gathered at the door. Even Nelson felt the curiosity to stand. What was Adam doing?

He turned to the People of Bliss. "Okay. First, we need a team to find everyone left on the Servo Clementia list and recruit them. Second, we gather a team to survey the Union castle. Third, we devise a way to bring more followers here from foreign countries.

Through wet eyes, Royal asked, "What are you talking about Adam?"

With his back straight, he answered loud so everyone could hear. "Listen up. People of Bliss! We are not going to *knock* on Marcel's door." Through gritted teeth, Adam whispered, "We are going to break it down."

Made in the USA
Columbia, SC
12 February 2019